Praise

The Eighth Texas Red River Mystery

"Wortham adroitly balances richly nuanced human drama with two-fisted action and displays a knack for the striking phrase ('R.B. was the best drunk driver in the county, and I don't believe he run off in here on his own'). This entry is sure to win the author new fans."

—*Publishers Weekly*

Gold Dust
The Seventh Texas Red River Mystery

"Center Springs must deal with everything from cattle rustlers to a biological agent that the CIA said was safe but were wrong, and a real fight between the government and those who actually know what the term 'gunslinger' means. Murder is everywhere, and readers will never forget this Poisoned Gift once they see it in action. Wortham has created yet another [Texas] Red River Mystery that hits home in a big way, making [it] all the more terrifying."

—*Suspense Magazine*

"Richly enjoyable... Reads like a stranger-than-strange collaboration between Lee Child, handling the assault on the CIA with baleful directness, and Steven F. Havill, genially reporting on the regulars back home."

—*Kirkus Reviews*

"It's a pleasure to watch [Constable Ned Parker and Texas Ranger Tom Bell] deal with orneriness as well as just plain evil. Readers nostalgic for this period will find plenty to like."

—*Publishers Weekly*

"Reading the seventh [Texas] Red River Mystery is like coming home after a vacation: we're reuniting with old friends and returning to a comfortable place. Wortham's writing style is easygoing, relying on natural-sounding dialogue and vivid descriptions to give us the feeling that this story could well have taken place. Another fine entry in a mystery series that deserves more attention."

—*Booklist*

Unraveled
The Sixth Texas Red River Mystery

"The more I read of Reavis Wortham's books, the more impressed I am by his abilities as a writer... His understanding of family feuds, how they start and how they hang on long past their expiration date, is vital to the story line. Wortham's skill as a plotter is demonstrated as well. He's very good at what he does, and his books are well worth reading."

—*Reviewing the Evidence*

"This superbly drawn sixth entry in the series features captivating characters and an authentic Texas twang."

—*Library Journal*

"Not only does Wortham write exceptionally well, but he somehow manages to infuse *Unraveled* with a Southern gothic feel what would make even William Faulkner proud... A hidden gem of a book that reads like Craig Johnson's Longmire mysteries on steroids."

—*Providence Journal*

Dark Places
The Fifth Texas Red River Mystery

"Readers will cheer for and ache with the good folks, and secondary characters hold their own... The novel's short chapters fit both the fast pace and the deftly spare actions and details... the rhythm of Wortham's writing, transporting us back in time, soon takes hold and is well worth the reader's efforts."

—*Historical Novel Society*

Vengeance Is Mine
The Fourth Texas Red River Mystery

"Wortham is a masterful and entertaining storyteller. Set in East Texas in 1967, *Vengeance Is Mine* is equal parts Joe R. Lansdale and Harper Lee, with a touch of Elmore Leonard."

—*Ellery Queen's Mystery Magazine*

"Very entertaining... Those who have read the author's earlier books, including *The Right Side of Wrong* (2013), will be familiar with Center Springs and its rather unusual denizens, but knowledge of those earlier volumes is not required. This is a fully self-contained story, and it's a real corker."

—*Booklist*, Starred Review

The Right Side of Wrong
The Third Texas Red River Mystery

"A sleeper that deserves wider attention."

—*New York Times*

"Wortham's third entry in his addictive Texas procedural set in the 1960s is a deceptively meandering tale of family and country life bookended by a dramatic opening and conclusion. C. J. Box fans would like this title."

—*Library Journal*, Starred Review

Burrows
The Second Texas Red River Mystery

"Wortham's outstanding sequel to *The Rock Hole* (2011)... combines the gonzo sensibility of Joe R. Lansdale and the elegiac mood of *To Kill a Mockingbird* to strike just the right balance between childhood innocence and adult horror."

—*Publishers Weekly*, Starred Review

"The cinematic characters have substance and a pulse. They walk off the page and talk Texas."

—*Dallas Morning News*

The Rock Hole
The First Texas Red River Mystery

"One of the 12 best novels of 2011. An accomplished first novel about life and murder in a small Texas town... Wortham tells a story of grace under pressure, of what happens when a deranged and vicious predator decides that they're his promised prey…a fast and furious climax, written to the hilt, harrowing in its unpredictability. Not just scary but funny too, as Wortham nails time and place in a sure-handed, captivating way. There's a lot of good stuff in this unpretentious gem. Don't miss it."

—*Kirkus Reviews*

"Throughout, scenes of hunting, farming, and family life sizzle with detail and immediacy. The dialogue is spicy with country humor and color, and Wortham knows how to keep his story moving. *The Rock Hole* is an unnerving but fascinating read."

—*Historical Novel Review*

Also by Reavis Z. Wortham

The Texas Red River Mysteries
The Rock Hole
Burrows
The Right Side of Wrong
Vengeance Is Mine
Dark Places
Unraveled
Gold Dust
Laying Bones

The Sonny Hawke Mysteries
Hawke's Prey
Hawke's War
Hawke's Target
Hawke's Fury

THE TEXAS
JOB

THE TEXAS JOB

REAVIS Z. WORTHAM

Poisoned Pen
PRESS

Published by Poisoned Pen Press, an imprint of Sourcebooks
P.O. Box 4410, Naperville, Illinois 60567-4410
(630) 961-3900
sourcebooks.com

Library of Congress Cataloging-in-Publication Data
Names: Wortham, Reavis Z., author.
Title: The Texas job / Reavis Z. Wortham.
Description: Naperville, Illinois : Poisoned Pen Press, [2022]
Identifiers: LCCN 2021023656 (print) | LCCN 2021023657
(ebook) | (trade paperback) | (epub)
Subjects: GSAFD: Mystery fiction.
Classification: LCC PS3623.O777 T49 2022 (print) | LCC PS3623.O777
(ebook) | DDC 813/.6--dc23
LC record available at https://lccn.loc.gov/2021023656
LC ebook record available at https://lccn.loc.gov/2021023657

Printed and bound in Canada.
MBP 10 9 8 7 6 5 4 3 2 1

This one is for my longtime friend, Captain/Division-Director, Union Pacific Railroad Police, Landon McDowell (Ret.). Thanks for being there through thick and thin.

"We sleep safely in our beds because rough men stand ready in the night to visit violence on those who would do us harm."

—GEORGE ORWELL

Chapter One

The buckskin's hooves landed with soft thuds on the sandy East Texas road. The early autumn air was unusually dry and cool as scissortails dodged and darted over a wide pasture on my left. A mix of hardwoods rose green and thick off to the right, watered by an unseen creek. Filled with the tracks of other horses, wagon wheels, and narrow tires from gasoline-powered cars, the dirt road had obviously seen a lot of business both going and coming in the booming East Texas oil fields.

I'd recently stepped off a train in the small town of Troup and was a stranger to one of the oldest sections of the Lone Star State. A gentle breeze that day in 1931 cooled my face under the wide black brim of one of Mr. John B. Stetson's best full beaver hats. The air was fresh and clean with the scent of pine trees intermixed with the hardwoods and damp earth.

Against the clear blue sky, black wings rode the thermals off to the right. Something was dead over near the heavily wooded creek bottom. The unusual number of buzzards indicated it was large. As was my new habit when thinking, I unconsciously smoothed a recently cultivated mustache that had come in thick and brown.

Likely a cow that drifted away from someone's farm, or maybe a deer.
It was a good day to be out in the old way, swaying along in

a saddle. I figured it wouldn't be much longer before traveling horseback would be a thing of the past. Wagons were already fading away as folks replaced their mule teams with cars and pickup trucks. Tractors were showing up in the fields as farmers realized they could cover a lot more ground with a gas-powered engine than walking behind a team.

My relaxed mood vanished when a young, black-haired boy wearing nothing but a pair of faded Sears, Roebuck bib overalls and carrying a short, single-shot .22 rushed out from behind a thick cluster of cedars and stopped in surprise. He almost scared the pee-waddlin' out of me popping up so fast out of nowhere.

I reached for the holstered pistol under my coat, but the rent horse shied, and it took me a second to get the gelding back under control. Lucky for me the boy wasn't a real danger, but I cursed myself for not paying attention. The boy waved his arm back toward where he'd come from.

"Whoa, son!" The horse threw his head up and down in fear. "Settle down and stand still before this damned knothead twists out from under me." I noted his battered rifle with an octagonal barrel was the same as a little single-shot .22 dad bought me when I was about the kid's same age.

Instead of listening to me, he shouted, gesturing again with his free hand back toward the circling scavengers. Three squirrels tied by their necks swung on a rope around his waist.

I checked the brush beside the road. Thick cedars grew close along with blackberry vines that could conceal armed men intent on robbing me. A quick look behind satisfied me that it was only the two of us, and I had time to study the barefoot youngster blocking the road.

He looked downright terrified. Sweat-soaked and hatless, the kid was plumb out of breath. He stuttered, trying to talk in a flood of expressions, and I couldn't understand a word he said.

Good Lord, he ain't much more'n ten or eleven.

"Sorry, son. I don't savvy what you're saying. Sounds like you're talking Indian." I wondered if the kid was a half-breed. There were a lot of Choctaw and Cherokees still living in East Texas, along with Coushattas, Alabamas, and Caddoes, and they weren't timid about marrying one another. "You speak English? Tu hablas Español?"

He wiped sweat away from his forehead with a palm and collected himself. Gathering his thoughts, he grabbed for breath. "Yyyes." He paused and added, "Sssir. I know English, and can write my name, too."

"All right now. Now, make sure that rifle's pointed at the sky and simmer down. Tell me what's got you so het up you almost got me throwed."

The youngster gathered himself. "I I ff..."

"You're doing better. Take a deep breath to settle your nerves and swaller." He did. "All right, now try again."

"I...I found a body back there. Somebody's dead."

I studied the barefoot boy, who looked like hundreds of other shirtless kids trying to survive cotton and scratch farms in the fall of 1931. Hair cut short on the sides and longer on top, it wasn't hard to believe someone just put a bowl on his head and cut off everything else they could see.

I figured a parent did it. Barbers cost money, and it was a good way to save money in a depression.

I didn't feel that prickling on the back of my neck when there was danger around I'd learned to listen to long ago, so I settled back into the saddle and patted the gelding on the neck. "You sure about that? Maybe it's a cow, or something else like a panther kill."

"Nossir, Mr. Man. It's one of my people. A woman."

"My people." I couldn't help it, and checked my back trail, *still* not convinced we were alone. That kind of caution kept me alive down on the Mexican border. With the recent East Texas oil boom, thousands of men flocked to the Pine Top area in search of work or money. There were always a few who lived off others, stealing, robbing, or murdering for what little money a man might have in his pockets.

I finally relaxed when the gelding blew a couple of times and settled down under me. Giving the kid another minute to calm down, I studied the road cutting through the patchwork of woods, pastures, and fields. The busy oil town of Pine Top wasn't far, but still out of sight in the distance, as were the massive oil derricks I'd heard about, ones that strained upward like skeleton trees stripped of their limbs.

I wasn't there to see the derricks, though. I'd already seen the oil fields that swallowed Teague and sprouted so many rigs around the town of Gladewater tha the buildings were literally shaded in the evenings by the tall steel frames.

I softened my tone. "What's your name, son?"

As if the question had no relevance, the youngster blinked at me in silence.

Finally, the kid licked dry lips and took a deep breath. "Booker Johnston."

"Fine then, Booker Johnston. You got some Indian in you?"

"Yessir. Some. Half."

"Choctaw?"

The kid was surprised. "Cherokee."

"Figured with them high cheekbones. Got some Choctaw in *me*. Who do you get most of your light complexion from?"

"My daddy. My granny's where the Indian comes from."

"How far back yonder'd you find this body you're talking about?"

The kid swallowed and bit his bottom lip. "About a mile. You go over there a little ways down that path, and you'll cut a trace that leads to the creek."

"That where the body is?"

"Yessir."

"We're still about two miles from Pine Top, right?"

"Yessir." Booker pointed down the road with the rifle. "Two miles as the crow flies."

"That means around four or five on the road."

"Yessir."

"You live there?"

"Yessir."

I flicked a finger toward the squirrels hanging limp and fresh enough they hadn't stiffened up. "Guess you walked out here to hunt squirrels."

"Yessir. I'm the best shot in the family. I'd rather have rabbit, but Daddy won't let me shoot none 'til we get our first freeze."

"Your mama taught you good manners. Well, my name's Tom Bell. I reckon you better climb up here with me so we can go take a look at what you found. Hand me up that single-shot. Is it loaded?"

"Yessir."

"Then hand it up careful."

Booker passed the rifle up, and when I offered my hand, he grabbed and jumped at the same time I yanked. It wasn't the first time the youngster had mounted a horse in such a way, and he swung up behind me, smooth as oil.

I reined the horse down a game trail winding through the trees that closed in overhead, making it feel like a cool, shady tunnel. Their colored leaves covered the ground below. With the rifle resting across the seat rise in front of me, we fell silent as the horse's steady pace ate up the yards, and more leaves drifted down around us.

The boy settled in and steadied himself by holding my dress coat. His right forearm bumped the holstered revolver on my hip, and I reached back and adjusted Booker's hold without a word. He didn't react to the pistol, and I didn't expect him to. Guns weren't unusual in the country. They were as much of a tool as a hammer, saw, or those cast-iron monkey wrenches everyone carried to work on their T-model cars. Some men carried them for business left unfinished, and others for new business. I carried mine as part of the job.

Folks think the woods are quiet, but they're a symphony of natural sounds. Wind sighs through the trees. Limbs creak and rub against each other. Birds call and flutter through the branches. Insects buzz, water gurgles, and unseen animals rustle through the understory. I'd long ago learned to pay attention to the sounds around me, unconsciously filing them away when everything seemed normal. But when those sounds suddenly ceased on that downward slope, I reined in to figure out what was wrong.

The boy leaned around me. "What?"

"Shhh. Listen."

Not a bird called, and even the insects quieted. I tensed, trying to locate whatever it was that caused the silence. Movement catches the eye, and I slowly scanned the trees. I recalled an old woman down in the Valley once told me that when the world goes quiet, it's because the ol' Devil is close by.

I wasn't scared of the Devil himself. The things he made people *do* was what worried me. I rested my hand on the butt of the pistol and waited.

The boy shivered. As someone who spent a lot of time on his own in the woods, he felt it, too. I felt him turning to look behind us. Good for him.

Something was out there. Maybe a lion, or a bear. Cougars sneaking up on unsuspecting people in the woods was still pretty common. Both still lived in deep East Texas and down in the Thicket, and every now and then you'd hear of someone running into an irritable old black bear.

Here and now, though, it was most likely it was someone staying out of sight and sneaking around so I couldn't see him. The hair rose on my neck, thinking a rifle could be trained on us.

The horse shifted and stood hip-shot. He casually flicked an ear. If he'd sensed any danger, those soft ears would have pricked forward, giving me an indication of what might be coming, and from where.

He was completely unconcerned, and I relaxed. A late-season grasshopper buzzed across in front of us, wings rattling like dry paper. Somewhere in the distance, a woodpecker hammered at a tree, and a blue jay screeched.

The Devil had passed on by.

My heels urged the gelding forward, and the world woke back up. The trail led down a swale, then intersected an old two-track that likely began as an ancient foot trail before being cut deep by wagon wheels.

Tread marks in the dirt caught my attention. Out of habit, I reined up to study two sets of distinctive, narrow rubber tire tracks made when the ground was damp several days earlier. One set was slightly wider and overlapped the other.

"This where you're talking about?"

The boy leaned around him and again pointed upward. "It's the road that runs close to the creek. Now you can follow them."

"When did it rain last?"

"About a week ago. Rained purdy hard."

"Umm humm." Taking in the countryside, I heeled the gelding forward. We rode across the two thin lanes and back onto the beaten path. The ground sloped downward, and soon we caught the sound of water chuckling over a tangle of drifts that backed the stream into a shallow pond before spilling over a fallen log. The horse's ears pricked forward, and he snorted again, thirsty.

Here the path narrowed, becoming nothing but a game trail widened by hundreds, if not thousands of footprints through the years. The boy tensed behind me, and I realized we were getting close to the body.

I didn't intend to make the kid look at the remains again, and hated that he'd seen them in the first place. The first human corpse I'd ever seen as a result of violence was when I was nearly eighteen, and I figured that was a mite too soon for anybody.

Minutes later, we caught the distinctive odor of a rotting corpse. Whether it be human or animal, it's a smell that stays with a person long after they smell it for the first time. It brought back the memory of the first time I'd encountered it in an overgrown fencerow on a sunbaked gravel road in Center Springs, Texas, back when I was five, not long before Dad moved us down to the Valley.

I kept that memory, not because I found a dead coon rotting in the weeds on that sweaty summer afternoon, but because my dog rolled in it and Dad made him stay away from the house for more than two weeks until the stench faded away. It came back every time it rained, aggravating Dad to no end.

Our trail paralleled the muddy little creek, and fifty yards later I reined up. From high on the horse's back, it was easy to see how the boy had stumbled upon the corpse lying beside a downed tree trunk. With the wind behind him, and being on the ground, he wouldn't have been able to see the body until he was almost upon it.

Buzzards rested on the bare limbs sticking out from the split trunk, with their wings spread to catch the warm sun. They launched themselves into the air, followed by those who'd been feeding. One reluctant scavenger pounded the air and soared across the creek only a few feet above its surface. Booker slid to the ground, and I handed him the little rifle.

Swinging down, I passed the reins to the boy. "Hold him for a minute." Breathing through my mouth, I walked to the body and stopped by the corpse's feet.

Good goddlemighty.

"It's a woman." My quiet comment was more to myself than to the boy holding the horse. It's the way I work out a problem sometimes, talking to myself, or thinking about it so loudly in my head, it's a wonder people can't hear through my ear holes. "Poor thing."

She'd been laying out there for several days. The bloated corpse was dressed in a long skirt that would have reached to her calves had she been standing. Tangled, windblown hair covered most of her face. A large exit wound had taken most of her nose and upper teeth, telling me the gunshot came from behind. She would have been unrecognizable to her closest family members. A patchwork quilt half underneath her body was fouled with blood, fluids, and rotting tissue.

She wore bright red shoes.

She has…had…a little money.

I straddled the tree trunk after checking for snakes and circled the body, scanning the ground. Finding nothing else, I returned to the boy holding the horse. "Well, you were right."

"I done tol' you." Booker was staring off across the creek, his back to the body not far away. "I know what dead people look like."

"Just needed to see, so I can tell the sheriff when we get to town. I'll take you home. Said you live in Pine Top, right?"

"Yessir, on the far side and out of town a piece."

"And you came all this way on foot."

"Hitched a ride most of the way. Papa lets me hunt when I finish my chores on Saturday. Cotton won't be ready for a couple more weeks."

He was startled into silence when a covey of bobwhites exploded into the air. I turned toward the scattering quail and squinted. Something was out there.

The crack of a gunshot and a buzzing bullet shocked the still morning air. My Colt revolver was in my hand before I knew it. Another round whined off the log and into the woods behind us, telling me it wasn't a hunter, unless they were hunting *me*.

I threw two shots in the shooter's direction and waved back at the boy. "Get down, but hang on to them reins!"

Two more shots from the concealed shooter rolled together in a rumble of gunpowder-fueled thunder. The best cover was behind the log, opposite the woman's body. I dropped behind the silvery trunk and was immediately wrapped in the sickish-sweet odor of corrupted flesh.

Four rounds left in the Colt. Though I was practiced in fast reloads, I didn't want to be caught with an empty weapon if there was more than one shooter. I returned fire twice more and reached my free hand back toward Booker, who was flat on his belly and using the stream bank for cover.

"Stay down and slide your rifle over to me!"

He'd wrapped the reins around a tough sapling to restrain the anxious horse. Holding on with one hand, he pushed his little .22 toward me through the grass.

Staying low, I folded in half to reach the rifle. "You have more hulls for this?"

"Yessir. In here." From the front pocket of his overalls, Booker withdrew a wheat-colored Bull Durham Tobacco bag half full of .22 shells. Staying low, he sidearmed the ammunition, which bounced off my leg like a beanbag.

The hidden assailant's gun spoke again. The bullet struck the trunk only inches away and whined off into the woods. Rolling onto my side, I reloaded the revolver and jammed it back into the holster. Because there was so much cover between me and the shooter, I didn't trust my aim with the pistol. But a rifle was a different story, especially since I had learned to shoot with a .22 just like the one in my hands. I pulled the bag's drawstring loose, shook out three fresh rounds, and stuck them between my lips. I dropped the bag onto the ground.

The stub of a short branch was just long enough for me to hang the Stetson in view to offer a half-hidden target. Staying low, I crawled to the broken end of the log at the same time the shooter put a round through the branch, flipping the hat onto the ground.

Thankful he wasn't a great shot, I slowly pushed past the splintered end of the log and tucked the short rifle against my shoulder. Hoping its sight was accurate—and I figured it was since Booker took three squirrels with it that morning—I aimed through a tangle of dewberry vines and waited.

A minute passed, though it seemed like an eternity. A jay called in the woods, the harsh cry lonesome and loud.

Holding still and looking down the rifle's iron sights, I searched the understory bushes and waited. Finally, a flicker of movement told me where the rifleman was hiding. The man moved from behind a tree and studied the scene from his new vantage point. I hoped the guy thought he'd put a round through my hat and skull.

The would-be assassin leaned farther around a pine, aiming his rifle at where my hat had disappeared. He moved a little more into view and put one foot out to the side, providing a big belly that gave me more than enough target area. But something told the man to look left, and he saw enough there to make him jump back, half a second after I pulled the trigger.

The crack of the little .22 rifle was followed by a grunt. I broke the rifle down, pulled out the empty hull, and thumbed in one of the rounds from between my lips. Snapping it back, I lined up on that same tree and fired again, knocking off a chunk of bark. Loading again, I waited as a squirrel scolded us from high above.

It wasn't long before the shooter shoved off, running hard at an angle to my log. Nothing more than a flicker of blue movement between the trees, he offered little in the way of a target before he vanished into the woods. Frustrated, I finally rose to one knee.

"Stay there, Booker."

"Ain't got no place else to go."

Admiring the boy's grit, I left the cover and crept though the underbrush until I reached the shooter's vantage point. Expended brass was scattered around the tree, along with boot prints and a small drop of blood. Waiting, I kept an eye out as the unseen blue jay complained from somewhere back in the woods, signaling that the danger of more gunfire was likely over.

I picked up the empty hulls and went back. Booker rose.

"You hurt?"

"Nossir. He was shooting at you, not me."

"Well, had he hit me, you'd-a been next. Let's get on out of here." Taking the reins, I swung back into the saddle and helped the boy mount.

We rode back upstream until the corpse was far behind and the air cleared. I finally relaxed and reined the horse to the edge of the creek. The gelding smelled the surface, snorted, and drank. Booker dropped to the ground, walked a few feet upstream, and dropped to his stomach to reach the water for himself. Finished, he stood, wiping his mouth. "Mister, are you a lawman?"

Heart still pounding, I didn't want the kid to know I'd been scared back there. I tilted the black hat back on my forehead to show I was relaxed, though inside I was wound tighter than a mainspring. "Why do you ask that?"

"The way you fought back, and that pistol on your hip." Booker squinted upward. "You know how to use it. Most folks around here don't carry them low like you do. Them that do, just stick them in a pocket or under their belt."

"You're a right smart little feller." I lifted my lapel to reveal a badge. "I'm a Texas Ranger. Came up here after a murderer named Clete Ferras. Ever hear of him?" I unfolded a wanted poster and handed it down to him.

Booker shook his head. "Not so's I remember. You think that was him back there?"

"Could be, but I doubt it. He wouldn't know I'd be there. That was someone keeping an eye on the body, or something else. You know the sheriff around here?"

"I know Sheriff Dobbs in Pine Top. You want me to take you to him?"

"I'd be obliged. We'll both need to tell him what happened."

"I'll take you, but don't expect much out of him."

I felt the corner of my eyes wrinkle into crow's-feet. "How old are you, son?"

"'lebem."

"I 'magine you'll do well in life."

Chapter Two

Quinn Walker stepped outside onto the large covered porch of his four-square, two-story Craftsman, shipped as a kit from Sears, Roebuck and Company on a flatbed railroad car and assembled by experienced carpenters on-site. He smoothed his oiled hair back with a palm and plucked a gold watch from the pocket on his vest. Snapping it open, Walker bounced on his toes for a second, replaced the timepiece, and adjusted his suit coat.

He glanced up and down the brick street. Model T Fords and more than a few of the newer Model A's chugged past, dodging wagons, saddle horses, and pedestrians. Two blocks over, Pine Top's main street was even busier and working alive with cars. Not ten years earlier, his town had been nothing but a cluster of wooden buildings lining a wide dirt street huddled in the middle of the piney woods.

Now it had brick buildings, brick or oiled roads, and an overhead tangle of telephone poles and electric power lines, though Main Street was still hard-packed dirt in the summer and a mire when it rained. The city planned to start bricking Main on January 1, but most of the locals wondered why it hadn't already been done.

The truth was that Quinn Walker and his associates slipped enough cash under the table to brick their own residential streets first, with the promise of more to come for other projects if the city council would continue to cooperate.

He thought of it as his town, and he planned to own a lot of it in the years to come.

The familiar odor of frying chicken wafted through the open windows behind him, reminding Walker of how much he loved having an on-premises housekeeper. That's how civilized people lived, with someone to keep the house and yard. The lot was extra-wide because he'd purchased four of them at the same time and plopped the house right in the middle.

His grin widened. Mine. The house, grounds, and swelling bank account were his, or would be someday soon. Glancing back, he saw his plump wife settling into a rocker beside the window. Mallie enjoyed sewing or reading there in the breeze where the light was good and she could see the tall oil derricks rising over the town only two blocks away, pumping oil from the ground at an astonishing rate.

Walker was originally from nearby Hog Eye, where dozens of wells were changing the landscape of East Texas. He had missed the initial opportunity to get in on the ground level of Pine Top's oil business. Until he married Mallie Whitehorse, he didn't have two nickels to rub together, but her family had the incredibly good fortune to own fifty acres out west of Pine Top that they worked and sweated over for decades to make a few hundred dollars each growing season from cotton or corn. When her old man signed an oil lease and they struck crude, their whole world changed.

It changed even more when Quinn Walker swept her off her feet. Now Pine Top had four hundred wells within sight of the town, employing eighteen thousand new arrivals. That would soon be Hog Eye. He didn't intend to make the same mistake twice and miss another opportunity to be wealthy. With Mallie's money, he would soon be one of the richest men in Texas.

He scanned the horizon, then turned back to the house.

Mallie's dimples appeared. She waved one plump hand at her relatively new husband and spoke through the screen. "I thought you were gone."

Walker checked his watch again. "Gene's coming to pick me up."

"He's always late."

"Yep, but this time he was getting up a few things for me."

"Okay. Don't be late for dinner. I may go to bed early. I'm still not feeling good. I just don't know what's wrong with me these days."

"I won't." Instead of getting hooked into another conversation about her health, he paused and heard the squeal of brakes as a large truck carrying a load of live trees pulled to a stop out front. The driver killed the engine and spoke across the seat. "Here're your sycamores, Mr. Walker."

"They look smaller than I ordered."

"Well, sir. It was a chore digging these up down in the bottoms. Like I told you, it's too early to be transplanting them, so I chose smaller trees so we could get a bigger root ball. Even that ain't gonna guarantee they'll live. Now, if you'd-a waited 'til January…"

"Nope. I want 'em now." He pointed at the bare yard. "I got it marked where I want 'em."

"We'll get to it, soon's my hand shows up."

"I'll be back in half an hour." A black 1930 Ford sedan pulled to a stop in front of the house. "There he is." With a quick wave back to his new bride, he trotted down the front steps. Gene Phillips was watching Mallie as Walker opened the door.

Even the unfamiliar could see that Phillips's car was a step above the common Model A Fords in town. In fact, his was the top-of-the-line town car that cost over $1,200, but Walker's car would be much better still, once it was delivered.

He stepped up on the running board and slammed the door. Hanging an arm out the open window, he looked straight ahead. "You get it?"

"Said I would."

"Where?"

"What difference does it make?" Phillips pushed on the foot-feed, and they joined the stream of cars.

"I just want to know where it came from."

"Lyall Brennen made it. He said if you mix it with something sweet, she won't taste a thing. Just be sure you don't drink any of it."

"I won't. How fast will it happen?"

"Well, pretty fast now that you're dosing her with that other stuff. If you give her a little at a time, though, it might take two or three weeks. That could buy enough time for you to set up a solid alibi."

Walker's head snapped around. "What? How'n hell am I gonna get her to drink so much of this stuff?"

"Hell, she's part Indian, ain't she?" Phillips pulled around an ice wagon. The deliveryman reached inside, clamping tongs around a white chunk of ice that was heavy enough it took some effort to lift it up to his wet shoulder. "You know how Indians are. Once she gets a taste of good white lightning, you'll have to chain her to the house if you run out, or she'll be bird-dogging every driller that'll buy her a drink."

"Hell, I don't think I can take being around her for that long. I might just get a funnel and pour it in."

Phillips laughed and stuck his left arm out the window to

signal a turn. Muscling the car around the corner, he almost ran head-on into a butter-yellow Nash. Both drivers hit their brakes at the same time, and the vehicles stopped parallel to each other with the drivers close enough to touch.

Jack Drake nodded at his third cousins Quinn Walker and Gene Phillips.

The heavyset man nodded and shifted into neutral. "Howdy, Gene. I was just coming to see you, Quinn. When's your new Duesenberg coming in?"

Refusing to drive a common man's black Model T, Walker had ordered his own red Duesenberg Convertible Victoria with a cream-colored top, ignoring Phillips's argument that the car was too long and ostentatious for East Texas folks. It didn't matter, though, because Walker's new up-and-coming status required something few others had.

He'd pushed for the expensive vehicle he'd read about in *Autocar*, but Mallie refused because it would be too showy and expensive. He gave up for a while, because her name was on their bank account and the titles of everything they owned, but one day he slipped over to the Ford house and talked one of the salesmen into calling all the way to Indianapolis to find they had the car that had been sitting in a showroom for over a year.

He bought it on the spot, using the house as collateral until the car came in. Though his signature at the bank was useless on the account, bank president Emsworth wasn't above a little financial sleight of hand when he suspected someone was about to come into even more money than they already had. Oil money flowed through his hands on a daily basis, and he knew Walker would be good for it, because they were working closely together on what they called their "Project."

It all came from the oil that was virtually under their feet, because Pine Top was a boomtown straddling Gregg and Rusk counties. Landowners in those counties and others stretching from north of Pine Top all the way down beyond Henderson, an area forty-three miles long and nearly thirteen miles wide, were signing drilling leases every day, if the owners were truly attached to their land. Others completely sold out, took the cash, and left for brighter days somewhere else.

Then again, those like Walker were more ambitious. Marry into a land-rich family and enjoy the spoils. It was happening more and more throughout the area. Truthfully, it wasn't *his* idea, but he'd arrived a year earlier as the drilling was spinning up, and met a few others who decided to form a loose organization and work together to satisfy their dreams.

Once Mallie and her mama were out of the way, he'd inherit everything, and he couldn't hardly wait.

Walker thought about how he'd look sitting in the car with a chauffeur behind the wheel. "It'll be here just in time. You do what I told you?"

Drake's expression went flat. "I don't work for you."

He'd done it again. Growing up, they were partners, but Walker tended to be the thinker. A year younger, Drake didn't mind it until Walker started ordering him around, then he always dug both heels in, stubborn as a turtle that won't let go of a bite until it thunders.

"I'm sorry. You're right, and I stepped out of my place. Did you do what I *asked*?"

"Kind of."

"What's that mean?"

Drake wiped a hand across his forehead. "I intended to, but listen, there was a guy there. Some stranger in a black hat."

Phillips stiffened. "Doing what?"

"Poking around." Drake glanced at the pedestrians passing

close by. He lowered his voice. "I'm afraid the cat's out of the bag on that one."

"Dammit." Walker shook out a Lucky Strike and lit it. "How'd it happen?"

Drake shot him a disgusted look. "I didn't hang around to *ask* the man. Some kid was with him, though."

"Kids. Always messing things up. Did he see you?"

"Not enough to recognize me, but the guy put a hole in my stomach with a damned .22. I was lucky it was so small. If it'd been a bigger rifle, it woulda killed me."

"He shot you?" Phillips's voice came loud and shrill.

"That's what I said."

"Shhh." Walker checked their surroundings. "Why'd he shoot you?"

"I shot at him first. Missed. Then the next thing I knew we're in a damned gunfight, and I was hit. The old woman who doctored me up said it was a .22. I went to her instead of Doc Patton. I didn't need anyone asking questions."

Walker nodded. "Good idea."

"How bad is it?" Phillips leaned forward as if to look at Drake's abdomen. Since they were still in the idling cars, the movement was more instinct than a genuine attempt to see the wound under his clothes.

"Went through the fat here on the side. Hurts like a son of a bitch, and it still leaks, but I'll live."

"What's Calpurnia say about that?"

"She don't see me without my clothes. We don't exactly have *relations* these days 'cause she's so sick."

"Fine then." Walker leaned back, relieved. "Everything's all right for now. We're still on track."

Nodding in thought, Drake built a wry smile and rubbed the side of his ample stomach. "How's Mallie'n them?"

Walker and Phillips exchanged looks, but Quinn saw something in the man's eyes he didn't like. Fear. "They're fine, for now."

Despite his concern, and Drake's bullet wound, the three men laughed, but Phillips was the last to join in.

Chapter Three

My rent horse was skittish, so I kept a tight rein on the gelding as we came into the fringes of the bustling town. A couple of miles out, trees gave way to open fields and pastures divided by bobwire fences stapled to bois d'arc posts cut from tough Osage orange trees. Everywhere we looked, oil derricks towered over the land. Here and there, new rigs bored deep holes in search of the next gusher.

On the outskirts of Pine Top, we passed a tent city full of oil workers squatting in a sea of dried mud. Rough, unpainted wooden walls covered by new or rotting canvas, or corrugated tin, called "sheet iron" in that part of the state, lined narrow dirt traces substituting for roads. Smoke drifted from dozens, if not hundreds, of fires, leaving a haze in the air that joined the chemical smell of spilled crude. Rough outhouses scattered through the camp added the foul odor of human feces, no matter where anyone stood.

"Stay out of these camps, young Booker. They're no fit places for a boy, and before long you'll see cholera and typhus here and, I'll allow, dengue fever on top of all that."

"I've heard of those sicknesses."

"You'll hear more about 'em, too. When all this plays out and everybody leaves, it'll be the worst dump you ever saw."

As we got closer to town, the camps gave way to a number of sun-faded, boxlike wood-frame buildings scattered alongside the road. A young boy was playing in front of a porch-less church identified only by a hand-painted sign nailed over the front door that opened right onto the road.

Older, more established frame houses increased in number, some were on the road, others at a distance, but all were within sight of an oil rig. A neglected farmhouse that had obviously been there for thirty or more years was boxed in by wells drilled mere feet from all four corners. At the outskirts of town, scattered farmhouses separated by fields and pastures were dwarfed by oil rigs. Looking straight ahead, I counted nineteen wells within the distance of only half a mile.

This town'll be rougher than any of them border towns ever were, Progresso and Ciudad Juárez included.

Near what amounted to downtown Pine Top, the unpaved road finally led through a tent city of businesses. It widened slightly, passing between several hundred yards of temporary buildings with plank sides and newer tin roofs, proof there was money to be made and it was.

Mary Glenn's Coffee and Doughnuts was doing a brisk business under a derrick, the canvas sides rolled up for ventilation. The doughnuts sure smelled good, until the wood smoke from a barbecue barrel built directly in the street took over.

What could be lanes or alleys intersected the busy street, leading to even more businesses deeper in the boomtown camp. Next came a line of quickly erected structures with false fronts. Built only two feet apart, and in some instances against one another, they ran the gamut from diners and stores to tents where workers could rent twelve hours on a cot at the end of their shift.

Booker read the signs to me as we passed to show me he knew his letters.

"Pine Tree Bath House, Texas Café, J.R. Crane: Groceries, Tools, Hats, Circulating Library, Louis Pond and Co. Merchandise."

"Looks like a gold rush town."

Cars and trucks parked haphazardly along both sides of the street. Loafers on wooden sidewalks watched us pass, while others, bent on their individual tasks, ignored the horse. To a man, they all wore hats, some battered and sweat-stained, others fairly new fedoras and cowboy hats.

A bent corner of one piece of a sheet-iron roof rattled in the slight breeze, a sound that makes me feel low, no matter when or where I hear it. The horse tolerated motorized vehicles, but he didn't like them one damn bit. The rattling tin spooked him, and only my experience kept him under control.

I spoke to Booker over my shoulder. "I don't know how you stomach all this."

"Don't, much. We stays mostly on the farm, except for Saturdays, when we come to town for supplies or when it rains us out of the fields."

Horses and riders were still common enough that most people paid us little attention amid the steady stream of activity on the street. Even Booker riding behind with the .22 rifle across his legs went unnoticed.

The growth nearer the center of town was astonishing. The town sprouted a grove of steel derricks that were in places only feet apart, towering amid clusters of buildings as far as we could see.

It was impossible to look up at the sky without seeing dozens of derricks. I craned my neck until it ached, awed by what men had constructed in only a few months. A tall brick church to the left was overshadowed by fourteen rigs that blocked the view from any direction. Cars lined up on the street were dwarfed by the structures.

To somebody with a vivid imagination, the derricks could have been foundation columns for an entire world to be built high above.

Adding to the overhead turmoil, power lines and telephone lines ran every which way in a spiderweb of confusion, sagging between fresh posts that hadn't been there long enough for the creosote to cure.

Unfortunately, the infrastructure hadn't caught up with the town's construction and booming population. The streets were still dirt and packed with wagons pulled by horses and mules, along with T-model cars and the newer Model A Fords.

"I bet this is a mess when it rains."

The boy chuckled. "Everything buries hub deep. I was here one Saturday and sat right over there and watched all day long. They's using mules to pull cars out, and they'd bury right back up again before they could get out of town.

"My uncle made a small fortune that day with his mule. He prays for rain every day now. Back before the drillers came, everyone stayed in and did inside chores when we had falling weather. Now getting muddy's worth more'n chopping cotton."

The noise increased as we passed particularly close to a drilling rig, and I had to raise my voice. "You're gonna have to tell me where the sheriff's office is."

"It's still a ways up here, by the town hall."

"Makes sense."

Two-story brick buildings were dwarfed by buildings five stories tall rising on both sides of the streets, and more were under construction. The air was thick with smoke, almost invisible particles of oil, and the constant chemical scent of crude.

The gelding shook his head and snorted at the chaotic

activity that increased the closer we came to the downtown area. "Easy, son." I stroked the restless horse's neck to calm him down again.

Booker settled himself behind the saddle. "Ridin' this way's wallering out the insides of my legs. Why're you ridin' a horse anyway? I'd be in a car myself."

"Because I took a train from Tyler over to Troupe. I had to go someplace a car wouldn't, like when this street gets wet. I didn't want the feller I'm after to know I was coming if he was hiding out in the woods or a thicket. A horse walks quiet."

"You gonna keep ridin' him?"

"Some, but I have a feller bringing a car in for me. He should be here by now."

"You better hope it don't rain." The boy pointed. "There's the sheriff's office."

The old brick building was under renovation. Across the street, a large, well-dressed man in a cowboy hat and boots leaned on a post amid the clamor of drilling, watching the works and the traffic passing by. His brown suit looked expensive, cut to fit the big man's three-hundred-pound frame. With thick hands, red nose and cheeks, he gave every indication of being an experienced brawler.

"The fat guy there's Sheriff Dobbs."

I waited for an oil tanker to rattle by, then reined across the street. As if he'd been there before, the horse stopped at a concrete sidewalk rising a foot off the ground and sniffed the iron tether ring anchored there.

Sheriff Dobbs tore his attention from the construction and derricks as if they'd sprouted while he was standing there. He focused on us and spat a stream of tobacco juice. "Won't be long, there won't be horses in town no more. They turned the blacksmith shop into a garage that smells like dirty old grease.

Gimme the smell of horseshit any day. When they brick this street, there'll be electric streetcars. I won't even recognize the place in five years."

I heard the resignation in the man's higher-than-normal voice. "Times are changin', that's for sure. They building you a bigger jail?"

Sheriff Dobbs grunted and peered upward from under his hat brim. "They're shortening the damned thing to accommodate the wells they're drilling back behind." He jerked a thumb toward the street corner. "Can you believe it? Cuttin' off the backs of buildings to make room for another rig."

He nodded back the way we came. "They're tearing a whole bank down over there. Tearing it down to drill another damned well right where it sits. I never saw anything like it.

"A year ago we had about seven hundred folks living here. Now I figure there's about ten thousand people tearing this town apart, and I don't like it one damned bit. Hell, there's more'n three hundred water and sewer connections in the city right now and more going in every day. If they ain't drillin', they're digging ditches to bury pipe."

Pulling his suit coat back to expose the ivory-handled revolver in a relatively new hand-tooled leather holster on his hip, Sheriff Dobbs rested a fist on his belt. The badge pinned to his left lapel glowed in the sunlight. "Now, you looking for me with that pistol under your coat there, Mister?"

"I am." I pulled back the coat's lapel to show the Ranger badge pinned to my shirt. "Tom Bell."

"J. L. Dobbs." The sheriff tilted his head to see the boy behind me. He pulled the coat back to cover the pistol. "That's Booker Johnston behind you. I've knowed him since he was a pup, and his daddy before that. He a prisoner? I can't lock no half-breed kid up with those hard cases. Right now, all I got is a concrete building to hold what I got, and it don't have no windows, only a little bitty door you have to duck through."

I shook my head. "Nope. Mr. Johnston here waved me down out west of town. He found a body, so I brought him in with me."

A crease formed between the Sheriff's eyebrows. "*Body?* I'm not of a mind to take a shavetail kid's word on finding *bodies*. Especially this one, or his buddy Hut Parsons. Seems like ever time I turn around, one of these two scalawags are into something."

"Well, you'll take my word, then. He took me to it, and it's there, sure enough. Looks like murder to me."

He sighed, as if put out by the notion of somebody being dead out of town. "Well, then. I'll have to check it out." He explored a tooth for a minute with his tongue. Finding what he was looking for, he spat the particle into the street. "Now, you ain't here huntin' bodies in the woods. The Rangers send you out here to help Delgado wrangle these roughnecks? A lot of that trouble's already handled. He's done shot two or three."

"He doesn't have much of a sense of humor, that's for sure."

I knew Ranger Enrique Delgado had arrived in Pine Top a month earlier to rein in what some called the most lawless town in Texas. I figured the slight but formidable Ranger, nicknamed Iron Eyes, had already made a significant impact on the wide-open town.

A passing tanker truck rumbled past, and I waited so I wouldn't have to holler over it. "I don't believe he needs any help with roughnecks trying to tree the local constabulary. I imagine between the two of you, y'all have everything handled. I'm here looking for a murderer on the dodge. Heard he was seen here in town a couple of days ago."

"Delgado don't need no help, for sure. He wrapped up

an investigation here a while back and walked a hundred chained-up men through town like a circus parade. Like I said, people are still pouring in looking for work or just money, and I'll allow a good number of 'em are criminals. What's this feller's name you're looking for?"

"Clete Ferras. Wanted for murder down in Laredo."

"Don't recognize the name, but that don't mean nothin'. Whyn't you just call up here and get Iron Eyes to arrest him for you? Save you some trouble."

"He has his own job to do. I have mine." I reached back to pat Booker's skinny leg. "Hop down."

The youngster slid off, and I handed down the rifle one more time. "Sheriff, he can tell you where to find the body, or I can go with you once you round up a deputy or two. The woman looks like him." I nodded toward the youngster who held the .22 one-handed by the fore-piece, with the muzzle pointed down.

Dobbs frowned. "Well, then. That information changes everything. If it's just an Indian, I'll send some of the boy's people to pick it up."

"Her." My ears grew hot, and I had to choke down the anger trying to rise like steam from a kettle. "It was a woman murdered, and it don't make no difference what color her skin is, yellow, black, white, or red. You're the law. Don't you want to look around before you bring her back?"

"I got lots to do. This town's a-boomin." Seeing a look in my eyes, Dobbs rubbed his chin. "Well, I guess I can take one of my men with me to look. Still need somebody with a pickup or a mule to bring her to her people."

"Y'all don't have a funeral home? Looks like you would, town this size."

"Naw. Lots of these folks out in the woods and down in the Thicket take care of one another. Somebody'll knock a box together for her." The sheriff fixed Booker with a look. Once a million acres in size, the Big Thicket was a virtually impenetrable woodland of hardwoods and understory plants that hid generations of people who originally hid from the law and seldom emerged. "You reckon she's your kinfolk?"

"Don't know, sir, she's. She's, she's..."

I answered for the boy. "Pretty ripe."

Booker shrugged. "I don't know of anyone who's missin', and didn't recognize the clothes. Not from church ner anywhere else."

A truck backfired, the report loud even over the chaos around them. The gelding jerked and fought the reins for a moment, then steadied.

"What is it with you Rangers and horses? You need a car here in town."

I sighed, not in the habit of explaining myself. The man was irritating me even more, and I'd already answered that question once. "I have one." I gathered the reins in my hand. "I'm going to the hotel after I return this horse. You can find me there."

"They're liable to be full up."

Done with the man, I ended the conversation. "They won't be." I studied Booker standing there with his squirrels. "Come on, Deputy."

Chapter Four

After checking in to the hotel, Booker and I walked back down to the sheriff's office to talk with Dobbs about how many independent oilmen might be drilling in Pine Top. He was standing behind his desk when I left the boy outside and stepped into the office, bringing the outside noise and odors with me.

Smoothing my mustache, I fully expected to feel oil on my fingers. "I believe there's a few more rigs popped up while I was checking in."

"Wouldn't be surprised." Dobbs picked up his hat. Like mine, the brim on one side was creased into a permanent curl from handling. "What can I do for you?"

"I'd like to get an idea who to talk with, who might have hired the man I'm looking for, if he's working."

Dobbs shoved a handful of wanted posters across the cluttered desk. "Didn't find anything here on Clete Ferras."

"Didn't expect you to." I dug the wanted poster from my coat pocket and handed it over. "I don't need another picture on a wanted bill. I'm looking for the man himself."

"Well, I didn't get to study on it very long. There's a lot of sheriffin' to do around here without having to track down strangers running from the law."

His attitude irritated me, but I tried not to show it. "All right, then. I'm going to start nosing around. How many independent drillers are hereabouts, you think?"

"Good goddlemighty. I can't even take a swing at that one. Too many to count. A couple of the bigger outfits might be where you'd start, but come to think of it, does this Ferras have any drilling experience?"

"None that I've heard of. I'm not even sure if he's working, but a man needs money, so if he's not rolling drunks, he'll be doing something to make a little pocket cash."

"Well, then. I'd think about talking to the smaller operations. They might be more inclined to hire a boll weevil first."

"Inexperienced drillers, right?"

"That's it. The bigger companies might pay more for experience and shy away from someone they're gonna have to teach. Them weevils who don't know what they're doing tend to get hurt or killed pretty fast. They don't want none of that, if they can help it."

"Good idea." I shoved the stack of posters back across the table. "You let me hear if you run across that name, and I'll look around."

"You might want to talk to Delgado. He's brought in a bunch of 'em."

"I will. I've already been by the boardinghouse where he lives, and the woman there told me he usually comes in close to dark. I'll be waiting for him there. Hey, did you get out there to pick up that body?"

"Sent some deputies. They're already back, and they have her over behind the funeral home."

"*Behind* it?"

"White folks ain't gonna let a half-red nigger body lay in the same room as their kin."

My face flushed, and I forced myself to speak softly. "You use that word around me again, Dobbs, and it'll be you and me. Didn't like it around me down in the Valley, and won't allow it here."

Though he was bigger than me, the sheriff's eyes slid off my face and down to the black-and-white wanted posters. He licked his lips. I let him squirm for a few seconds before continuing. "Did your deputies draw the same conclusions I did?"

Dobbs shrugged. "They didn't draw nothin'. Just picked up the body, like I told 'em to."

"Aren't you gonna investigate? It's a homicide, if I ever saw one."

"It was." Dobbs straightened with pride. "Already made an arrest."

"How'd you do that so fast?"

"Last night I got word that a feller by name of Stanley McCord was talking about taking that...Indian gal out for a good time. Heard that she's a pro skirt. Picked him up over in Shantytown, and he broke down and confessed, said they'd got to arguing and he threatened her with a pistol from his pocket. Probably about price. Anyway, she grabbed it and fell, and it went off. He'll go before a jury, but I imagine they'll rule it an accident. You know, she was an Indian."

"I don't know that at all. She had black hair's all I know. Is he white or colored?"

"White. Sure's hell won't have no Indians or nig...Negroes on a jury around here to get him off. They all have their places, and it ain't in no court of law, 'less they're on trial." He grinned.

"You have him in jail?"

"Naw, he works for J. R. Rupert. They posted bond and said they'd keep an eye on him until the trial next month. No reason for the county to feed him all that time. Took the bracelets off and sent him on his way."

"You know she was shot in the back of the head, right?"

Dobbs shrugged. "No telling how it happened. She could have been falling, or he dropped the pistol for all I know. It'll all come out in the trial."

I watched Sheriff Dobbs's expression, but saw nothing in there. "Well, since you gave me a name, I guess I'll just start with Rupert and see if he's heard of Ferras."

"Good hunting." Dobbs went back to shuffling through a sheaf of papers.

Trying to cool down, I stepped back outside and found Booker Johnston sitting on the sidewalk, waiting for me. "Howdy, son."

"I heard y'all talking in there. Deputy Knott and some other feller hauled her out of that creek bottom and brought her back in the bed of the truck. She's in a box full of ice over behind the funeral home."

"I heard."

"You going over there to look at her?"

"Seen her already, and the sheriff's already got a confession."

"I heard that, too, but Mr. Bell, Hazel Freeman weren't no hoochie coocher, like they said."

"Where'd you get that language?"

"Heard on the radio."

"Them blamed things are gonna ruin kids. Now, you didn't know who she was when we got to town. How do you know who she is now?"

Rubbing his hair in thought, Booker found something buried in the tangle and examined it between two fingertips. "Well, I suspicioned then who she might be, but I didn't want to say for sure. When we got to town, Miz Nellie Freeman'd already come in looking for her daughter Hazel. She's been gone a while. She talked to Sheriff Dobbs, but I doubt he even listened to her.

When Miz Nellie heard there was a body, she got somebody to bring her to town, and I heard her a-wailin' a little bit ago when she recognized them red shoes."

"What about Nellie's husband, Hazel's daddy? He in the field?"

"Not no more. He came to town a few months ago to work the rigs and got killed in a drillin' accident. It's just them and a boy who ain't got sense enough to know the difference between 'come here' and 'sic 'em.' He was kicked in the head by a mule when he was just a little feller and ain't been right since."

"Well, I hate to hear all that. Now, have you ever heard of J. R. Rupert?"

"Sure 'nough. Runs one of the biggest drilling operations out here."

"You know where to find him?"

Booker adjusted his overalls' one gallus over his shoulder. The other one was missing the buckle loop. "He's drilling a new well a few blocks over."

"Take me there, and I'll give you two bits for your trouble."

"A quarter? That ain't much to pay a guide."

I couldn't help but grin at the little businessman. "All right. I'll make it a fifty-cent piece, but don't try to hold me up for more."

"Done." The boy rose as smooth as a cat and led the way.

Chapter Five

Heavy gray clouds over Pine Top darkened the ravaged landscape of change. The sun winked out and the air immediately cooled several degrees. It had been windy out of the south for the last couple of hours, and now the breeze seemed to come from everywhere.

The clamor of drilling filled the air as roughnecks slung chains and rattled pipes. Three men in khakis and waist-length jackets were leaning over a map spread across the hood of a Model A Ford when me and Booker Johnston came down the side street off Main.

Booker pointed. "That there's who you're looking for. Mr. J. R. Rupert there in the middle."

"I figured as much. Looks like a man in charge."

I found out later that the gruff, hard-drinking man with scarred knuckles and a crooked nose had been a roughneck himself, working for a crooked con man by the name of Billy Harden back in 1927. That was after the wildcatter gained the mineral rights to thousands of acres of land by creating a syndicate and offering a one-acre interest in the lease block. He convinced investors to join the drilling lease for twenty-five dollars each.

Once Harden had enough money in hand, he paid a spurious geologist for a false report that promised the existence of oil-soaked strata far underground. He mailed the bogus report to hundreds of names on his sucker list and re-sold the same shares again and again, claiming that major oil companies were already drilling.

To keep up appearances, Harden paid Rupert a quarter of what he collected to drill a bogus well, so they'd have something to show future "investors." Unfortunately for Harden, the scheme fell through when a widow-woman by the name of Grace Atwell gave him every penny she had, but then regretted her decision and killed herself with her late husband's pistol.

The suicide prompted an investigation that eventually led to Harden's arrest. The authorities felt Rupert wasn't part of the scheme, merely a hired driller, and let him go, but he went with his pockets full of cash. With that seed money, Rupert went straight, drilled his first well, and struck it rich.

At the time, though, I didn't know a thing about the driller or his shady past when I stopped in front of the trio. "Gentlemen."

Rupert straightened from the papers on the hood. The others turned their attention from the geologist's report and waited. Rupert nodded. "I know a lawman when I see one."

"Yep. Tom Bell. Texas Ranger. You're Mr. Rupert."

"I am. How can I help you?"

"Looking for a man named Clete Ferras. Murdered a man in South Texas, and I trailed him up to this part of the country. Sheriff said you run one of the biggest operations here in Pine Top and thought you might have him working for you. He suggested I start with one of the smaller outfits, but I prefer to start at the top."

I didn't bother to tell Rupert that I didn't trust Dobbs and figured he was trying to lead me somewhere I didn't want to go by suggesting I start with smaller companies.

Rupert slid a hand into the pocket of his khakis and jingled the change there. "Well, the name don't ring a bell, but we hire a lot of men. I don't know all their names."

I handed him the wanted poster. "Maybe you've seen him. Hawk nose. Long face that ends in a narrow chin that juts out and curves up. Graying hair he oils back. Prominent cheekbones and sunk-in cheeks, because he's missing so many teeth. The man just looks mean, and I doubt he ever smiles."

"You're describing half of the men working here, and about a quarter of my own kinfolk." Rupert barely glanced at the paper before returning it. "You need to speak with my rig manager who does the hiring and firing."

"I appreciate it." Looking past him at a nearby rig, I saw one of the drillers who should have been paying attention to the job at hand, but was instead watching us, or rather, me.

Rupert tilted the spotless fedora up on a long forehead. "You're not with them Rangers they sent out here a couple of months ago to shut the field down."

I knew the story. Overproduction had sent the price of crude down to thirteen cents a barrel. To stabilize the market, Governor Ross Sterling sent the Rangers and National Guard to limit the East Texas production to market demand and stabilize the price of crude by shutting down nearly seventeen hundred wells before opening them back up in September. Disgruntled operators filed lawsuits in protest.

Others had a different idea. They simply shipped hot oil, or crude produced above the legal limit, out of the field in a variety of creative ways such as bribing truckers to haul at night using company rigs, or railroad and pipeline employees who filled barrels and loaded them on trucks. One enterprising company stole tankers from others and sold the contents in backdoor deals that brought high profits for little capital outlay.

The governor shut the operation down pretty fast by sending Ranger Enrique Delgado to Pine Top to clean things up.

"Nossir. I work out of Company D, not B. My company's assigned to the Rio Grande Valley. I haven't been up this way in years."

The rigger beyond Rupert kept watching the exchange until one of the roughnecks on the platform with him shouted for the man to get back to work. Throwing one last look over his shoulder, the man rejoined his crew.

It wouldn't hurt to keep my eye on him as we talked, though I tried not to look past Rupert. You want to end a conversation pretty fast, just look away from the man you're talking to, and it'll be over in no time. I owed him the courtesy of paying attention to our conversation. "Who's your rig manager, Mr. Rupert?"

"Name's Andy Fontenot. You'll know who that crazy Cajun is as soon as you hear him talk. He's over in a rent house off Elm Street that we use as our headquarters."

"I'll drop by."

Rupert turned back to his map, then pivoted back, brow furrowed. "Arrest Ferras if you want, if he's one of mine. I don't need no trouble around here, but try not to take too many others. That Ranger Delgado's wearing me out. I've lost two dozen men in the past two weeks."

"What for?"

"Drinking, fighting, cutting…the same thing you see in all these boomtowns."

"You might have your man cull 'em a little better when he hires 'em, then." Still concerned with the man on the oil rig a hundred yards away, I shifted to a new line of thought. "What time does this shift end?"

Rupert frowned and flicked open the cover to his pocket watch. "In about ten minutes. Why?"

"No reason. Just trying to get an idea of the comings and goings around here." I nodded a thanks and left, followed by Booker. When we were out of earshot, I stopped and turned back to the rig I'd been watching. Taking Booker's shoulder, I twirled the boy to face me. "Look past me and tell me if you see that redheaded rigger on that platform. See him? Bright-red sunburned nose."

"Yessir."

"Good. I'm gonna ease over here where I can watch a while without him knowing it. When they get off shift, go tell him I need to talk to him. I want to see what he does."

"You ain't paid me my wages for bringing you over here yet."

"Good Lord, boy. I'm not made of money." I handed him a fifty-cent piece. It disappeared into the pocket of his overalls.

Booker squinted up at me. "Now that we've settled for past wages, you need to know that telling him, that'll cost you another two bits."

Without expression, I held my hand out, and the crestfallen youngster dug in his pocket and returned the coin. "I'm sorry..."

I sifted through the change in my pocket and held out a silver dollar. "A man has a right to be paid for his job. That oughta cover it."

Booker's face lit up. "Done!"

Knowing that a youngster with a solid dollar was a rarity in that area, I tapped the coin in his palm. "Show that to him so he'll know you're there for me."

The boy left, and I leaned against a bollard, absorbing the beehive of activity around me. The number of men on the street increased with the shift change, many rubbing shoulders as they passed. On the elevated sidewalk on the opposite side of the dirt lane where they were drilling, I watched Booker wait for the redhead to come down off the platform with his buddies.

Fat raindrops landed with soft splats on the sidewalk shed overhead. Others exploded on dusty cars and in the dirt road, quickly soaking into the dry ground.

The shift ended, and covered in dirt and grease, the redhead paused when Booker stepped in front of him. They talked for a moment, and the man stiffened. Booker held up the silver dollar, and Red snatched at it. The boy jerked away just in time and the rigger tried to backhand him out of the way, but Booker jumped back and trotted off. Red scanned the area and hoofed it for the next dirt intersection to his left. He dodged a truck and jogged out of sight.

I dropped down in the street and jogged in the same direction, paralleling Red one block away and keeping an eye on the vehicles that flowed eastward. At the next intersection, I turned left and sprinted down the busy street for the corner. The number of men lessened. Red soon appeared, looking back over his shoulder.

Stepping out, I grabbed the man's filthy shirt and slung him around and against the wall of what was once a blacksmith shop, now an automobile repair shop. "Hold up there, amigo!"

The man threw his arm up, breaking my hold. He swung a grime-covered fist at my jaw, but I was expecting something like that. I slapped it away with my left hand and cracked him in the side of the head with a lead-weighted leather sap I use to get people's attention. Red's knees sagged.

Holding him upright, I cocked my arm again. "We still fightin'?"

Breathing hard, Red shook his head and blinked to clear his vision. "Naw, we ain't."

"Good." I lowered the sap. "What're you running from?"

"Nothin'. I ain't running from a damned thing."

"I know that boy said I wanted to talk with you."

"I don't believe nothin' a strange kid tells me. Who are you, and what're you bothering me for?"

"I'm a Texas Ranger. Name's Tom Bell." I pressed harder as a group of men gathered around us to watch the excitement. "He show you that silver dollar?"

"Yeah, but I figgered he stole it."

"You sure was watching me while I was talking to your boss."

"No I wasn't. I's thinkin' 'bout gettin' a drink after I got off that damned platform."

One of the roughnecks behind me snickered at Red's answer.

Ignoring all for the moment, I wouldn't take my eyes off Red. "Look, we're not kids in a schoolyard here. How come you to stare at me for so long, then take off runnin' when you should've come straight to me instead?"

"I don't like for the laws to mess with me."

"So you recognized me as a lawman."

Red glanced around, likely looking for a way out, or help. I didn't intend to let either of those things happen. Releasing his shirt, I stepped back and glanced over my shoulder at the ring of men around us. One particularly rough-looking driller was standing too close, arms folded across his chest.

Keeping one eye on Red, I angled myself toward the driller. "I'd appreciate it if you wouldn't stand so close."

The driller leaned over and spat. "Free country."

"Red, you move one inch away from that wall, and you won't walk right for a week." I made sure he heard, then without waiting for an answer, scanned the crowd and addressed everyone at the same time. "I'm a Texas Ranger. Name's Tom Bell, and if any of y'all give me any trouble, I'll knock the first one out and shoot the rest."

Using an old trick taught to me by a retired Ranger, I bored a hole with my eyes through the driller until he gave an almost imperceptible nod and stepped back. "Thank you."

More scattered raindrops fell as I swiveled back to the redhead. "You've been in the pen before, right? What's your name?"

"Folks call me Red."

"I figured that, but what's your given name?"

"Harold Guinn."

"Where'd you do time, Harold?" I'd learned from an old Ranger that if you use a man's first name in conversation, he'd be more likely to respond and even relax, if the situation hadn't escalated to a point where physical violence came into play.

Red frowned and started down at the worn shoes barely together enough to cover both feet. "Huntsville."

"What for?"

"Armed robbery. Just got out and come up here to get work."

"Hard times for sure, both in *and* out of the pen. Harold, I'm gonna check on your story, but right now I want to know if you've run into a feller named Clete Ferras?"

"Uh, no. Never heard of him."

I laid the sap against Red's head again, not as hard as the first time, but enough to stagger him.

"Goddamn!" Red rubbed his head. "What'd you hit me for that time?"

"Because you're lying to me." Men chuckled behind me.

"If his mouth's moving, he's lyin'."

I ignored the speaker and waited.

"Am not." Red's fingers probed his short hair.

"Look, the name Clete's familiar, is all. I just don't like lawmen and figured you were asking about me, seein's I just got out and all. I don't want no trouble."

"Fine, then. Here's what you're gonna do, though. You spread the word that I'm here after a murderer." I spoke up so the others could hear. "If anyone knows Clete Ferras or where he is, they need to tell me. Then I'll arrest him, or shoot him, and be gone, and y'all'll only have one Ranger here, for the time being. Now, you can go, Red."

Rubbing the growing knot on his scalp, Red slunk away like a whipped dog. A light shower spotted the onlookers' hats and shoulders. The other big driller was still standing nearby, but instead of facing me, he was eyeing the crowd that still hadn't completely drifted away.

Face impassive, arms still crossed, the man was a couple of steps away, like I'd asked. Pleased that the stranger was watching my back, I gave him a slight grin. "Now, sir. What's your name again?"

"Harvey McKnight."

"Well, Harvey, if a man wanted to get a drink around here, where would he go?"

The man's chiseled face broke into a white grin of perfectly straight teeth. "Well, I wouldn't know nothing about that, seeing's how there's a prohibition and all."

"Funny, the young man here named Booker tells me there's several speakeasies not far away, and a few stills out in the woods, too. I like a good whiskey every now and then myself, though I can't legally imbibe anymore, either. I thought I'd drop by and talk with a few folks with lesser morals, so I can find Clete and leave all y'all alone."

"Well, sir, I believe if you'd follow this street a ways back to the east, you might kick up a doughnut shop or two. Might find something else there, too."

"Much obliged." I motioned to Booker and tilted his hat so the rain would run off the back. "Deputy, come go with me."

Booker smiled and followed along. The ground was wet as

we neared the edge of town, then traveled back into the tent city that stretched into a long maze of twists and turns.

The shower became a light, steady rain that soon turned the road into a mire of rutted mud. An hour later, we hadn't found anyone I wanted to talk to, though we'd passed tent after tent, and shack after shack. The sky had been growing darker as the clouds lowered. Thunder rumbled and the rain increased.

We stopped beside a plank-walled tent between two dough-nut shops and I caught the odor of fresh coffee. "I believe I need a cup of that coffee we're smelling."

We found ourselves wrapped in the smell of frying food. Booker craned his neck upward at a hand-painted sign on an old board. HATTIE'S HASH HOUSE. "I'll be right out here when you get done."

Knowing the youngster wouldn't be admitted to a white-only business, no matter that it was nothing more than tables covered with canvas, I didn't invite him in. It would be too much of a disruption with little to gain. All we'd end up with would be an angry owner, and possibly angry customers, and an embar-rassed kid.

There were better battles to pick.

An empty freight wagon was parked nearby. "Duck under there out of the rain and holler if it looks like something bad's about to happen."

Booker folded himself under the wagon and sat with his legs crossed, facing the street. "Bad how?"

"You'll know if you have to holler."

Stepping inside, I paused to get used to the dim interior's fil-tered light coming through openings in the sides. Rough tables knocked together with whatever planks the carpenter could get his hands on provided a place to eat. Seating consisted of a couple of worn cane-bottom chairs, hammered-together stools, and plank benches.

On one of the benches, Harvey McKnight was finishing a plate of beans and fried potatoes. He displayed those white pearlies again. "I figured you'd show up, but there ain't no whiskey in here."

Puzzled, I settled onto a stool on the opposite side. "What made you think I'd come in this particular establishment?"

"'Cause if you understood the doughnut reference, you'd find me. If you didn't show up, I'd find you."

"Why?"

"Because I've been working in this town for months, and the whole place is a swarm of crooks."

"What do you mean?"

"Well, my old daddy always said that if you look under the covers before you crawl into bed, you likely won't get scorpion stung. Mister, there's a whole mess of stinging lizards in this place."

As I listened, Harvey told me about what he'd encountered since he arrived in Pine Top, and I realized I was in the middle of something other than chasing down a fugitive.

Chapter Six

Booker Johnston slid up to the edge of the Model A's front seat late that evening so he could see through the windshield. "This is a fine car. Where was it yesterday?"

"Parked out by the livery. Left it there when I rented the horse."

Following the Ford's headlights, I drove slowly down the dirt road.

He frowned and shook his head. "You're rich! Man has a car like thissun, he's on the way up."

"I'm far from rich, son. And this is just an automobile made to do a job and nothing else. It's a machine. That's all it is. Problem is it ain't like a horse. If it rains, it'll cost me some elbow grease to get it cleaned up."

"I'll do it."

I couldn't help but grin. The kid was a cyclone. "How much'll that cost me?"

"Four bits."

"Boy, dealing with you's a serious drain on my bank account. I don't think I could lose money any faster if I had a hole in my pocket."

"Nah. You Rangers always find gold the outlaws have hid. I know you don't give it all back."

"Easy, hoss. If I find stolen money, and I have, every penny goes back to the owner. That's the right thing to do. Always do right, and you won't have to worry when the good Lord comes back."

The boy nodded, solemn as if listening to a preacher on a pleasant Sunday morning. "You read the Good Book, too? I figgered Rangers didn't have time for such."

"Every night." The headlights lit the country road, but fog was forming, making it hard to see. I slowed even more as our turn came up. "Where's that cutoff to your house?"

"Right up yonder where that barn sits." Booker deflated as we neared his house. "My daddy's gonna wear me out for coming in after dark."

"I'll talk to him and make it right. He might be aggravated at you, but he's liable to change his mind after I talk with him."

"Mama'll cool him down. She's pretty good at it."

"Sounds like they got things worked out just fine between the two of 'em."

"Turn right at that bull pine up there."

The rural farm road narrowed even more as I steered down what amounted to not much more than a pig trail cut deep by wagon wheels for decades. Steep banks rose head high as we passed, then opened up into a cotton patch that would have been white with open bolls had the weather been dry.

Sitting at the edge of the field that would soon need picking was an unpainted shack on bois d'arc posts. The headlights lit a rusting sheet-iron roof dripping water. A weathered outhouse fifty yards beyond leaned against a dying chinaberry tree.

Yellow light from coal oil lanterns spilled onto the front porch through the screenless windows. The door stood open, and the backlit shape of a slender man leaned on the frame, watching the lights come toward him.

As I stopped in what passed for a front yard and killed the engine, the man stood erect, watching.

"He don't know the car." Booker opened the door and stood on the running board. "It's me, sir."

"That the law bringing you home?" A deep bass voice that should have come from a much larger man revealed neither anger or concern.

I opened the door and stood beside the car, waiting as Booker stepped out and jogged to the house. Once on the porch, he broke open the rifle so his daddy could see it was unloaded, "Nawsir. Well, you might say that." He waved back at the car. "This here's Mr. Tom Bell. He's a Texas Ranger, but I ain't in no trouble."

"From *him*, anyway." The dark shape shifted slightly. "How-do. Mr. Ranger, come up here on the porch and get outta that dampness."

The man reached inside the door and picked up a lamp to bring light onto the porch. Booker leaned the rifle against the house as I approached. "Got three squirrels, sir."

The man looked down on his son. "Meat'll likely be spoiled this late in the day."

"Nawsir. Mr. Bell had someone at his hotel put 'em in the ice-box after I cleaned and skinned 'em. They even cut 'em up and wrapped these fluffy-tails all nice and neat in butcher paper, like store-bought if somebody was to sell squirrels from the meat counter."

I climbed the two rough plank steps and ducked through the drops running off the shed roof. I stuck out my hand. "Like young Mr. Booker said, name's Tom Bell."

Light from the burning lamp in his left hand revealed the man made of hard bone and corded wire. When we shook, his grip was almost painful, hammered into hard anvils by a lifetime of heavy work. "John Henry."

"Pleased to meet you. Booker's a good boy."

"Most of the time." John Henry eyed the eleven-year-old. "Good thing you brought him home. I was thinkin' I'd need to take a belt to him for being so late and worryin' his mama."

"Not this time. It's my fault he's here so late, and I truly am sorry for any worry. He's been acting as my guide today."

"He paid me, too." Booker held up his day's wages and jingled the change. "And I found a body, Daddy."

John Henry frowned. "Whereabouts?"

"On the other side of town. I's following a branch and come across one of our people, dead."

I still wondered if the boy meant "our people" as Indians, white, or family.

John Henry studied me, as I would a stranger who brought my son home after dark. "Drowned?"

"Murdered, I believe."

"Who was it?"

I picked up the narrative. "The boy didn't recognize her. She'd been out there a while. Name's Hazel Freeman."

The sadness in John Henry's face said he thought a lot of Hazel, or the Freemans. A sharp intake of breath inside the house told me his wife was listening to the conversation on the porch. The unseen woman choked back a sob, and pans rattled in the kitchen.

"I hate to hear that, Mr. Bell. She was a fine woman. Good Christian girl. Who'd want to do that to her?"

That was a question no sane man could answer. Dobbs said she was a loose woman, but Booker disagreed. Now I heard an unsolicited description that told me two and two wasn't adding up the way it should.

I tilted the hat back and itched my forehead where the band rode. "Mr. Johnston, someone shot that woman. Man named

Stanley McCord was taken into custody for it. The sheriff told me about the Freemans' troubles. It sounds like that poor family's been snakebit."

The sun-browned skin on John Henry's face tightened, and he recrossed his arms. "And I bet you McCord ain't in jail no more, neither."

"You got second sight, or is there something I need to know?"

"It's that Sullivan land.

"Me'n some of my wife's people think there's something going on, and now I'm sure of it. Mr. Bell, me and Olivia're kinda tight in this house with all these young'uns, but I'd be obliged if you'd come in for a little bit so we can talk. I think you're gonna find out Pine Top's a cesspool, and I don't see no way to drain it."

Chapter Seven

The morning dawned moist and cloudy.

Choking back a sob, Gene Phillips stepped into his living room a couple of blocks from the sheriff's office and lifted the phone's receiver with a shaky hand. He waited for only a moment before the operator picked up on her end. Since the central switchboard was only four blocks away, the operator's voice came through as clear as if she was in the house with him. "Switchboard. Hey Gene, who you need?"

"Get me Quinn Walker's residence."

"One moment please."

Grinding his teeth together to maintain the tenuous grip on his emotions, Phillips listened to the click as she pulled a phone plug from the panel in front of her and plugged it into the appropriate jack.

A hum told him the connection was complete. It rang on the other end several times before Mallie's voice came on the line. "Hello?"

Phillips swallowed and cleared his throat to calm himself. "Mallie. This is Gene."

"Hey, Gene! How are you doing?"

"Not so good right now. Is Quinn home?"

"I'm sorry, hon. I'll get him. Hold on a minute."

Walker's voice came on the line and Phillips's legs went weak and watery. "What?"

He dropped onto the telephone table's seat and rested his elbow on the small tabletop. He looked through the front window without registering the brightly colored leaves falling from the sweet gum tree in his front yard. "We got problems."

Recognizing Phillips's voice, Walker answered without hesitation. "What kind?"

"Can't say." The man's voice quavered. "I'm fixin' to come by and pick you up."

Walker paused before answering. "I'll be out front."

———

Walker was waiting out front when Phillips pulled up. The air seemed particularly greasy from floating oil particles when he opened the door. He slipped into the seat and fixed Phillips with a worried look.

"What's wrong?"

Phillips steered onto the street, then turned left on Pine Top Street and headed out of town. "We got troubles."

"You've done said that." Walker's glower bored into the side of Phillips's face, but he remained intent on the road.

"I know it." He paused to gather his thoughts. "Look." Phillips's voice broke, and he had to clear his throat. "I've been trying to do everything just like you, but I guess I'm too impatient. I can't stand to be married with Ruby for much longer. Her mama's wearing me out, and I can't wait to get the place."

Terror filled Walker with electricity. "What did you do?"

They were completely out of town and in the country when Phillips licked his lips. "We were sitting around last night, and I figured I'd kill two birds with one stone. So me and Ruby mixed up some of that doctored-up white mule I brought you, and I dosed her with it. Not enough to kill her right then. I wanted to do it like you planned, a little at a time until it finally took her down, you know, to make it look like she was getting sicker and sicker."

"So what's the problem?" Walker frowned. "You didn't drink any of it, did you? You sick?"

"No. It's too strong, so I mixed it with Co-cola. She liked it just fine, and I reckon she sucked a couple down right quick."

"Oh, shit. Did it kill her right away?"

They left the busy town behind them and drove into the country, passing fewer and fewer rigs and more cotton fields. Phillips finally found the words he was looking for. "No. Worse."

"What're you beating around the bush for? Tell me, dammit!"

Phillips let off the gas and the car slowed. "You know her mama, Claudine, lives with us, right?"

Growing frustrated, Walker made a fist with his right hand to control himself. "Quit telling me what I know and get to it!"

"All right. Her mama wanted some, so she drank twice as many before she went to bed." He turned down a dirt road running between cotton patches. The field was white with cotton fluff ready to be picked. "They were mostly alcohol and not much Co-cola."

He slowed the car and stopped. "Claudine was already slurring her words when she said she was going to bed. We didn't know it, but she took our Baby Sarah to sleep with her and Claudine rolled over on her in the night." Phillips broke down and leaned over the steering wheel, sobbing. "I don't know if it was the whiskey mix, or her heart, or whatever else was in that bottle, but she died on top of the baby, and my daughter's dead, Quinn."

Stunned, Quinn got out of the car and walked down the rows, thinking.

Phillips regained control of himself and killed the engine. He got out and followed Walker into the field. "What are we gonna do?"

He turned and tilted his fedora back. "They say anything when they came to pick them up?"

"No. Ruby found them and went all to pieces. I called the sheriff. He came over, looked at them laying there in the bed and said it looked to him like Claudine had a heart attack."

"Well, maybe she did. Maybe it wasn't that doctored whiskey in the first place."

"No. I believe it was the whiskey, 'cause Ruby got sick in the night. Sweats and aching muscles."

"Could be something else, you don't know. But that's the whole idea of what we're doing, and maybe Claudine had a heart attack after all. The truth is, she had to go too, for you to get the land, so that gets her out of the way." Realizing how it sounded, Walker backtracked. "I'm truly sorry, Gene. I know you never meant to hurt that baby."

Phillips wiped his sweaty forehead. "I surely didn't."

"But what's done is done. You can't take it back."

Phillips tried to read his face. "What are you saying?"

"Son, you done paid the price, so there's no reason to quit now. I'm not pouring mine out. There's no point in it. We all need to stick with the plan."

"What if we get caught?"

"We won't. It's all working just fine. You shoulda come to me, and I'd've told you to get Claudine off somewhere and put a bullet in her head six months ago."

Phillips recoiled. "I couldn't do that!"

"You wouldn't have to. Jack'll do it for you. Just like when he took care of Hazel a week or so ago."

"Good God."

"It had to be done. He's done spent a year getting everything ready and they had everything worked out just right. Shit, she's still missing and you can bet that once they find her body no one'll have any good idea what happened. Emsworth oughta get that land for a song.

"Look, you shut one door, but now another'n's opened up. Dose Ruby with a little of that whiskey every day to help her deal with it, then in a month or two, she'll die of heartbreak from missin' her mama and baby, and no one will know the difference."

Knowing what he meant, Phillips broke their gaze, spun on his heel, and took a few steps back to the car. "I don't think I can go through with this."

"You can, and will." Quinn Walker's voice went flat and cold. "Damn, son, it's working, and if all of us stick together," he pointed at several oil derricks rising above the tree line, "we're gonna own half of these rigs before long and come out smelling like a rose."

He waved a hand toward town in the distance. "We're gonna be *rich* soon. They'll be drillin' in this field by Christmas, and all the money they pump out of the ground'll be in the bank under your name. Once Ruby's dead, it won't be Youngblood land no more, it'll be Phillips land. Then you can get married again, this time to Melba Lee, and y'all can have a house full of kids and won't have to work 'em in a cotton patch to make ends meet."

Phillips surveyed the fields around them that had belonged to Ruby's family for over sixty years. Her dad had died a year earlier when the barn caught fire and he'd rushed inside to save his mules. At least that was the story that made the paper. The blackened ruins of the barn and the half-burned-out house were a hundred yards away.

Philips sighed. "I'll get in trouble for having whiskey in the house. When they do the autopsy, they'll find the alcohol and poison in her system."

"Nobody's gonna autopsy her. There's no reason to. Ruby thinks it was a heart attack, and Dobbs said so himself. If you're lucky, maybe they'll find Ruby in the bathtub in a few months with her wrists cut. She couldn't take it. Damned Indians, they don't have the sense to come in out of the rain, let alone deal with problems. One way or the other, you have nothing to worry about. Just act natural from now on so's you don't mess things up for the rest of us."

Walker met Phillips's gaze and raised an eyebrow. Phillips went cold. He'd just been threatened without hearing a word. He swallowed. "You think it'll work?"

Walker flashed him a reassuring smile. "Of course it will, and before long, we'll all be some of the richest men in Texas." He reached out to pat Phillips on the shoulder. "It'll be all right." He pointed at the car parked at the end of the turn row, and the oil derrick beyond the trees. "Now, let's go bury your little girl and mother-in-law and get on with it."

Chapter Eight

I stepped outside the Pine Top Hotel not long after daylight pushed through the gray clouds. A blue neon sign hanging above the window identified the four-story brick building as a place to stay for those who were new to town and had money in their pockets.

Setting my hat just right, I made my way down the busy sidewalk toward Charlotte's Café, an establishment recommended by the desk clerk. An ice wagon rattled past. The clamor of drilling, construction, and business hadn't lessened any.

The haze from smoke, drilling, and dust hid the far end of the street. I could actually taste the air. Breathing through my nose, I waded upstream, passing another mercantile, a dentist's office, and a photography studio on the way.

A bell over the café's door jangled when I pushed inside. Inside the crowded café was a different kind of noise, but the air smelled better from coffee, frying meat, and onions. Several stools at the counter were vacant, but I chose a small table in the corner to the right of the door. There was a folded, well-read newspaper in the chair. My back to the wall, I scanned the room full of drillers, roughnecks, and even the oil workers Sheriff Dobbs called boll weevils.

Thousands of inexperienced farmers left their plowing and poured into boomtowns, drawn by the smell of oil money. Once they learned to sling heavy cables and pipes on the derrick floor, the farmers became oilmen and graduated from weevils to *roughneck* status.

An attractive black-haired woman wearing a stained apron soon arrived at the table. A strand of hair hung free over the side of her face. She absently wiped it away and tilted her head as she studied my face. Her tired demeanor brightened when our eyes met. "What'll you have?"

I picked up the paper menu and pointed. "Steak and eggs?"

"We don't mess that up too bad. Scrambled? Coffee?"

"That'll do." I liked her wit.

"You a Texas Ranger?"

I glanced down to see my coat gaped open, revealing the *cinco peso* badge. I waved a fly away. "Yes, ma'am."

"That Mexican Ranger comes in here to eat every now and then. You waiting on him?"

"No. And his daddy was from Spain."

She rolled her eyes. "I'd like to go there sometime and get out of this place. Where you from, Ranger?"

Leaning on the table, I laced my fingers. There was something about the woman that felt instantly comfortable. A tingle ran down my back. I liked her look. Hands neither too soft or work-hardened caught my attention, as well as the fact that she wasn't wearing any rings. She'd taken two orders since I came in and didn't engage any of the previous customers in conversation.

"Born up in Grant, Oklahoma, but my old man took me down to the Valley when I was still on all fours."

"The Valley's a good-sized place, I hear. I'd like to go there, too. What town did you call home?"

"Falfurrius. Am I being deposed?"

She frowned. "I don't know what that means. Oh, you think I'm being nosy."

I grinned. "Nah, I think you're being friendly."

She returned the smile, revealing two deep dimples at the corners of her mouth, and I had to force my attention back up to her eyes. "I'll be right back with that coffee."

As she headed to the counter, I opened the paper. Several articles were on the dry conditions in the Texas Panhandle and western Oklahoma. I glanced out the window at the cloudy skies that promised rain. Articles I'd read in the past months were concerned about the dry conditions that moved east as steady as a clock. An article quoting *Progressive Farmer* magazine predicted an upcoming drought that would rival anything the country had ever seen.

Dust storms had already reached East Texas more than once, covering the town with what was once topsoil supporting thousands of wheat fields on the high plains and Oklahoma. The current rainy weather was a fluke, and the old men loafing in front of country stores across Texas predicted the drought would be the last for a long time once this storm settled in and took root.

The other top story of the day concerned Al Capone, who had been sentenced to eleven years for tax evasion. I grunted and made the mistake of speaking aloud to myself. "Somebody shoulda shot him years ago."

A sun-browned man in a worn-out fedora; faded, oil-stained shirt; and overalls nodded. "Lots of folks need killing. I read that paper yesterday, and if you're talking about Capone, somebody shoulda put him in a shallow grave years ago."

Across from him was another driller working his way through a plate of beans and greasy fried potatoes. It was clear the man hadn't used water for anything other than drinking in months, and his cowlicks hadn't seen a comb in that length of time, either.

Annoyed that I'd been overheard, I sighed and folded the paper. I'd planned to relax and read the funnies before my meal arrived, a guilty pleasure I hoped no one would discover. Instead, I was back on the job in an instant. "I know of a few in particular who need planting. You ever hear of someone named Clete Ferras? Maybe working the rigs around here? Likely got to town a week or so back."

Finished with his meal, Fedora lit a ready-made cigarette and blew smoke down at the table. It washed across the other man's plate in a wave, but he never looked up.

Two men at a nearby table argued with enthusiasm, their voices rising above the cafeteria noise. Those nearby watched with care, likely expecting the disagreement to amplify to the point of fists, in which case the other customers would have to rescue their plates and give the two roughnecks room to finish their disagreement.

Taking a folded wanted poster from inside my coat pocket, I passed it across. Fedora and his companion shook their heads after giving it the once-over. Fedora handed it back. "Most roughnecks don't eat here very often. Can't afford it. Hell, me'n Bruce here saved up to treat ourselves today. You're gonna find out when you get the bill for that steak."

"Any idea where I go to looking?"

Fedora shrugged. "Well, I wouldn't waste my time in eateries, there's more'n you can shake a stick at. He a drinkin' man?"

"I've heard tell."

My coffee arrived. The waitress put a mug in front of me and frowned toward at the men who were arguing at a table only feet away. She planted her feet as if preparing for a charge. "You boys settle down over there or get your asses outside. It's loud enough around here without y'all adding to it."

The men lowered their voices and continued their argument as she disappeared into the kitchen.

I liked the way she handled that. My attention flicked from the disagreement back to Fedora, who sucked in a lungful of smoke as if we hadn't been interrupted. "Well, your Ranger friend's closed down most of the speakeasies around here, but there's a couple of places you can find a sip or two of mule, or bathtub gin. That's where I'd start looking...or the cathouses out in Tent City or the other camps. I hear they're doing a pretty fair business for a reasonable price, or it seems to me reasonable, though I never partake myself."

Our conversation stalled again when the oil workers' voices at the other table rose in anger. They planted their feet and grabbed each other's clothes. Men from adjacent tables snatched up their plates and stood as the roughnecks went at it.

One of the others still seated at that same table reached down for his ankle. I saw the motion, and years of experience told me there was some kind of weapon hidden there.

My whipcrack voice was like a pistol shot. "Hey!"

I'd had it already. With barely a sip of coffee in me, and hungry as a bitch wolf, I didn't want a fight to break out and ruin my breakfast. The two men stopped as if someone had doused them in ice water. Aggravated, I stood and pulled my coat back to reveal my badge. The café went silent as the oil-covered crowd watched to see what would happen.

Seeing the unmistakable Ranger badge, the roughnecks slowly settled back down into their seats, still angry but respectful of the law and what could happen. The man reaching for his ankle straightened, but wouldn't make eye contact.

I stayed where I was until the combatants lowered their gazes to the table and their plates. Once things quieted down, I sat back down and the café's noise level resumed, but not nearly as loud.

I turned back to my original conversation with Fedora and Bruce, who hadn't moved. Bruce sopped up the last of his egg yolk with a biscuit, and Fedora jerked a thumb back to the empty street. "Guess you'll ask for a good long while. This place is working alive with oilmen, operators leasing from the land-owners and farmers around here. Lots of places to look. Folks weren't making any money raising cotton or row crops, but they're making a killin' on mineral leases.

"There's big and small leases, some by the acre, and others even by the foot. You might recognize some of them like Humble Oil, Sinclair, or Gulf. Then there's the little outfits you likely never heard of. Texas Services, H. L. Hunt, Atlantic Production Marco-Doss, Halliburton, J. S. Caruthers, Kathleen Oil, Stranolind Oil, Fine Oil, Cabinsas Oil, and those are just the ones come to mind right this second. You're gonna wear out some shoe leather before you find your man."

Bumfuzzled by all the names, I could only shake my head at the number of oil companies drilling in such a small area. "Guess I'm gonna have to dig in and root hog."

Fedora took a deep drag on the butt and let it out again. "Like I said, if I's you, I'd find the watering holes, or cat…" he paused when the waitress passed, "uh, social clubs, in the red light district to look for a man like that."

There was something in the way he spoke that raised my eyebrow in question, and the man grinned. "I wore a badge once."

The waitress returned with a sizzling steak that hung over the plate. The eggs were on another. "That's on the house, and the pie I'm gonna bring you, too." She paused, appearing to gather her thoughts at my unspoken question.

"You saved me the cost of a few chairs and maybe a table when you cooled those boys down." She cocked a hip and tilted her head again, letting me know that there was more to her next statement than just conversation. "In fact, you can eat here free from now on, if it's this quiet ever' time you come in."

"Much obliged." I picked up the utensils. "I don't want to say 'Hey, waitress' every time I come in. What's your name?"

"Charlotte."

"So you're not a waitress. You own the place."

"I do, but it's wearing me down." A fly lit on the table, and she killed it with a damp cup towel. "Blood and guts. I live over in Hog Eye and travel back and forth every day."

Knife and fork still hovering above the steak, I matched her head-tilt, just to see if she'd notice. "Where's Hog Eye?"

She did, and in response, tilted hers the other way as her dimples re-formed. "It's not but six miles away, but it's a slow six when it rains or snows."

"Not much of a name for a town."

"I heard they're going to change it to Liberty City, 'cause it's booming just like this place. Speaking of names, you didn't say yours."

"Tom Bell."

"Howdy, Tom Bell. My last name's Cain. I look forward to seeing you in here again."

"Many thanks. I don't believe I've ever seen too many women with eyes that green."

"Skeletons in the closet." She gave me a wink. "Maybe I'll see you in my other place in Hog Eye. It's called the Southern Café. My cousin runs that one, when I'm here."

"You're spread pretty thin."

"I was thinking the same thing. Enjoy that steak."

"I will." She whisked off to wait on another customer as I cut off a bite and addressed Fedora one last time. "Place don't seem too expensive to me."

Fedora and his quiet friend Bruce laughed as I went to work with the cheap utensils.

Chapter Nine

Clete Ferras rode on the passenger side of Jack Drake's Nash. Employed by Quinn Walker and the Corporation, the two hard-cases had a job to do that evening. Armed to the teeth, they were headed northwest out of Pine Top toward the booming town of Hog Eye. An up-and-coming oil company was getting in the way of a lease Walker was interested in.

"Here's what Quinn wants to do." Jack took a drag on the ever-present cigarette in his hand. "He doesn't want what happened in Pine Top to happen out in Hog Eye. Those oilmen out there are drilling wells as fast as they can to keep the next guy from sucking up their oil. Quinn wants to get this whole farm and start drilling along the outside edges, so he can draw up all that oil that's *not* under his land."

A farmer by name of Herb Nelson there in the bottomlands of the Sabine River stubbornly held out to raise cotton until his family finally convinced him to lease the oil rights so they could get in on the fabulous wealth pouring from underground. The Great Depression debts those cotton farmers had accumulated over years of cheap cotton gave ample opportunity for bankers and other people in positions of power to seize their lands.

After hearing how much money was being spread around by

the oil companies, Herb Nelson wasn't going to simply lease his family land to the first person who offered him a contract. He'd made it clear that he had no intention to sell to the half a dozen oilmen who'd already come by with signed checks in their hands. That was their first offer that, all too often, was snapped up by those desperate for money.

Herb had already talked to a number of farmers who wished they'd known enough to haggle. He shook his head at every offer after that, letting the bidders know he had a figure in mind, and they weren't even close.

Every time an operator offered a higher amount, he made it known that the money was way below his expectations. He'd also staked the field into the small mineral leases he expected to get. Each was measured in feet, and he'd already turned down what would have amounted to three thousand dollars per acre.

Herb was an even bigger problem to the drillers because, unlike some landowners who lacked clear titles to their land because they'd never been able to afford a lawyer to examine their paperwork, the sunbaked father of ten grown children was the exception. During one bumper crop year a decade earlier, he'd done just that, and the clear title to his farm was faultless.

He'd been to Pine Top, where one city block contained forty-four wells drilled into the yards of homes so thick that derrick legs touched those of the next drilling unit. He knew good and well what he wanted, because he made it clear that he was finished with stoop labor and was done raising cotton. He intended to lease to several outfits at the same time, and they could drill all the wells they wanted, even if the rigs were only feet from one another.

Jack Drake explained. "Walker's gonna buy the farms on the *other* side, like a checkerboard, where he's slant-drilling on the Blacks and under the Reds that're just sitting there, holding out for more money. This thing won't last forever, and when it goes bust, and the oil's all gone, well, he's gonna be one helluva land-owner when cotton comes back."

Drake took another drag. "That's where we make our money, too. Calls it a consortium, whatever the hell that means."

Clete watched the fenceposts flash past, rubbing his hawk's beak of a nose. "Where'd he get that kind of money in the first place?"

"Well, you know Quinn married Mallie, and she's rolling in the dough. She won't turn loose more'n two bits at a time, but we're working on that. When she's gone, he'll be the sole owner and sitting pretty."

"How's he gonna pay for these leases right now if she's so tight?"

"The money'll be there before you know it. What he's using for capital right now is from some of the other members who've already wormed into their own deals." Drake grinned. "There's eight of 'em, and it's like the legs of one of them octopuses, all feeding toward the head that's O. L. Caldwell."

"So what're we supposed to be doing? I don't feel like shooting nobody today."

"There's one hardheaded old boy who won't quit pestering Nelson about signing a lease. Name's Barney Chadwick. He's raising the bid about two dollars a foot every time Quinn makes Nelson an offer, and Quinn's tired of it. The truth is, he's afraid that oilman's gonna get the lease right out from under him, because Chadwick and Nelson are talking so much. We're gonna persuade that particular small-time operator enough is enough."

Ferras nodded. "We're gonna muscle him out, then."

"Maybe a little more'n that."

"Understood." Ferras checked the loads in the Colt and tucked it into his waistband.

Chapter Ten

Jack Drake parked Gene Phillips's borrowed Ford in front of what passed as a hash house in the corrugated-iron shantytown named Hog Eye, which only months earlier had consisted of nothing more than a few buildings and one general store. His yellow Nash was too recognizable for what he and Clete had to do, and the black Ford was as common as sparrows. Heavy dark clouds filtered the light, giving the bustling community a medieval appearance.

Thousands of people were streaming into the newly tapped oil field, with little infrastructure to accommodate so many workers and support businesses. Those who had no desire to join the flood of roughnecks made money in the time-honored businesses related to boomtowns, including what were popularly known as cathouses, drinking establishments disguised as candy stores, places to eat, and barely concealed gambling houses.

What was once a rutted dirt road winding past pastures, fields, and woods had evolved into a newly minted Main Street lined on both sides with flimsy buildings that looked as if they would blow away in a strong wind.

Towering above, a forest of oil rigs polluted the air for miles around the new town. It was nauseating when you could smell it, and dangerous when you couldn't. The town's one doctor spent most of his time treating gas blindness and injuries on the dangerous wells. More than a few limp roughnecks were brought in by frightened friends, victims of gas-induced death.

"This stink is gonna kill us all before we get out of here." Jack took off his hat and fanned with it, as if that's all it would take to clear the air so he could take a deep breath.

Clete Ferras, ignoring the statement, pointed at a bubbling vat in front of a table made from warped planks and homemade sawhorses. "Look at that. Fifteen cents for what they're calling bean soup. That's highway robbery."

The door of a corrugated building flew into the street when two men fell through, grappling at each other on the board sidewalk. An innocent bystander walking past got tangled in their disagreement, giving one of the combatants just enough edge to plant his feet and drop the other with a haymaker. For good measure, he slammed a fist into the jaw of the innocent man, who landed with a thud, out cold before he hit the ground.

Jack grinned. "Somebody made that feller mad."

Clete grunted. "I could take him."

"Well, hell, Jack Dempsey, go on over there and show him what's for."

Clete opened the door and stepped out. "Watch this."

"Hey, wait! I was just aggravatin' you." Jack was shocked upright when Clete called his bluff. "Dammit, we don't have time for this. That man's gonna come by here any minute."

"Won't take a second." Clete pitched his hat onto the seat and approached the winner. "Hey, feller. That's my friend you just knocked out."

The red-faced roughneck pivoted to face Clete, fists raised. "I don't care."

"Well, me neither." Clete busted the man's nose with a straight left, then followed it with a hard right. The rigger stumbled back, shaking his head as blood poured from his broken nose. Not hesitating for a second, Clete jabbed twice more with a left, and when the rigger staggered, he hit him with a piledriver right. The man went down between the other two and didn't move.

Grinning, Clete went back to the car, sucking on one scraped knuckle. "See? I told you. Punch 'em in the beezer a couple of times and add a little chin music, and they're down for the count."

"Damn, boy. You're gonna draw the law down on us."

"Ain't no law here." Clete made a fist. "This is the law now, and this." He pulled his jacket back to reveal the butt of a Colt revolver.

Disgusted, Jack lit a ready roll with a wooden kitchen match and inhaled at the same time a Ford drove past. He recognized the man in the passenger seat. "That's Barney Chadwick. He's our man." Squinting through the smoke, he started the car and pulled in behind the Ford.

Scattered raindrops splattered against the windshield as they left the main part of Hog Eye and passed through a cluster of tents and big cardboard boxes draped around trees. Two children peeked out of an eight-foot-square doorless shanty that was nothing but sheet iron wired to posts supporting a corrugated roof.

The clouds lowered, and the bottom fell out. The deluge quickly became tropical.

Jack let the car gain some distance as they finally left the town behind. The number of drilling rigs dwindled, but they were never out of sight of producing wells. "He's heading for Herb Nelson's place."

"We need to stop him before he gets there."

"You got that right." The driving rain gave Jack Drake an idea. "You can fight, but can you hit with that gat you're carrying?"

"Wouldn't have it if I couldn't."

"Good. Everything'll be jake if you do what I tell you." Jack pushed the foot-feed and they sped up. He caught the Ford and passed them, pulled in front way too close, throwing a spray of mud over the other car's windshield before tapping his brakes.

The driver hit his own brakes and swerved, sliding the Ford into the bar-ditch. Jack continued out of sight, disappearing in the deluge. Half a mile farther on, he came to a pasture with a gate turnout. He made a three-point turn and returned to the stuck car, knowing that all Model A cars looked alike, especially when covered in mud. Barney Chadwick and his driver were already out beside the right front wheel, which was buried to the hub in the ditch.

Jack Drake pulled to a stop in the middle of the road that was already turning to bog. "Let's go." Pulling the brim of his hat down, he pointed at the driver. "Put one in the right side of that man's head and don't mess it up." He stepped out from behind the wheel and pointed. "Do it fast."

The pouring rain immediately soaked their clothes.

Barney Chadwick was standing by the road when they approached. Red-faced and angry, he pointed in the direction they'd been traveling. "Did you see that fool driving like hell in this weather? He ran me off the road."

"I saw him when he passed us." Jack threw a thumb over one shoulder. "He was a-flyin'."

The driver shook his head and raised an eyebrow at Clete. "Damned lunatic is what he was."

Clete nodded in sympathy.

The other man who was about to be a corpse pointed at their car. "Would you look at this?"

Jack acted surprised. "Hey, I know you. Your name's Barney Chadwick."

The oilman frowned. "I don't know you, though."

Jack stuck out his hand. "Name's Jack."

Barney instinctively took the hand, and Jack held on. When the driver waited for his turn to shake, Clete raised the pistol and put it against the man's head. He pulled the trigger. The crisp report was muffled by the rain. The driver collapsed in a heap.

At the same time, Jack held tight to Chadwick's hand. "Him, too."

Clete stuck his arm out and shot Chadwick in the heart. Face shocked white from the impact, the oilman fell straight back into a stream of water running down the ditch.

Watching to make sure he was dead, Jack waved a hand toward their car. "There's a bag behind your seat with two pistols in there." He glanced up and down the road. "Get one of them, and hurry."

Clete jogged through the rain, returning with a revolver. "What now?"

Jack took the pistol and fired two times into the air and dropped it beside the driver's hand. He pointed to Chadwick, then the driver. "Murder, suicide."

"Yep. People do strange things for no reason. Let's get out of here."

They jumped in the car and headed back to a crossroads they'd passed earlier. Jack Drake turned left, and they disappeared into the storm.

Chapter Eleven

It was late that rainy evening when Clete Ferras and Jack Drake met Quinn Walker in Sheriff Dobbs's office, where he was seated behind his desk. From that position, he could see outside when the paper shades were open and watch the street. Right then, they were all pulled. The room was lit by a white schoolhouse-style light suspended from a long chain.

Duke Ellington's "Three Little Words" was playing on the wooden Radiola 20 sitting on a table beside the desk. Dobbs reached over to move the tuning wheel with a thumb when the back door opened, admitting the sound of rain on hard surfaces. He'd been expecting the visit, but picked up the .38 revolver lying beside the black Ericsson Bakelite phone on his desk, just in case.

He swiveled the wooden chair to see the three men step inside, shaking water from their hats. Recognizing them, he replaced the pistol close to hand, as one after another, they hung their hats on a coatrack and trailed around to several wooden chairs on the other side of the desk. The sheriff thumbed the volume wheel down and spun in the chair to face them.

Walker dropped into one of the hard seats, but Ferras and Jack Drake remained standing.

Wanting to be the aggressor in most situations, Dobbs pointed at Ferras. "There's a Texas Ranger in town looking for you."

Rubbing his stubbled chin, the gray-haired man frowned at the information. He shifted his weight as if that would help him think more clearly. "Me?"

"He called your name."

"What'd you tell him?"

"To go pound sand. I said I'd never heard of you, but you likely worked for one of the small oil companies like the other ten thousand sonsabitches that are making my life miserable around here."

Walker's gaze flicked from the sheriff to Ferras. "Quick thinking."

"Quick thinking or not, Ferras, you need to get your ass out of here. I don't want no more trouble from these damned Rangers. Having Delgado running around arresting folks is one thing, but two of these Ranger bastards hanging around here spells *dangerous*."

The back door opened again and bank president Albert Emsworth squeezed inside, dripping water. The big-bellied man with oiled-back hair paused when he saw the other two visitors. He stopped cold. "What're y'all doing here?"

Hand once again on the .38, Sheriff Dobbs swiveled the chair to face the shocked banker. "We're talking, and shut the damned door. Lock it, too."

"Are y'all nuts?" Emsworth's quavering voice was soft. He did as he was told, but instead of coming around to join the others, he huddled against the wall like a caged rabbit. "Drake, you ought not be here. We can't be seen together in this town. We all agreed none of us'd never be in the same place at the same time."

"Front door's locked, and I doubt anybody'll be coming by

in the next ten minutes or so in this rain." Dobbs leaned back, the chair creaking under his bulk.

Emsworth shook his head. "You don't know who's gonna come to the door."

Dobbs grunted. "Not in this kind of falling weather, unless something bad happens. Leave, if you want to."

"I need to talk with you before I go home to supper." The banker remained beside the back door, as if the other three would bite. "Well, uh, I wanted to talk to you about the Freeman land. I heard they found the daughter Hazel dead."

"A Texas Ranger did." Dobbs leaned back in punctuation.

Emsworth blanched. Fingers plucked at the pocket watch in his suit vest, then dropped. "Delgado?"

"No. Worse. There's another Ranger in town." Dobbs grinned and pointed at Ferras. "We's just talking about him. He's looking for our buddy here."

The information was almost too much for Emsworth, who turned white. "Who're *you*?"

"Don't matter." Ferras scowled. "I work for Mr. Walker."

Emsworth turned back to Dobbs. "Sheriff, is he under arrest?"

"Not so's you'd notice. But I bet I have cause." They chuckled as if he was a vaudeville comedian. "See, he don't have any bracelets on, right this minute. Like he said," Dobbs shot both Walker and Ferras a warning look to make sure they knew their place, "he's working for Walker, who works for me in our little business venture."

Quinn Walker frowned at the statement.

"I don't need to know that." The banker's hands fluttered up like small birds, first reaching for the round glasses perched on his nose, then the thinning hair barely covering a freckled scalp. He wiped his mouth with a thumb and reached for the doorknob before hesitating. Coming to a conclusion, he finally faced the men again. "I don't want to know what any of you are doing. That part isn't my business at all."

"What do you want, Albert?"

"Like I said, I came by to see if there's any chance that we can soon acquire that Freeman land."

Dobbs grinned at the men across the desk from him. "I believe it won't be long."

They returned the smile, and Walker spoke up. "I'm gonna have these guys drop by and see if they can't make a deal with Nellie Freeman in a couple of days."

Emsworth licked his dry lips. "I don't want to know anything about that. What I need to know is if Mr. Caldwell is ready to move on that property."

"Not yet." Walker's voice was flat. He didn't want to talk about the headman who'd moved in on his territory.

"How'd you come to know that?"

"Because, before Frank Freeman got killed a few months ago, he sold damn near everything he had to a cousin down in Dallas. Furthermore and all that, the cousin gave him a couple of thousand dollars on the come, so Freeman could hold on long enough for one of the companies to offer him a lease. His wife has the cash on hand, and she'll come out smelling like a rose."

Dobbs knew the man wanted that piece of valuable land and watched as Emsworth grew silent pondering the implications. He didn't much like the portly little banker who was foreclosing on farms and homes as the Depression deepened. Now the man was making money hand over fist as rivers of oil-produced cash flowed through the bank.

The sheriff held up a finger. "Don't worry. I have an idea how to speed this thing along, and Mr. Ferras here'll make sure it happens."

Walker sat straighter. "I think that Phillips's arm of our endeavor has dramatically changed, too. It's moving faster than we expected."

The sheriff's amusement vanished. "*That* wasn't planned."

Emsworth stepped forward, unconsciously rubbing both hands together. "Mallie?"

"No." Dobbs picked up the conversation. "There was an accidental death. Phillips's baby was smothered to death last night, and his mother-in-law's dead, too."

Emsworth backed up again, his heels hitting the wall with a thump. "A child is dead? I never signed up for anything like that."

Dobbs leaned forward. "We all know what you signed up for, just like the rest of us. It was purely an accident, that's all." He shot a look across the desk at Walker. "I don't expect anything else like that, neither."

Hands raised in a questioning manner, Walker shrugged. "Like you said, it never was planned, not like that gal was. Ol' Jack here comes through every time."

Nodding, Jack agreed. "Just like a little while ago out in Hog Eye. Sheriff, I hear there's been a murder and a suicide just west of town. Some scratch oilman and his friend did each other in. I 'magine y'all'll get the news later."

"I guess somebody likely called the constable out there." Sheriff Dobbs leaned back again. "He'll holler at me soon enough. You know, Emsworth, this snowball's rolling downhill pretty fast, and there ain't no backing out now. You just make sure you hold up *your* end of the deal."

White-faced, Emsworth licked his lips. "Y'all just keep all that out of my bank. I only move the money and titles. I don't want to be seen with any of you."

"You're gonna move an awful lot of it soon." Quinn Walker's

voice was low, but full of excitement. "My wife hasn't been feeling too good lately, and I heard there's another piece of property that's liable to come up for auction. Emsworth, do you hold the mortgage on land owned by the Sullivan family, south of Longview? It's over the Hart field."

The banker nodded. "I do. They're in trouble and behind on about eight months' mortgage. Why?"

"I want to make an offer on it. Figure out what it's worth, and I'll buy it out."

"Quinn, you're overextending yourself." In an instant, Emsworth ceased being a mouse and became a banker full of confidence. On solid ground dried by experience, he'd honed such responses in the past several months as struggling farmers came into the bank, hat in hand, to ask for mortgage extensions or loans. "You don't have that kind of money yet. I worked with you to order that car because you said she was getting close to…" He paused, gathering his thoughts. "…where we want her, but your name's not on any of her money, yet."

"I'm *married* to the woman."

"Yes, you are. But you can't be buying farms without her consent. It's the law."

Clete Ferras snickered at the last sentence. He glanced over to Jack Drake, who'd been silent for the entire conversation. "It's the *law*, he said."

Drake finally spoke. "I have the law in my pocket."

Dobbs frowned, wondering if Drake was talking about the revolver he carried, or *him*.

Walker nodded, staring at the floor and biting his lip. "There's a little oil company I heard's interested in getting the lease rights for that piece of Sullivan property. I want to get in there before they do, so I can buy the land out from under them."

Sheriff Dobbs leaned forward and laced his fingers. "That's part of the Sabine Bed Lease, right?"

Emsworth agreed. "It is, and there's a half-million-dollar offer on that riverbed, even though Senator Neal's trying to stop drilling there."

Senator Margie Neal was the first woman to hold a senate seat in the state of Texas. She was elected on four platforms: education, good roads, welfare, and progress. She was convinced that drilling would pollute the water supply for the city of Longview, which took most of its water from the Sabine River.

Governor Sterling, in an attempt to increase state revenue from oil and gas leases, called the legislature together to ramrod a deal through, increasing drilling in state land in the Sabine Riverbed. Unfortunately for him, most of it lay in Senator Neal's district, who was fighting like a she-bear protecting her cubs.

Quinn Walker and Longview businessman Andrew Mathews wanted to get rigs in there before drilling froze from the landslide of anticipated lawsuits. Senator Neal had already called for a moratorium on cotton production, citing an oversupply that threatened farmers' very livelihoods, and it passed. Now they were afraid she'd win in the battle to protect Longview's water rights.

"Well, me and a partner you don't need to know the name of intend to get that farm." Walker stared at Ferras.

Without expression, the man slow-blinked at Walker and nodded in understanding.

Walker turned back. "And I figured we might make that offer day after tomorrow, when a certain farmer might be looking to sell out."

Chapter Twelve

East Texas is hillier than most people realize. In places, the Sabine cuts through bluffs thirty and forty feet high. Just such a bluff defined the opposite side of the river behind the little scratch farm owned by Bradley Sullivan.

Low clouds scudded across the heavy gray sky obscuring the top of the bluff, giving it the appearance of being the base of a tall mountain. A heavy mist turned the world to water and promised to ruin the man's cotton crop that drooped into the wet middles.

Sullivan owned forty acres that backed up against the Sabine River. The house itself sat by the dirt road on the edge of the field, devoid of shade when the sunshine returned, or grass. Rows of cotton beginning only yards from each side receded into the distance, reaching all the way to the riverbank lined with tall oaks and elms.

Clete Ferras drove and Quinn Walker rode in the Model A's passenger seat as they pulled into the soggy yard. A dirty, shaggy mutt rose from under the porch, barking at the strangers. A tired barn, a plank cattle pen, and a slapdash hogpen settled into the earth behind the tin-roofed unpainted house.

Ferras honked twice, and they stayed in the car until a lean man in faded overalls came to the screen door. "Shut up, Shep!"

The sunbaked farmer stepped onto the porch behind rivulets of water pouring from the shed roof. He angled his head in
question as Ferras opened his door and stood on the running
board. Walker did the same.

"Help you fellas?"

"Howdy!" Frowning at the mud, Walker stepped down into
the mire. He sloshed to the porch and climbed the steps uninvited. "You Bradley Sullivan?"

"I am." Sullivan shifted his weight, brogans grinding wet sand
into the raw wood porch, so that he was between the impolite
stranger and the door.

"I'm here to help you out."

Suspicious, Sullivan tilted his head back and studied Walker.
"How so?"

Walker nodded toward the cotton field. "Your crop's gonna
rot out there in this rain, and I have it on good authority from
the bank that you're in foreclosure."

Sullivan's expression became even more suspicious. "How
do you know that?"

"Because I'm a businessman. Look, times are hard, and we
both know you don't have the money to pay your mortgage.
It's a crying shame what the bank's done to you." He reached
into the inside pocket and produced a folded piece of paper.
"Here's what I'm gonna do. I can buy you out right now, with
enough money to pay off the mortgage and get shed of this
place once and for all. You sign this bill of sale, and I'll take
it to the bank, and you're free and clear with a pocket full of
cash."

"Mister, what's your name?"

Walker hesitated for a moment. "I'm sorry. Forgot my
manners." He held out his hand that was ignored. "Well,
anyway, name's G. W. Middlebrooks. I'm here representing

a consortium of investors out of Longview who've gotten together to help farmers who owe the bank. You know Mr. Emsworth, of course."

Sullivan refused to shake. "I know 'im."

"Well, I work for him, but he represents the bank, and we all know how they are. But me giving you his name's my bona fides. The reason I'm here is because he sent me out here to tell you that you'll have to be off this property in two months."

The farmer stiffened, both work-hardened hands folded into fists.

"Yeah, I know you have a crop in the field, but with this rain and the price of cotton these days, you won't clear enough to make your nut. We both know that. You're finished. Now, here's the deal I'm gonna offer you through my investors that Mr. Emsworth doesn't know about. I've been authorized to give you twice what this farm's worth right now." He unfolded the document and held it up for Sullivan to read. He repeated himself so the farmer could hear it aloud once again. "Like I said, that'll give you enough money to pay the place off and still have enough to start over somewhere else."

"I cain't read much more'n my name, but my note ain't due for two months." Sullivan shook his head. "Never was much punkin' at school. Been a workingman all my life."

"Well, I understand, but I'm here to help you solve this problem. Can your woman read?"

"Naw."

"How about your kids? Mr. Emsworth tells me you have eight kids. One of them can read it for you."

"Naw, the oldest's only nine, and he didn't take to his letters much. He can cipher better'n the rest though."

"Well, you know your numbers, don't you?"

"Mostly."

"Good. That's all you need." Walker held up the bill of sale and turned it so Sullivan could see it. "You know this number here?"

Sullivan peered at the figure at the end of Walker's finger. "Fifty."

"That's fifty dollars *an acre*. Now, you and me both know your place is only worth about thirty dollars an acre right now. That'll put thirteen hundred and twenty dollars in cash in your pocket right this minute. Hell, I want to help you out. I'll make it an even fourteen hundred. How about that? You sell it to my people, and we've both screwed the bankers."

Walker rose up on his toes, burning off hot energy. "I dislike banks as much as you do. One took my family's farm just a year ago, and from what I'm seeing on Emsworth's desk, there'll be a steady stream of foreclosures in the next few years.

"This is my way of getting back at them. You take the deal, and you'll get enough money to settle up with those sonsabitches and get gone with lots of cash in your pocket, and *my* people will get this land the bank wants, because Emsworth intends to get you off your land one way or another so he can lease it to these oil companies."

The farmer took the paper and looked it over, then handed it back. He scowled. "That's too low, even if I did take this deal."

Walker almost rose up on his toes again in excitement. He was an experienced fisherman who loved to take a cane pole down to any river or pool and throw in a line baited with a fat worm, or crawdad if he felt like seining a few. Once the bobber settled onto the surface and the rings disappeared, he'd sit on the bank with the pole in his hand, waiting for that first nibble and thinking of all the money he would have once his wife was out of the picture.

Like a hungry fish under the surface of the water, Sullivan had already nibbled at the bait, and with that, Walker knew he had him. Forcing himself not to smile, Walker figuratively jig-gled the bobber, maintaining the farmer's interest.

"I see you're a businessman down deep inside. How about I offer you seventy-five an acre? If my arithmetic is right, that's three thousand simoleons. Now, I've stretched it about as far as I can go, and while we're standing here talking, some of your land's washing off right now into the Sabine.

"Your signature on this here bill of sale gives us the land so the bank can't have it, and you'll be sitting pretty to start over somewhere else."

Sullivan's attention bounced from the contract to the water-logged rows within view of the porch, then back to the slick-talking man in a well-cut suit.

Walker pressed on. "Look, you've had this place for only ten years. You take the deal, and you're making a killin' here in this depression and screwing the bank, to boot."

Sullivan's eyes flicked from Walker to Ferras still standing on the running board, watching over the open car door. "I don't believe I want to sell. Cotton might go up. This rain might not last very long, and I'll get to pickin.'"

"I've been talking to forecasters. Those are scientific people who have figured out how the weather changes. We're gonna get rain right through 'til after Christmas, and then it's gonna set-tle in hot and dry. It's already happened out in West Texas and Oklahoma. There ain't been no falling weather for a good long while, and big winds have started to blowing folk's land away. They're calling them dust storms, and they reach all the way up into Nebraska.

"Mr. Sullivan, we're in for a long dry spell, and farming is going to come to an end pretty soon. I know how you feel, but if you don't take this offer, Mr. Emsworth is gonna send me and the sheriff back out here in about a week or so with the papers to throw you off this property. You know as well as I do he's given you more time than most of his other farms."

Walker glanced around, as if someone might be listening to their conversation. "They're working crooked deals with these oil companies left and right. They want to cover this whole country in those nasty oil wells, and my people don't want that."

Walker looked inside and saw three barefoot kids watching them through the open door. Two were shirtless boys in patched and faded, hand-me-down overalls. The third was a little blond girl in a shapeless feed-sack dress. He wondered where the rest were.

"My people believe in farms and farming; they believe in the little man, and not banks. If you sell, they're gonna hold this land until the time is ripe for planting more cotton, and take care of it instead of drilling holes everywhere, but if *you* wait that long, your family's gonna go hungry."

The mist changed to light ran that rattled on the tin overhead. He jiggled the figurative bobber again. In his mind, Walker could see a fish named Sullivan fin a few inches closer to the fat worm wriggling on the hook.

"Look, those kids won't have to work stoop labor for the rest of their lives if you take this cash and start over somewhere else. Cash, Mr. Sullivan, right here in my pocket. You wonder why there's two of us here? That man out there is a guard my investors sent with me to make sure I didn't get robbed. That's how serious they are.

"Take the money and go buy a small place just big enough for a truck garden and a two- or three-acre pasture to raise some pigs and cows. Or maybe move to town and open a hardware store in Longview or Pine Top.

"Do that, and you'll have a better house with less work. You can have electric lights and indoor plumbing, and go home at the end of the day. You'll have time to play with the kids and listen to a brand-new Philco radio. I bet y'all don't get a chance to do that very often."

He grinned for the first time at his cleverness. "You'll have time to go fishing. When was the last time you fished? I bet you're like me. I love to take a cane pole down to the river and catch me a mess of white perch or catfish."

Sullivan turned enough to see inside, then brought his attention back to Walker, who twitched the bobber one last time. "All right, Mr. Sullivan. I'm really not supposed to do this." Walker shuffled his feet on the rough boards, as if readying himself for a sprint. "Here's what I'll do. I'll offer you *ninety* bucks an acre. That's three thousand six hundred dollars in your pocket and all this'll be behind you."

Walker paused, watching Sullivan consider the offer.

"Mr. Sullivan, this is your chance to screw 'em once and for all. Not many folks in your position can do that."

Sullivan wiped a brown hand across his mouth, then stepped to the side of the porch. He studied the rain for a moment before turning back. "We ain't got much more'n beans and a little corn-bread in the house. I'll sell if you'll make it a hundred an acre."

"Well." Walker opened the bill of sale and studied it for a good long while, looking doubtful. He bit his bottom lip. "That's *four thousand dollars.*"

"Take it or leave it." Sullivan swallowed the hook. "I can sell one of them pigs in the pen out there and get enough money for another month and maybe I'll get that crop in after all."

Walker tilted his fedora back and scratched the back of his neck as if he'd been backed into a corner. "If I give you the four thousand, you'll sign the papers?"

"I will if it's cash."

It was silent, except for the rain on the tin roof, and the water splashing into the yard. Walker took a deep breath and walked to the opposite side of the porch. Letting the silence stretch, he studied what was left of a stripped-down tin lizzie sitting on blocks. It looked as if Sullivan had been selling parts off the old T-Model to keep food on the table.

The hood was folded back and two electrical wires trailed from the battery and into an open window. He knew that inside the house, a radio was attached to those wires so they could listen to music or a program every now and then. His mind wandered, first to a bottle of gin back at the house, and then to a James Cagney picture playing at the Rio that he'd been wanting to see. Deciding he'd let Sullivan stew long enough, Walker turned back to the farmer. "It's a deal. You sign this, and the money is yours."

"I need to see the cash."

Walker bit his lip again, appearing to be deep in thought. He finally motioned for Clete Ferras to join them. Watching through the rivulets running down the windshield, the sour-faced man left the car and slogged through the mud. When he stepped onto the porch, Walker flicked his fingers toward Sullivan. "We've made an agreement. Four thousand dollars."

"Mr. Emsworth'll have a conniption fit over this." Ferras shook his head. "I wouldn't want to be in your shoes when we get back."

"You won't. Count out the money."

Sullivan watched the exchange and looked surprised when Ferras took an envelope from inside his coat and opened it up. The farmer whistled low and soft. "You fellas really do carry that much cash?"

"Yessir." Walker unscrewed the cap from a fountain pen. "But you've taken almost all of what we have. You're a shrewd businessman, that's for damn sure."

"Let me ask you a question."

"Go ahead, Mr. Sullivan."

"I think y'all might be from one of those oil companies. I know they're buying up land, or at least paying folks for leases. What if I talk to some of them about leasing my place?"

"You could, but they're offering a lot less than what I'm giving you here. And I don't know if you know it or not, but a lot of those wells are coming up dry. You're right at the far edge of the oil field, and the odds are against you here.

"If they drill and don't make a strike, your lease is void, and they'll pack up and leave, putting you right back where you are now, fighting the weather and dryland farming." Walker pointed into the rain. "There's not a rig around here for miles. If they thought you had oil under your feet, they'd have already been out here, don't you think?"

He held out the pen and paper. "Put your name on that bottom line there."

With the pen and paper in hand, Sullivan shifted his weight. "I'll have to go in and sit at the table to write my name."

The man's wife appeared in the doorway. Her face looked as tired and washed out as the faded cotton-sack dress she wore. Something in her expression told Walker that if they went inside, the price would go up, or they might not sell at all.

"Turn around, Clete. Let the man use your back."

Ferras turned around and bent slightly as Sullivan placed the paper on the back of his damp coat and slowly signed his name. When he finished, Ferras stepped back and Walker handed over the cash.

"Here you go, Mr. Sullivan. That's four thousand dollars right there, and I thank you for your business. Now, if I's you, I'd get to the bank first thing in the morning and pay off your loan. Then you can get out from under this place and be sitting pretty."

Sullivan handed the money to the woman, who disappeared with a soft cry of joy. "We'll be gone tomorrow."

Walker stuck out his hand. "Much obliged."

This time Sullivan took it. "Thank *you*, sir."

Walker and Ferras left the porch and trotted through the rain. Ferras started the car and they pulled slowly onto the muddy road.

Taking off his hat, Walker shook the water into the floorboard. "Did you notice how high that river is?"

"Sure did."

"Folks who go off in there'd be washed plumb down to the coast, I imagine. A man distraught over money might do some terrible things."

Playing into the imagery, Ferras leaned over the steering wheel as if it would help him see past the screeching wipers. "What kind of things?"

"Well, I read in the paper here-while-back that a man killed his wife and kids, then himself when he realized he'd lost the family farm and they were going to be living in a tent camp somewhere."

"Killed 'em all, huh?"

"Yep. Shot 'em every one and then burned the house down on them all. Happened out there around Guymon, Oklahoma, I believe." He and Ferras exchanged a knowing look. "Come out here and get that cash back tonight, and I don't care how you do it."

"Be glad to."

"I'm looking forward to inheriting this little place." Tucking the signed document away, Walker barked a laugh. While the farmer was mesmerized at the sight of so much cash, he'd switched the fake bill of sale with a Last Will and Testament that named Quinn Walker as the sole beneficiary of Sullivan's estate, dated six months earlier.

"That was easier than I thought." Walker glanced out the window. "Let's go to Lee's place. I believe we need to celebrate with a little gin."

Chapter Thirteen

Booker was right. Main Street was a morass full of stuck automobiles and people muddy from their knees down. Mules struggled to pull loaded wagons around the vehicles buried to their hubs, while cursing men used teams to pull the cars and trucks out of the mudholes.

It wouldn't quit raining, which kept things interesting. Usually, a hard rain turned the street into a quagmire that soon dried in the hot Texas sun, but this time, the clouds refused to part.

A light shower pattered on the sidewalk as I stepped from the hotel the next morning. By the time I walked down to Charlotte's Café, water again dripped off my hat brim. The café wasn't as noisy as before.

Wondering why the men were so subdued, I scanned the crowd to see a familiar face. Iron Eyes Delgado was seated at the same table I'd used the day before. A mug of steaming coffee hooked around his forefinger.

"Capitán Ohos de Hierro."

The slender Ranger glanced up. Humorless green eyes in a scarred face relaxed as he moved his hat from the table to an empty chair. "Morning, Ranger. Have a seat."

Dropping my own hat into the other empty chair, I sat across from the captain and was barely finished adjusting my gun belt when Charlotte Cain appeared with a fresh cup of coffee. This time her hair was brushed, and the aggravating strand of hair she'd fought the day before was held back with a bow.

It was good to see her, and somehow I knew she'd done her hair for me. "That was fast."

"Didn't want your friend to get too far ahead of you." She inclined her head toward Delgado. "He's having bacon and eggs, and they're already cooking."

"Sounds good. Two over easy, and some biscuits and gravy."

"Done. I didn't ask yesterday, you want cream or sugar with that coffee?"

"No, ma'am. I just want coffee in my coffee, and a few grains of salt."

"What for?"

"Cuts the acid."

"You'll have to salt your coffee yourself." She spun on a heel with a wink.

Delgado laced his fingers back around the steaming mug. "I heard there was another Ranger in town. They didn't say anything about sending *you* out here."

"Came up from the Valley after a murderer by the name of Clete Ferras."

"Don't know him."

"Didn't figure you did, or you'da already had him in chains or laid out over at the undertaker's. Ferras is on the run for a killing down out of Laredo."

"It wouldn't surprise me if he was here, all right. This town's full of all types."

"You ain't a woofin'. Half the men I see here have crossed the line a time or two."

"There are some rough old boys out here for sure. Had to shoot one or two to get their attention when I first got to town." Delgado sipped the steaming coffee. "I'm starting to put a dent in all the meanness going on here. Shut down most of the whiskey rings, and getting a handle on the gambling. There's still a lot of crime around here, though. That's what boomtowns bring."

"You getting much cooperation from the sheriff?"

Delgado's face tightened, a rare display of emotion. "We don't gee haw. He takes care of what he can, and I do the rest." He took another swaller and put the mug down. "I don't like him, though, and wouldn't trust the man any farther than I can throw him."

His five-foot nine-inch frame told me that Delgado couldn't throw the big man very far. Charlotte returned with a plate in each hand, and a third balanced on her forearm. She placed them on the table just as a nearby patron complained. "Hey, I ordered before he did."

She placed a hand on my shoulder and grinned at the irritated customer. "You sure did." She reached across the space between the tables and lightly whacked the back of the man's head. "Hold your horses." She turned back around as the other customers laughed. This time her face was serious. "Did y'all hear about the farmhouse that burned down over in Hog Eye?"

Forks in our hands, we shook our heads.

"Word travels fast around here. These drillers are worse than a bunch of old women. Heard that the farmer lost his mind and killed the whole family, then burned the house down on top of 'em all. They say he was about to lose the place to the bank, and when this rain ruined his crop, he couldn't take it anymore."

"Who's 'they'?" Delgado tilted his head, waiting for an answer.

We exchanged glances, listening.

"Some guys who were in here talking about it first thing this morning. I know their faces. They called the man's name, Sullivan."

"I know of him." Delgado picked up his fork. "Saw him in town a time or two. His name was Bradley. Quiet feller. I wouldn't have thought he'd do something like that."

In my experience with Delgado, I knew the man seldom forgot a name or a face. I smoothed my mustache in preparation to eat, a habit I was trying to break, and paused. "Charlotte, would you see if you can get a name next time they're in here? I'd just like to know."

"Sure will." She gave my shoulder a little pat and left a tingling feeling from the warmth of her hand.

We ate in silence for a few minutes as the noise increased inside the café enough to drown out the sounds of drilling outside. Eating was serious business, and we had a lot to do that day.

Finished, I sat back with my coffee. "You know, I came upon a murder as soon as I got here. Indian woman killed out east of town."

"I heard about that." Delgado chewed on a piece of bacon. "I was going over to talk with Sheriff Dobbs this morning, to see what he found out since he locked up Stanley McCord. I have a notion he's not working too hard on it, though."

"Wouldn't surprise me." I tried not to watch Charlotte as she came back out with more plates. "I'm not getting into your business, but I think I'm going out to Hog Eye and look around a little bit. Somehow I have a sneaking suspicion that the feller I'm after may be involved somehow."

"What makes you think that?"

"Talked with someone yesterday who knew the Freeman woman who was killed. He told me about that scam you broke up, and said there might be another one. Maybe more."

Captain Delgado studied me for a second, and then threw a glance at Charlotte to let me know he'd seen my interest. "Tell me what you know, and I'll look at it, too."

Chapter Fourteen

Because it was still raining, John Henry Johnston was mending harness in his barn when a car pulled into the soggy yard. He moved to the door, wondering who the hatless stranger was who stepped out of the three-window Tudor sedan. When no one immediately came outside, the man with sunken cheeks and a prominent chin faced the house and reached inside to honk the horn.

Not liking the look of the hawk-nosed city slicker in a three-piece suit, John Henry picked up a hammer lying atop a barrel and slowly made his way outside.

His wife, Olivia, came outside in a shapeless front-button housedress, wiping her hands on a thin dish towel. Speaking from behind the screen door, she threw the rag over her shoulder and finished drying her hands on a stained apron. "Help you?"

"I'm here to see your husband."

The hair prickled on the back of John Henry's neck at the abrupt statement. In East Texas, there were certain courtesies toward others when meeting. He closed the distance between them and stopped about ten feet away. "What about?"

The man jumped and turned, reaching into a coat pocket.

Seeing the farmer standing close by, holding a hammer, he let the hand hang free. "You're Johnston?"

"What do you need?"

"Well, howdy!" The stranger's cheeks caved deeper in a forced smile. "I'm here to talk to you."

John Henry noted the man's appearance that was in direct contrast to the fine clothes he wore. Gray hair stuck up in the back and on one side. John Henry shifted his weight onto one foot. "All right. Here I am. What's your name?"

"It's, uh, it's Ferris. C. M. Ferris. Spelled like one of them Ferris wheels they have at fairs."

"I've seen one before. What can I do for you?"

"Is your wife there an Indian?"

Lips in a tight line, John Henry bit back the first response that came to mind. "I asked what you need here."

"I've always been partial to dark-skinned women myself." Ferris chewed lightly, as if there were fig seeds between his teeth. "I had a gal down in South Texas who was something else. Part Messkin and Lipan with the blackest hair you ever saw."

Behind Ferris, John Henry saw Olivia latch the screen and disappear back inside. Thankful that Booker wasn't there, he jogged the hammer up and down in his hand, measuring its weight. "I don't know you, and I don't intend to stand here in the rain and talk about wives."

"Well, invite me in the house, so we can get in where it's dry."

"No."

"The barn, then, though I think it's rude to talk business with the smell of horseshit in your nose."

"The air's clean out here. State your business, or get gone."

Ferris's eyes went flat. "How many acres you have here?"

"None of your business."

"It is, because I want to see about buying your place."

"Not for sale."

"Everything's for sale."

"Look, this land has been ours since my granddaddy built this house. It's not for sale for any price. Now, I bid you to leave so I can get back to work."

"Have you already been offered a deal by some oil company?"

"None of your business." John Henry's stomach tightened. The haggard man standing in the yard was validating his suspicions about the Freeman family. "Go."

"I don't believe I will." Ferris took a step toward John Henry, who held his ground. "It's a free country. I come and go as I please."

A distinctly furious female voice cut through the damp air like a slap. "Then, please, go."

At the sound of Olivia's order, Ferris turned to see the twin bores of a twelve-gauge shotgun pointed at his chest. John Henry kept it loaded with buckshot. Both hammers were cocked, and the woman who stood behind the two-shoot gun held it level and steady.

Ferris's face was full of fury, but he knew the street howitzer in the woman's hands was deadly at that range. "You keep watch, John Henry Johnston."

"You ain't foolin' nobody." John Henry jerked a thumb over his shoulder. "There's a Texas Ranger in town, and I'll allow he's looking for you right now. You better get gone, Mister Clete Ferras, out of this county, 'cause when I tell him you've been rootin' around here under a false name, he's gonna come knocking on your door."

"Nobody runs me off. I'll be back someday when you least expect. Keep watch over your shoulder, Johnston, and that damned red nigger wife of yours, too!" Slamming the door, Ferris/Ferras stomped the gas, spraying mud across the barn.

John Henry let out a long-held breath and stepped up on the porch. Completely familiar with the weapon in her hands, Olivia lowered the shotgun and lowered both hammers.

He rested a hand on her shoulder. "Good work, sweetheart."

The woman who'd been raised on a dirt floor and survived hardscrabble farms gave him a wan smile. "I despise rude men."

He laughed, releasing a gusher of pent-up tension. "I'm glad Booker wasn't here. He didn't need to see that."

Breaking open the shotgun, she rested it inside her elbow, keeping an eye on the muddy road stretching east and west. "Where is Booker, anyway?"

"Mr. Tom Bell came and got him this morning." At her raised eyebrow, he laughed again. "He's making more money leading that Ranger around than I've made all month."

Chapter Fifteen

Quinn Walker rested a hand on Mallie's shoulder and kissed her plump cheek as he stood to answer the doorbell. He had a *doorbell*, and it pleased him to no end. Those were the little things that made a man successful. "You'll feel better in the morning, dear. I'll mix you another of those toddies before you go to bed, if you want."

She gave him a slight smile. "I don't know why I feel so bad."

The doorbell rang again, insistent.

He thought about strangling her where she sat in her parlor chair beside the radio, then answering the bell, but it would be too soon. Forcing a serious look on his face, he frowned at the door, trying to see through the glass who was on the other side. "It's likely just a bad old cold coming on. Just a minute and you can have another drink."

She sighed. "I feel so...evil for drinking alcohol, and on a *week*night."

Torn between their asinine discussion and whoever was on his front porch, he wanted to explain to that dumb lump with piggy eyes that the patent medicines she liked to use were full of something just as bad as the doctored-up homemade whiskey, but he had to find out what was going on out front.

"Be right back." He crossed the room and foyer to find Clete Ferras and Gene Phillips standing beside the porch rail. Making sure his wife wasn't watching or listening, he slipped outside to join them in the shadows. "What?"

Even in the darkness, Phillips's face looked more strained than it had when he told Walker about his baby's death. "We have a problem."

"I wish you two would bring me a solution to a problem, instead of bringing more trouble to my house. What is it now?"

Ferras licked his thin lips and waited for Phillips to answer. The shine in his eyes was reminiscent of a hungry dog faced with a full pan of meat scraps.

Phillips cleared his throat and glanced around to make sure they were alone. "Clete here went out to John Henry Johnston's place to talk to him like you said. He found out something."

Frustrated by their game, Walker snapped. "What?"

"That Texas Ranger who's snooping around looking for me must have been out there." Ferras's voice was low and mean. "Johnston knew who I was and threatened to sic the law on me."

"You mean to tell me that you managed to find a house in the country he's been to, and that person *recognized* you!"

"Who would have thought that could happen? I guess it's 'cause this town's so small as far as farmers are concerned. They all know one another, and talk." Ferras had the demeanor of an often-kicked dog. His hollow cheeks seemed to sink in even more. "He's gonna tell that Ranger I was out there."

"So?"

Phillips was so nervous he couldn't keep his feet still. "Well, aren't you worried that if he's looking for Clete, he might stumble into what it is we're doing? We don't need that."

"Sheriff Dobbs'll take care of it when the time comes, but

you're right, it's not good to have him digging around anymore'n he already is."

They stood in silence, each man weighing his thoughts.

Walker felt his vest pockets for a cigar. Finding a fresh one, he bit off the end and struck a lucifer. He puffed it alight and studied the dark street, picking a bit of tobacco off his tongue. "All right. Do we know if he has any of our names already?"

Phillips pointed at Ferras. The killer shrugged. "I don't know. All I was told was that he was here looking for me. I used a different name, and was just doin' what you wanted, visiting farms and seeing if they were inclined to sell out."

Walker puffed on the cigar. "What name did you use?"

"Told him I was C. M. Ferris, spelled like a Ferris wheel at the fair."

"That the best you could do? You damn-near used your own name."

"It was all I could think of right then. I'd likely forget something I completely made up."

"You probably would." Walker took a deep drag on the cigar and let the smoke out through his nose. "Those Rangers are pretty smart, and tough." Walker recalled what had happened when Ranger Delgado arrived in town.

After meeting the sheriff and learning there was no jail, he hired a blacksmith to anchor a log chain across the length of the courthouse, as long as the Baptist Church building. Violent criminals, shackled to trace chains that were padlocked to the heavy linds, soon became known as Iron Eyes' Trotline. There, they were forced to endure the elements and were fed once a day.

"He'll be like a bird dog with his nose to the ground, working a quail. He won't quit until he finds something." Smoke rose straight up from his cigar. "Has anyone told Dobbs?"

"Not yet." Phillips scratched his cheek. "We figured to keep him out of it right now."

"Fine. Has anyone told *him* yet?"

They all knew who he was talking about. Caldwell.

"No."

"Don't. We'll handle it ourselves."

"How?"

Walker pointed at Ferras. "Get some boys and take care of it."

Ferras's grin was feral. "Will do."

"That'll bring more lawmen looking." Phillips ground his teeth and Walker could see the man was close to cracking. Everything that happened in recent days had him wound tight as a new fence. "Two Rangers are enough. If we have about twenty of them sonsabitches digging around here, the whole thing's liable to blow wide open, and Dobbs won't be able to cover it up. We don't want to get any of that on us."

Walker nodded, thinking. "Fine then. Ferras, here's what you do. Find some people, pay 'em up front to do the job and have them get train tickets to Florida. Keep our names out of it. Once they rub him out, tell 'em to hightail it on out of here. I'll see that Dobbs goes to the station during his investigation. The ticket master'll remember them and give him a description. The laws'll pick 'em up somewhere between here and Florida, and that'll keep the Rangers off our backs and lay off any suspicion. That'll lead everyone off on a side trail."

Satisfied with the plan, Phillips nodded at Ferras. "Ankle on out of here and handle it."

The killer nodded back and faded off the porch and down the street. They watched him go, and when he was completely out of sight, Phillips turned back to Walker. "This is all getting out of hand."

"It'll be fine."

"I don't think I have the moxie anymore."

"You'll be fine." Walker puffed his cigar back to life. "All the dominos are set up. Let 'em fall and we'll be even richer than we are now."

"I'm not sure it'll all be worth it. Now that my baby's gone, it's all ashes in my mouth."

"I don't have the time to go over this again. You go on home and think about how fat your bank account is going to be in a couple of months. I'm going in to make Mallie another one of her toddies. They seem to be working."

Phillips's eyes widened in understanding. "You're still doing it? With all of this going on around us?"

"I'm just dosing her a little at a time, and there's no better time than the present."

Chapter Sixteen

A knock on my hotel room door brought me upright. I flicked on the bedside light and checked my watch. Anyone calling after nine at night usually brought bad news. I habitually slept in my trousers, in case anything happened, so there was no hesitation if I needed to move.

Pistol in hand, I padded across the room in bare feet and paused beside the door. "Yes?"

A woman's voice spoke softly. "Tom, it's me, Charlotte."

Shocked, I didn't know what to say.

"Tom, I know it's late and improper for a single woman to come to a man's door at night, but I need to speak with you." Her voice lowered even more. "Please, I'm afraid someone'll see me out here in the hall."

I opened the door, and Charlotte slipped inside with a soft smile. I leaned out to make sure the hallway was clear. She was standing in the middle of the room when I locked the door and turned.

She considered my flat stomach and chest, eyes lingering on the two puckered scars from bullet wounds, and several long, white trails that defined where edged weapons had once laid me open.

Feeling unusually vulnerable, I picked up a shirt hanging over the footboard and slipped it on. "Well, it's good to see you. Sorry I wasn't presentable."

Charlotte's face flushed, and I could tell she was suddenly embarrassed. "I'm sorry to wake you."

"I was just laying there, staring at the ceiling, so you didn't wake me up. I'm surprised to see you here at this hour, though." I crossed back to the nightstand and laid the pistol on top of my well-thumbed Bible.

"We closed up and I started for home, but then decided I needed to talk to you…where we couldn't be heard."

I smoothed my mustache with one finger and stopped when I caught the habit. "We need to speak softly. These walls aren't that thick. I can hear people talking in the other rooms and having…" I paused in embarrassment at what almost came next. "Anyway, it isn't as private as you think."

Her shoulders finally relaxed, and when her dimples appeared, I melted like a spring snow and knew I was in over my head with her. I motioned toward a chair. "Please. I'll sit on the bed."

Back as straight as a board with both hands on her knees, she scanned the room. "This looks like a comfortable place."

"Better than most of the rooms I've stayed in. At least there aren't any critters in the bed or on the floor."

She was through with the small talk. "I don't think you know what you're up against here. This is a dangerous place, and getting worse."

"I was under the impression that things were changing, for sure after Ranger Delgado showed up."

"They are, but he's concentrating on the oil company men. This place blew up overnight, and brought in all kinds of men, both good and bad. I watched the good people who live here give over to those who came for the work. They brought in fights, murders, drinking and prostitution." She drifted off on the last word. "I don't fault the women. They're doing what they can to stay alive, but our world here in East Texas changed when all these strangers showed up. Ranger Delgado got astraddle of most of them and things calmed down, but there's more going on than meets the eye."

"You're talking about the Freeman murder?"

She nodded. "Yes, but it's not just her. There's been all kinds of death here, in addition to outright murder. For a town of our size, there are too many people dying. I didn't put it all together until my husband was killed."

I caught myself before she saw my reaction. Charlotte hadn't been wearing a wedding ring, so I assumed she was unmarried, or maybe divorced, though divorce was rare in small towns. The strong attraction grew, and I concentrated on not letting it show.

"Three months ago, he went down on the creek, where there's an iron bridge over a deep hole where he likes... liked...to fish. He'd been going down there since he was a kid. He didn't come home that night, and I knew something was wrong.

"I called Constable Burdine in Hog Eye, and he went looking for Gerald. He found him the next morning, laying half in the creek, drowned, but I have my suspicions."

"He could swim?"

"Like a fish, and I saw him swim the Sabine once in his clothes. He was strong, and they didn't slow him down one whit."

I ran the facts over in my mind, as if running a trotline. "You're saying someone *drowned* your husband?"

"Yes."

"Drowning a healthy man is a hard thing to do."

"But it was done, and I believe I know the reason why. We own a hundred acres of land just outside of Hog Eye, and the banker here in Pine Top tried to buy it, but we wouldn't sell. Gerald told him it was old family land and he wasn't interested.

"Well, it wasn't two weeks after the funeral when Albert Emsworth from over at the bank came to the café just before I opened one morning. Said he figured I'd find it hard to pay the taxes on the land with this depression on, and he wanted to make it easy on me. He offered quite a bit of money for it, but when I turned him down, I saw something in that man's eyes that revealed more than the truth."

"They say a person's eyes are a window to their soul."

She licked her lips. "I believe that's true. There was nothing behind there but darkness. He's been back a couple of times since then, raising the price a little each time. He seems friendly, and smiles a lot, but his eyes are always flat."

"You think this Emsworth shot Gerald, then."

"Oh, no. Albert Emsworth don't have the guts to do it, but he has the money to have it done."

"And you've said no every time he comes around?"

"I have. Then, a few days before you came to town, I was approached by an oilman who asked to lease the land for drilling. He was polite and to the point, but I declined his offer, also."

"There's oil under your place?"

"They think so. You've seen the drilling around here. It's moving in our direction as sure as rising water, and I expect the oil companies to start boring their holes in our area soon."

"You don't want them drilling on your husband's land."

"Oh, you misunderstand. It's *my* family land. My granddaddy settled the family there when they moved up from the Big Thicket. Gerald never wanted to farm. He's the one who opened this café and the one in Hog Eye. But that's neither here nor there. I listen and watch the men in town, and have heard some disturbing things. Suppositions."

"Such as?"

She lowered her voice, and they leaned in. "There have been a lot of folks dying, as I said. There's a family out of town that had a run of bad luck ten years or so back. The Roberts family. Most of their men passed away in one way or another. One had a heart attack. Another was killed when his horse threw him. There was one who cut his leg with a chopping axe and died of blood poisoning."

The story poured out of her as if a dam broke.

"The two oldest just died of old age, and before you know it, the only ones left were women, some of marrying age. The youngest of those men passed away from Old-Timer's Disease, which was odd, but not unheard of. He simply started losing his memory and wasting away, and before they knew it, he was gone.

"The family had already leased the land, and the drillers struck so much oil the widows were millionaires within a few months. They had money, but no husbands. They bought new cars every two or three months or so, built big houses, and wore the finest clothes they could buy, and ordered everything they wanted by catalog from New York City and even France and Italy.

"The youngest girls were something else, let me tell you, and drew men like bees to the sugar jar. A couple of them remarried last year and everyone thought things were looking up for those gals. One named Florence married a feller out of the territories up north of Oklahoma City and her sister Bobbi Jo hitched up to a man from Fort Smith, Arkansas."

As she talked, her slender hands fluttered up on occasion, laced their fingers, and then she wrung them as if soaping up. I'd seen that kind of behavior before. Nerves.

"I hope they married good men."

"Who knows how *good* they were. Florence passed away from diabetes back in May. Bobbi Jo from alcohol poisoning several days later. They found her in the bedroom with three empty quarts of white lightning on the floor beside the bed."

"That'll do it. At 190 proof, that much booze'll kill a person pretty quick. They think it was suicide? Still grieving over the loss of her sister?"

"We all wondered, but nobody said a word. The thing is, those men inherited everything when the girls passed. Men from other states are now the millionaires, and getting richer each day as those pumps just keep sucking the earth's blood out into barrels."

The room was silent as we considered the implications. It was that silence that saved our bacon. The floor creaked in the hall, and my head snapped up. The same board creaked again, telling the me that it wasn't simply a person passing by. Someone was standing in one place just outside the door, shifting his weight.

Putting one finger to my lips, I twisted from on the bed and picked up the revolver and raised my voice loud and clear. "You know, I really liked that coconut pie you served me this afternoon."

Quickly understanding, she nodded and spoke louder than before. "It's my mama's recipe."

The doorknob turned slightly and the creak came again. Stomach in a knot, I stood, flicking my empty hand, telling Charlotte to get between the bed and the wall. She understood and hurried around. Dropping to her knees, she disappeared behind the mattress.

When she was down, I switched off the table lamp, plunging the room into darkness, and waited to shoot the first person who came through that door.

When I was a boy, I learned to shoot from an old man named Fitzhugh Buckner, who once lived in Langtry, Texas, and said he'd been good friends with Judge Roy Bean. Fitz, as he was known, showed me how to stand when faced with a duel or shooting challenge, and repeated over and over that being ready to shoot was the first step in surviving. The second step was not speed, but marksmanship. We practiced in the evenings when the chores were done, and I soon found I had a knack for hitting what I was aiming at.

That knack, preparation, and years' worth of practice saved our lives when the door exploded inward, followed by three armed men silhouetted in the doorway by faint light coming from sconces in the hallway.

There was no time for useless shouting or orders. Standing in a dueling pose, my Colt .38 barked twice, punching two bloody holes in a stranger's shirt. The revolver's muzzle flash lit the room like flashbulbs.

The assassin of medium build got off one shot before his brain and fingers ceased to work together. The fresh corpse dropped straight down in the doorway, a sudden impediment to the two others rushing to get inside.

A second man, twice as large as the first, ducked back out of sight, allowing the third to step forward and raise a Colt .45 semiautomatic. Thunder rolled from the big pistol as the stranger pulled the trigger as fast as he could, apparently hoping that a steady stream of lead would overcome my response.

Flashes like lightning filled the room, freezing the action in a sequence reminding me of a flickering picture in a penny arcade.

Unfortunately for the would-be murderer, every round missed, though wallpaper puffed from the impact of the big slugs. A picture jumped off the wall, and a windowpane shattered. Still rooted to the floor and angled with my right shoulder facing the man, I centered the pistol's sights on the middle of the huge silhouette and fired.

The bullet's impact staggered the assassin, and he fired again. The automatic continued to spray lead as the outlaw stumbled backward to fall across the hallway.

Legs splayed and somehow still alive and with his back against the wall, the determined son of a bitch raised his arm to shoot again. I put still *another* slug into the big guy, and then another in his bloody chest to anchor him to the floor.

The twin muzzles of a sawed-off twelve-gauge stuck around the doorframe. Those twin bores scared me worse than seeing the other two. The guy stiff-armed the shotgun sideways into the room and, still hidden, pulled the triggers. The first barrel belched fire, lead, and lightning with a hard slap of thunder.

The Colt revolver was empty, but I wasn't out of the fight, not by a long shot. I dropped the empty Colt revolver and bent to pluck a smaller .32 caliber pistol from one boot sitting half under the bed. The shotgun's second barrel went off, also missing by several feet.

I judged how far back the man was from the door and shot three rounds through the wallpaper where I figured he stood. Puffs of plaster dust rose from the impacts.

In the sudden silence, the shotgun fell and unseen footsteps stuttered across the floor for a moment, followed by the thud of a third body. I waited, the backup pistol trained on the opening, but only the sound of a death rattle reached my ears.

Shouts and screams from down the hall and other parts of the building filled the air. Doors opening and slamming told me that the hotel's occupants were emerging from their rooms to find out what was going on, or they were running away.

Moving cautiously, I approached the door and checked the hallway to find three men cooling on the polished wooden floor.

Heads poked out from rooms up and down the hallway, looking for the source of the gunfire. Someone flicked a switch. White lights hanging from the hallway ceiling washed the slaughter-house with sharp definition.

"Y'all stay in them rooms for a minute! Texas Ranger at work here!" I saw the outlaw's 1911 pistol lying on the floor. A full magazine was still clasped in the dead man's hand. I picked it up by the ivory grip and pushed the release button to drop the magazine, then reloaded the pistol and chambered a round. He had two more full magazines in his pocket, and I took them as well. That done, I went back into the room, more heavily armed than before.

"Charlotte, you can come out now."

White-faced, she rose from behind the bed. A round bullet hole perforated the iron headboard only inches away from where she hid. "Are you hurt?"

Startled by the question, I glanced down to find no new holes in my shirt or pants. "I'm fine. How about you?"

She nodded with short, jerky movements. "I'm all right."

Absentmindedly smoothing my mustache and thinking, I studied the scene outside of the hotel room. "I believe I've poked a bear."

Chapter Seventeen

Sheriff Dobbs was mad as an old sore-tail tomcat. "Well, Mr. Bell, this is a mess, ain't it?"

All I could do was shrug. "Not one of my making."

Two hours after the shooting, the bodies were gone, leaving nothing but bloodstains on the hotel's wooden floor, along with more than a few bullet holes in the walls. We stood inside my room to get away from the onlookers who still milled around at the far end of the hall.

Dobbs stuck his forefinger in one of the holes put there by my .38. "No, I don't suppose it is. I thought I'd seen it all when these drillers showed up with a train-car full of troubles, but this takes the cake. I've never seen three men killed at one time in a gunfight."

"Well, you've never been down on the Rio Grande."

"Say you collected all their guns?"

I pointed at the bed as if he couldn't see them without my help. "Right there."

"I'm gonna need all those."

"You can have all but that .45. That's mine now."

"Nope. All of them."

"It fits my hand. Governor Sterling don't care if we keep

weapons we take from outlaws. I'll write you out a receipt, and if you want, I'll wire the major and have him send you a letter. I doubt those three had family that care."

The sheriff slid both hands into his pants pockets, studying me like I was some kind of new animal. "You Rangers sure are full of yourselves."

"Comes from riding alone."

"I figure y'all won't be around much in a few years. You know how some people down in Austin feel about all y'all." Dobbs almost rocked up on his toes, looking for all the world like he'd be glad for the Rangers to disband.

I tamped down my rising anger. I for sure disliked pompous lawmen, and the more I was around Dobbs, the less I thought of him. "You can investigate from your end. It's your town, and you'll likely have to explain it to the mayor and city council, but it's my encounter, and everything will go into my report."

"Fine, then." Dobbs checked his pocket watch, as if he had somewhere to be that early in the morning. "Why do you think they came after you?"

"I'm getting close to something, and it's not just Clete Ferras. I suspect he's mixed up in something pretty big, to bring this kind of firepower. He's mean as a snake, and would have ambushed me by himself while I was out somewhere, but he's small potatoes. Whoever sent three guns in the middle of the night is scared, and all this speaks volumes. You working on anything that draws this much attention?"

"Naw." Dobbs rubbed the early-morning stubble on his chin. "The usual small troubles, but this smells like what they have up in Chicago. Gangster stuff."

"Those boys I shot have never been north of Arkansas, I'd bet."

"They didn't look familiar to me on those slabs."

"Don't doubt that. Men like that generally stay under the surface."

"These didn't."

"They would have, if I hadn't been awake." I kept Charlotte out of the story from the outset. She slipped out the door during all the confusion, avoiding the pools of blood spreading out from under the bodies. "It was lucky for me that the floor creaks, so I was ready."

"How do you think they planned to do it?"

"Don't start me to lying. All I know is they tried the doorknob at first, so I imagine they'd've just waltzed in and shot me in the bed if it'd been unlocked. When they couldn't get in, they had more than one choice. Knock or call to me. One of 'em just shouldered the door and busted the frame, hoping to catch me before I could clear the cobwebs out of my head."

"I'd have knocked on it, and when you answered, plugged you through the door."

"If they'd been smart, they would have ambushed somewhere else and shot me in the back. Whoever sent them wanted it done fast. Didn't want to wait for a day or two and set it up right, so that tells me they were getting nervous."

The sheriff didn't get any of the information Charlotte told me earlier in the evening. I wanted to play my cards close and not get her involved if I could help it. The truth was, something about Dobbs raised the hair on the back of my neck, and I couldn't explain why.

Hands in his pockets again, Sheriff Dobbs surveyed the room. "The Rangers have a pretty good expense account, looks like."

"I pay my own bills for rooms like this. They don't like to part with as much money as you'd think, though we get free railroad passes."

"Sounds like a vacation to me, free passes."

I started to get prickly again. "If you call getting shot at a vacation, you need to look up the word."

"Say you were in here alone?"

"Didn't say."

"Were you?"

"Why do you ask? This late at night, wouldn't a man be in bed?"

"Well, there was a lot of shooting and you came out on the winning end. It woulda evened the odds if there's been two gunhands instead of one."

"I'm not a gunhand, and it was just me, though I used two different pistols. Count the bullet holes in the walls and the empty casings there on the night table that fit my pistols. They'll add up."

"Two different pistols. Two calibers?"

"That's right, and Dobbs?"

He appeared to notice I didn't say *Sheriff* Dobbs.

"I travel and work alone, so I carry more than one weapon, along with a rifle or shotgun in the car if I think I'm gonna need it. But listen to my words, I don't intend to be deposed by you or anyone else tonight. The door's right there. I'll come by in the morning if you want to talk further."

"No, that's all right. I have all I need."

"You bet you do."

The sheriff made a show of studying the entry and exit holes before taking his slow time down the hall.

Chapter Eighteen

The morning fog was thick. An extremely nervous Quinn Walker waited beside Gene Phillips's car, smoking one cigarette after another. Phillips stayed behind the wheel with the window down to let his own smoke blow out and into the damp, dripping tree branches. They were parked on the back side of a forty-acre field owned by Walker's wife.

It had been their meeting place for months, because the muddy dirt road took them down in the bottoms, where it ended abruptly right where they parked. There was no reason for anyone to be there, and was therefore the safest place they could talk without being seen.

Though Walker ran the operation in Pine Top, he answered to the moneyman and brains of the outfit, O. L. Caldwell. The old man was going to be madder'n hell about the missed attempt on the Texas Ranger.

It wasn't that far from Longview, but Caldwell was late. Walker stubbed out a butt with his shoe and reached into his shirt pocket for another. He spoke through the open window. "Gene, what do you think happened last night at the hotel?"

"It balled up because Ferras didn't do the job himself. When you go to hiring people you don't know well enough, things can go bad."

"I told him to get some men."

"Looks to me like he got the wrong ones."

Walker straightened at the sight of a Cadillac coming through the fog. "I'm afraid it's gonna get bad for a few minutes. Here he comes. Let me do the talking."

"I don't intend to say a word."

O. L. Caldwell never drove himself because he had never learned. The driver pulled up behind Phillips's town car, the Cadillac's V-16 engine humming with power. Caldwell opened the back door. "Don't kill it," he ordered and stepped out.

Walker met him between the cars. "I'm sorry I had to call you, sir."

In his seventies, Caldwell still stood straight and tall in a tailored suit. His white hair was mostly hidden by an expensive fedora. "What happened?"

Walker explained about Tom Bell and the botched ambush.

"So you tried to bump off a *Texas Ranger!*" The old man's eyes flashed. "Quinn, I thought you had more sense than that. Those old boys are made out of spring steel and wire."

"I's afraid he'd nose around and get into our business. See, he's looking for a man named Clete Ferras, who's from South Texas. Ferras killed someone down there and came up this way. He knew one of my men, who vouched for him, and I needed someone like that, but I didn't know he had a Ranger up his ass."

Walker described the plan they'd cooked up that would lead any investigation away from town. "Ferras was the perfect guy to handle it. New in town. He's only been here a couple of weeks, and nobody knows him. He's been a solid hand. Does what I want without questions."

"Up until last night."

"Well, sir, like I said, he hired men to do the job. At least he knew how tough Rangers are, so I guess he figured three people could get the job done."

"But they didn't."

O. L. Caldwell liked to point out the obvious, leaving his employees to squirm on the hook whenever they were trying to explain a mistake. Walker had seen him do it numerous times, but now he was on the receiving end, and he didn't like it one damned bit.

"Is Ferras one of the dead?"

"Nossir. He hired those amateurs, but stayed down in the car as the driver. After all the shooting, and when they didn't come right back downstairs, he took off."

"And now you've started a blood feud with a Ranger." His tone was flat.

"I don't know if you'd call it that."

"I'll call it what I want." Caldwell took a cigar from his inside coat pocket and used a small metal figurine of a nude woman to cut the end. Walker watched in fascination as the old man raised the figure's left leg to insert the small end up close to her crotch. With a snap, the severed end dropped to the ground.

The businessman's yellow teeth flashed in a grin, and he wriggled the clipper. "I knew an old gal like that once." He returned the clipper to his pocket and the hand reemerged with a Douglass lift-arm lighter. A quick flick of his thumb produced flame.

Puffing the cigar alight, he studied the fog-enshrouded trees around them. Crows called in the distance, their harsh cries deadened by the moist air. "Well, I believe that once you start a job, you're duty bound to finish it. I sure wish you hadn't started this one, though."

Instead of arguing, Walker waited in silence as the cherry on

Caldwell's cigar glowed in the flat, gray light. He exhaled and the cloud of smoke matching the color of the sky hovered between them before finally dissipating.

"This has all been going smooth, until now?"

Walker swallowed. "Yessir."

"If any of this gets on me, you won't like what happens next."

"I know that, sir."

"This Ferras. You send him out to get the job done right this time, but I want him on one of the triggers, and I don't care how many others he takes with him." Caldwell studied the hot end of his cigar. "In fact, I'm going to send the men down here to do it along with him."

Walker felt much of the tension drain away. He'd been dreading the job of finding enough toughs to do the job. He preferred to limit the number of dimwits he had to work with. Criminals had a bad habit of turning into blabbermouths and ratting people out if they got caught, and he didn't intend to spend the next twenty years down in the Walls Unit in Huntsville, or on death row waiting to see Old Sparky. Caldwell had an organization that rivaled those of the Chicago gangsters, and his shooters would be top notch.

"You plan it. You. Not Ferras, and then you go with them to make sure that happens."

The fear came back in a tidal wave. Walker wasn't a man of violence. He preferred to pay others to do his bidding, but he knew better than to argue with Caldwell. "Yessir. We'll get it done."

"Do it fast. I don't want this hanging over my head, and I damned sure don't want this lawman to go poking around any more than he has. If he stumbles into our plan, then we're blowed up."

"We'll do it as soon as your men arrive."

"They'll be here tomorrow. Coming from Hot Springs. I want it finished then, so we can get out from under this and back to making money."

They stood in silence for several moments before Caldwell spoke again. "You remember I said I didn't want any of this to get on me, but if it gets all the way up to Hot Springs, and gets on Himself, we're all dead men."

Chapter Nineteen

The afternoon clouds hung low, resting on the tallest pines as I drove over to Hog Eye. This time I traveled alone, not needing Booker Johnston as a guide. The windows were down, and cool air flowed through. Unused to piney woods, I relaxed and enjoyed the smells and sounds of East Texas.

Mind running free, I thought about the newer cars that were coming out with radios, and wondered how anyone could concentrate on their driving with music and voices blaring from the dashboard.

Music made me think of dances, and though I wasn't much of a dancer, I enjoyed the events just the same. I wondered if Charlotte liked to dance. If she did, we might have a chance to take a night off, if someone was making music close by. They usually were, playing in barns or out in open fields when it was dry.

If that wasn't the case, maybe she'd like to drive into Longview for a picture show. Lots of talkies were coming out, and she might be interested in seeing one. Of course, I couldn't tolerate it if she wanted to watch such nonsense as *Dracula*, but I'd enjoy E. G. Robinson in *Little Caesar*. It'd be interesting to see how they presented gangsters on the screen.

Rain made the road muddy, so I kept the speed down to avoid caking any more on the car than was necessary. A covey of quail crossed the road ahead, rushing from the wet grass on one side to the other. They cross open areas like paths and roads one at a time, and, in no hurry, I stopped even more to give them time. Sitting there beside a field, I saw three deer watching me.

It felt good to be out in the country, and I was looking forward to the return trip after nosing around Hog Eye for a little while. It was a pleasure to see so much peaceful green after spending time in the bustling oil town. The deer disappeared, and I shifted down into low gear and gave 'er the gas.

There were trees down in the Valley, of course, but mesquite in the pastures and cottonwoods and willows along creek bottoms didn't hold a candle to what surrounded me there in a world of water. That's what Dad called East Texas, a world of water, for if it wasn't falling, there were branches, streams, creeks, springs, and rivers everywhere.

Down south where I grew up, it was mostly flatland and row crops, some fields as far as you could see. I sighed at the sight of cotton on both sides of me, hanging heavy with water. I never wanted to be a farmer, though, couldn't tolerate the idea.

Dad had me hoeing when I was a kid, but as soon as I could get gone from farming, the Old West called, so I took off to become a cowboy in the high plains. After chasing the stupidest animals in the world through the heat, cold, snow, and rain, I was already looking for a way out when the Great War came along. Full of a kid's piss and vinegar, I signed up and went to France, where I lived in hell on earth until the Armistice in 1918.

When it was over, I was right back where I started. With Texas under my feet again, cowboying didn't hold the same appeal. I needed an honest job but had no intention of farming or ranching. Running a store wasn't my idea of a career, either.

That's when trouble along the border prompted Governor William Hobby to hire Rangers under special commission by the hundreds. I was one of 'em, and entered the service, where I soon picked up a reputation as a calm, clear thinker and a good hand when the action got hot.

Despite the danger, I loved the job and always looked forward to every case that came my way. The law was the law, though in my consideration, it was not as black and white as some folks thought. I enjoyed putting criminals away to pay for their crimes.

This case running down Clete Ferras hadn't been bad until a few hours earlier.

My mind continued to drift, and I wondered who was scared enough to hire three assassins in a small oil town.

That's it. It has something to do with oil.

I couldn't come up with any other crimes that would have such financial backing. If it was out west, it would be cattle or land. Here it was what's *underneath* the land.

Hog Eye was getting close. The muddy road curved around a pasture beside a typical East Texas farmhouse. A woman shelling peas on her porch waved, and I returned it. There are folks who'd turn their head to avoid saying howdy, but that wasn't me, ever.

Towns in that part of Texas were never more than twenty miles apart, the distance a horse could easily travel in a day. Between them, smaller communities popped up based on need. Sometimes it was a general store or two, and those evolved into larger settlements with the addition of a cotton gin, churches, and schools.

Hog Eye was such a town that grew slowly, then suddenly blossomed with the discovery of oil. That's where I came to, still another now-familiar shantytown stretching out from the center of the original community. Traffic increased, mixed with horses and wagons weaving around one another in the muddy street, and it took all my concentration to find a place to stop, angled nose in to the sidewalk.

Stepping out, I paused to take stock of the surroundings. There were two good places to get information in a small community. One was at the post office, the other was the general store. If there was a domino hall, then all the better. Here, the post office was in the back of a board-and-batten store, giving me a twofer.

Across the muddy street clotted with cars was the Grand Hotel, which wasn't much more than a two-story wooden building. A few doors down the boardwalk from where I stood was the Southern Café, where I intended to eat later in the day.

I stepped under the porch just as it started to sprinkle. Two men were loafing outside, leaning their cane-bottom chairs back against the wall covered with tin signs advertising Scotch Snuff, Chesterfield cigarettes, Beech-Nut, and a dozen more, all over-shadowed by an overabundance of Coca-Cola ads.

"Morning, gentlemen."

"How do?" answered a farmer in faded overalls with frayed cuffs. The other similarly dressed man with matching gray hair threw up a hand in a silent wave.

"Name's Tom Bell. Texas Ranger. I'm looking for a feller named Clete Ferras. Y'all ever hear the name?"

The farmer shook his head. "Nossir. But that don't mean nothin'. I used to know ever'body who lived here, but there's so many come to work the rigs, I can't keep up with them."

I handed them the creased wanted poster. The first farmer took it with gnarled fingers, studied it for a second, then handed it back. "Ain't seen him."

"Y'all got a constable here?"

"We do. D. R. Burdine. With those two initials, folks call him

Doc. He's usually on a tractor, but since it's raining, I 'magine he'll be here directly. He usually drops by here two or three times a day when it's weather like this."

"Much obliged." Using two fingers, I plucked the flyer from his hand and opened the wood-framed screen door. The spring squawked in protest, and I stepped inside, letting it slap closed behind. The interior was a typical country store with shelves stocked with everything from overalls to canned goods to fresh vegetables, harnesses, and everything necessary to maintain a house or livestock.

Behind the counter, half hidden by a head-high cash register, the bald owner was weighing tomatoes for a woman who was digging through her change purse. "Be right with you, sir."

"No hurry."

Instead of waiting, I went on back to the post office at the rear of the store. A woman under a thick bun of brown hair was sorting mail behind the wrought-iron cage window. She picked up a pair of glasses and perched them on her nose. "Can't see up close with these, but they sure make it easier to see past the end of my arm. Help you?"

I pulled back the coat's lapel to show my badge. "Looking for this man." I passed the flyer under the metal arch. "I was wondering if he called for mail here in Hog Eye at any time."

"I never liked that name. Come this time next year, we're gonna be called Liberty City, and that's a proper name for a town. *Liberty City*. It has a patriotic ring, don't it?" She passed it back. "Clete Ferras, let me look." She rummaged around and flipped through a thick book. "Haven't heard the name, nor seen any mail for him, neither."

"Just marking places off my list."

"You staying at the hotel? If you are, and I see him, I can send word."

"Not right now. I'm at the Pine Top Hotel in town."

"I'll send word to old Dan there. He's the owner. I've known him for years."

"He's a good man."

"I'll be a-lookin.'"

The woman with the change purse was gone with her tomatoes when I returned to the front counter. The bald proprietor adjusted a display of cigars and produced a flicker of a smile. "No mail for you today?"

"Didn't expect any." I went through the familiar pattern of passing over the flyer. "Looking for this guy. Has he come through here?"

The owner took it. "Sure have. Came in this morning. Bought two packs of Chesterfields and a Co-cola. Paid for it with a silver dollar."

The hair rose on the back of my neck. "Has he been here before?"

"Once, I believe, that I know of. Sometimes my daughter runs the store when I'm not here, so she might've seen him."

"Was anyone with him?"

"Not in here. He got in a car out front. I noticed because a truck backfired out in the street, and I looked outside to see if it was that or some dern fool shooting off his gun."

"Notice what kind of car it was?"

The man laughed. "Like all them others out there, 'cept, for once, it was blue."

Ford colors had been black on all T-Models. When the Model A came out, there was some variety. You could choose blue, green, gray, and of course, black. I joined him, laughing a lot more than the weak joke required.

When I quit laughing, I realized that was the first time I'd felt such pleasure in a long time. It came to me that I was finally over the hump of losing my wife two years earlier. My lungs finally felt free and light, and I drew a deep breath that seemed to wash away the last vapor of sadness.

Free from of a weight that had been draped over my shoulders for months, and hoping that a million more inhalations would be drawn with Charlotte close by my side, I felt giddy for a moment. "Don't suppose you can describe the driver?"

"Nossir. Just a shape in the car."

"Describe how Ferras was dressed."

"Dark suit. White shirt. No tie. Hat."

"What kind of hat?"

"Pinch crown. Snap brim. Dark gray."

"Much obliged. Call Constable Burdine if he comes in again, would you? I'll make sure we talk, and then he'll know how to get ahold of me. But don't let on you know who Ferras is when he comes in. He's a bad outlaw."

"Yessir."

The rain stopped again by the time I got back outside. The two farmers who were still leaning back against the wall were joined by three others, so I stopped to speak one more time. "I sure would appreciate it if one of y'all'd tell Constable Burdine that I'm over there in the café if he drops by."

"Sure 'nuff." The gray-haired farmer nodded in agreement.

The covered boardwalk was as crowded as the one in Pine Top as I made my way down to the café. Choosing a table against the wall, I sat facing the room. Less than two minutes later a waitress with dark hair and fine features came around the counter. I figured she was Charlotte's cousin. After a few minutes of watching her work, I knew I was right, meaning Charlotte was likely at the larger café in Pine Top. That was fine. I'd see her tomorrow. The cousin finally had time to come by for my order, and as soon as she got a good look at me, her face brightened into a wide smile.

"I'm Charlotte's cousin." She absently wiped her hands with a thin cup towel and cocked her head. "Someone we both know described you to me. She says she'll be working here tomorrow, and you can see her then."

"What's your name, Charlotte's Cousin?"

"Dorothy."

"Pleased to meet you, Dorothy."

"My pleasure, Mr. Man. Steak and potatoes, sir?"

"You bet."

———

I was sipping coffee when D. R. Burdine came into the café, dressed like most East Texas constables. Black slacks, blue shirt, and a leather pistol scabbard threaded through a belt finished the deal. Seeing me, Burdine tilted his narrow-brimmed western hat back on his head.

"Well, a Texas Ranger, in our little ol' community." He crossed the busy room and pulled out a chair across the table, and we shook. "Name's Doc Burdine."

"I've heard of you. Have a seat, Constable."

He sat down, adjusting what appeared to be a fairly new holster.

That got my interest. I pointed at the revolver on the man's hip. "Looks like fresh leather."

"It is. Got it just this week from a saddlemaker down the street. He makes them for all kinds of pistols and knives. Says since folks are buying fewer and fewer saddles these days, he had to make ends meet."

"I might drop by in a little bit, then."

"Wouldn't blame you if you did. Cliff over at the store says you're looking for me."

"I am. Really more looking for this fugitive."

Burdine took the flyer and studied it. "Yep. Saw him a day or so ago. Didn't like his looks, but then again, I don't know what to think about all these old boys coming in and out around here these days. Some of 'em look rough as a cob, but life's hard since the crash. I'm wrong ever' now and then, and I find out some of 'em are all right."

"Sounds like you're a good judge of character. Ferras is mean as a snake."

"Saw that right off."

"Any idea where he works, or if he has a job?"

"Naw. Just seen him on the street."

"Coffee, Doc?" Dorothy stood there with an empty cup and the coffeepot, and neither of us had seen her coming.

"Sure."

She poured him a cup, gave me a wink, and went back to the kitchen. Doc grinned at the look on my face. "Well, I guess it's true, then."

"What's that?"

"About you and Charlotte."

I frowned. "And that is..."

"This is a small town, son. News travels like wildfire, and I was in here last night when Dorothy and Charlotte were closing down. Charlotte came in from Pine Top early to help. I overhead them talking about a Texas Ranger with a thick brown mustache and cold gray eyes. That'd be you."

"Don't know about the cold eyes part."

"I do, and you breathed some light back into Charlotte. That's the first time I've seen a spring in that gal's step since her husband died."

Never much for discussing personal matters, I wanted to let the matter drop, but like any good lawman, I dug for information. "What do you know about that?"

Doc shrugged. "Her spark, or her husband?"

"Husband."

"Probably everything she told you, since that wasn't news to you. I looked into his death, but a body in the water don't carry too many clues as to how it quit breathing. The only thing I know for sure is that I don't believe he just drowned. I've known that boy all his life, and he can...could swim like a fish."

"Those are the same words she used. Suspects?"

"Nope. Let me tell you, with this many people coming in, I'm dealing with more and more meanness than I ever saw since I put on this badge. I mostly dealt with bootleggers and family fights before this. Now, it's a whole 'nother world, and I doubt I'm gonna run for constable next election."

"Wouldn't blame you for that. This place is booming, and I imagine y'all are going to need your own police department one of these days."

"I'm hoping the sheriff's department'll assign some deputies out here until then, just to give me some help."

"Seems peaceful enough right now."

"It's daytime. Come dark, these boys get to drinking and gambling, and before you know it, somebody'll bust somebody else in the mouth and the fight's on."

Prohibition did little to slow down folks' drinking. The Volstead Act didn't prohibit the *consumption* of alcohol, though some municipalities insisted on arresting citizens for drinking. Instead, it forbade the manufacture, sale, or transportation of intoxicating liquors within, the importation thereof into, or the exportation from the Unites States.

Like most everyone who enjoyed a drink every now and then, I kept a bottle in the trunk of my car for *emergencies*, preferring to call it my snakebite kit.

"I can't farm and spend all night prowling the streets. I know of at least two gin joints right now, but the minute I show up, all the hooch disappears and the customers are just sitting there, drinking Cokes and talking. There's one right down the street from here, but unless it's something serious now, I tend to look the other way. A man can expect a certain amount of low-level crime, as long as everyone can tolerate it."

I finished the last of my coffee. "Well, let me know if you see Ferras, would you?"

"How'll I get in touch with you?"

"I'm going over to the Grand to see if they have any rooms. If they don't, I'll go back to where I've been staying at the Pine Top Hotel. You can get me there."

"They'll have you a room here, if you want to stay close." Doc laced his fingers on the table. "Tell Malcom I said to give you one."

"If they're not full up."

"He'll empty one for you, if you use my name."

"How're you so sure?"

"He's my first cousin. Double cousin to be exact." Doc leaned forward. "And just to let you know, we don't talk about nobody around here, 'cause everybody in this part of the world's kin to everybody else. Charlotte's kin, too, so I hope she don't see the inside of that room you're getting."

I thought about the room in Pine Top, and the gunfight, and how I felt about her. "That won't be happening."

Chapter Twenty

The phone rang in the Ohio Cigar Store located just down the street from Hot Springs' most luxurious hotel, the Hazelwood. The speakeasy had been a favorite hangout of Al Capone when he wanted to get out of Chicago for a while to enjoy the mineral springs in Arkansas. His associate, Lucky Luciano, had great plans to make Hot Springs a nationwide destination for gambling, drinking, and, of course, his favorite, prostitution. Only a few months earlier, Luciano had sat at a table near the oak staircase with Bugs Moran, discussing just how to do it.

At the rear of the smoke-filled room, a dark-haired woman huddled with three men, talking and laughing. Leaning against the wall beside them were cases for musical instruments. Even with the specially constructed wall, music and loud voices still leaked into the front, requiring the bow-tied clerk to keep a careful eye out on the street for any lawmen who weren't on the take. A soundproof wall separated the speakeasy's tables from the small, ten-foot-deep cigar store fronting the building.

The bartender answered on the fourth ring, then laid the receiver down. Catching the eye of a well-dressed man standing beside a table across the room, he pointed at a figure sitting in the shadows and flicked his fingers. Chic Marco crossed the dim club and picked up the receiver and listened. The bartender moved away from the dangerous man with a scar running from his left eye to the corner of his mouth to make sure no one thought he was eavesdropping. Marco hung up and returned to the table.

"Mr. Moretti, Mr. Caldwell in Longview has a request."

Cherubino Moretti insisted that no one use his first name, which translated into Little Cherub, though his doting mother's choice of names fit him perfectly. Soft, baby-faced, and slightly chubby, he'd always looked more like a cherub than the tough gangster he wanted to be.

He took a small sip of twelve-year-old scotch and replaced the glass. To prove he was in charge, he picked up the cigar beside his elbow and took a puff as if giving the statement deep consideration. "What's he want?"

Marco leaned in so the other patrons couldn't hear. There wasn't much chance of that. Both tables on either side were anchored with Moretti's own employees. "He needs some men for a job in Texas."

"How many and where? What kind of job?"

"He wants to rub out a Texas Ranger in Pine Top. He asked for six."

Moretti puffed on his cigar, his attention on a young woman climbing the steps headed for the casino above. She saw him and gave her hips an extra twist, adding a smile just as she went out of sight. "Who is she?"

"Never saw her. I think she might be one of Gracie's girls working down at the club."

Both snickered at the mention. The Hatterie Hotel was a known bordello overlooked by the corrupt Hot Springs police department.

"I want some time with her."

"I'll arrange it. Now, about that Texas job."

"How many did you say he needed?"

"Six."

"*Six?* For one guy?"

"Says he's tough." Marco shrugged.

"Sounds like bunkum to me."

"All I know is he killed three already who underestimated him."

"Then he *is* a tough guy. All right." Moretti turned to the table behind them. Several of his men were drinking and playing cards. He flicked two fingers. "Ermano, all of you go to Texas and burn down a Ranger. What was that hick town?"

Marco answered. "Pine Top."

"Pahn-toup." Moretti drew the word out in his version of a country accent. "You got a name for them to meet?"

"Quinn Walker. I have a telephone number they can call when they get there."

"Good. Genovese, bring this Ranger's badge to me. I've always wanted one of those."

Ermano Genovese squinted past the ready-rolled smoke rising from the cigarette between his lips. His hat brim caught and held the smoke. "You got it, boss."

"They say he's good. Take the heavy equipment."

"When do we leave?"

"Right now. Drive all night and get right back here when you're finished." Moretti finished his drink and rose. "All right, gentlemen, I'll be leaving for a little while. I have an urge to meet that cute little chippie who just wiggled her ass at me."

Chapter Twenty-One

The Grand Hotel in Hog Eye, soon to be renamed Liberty City, had a room after I mentioned Doc's name. I took it for two nights, even though the room back in Pine Top was still in my name. After that little altercation in the hall, they were gonna have to patch things up, and I'd kinda soured on being there for the time being.

Besides, the Grand would be close to where Charlotte lived.

As soon as I dropped my grip on the bed, I wrapped the newly acquired .45 Colt in a newspaper and hoofed it down the board sidewalk in search of the saddle shop. It wasn't far, across the main road and a hundred yards away. The sweet natural cologne of leather filled me up when I stepped inside.

A dozen or more hand-tooled saddles costing anywhere from fifty to ninety dollars set on wooden stands scattered throughout the small shop. Leather belts hung in a thick fringe from one wall opposite a wall of full cowhides. The skin of a huge buffalo bull tacked on the opposite wall behind a massive stone counter framed the slender owner, who looked up from tapping on a leather saddle fender.

The man with a face full of wrinkles didn't look big enough to heft a kid's saddle, let alone one for a full-size adult. "Help you?"

Breathing deep and enjoying the smell, I laid the newspaper-wrapped .45 on a bare spot beside the thick leather where he was working and stuck out my hand. "Texas Ranger. To start off, I wanted to find out if you've seen this man."

The saddlemaker put down a stamping tool he was using to detail a saddle skirt and took the flyer with a work-hardened hand. He studied it with the attention of a detail man. "Nope. He don't look much like a horseman."

"I doubt he is. Probably not worth the powder it'd take to blow him up, neither. Let me know if he comes in. I'm across over at the Grand Hotel for a couple of nights. I wouldn't let on if you recognize him, though."

"You bet." The man waited, eyeing the package on his counter. "Something else?"

"I have a .45 in there. Do you have any holsters to fit it?"

The saddlemaker unwrapped the paper and picked up the freshly oiled pistol. He expertly dropped the 1911's empty magazine and pulled back the slide to make sure it wasn't loaded. "I have one over here. Let's see if it suits you."

He came around the counter to a table full of hand-tooled holsters lined up side by side. A small shelf above held neat stacks of matching belts rolled up and tied. Reaching for one holster, he changed his mind and selected another. It was common for men to use holsters threaded onto the belt that held up their pants. This one was slightly different. Not exactly a one-piece frontier style, it came with a distinctive matching belt that seemed to be almost a part of the holster itself.

"I made this one about a month ago for a feller who didn't come in to pick it up." He slid the semiautomatic in without effort. It fit perfectly. He put it into my hand. "This is the one you want. How'd you carry it before?"

"Haven't. Just got it." I slid the pistol in and out, testing the fit for myself. "Been wearing this .38 for years."

"This holster has a guard to cover the trigger, but there's nothing to hang the boat-tail on. There's another one with a strap, but I bet you don't want that. You'd have to unsnap it, and that can slow you down. I believe you carry these with the hammer back."

"You do."

"You need this belt to go with it." The tooling matched the holster. He eyed my waist under the coat. "Take that dress belt off and try this one, too."

"Two belts? I thought I'd just get a holster and thread it through the one I already have."

"That'n you're wearing there's too thin for this rig. Answer me this, do you want it to sag and take your pants down with it?" He didn't wait for an answer. "You could, but in my opinion, this looks better with the two of them matching up nice and purdy. Put it on just under this thicker one. It's a good look 'cause they set each other off."

Thinking, I caught myself smoothing my mustache again. "And you'll sell two belts and a holster at the same time."

A wide grin cracked the serious little saddlemaker's demeanor. "Man needs one to hold his britches up, and the other'n for his gun. Like I said, if you don't, the weight'll drag your pants down on one side. That pistol's heavier than a little .38. Put 'em on and let's see."

Sighing, I pulled my plain old black belt through the loops and laid the holstered .38 on the table, then threaded the new one back where it had been and buckled it up. The new holster strapped around my hips, only an inch below the waistband. Settling everything into place, I rested my hand on the .45's butt.

"This rig does feel good."

"Told you."

I drew the semiautomatic easily. Sliding it back in, I felt it needed to be adjusted to ride a little farther back on the side. Nodding in satisfaction, the owner picked up two small magazine pouches. "These thread on the other side so you don't have to carry extras in your pockets. That'll be 'leven dollars. Two for each belt, five for the holster, and a dollar each for the pouches."

Thinking, I left my mustache alone and settled the new leather again. "All right." I dug the money out and passed it over.

"There's a mirror over there."

"I'm not buying it for the looks."

"I know that, but you can see how everything sets. The magazine pouches should help balance the pistol. See how it rides? Looking in the glass don't cost nothin.'"

Self-conscious, I stepped over to the mirror to see how the new rig set on my hips. Squaring both shoulders, I admired the workmanship and the way the tooling matched.

The owner came over and handed over my change. "If you ask me, that setup is the bee's knees."

I found myself cutting my eyes at him. "Aren't you a little long in the tooth to be talking like these kids?"

He grunted. "I have those kids still at home for a little while longer. That's all I hear. How about me saying that rig suits you?"

"That's better." My grin showed I was kidding. Slipping the jacket back on, I adjusted the lapels. "You can keep that old belt. One more question."

"What's that?"

"Can you point me toward the most popular speakeasy in town?"

Suddenly uncomfortable, he found somewhere else to look. "What makes you think I know about stuff like that?"

"Small town. Everybody knows everybody else's business."

"I don't drink."

"Didn't say you did, but you know folks that know folks. I won't say nothing about you steering me in that direction. I think that's my best chance to find somebody who knows this guy I'm looking for."

"Well," the man rubbed his chin while I loaded the magazine with bullets from my pocket. "I've heard about a bootlegger or two, but you know..."

"I need a watering hole." I seated the magazine into the grip and pulled back the slide to seat a round.

His decision came fast. "All right. Go over to the Hydroxy Mercantile. They got a little candy counter there on the right side. There's a door behind it that leads into the next building. Tell 'em Clarence sent you."

"Who's Clarence?"

"Nobody. Just the name to get in."

"Thanks." Re-setting my hat, I tucked the still-holstered .38 into the small of my back and left, feeling pretty good about the way the new semiautomatic rode a little lower and closer to hand.

Chapter Twenty-Two

The Hydroxy Mercantile was close, but I went back to the hotel room and changed clothes, putting on khakis and a blue shirt, trading polished boots for a pair of worn brogans. The .38 went into the front pocket of my britches, and the new rig stayed behind. Minutes later, I wasn't a Texas Ranger, but just another man on the street.

I didn't like the clothes one damn bit, but it was the only way to keep from drawing attention. It worked, because not one person on the busy sidewalk noticed me. Still invisible, I crossed the mercantile's black-and-white penny-tile entrance to step through the glass doors.

Just as the saddlemaker said, there was a plain door behind a small oak-trimmed glass candy counter on the right. A wooden radio near the door blared new jazz into the air. Memphis Minnie was just finishing "Bumble Bee Blues," part of a wave of southern blues performers who pushed up to Chicago from the South, changing the sounds of popular music.

An oily-looking man came down the long counter from the dry goods section. "You need something?"

"Radio's kinda loud."

"That it is. I'm hard of hearing."

Putting a hand behind my ear, I leaned over the counter. "What?"

"I said I'm…oh, a wise guy, huh? Like I said, you need something?"

"Yeah, but I don't see it here." Acting uncomfortable, I glanced around the store, and then back to the closed door. I leaned in and spoke softly. "Clarence sent me. Said you could help."

I expected more discussion, or questioning. Instead, the oily man reached back without looking and tapped "shave and a haircut" on the door with a knuckle. When the cover on a judas hole slid back to reveal an eyeball, Oily jerked his head in my direction. "Said Clarence sent him."

"What do you want?" The man's voice was muffled by the wooden door.

"I'm thirsty. Heard a man could come in if he knew the right people."

The peephole closed and the door opened. Oily waved for me to come around the counter and stepped aside so I could walk into a dark bar that smelled of stale smoke, spilled beer, and whiskey. The door closed behind me, and a stump of a man gave me the once-over.

"No trouble in here." He picked up a weighted leather sap lying on a tall stool. "I'll knock you in the head if you start anything."

"The only thing I'm gonna start is my way down toward the bottom of a glass."

Stump smiled, revealing all four of his teeth. "That's the ticket. Have fun." He half-sat on the stool and opened a newspaper.

The interior was as wide as the mercantile next door, long and narrow. A dark bar took up the whole right side, and tables filled the remainder of the room. Three dozen people were there, drinking and laughing. Now I knew why the radio just outside the door was so loud.

Two men in dark vests and sleeve garters talked at the far end. One separated and came down. "What'll it be?"

"I'd like a beer."

"Coming up." The bartender turned to a barrel resting on its side and drew a mug that he sat down in front me. "That'll be two bits."

I put a quarter on the bar. It disappeared in the swipe of the man's rag. Turning to scan the dark room, I took a long pull of the warm beer and swallowed. It had been a while, and the toasted nuttiness of the bootleg beer was more than satisfying.

Most of the customers were involved in conversation. A poker game at the back kept half a dozen men busy. Several women were scattered around. Some were there with boyfriends or husbands, but more than one were likely working.

A gal with short dark hair appeared at my elbow. She wore an off-white dress with narrow straps that showed more shoulder than most women preferred. The look was well received by the patrons, though. "Buy me a drink."

"Sure." I dug out another quarter. "This beer's pretty good."

"I'd prefer something a little more stout."

"What'll that be?"

"How about a gin rickey?"

She was working the bar for sure, with too much lipstick and powder. The color in her cheeks was artificial. "Only if you let me have the first sip."

Her expression went flat, telling me I'd pegged her right. The drink that would likely cost between thirty-five and seventy-five cents would have been mostly carbonated water with very little liquor, if any at all. "You think I'm a bar girl?"

"Didn't say that." I took another sip of beer, not taking my eyes off her face. "I just like the first sip of a rickey."

The tightness in her face relaxed. "Well, how about I share that beer with you instead?"

"I said I'll buy you one."

"Changed my mind. A beer sounds good."

Neither of us waved toward the bartender, but he drew a mug full right on cue and sat it on the bar near her elbow. She picked it up. "I can only drink one. They bloat me up."

I considered her slim figure and skin not accustomed to the sun. "Looks like half a beer'll do that. You probably need to eat another biscuit. You're no bigger'n a minute."

She laughed and drained half of the glass. "You're new in town. Looking for work?"

"Just got here is right. Trying to find my uncle. He sent for me and said to meet him here."

"What's his name?"

"Clete Ferras. Gray hair. Long chin, collapsed cheeks. Heavy eyebrows and ears like the gate on a cattle pen."

She laughed. "Dresses well, but the clothes look like they hang on him."

The hair prickled on the back of my neck in excitement. "That's him."

"He was here last night with a couple of others. One of 'em's Quinn Walker."

"Don't know him."

"I wouldn't expect you to. He's a local that's making it big in oil. Lives in Pine Top now with a fat Indian wife who's worth a small fortune."

My eyebrow started to rise, and I forced myself not to react. This was exactly the information I was looking for. Finding a man who worked directly with Ferras was a surefire way of tracking him down, especially if he lived close by. Her information gave me more details I hadn't bargained on. They matched up with what Charlotte told me about what was happening in Pine Top. I'd have to study on it later and see how the dominoes lined up.

"You know who Walker married?"

"Sure do. Gal by the name of Whitehorse. Mallie Whitehorse. She and her folks lived in a dirt-floor shack until they found oil on her daddy's land. He died, and a month later her mama was out of cash and let one of those oilmen take out a drilling lease. Now they're rich as sin with more money coming in every month."

"Some folks have all the luck."

"Don't they though."

"Well." I took in the room, noting everyone. "Uncle Clete just might get us into the money here, then."

"I bet he'll be back in a little bit, but he's not a boll weevil or even a roughneck. He don't make money with his hands."

"That's what I was hoping for. There's easier ways of making money than working."

She laughed and drained the rest of her beer. Mine was still three-quarters full. I took another sip as she thumped the empty mug on the bar. "My favorite way of making money is doing what I like to do for fun and getting paid for it."

That eyebrow started back up, but I forced it down, pretending I didn't understand the obvious proposition. "Well, I'm just here to cut the dust until I meet up with Uncle Clete."

"Stay here with me until he comes in."

"I don't have that kind of money." I winked. "Or the time. Look, I'm here a little earlier than we both expected. If he comes in, don't tell him I came by. I want to surprise the old fart. I'll pop in every now and then, and you can tell me if he's showed up."

Her eyes twinkled. "I think that's the best description of him you could come up with."

I dug out a five-dollar bill. "You and me both will get our money's worth out of this fin if you see him."

She licked her lips in a flirt. "That's *all* I gotta do?"

"It is. And I'll give you another when he gets here."

"Deal."

"What's your name, Missy?"

"Louise Cherry."

"I believe the first name."

A lightning flash of anger flickered across her face. "All right. What's yours?"

"Tom."

"Tom how much?"

"Just Tom. I'm staying over at the Grand. Come get me if Uncle Clete shows up, or if I'm not there, leave a note."

"How about I bring a flask to your room when I come get you?"

"We'd get to having too much fun, and I wouldn't get to see him." I gave her a wink. "I'll see you in here again."

My glass was soon empty, and I was about to leave when two men approached the table. The Mutt and Jeff duo might have walked straight out of the newspaper comic strip, except their edges were harder and well-lubricated. Their demeanor was far from pleasant.

I was surprised when the shorter of the two thumped a hard knuckle on the table. Short and squatty, he was built like a blacksmith. His eyes flashed, hot and glassy. "Mister, I got a bone to pick with you."

The odor of cheap whiskey washed over me like he'd been pickled in it. Trouble was likely on the way, but I wasn't having it, though. "I don't think you do. I've never seen either one of you boys."

"You're cuddled up with my girl!" Cue Ball planted his feet.

"You sure do have a pretty girlfriend."

The statement caught Cue Ball off guard. It was obvious by his stance that he was ready to tangle, and the calm compliment was a surprise. "Well, yeah she is."

"I ain't your girl!"

Cue Ball ignored her. It took a second for his fogged mind to get back on track. "Well, you're standing here with her."

"That I was, but my beer's gone, and we don't seem to have much in common nohow. And being's how she's your girl, I don't have no designs on her. By the way, I surely like the smell of that cigar you're smoking. What brand is it?"

"Why, it's a King Edward."

"I believe I'll go find myself one." Using my left hand, I left a silver dollar on the table. "Sorry to be a bother. Y'all have a drink on me." I gave them a smile and walked away.

Behind him, the taller one I thought of as Jeff clapped his hands one time. "That sure was a nice guy. Let's have that drink."

I slipped the brass knuckles from my right hand, put them back into my pocket, and nodded goodbye to the doorman on my way out.

Chapter Twenty-Three

The next morning, two dark blue Fords rolled into Pine Top, carrying six well-dressed men who arrived from Chicago via Hot Springs. Ermano "Hermie" Genovese rode in the back seat of the lead car on that dark, gray morning. Frankie "Big Nose" Birder drove, with Alex Cardinella riding shotgun. They always wanted him ready for action, because Cardinella's nickname was Mad Dog, and he earned it.

In the following car, Michael "Easy" Andriacchi drove with Guiseppe "Joe" Alderisio in the passenger seat. Dominic "Gabby" Rio rode in the back seat beside two BAR rifles and a Thompson submachine gun. As they pulled to the curb in front of Quinn Walker's house, Gabby covered the weaponry with an old blanket and stared out the window.

Before they left Hot Springs, Hermie called Walker's house and told him they'd be there by daylight. Walker was less than enthusiastic about the news.

"Don't come to my house, for chrissake! Meet me somewhere else!"

Hermie snapped at him over the buzzing, static-filled line, his voice sharp as a razor blade. "No! We're not driving around town so everybody can get a good look at us. We will come to your house and you lead us to this Ranger."

"How about meeting at a café? You'll be hungry when you get here. We can have breakfast..."

"Do we have a bad connection on this blower? I said we will be at your house by daylight. You can make some sandwiches if you want. Yeah, that'll be good. Make six sandwiches. I want Italian beef, and top it with giardiniera peppers. Six sodas. Coca-Cola works."

"I don't even know what the hell *geronda* peppers are." Walker's voice was high and squeaky.

"Find out." Hermie broke the connection, and they left the Ohio Cigar Store moments later.

Now, in front of the new Craftsman house, Frankie Big Nose honked the horn. The front door immediately opened and two men rushed out carrying paper grocery sacks. The dark-haired man in the lead patted the air to stop them from blowing the horn again. He threw a quick look over his shoulder and rushed down the sidewalk, past newly planted trees held up with stakes and wires. Unsure of which car to approach, he hesitated until the back glass rolled down on the lead car. Hermie hung his elbow out. "You Walker?"

The man licked his lips. "Uh, yeah." He pointed with an elbow. "This is Gene Phillips, my partner."

"I don't care. You have my sandwiches?"

Walker cleared his throat. "Uh, yeah. But I couldn't find any of that Italian meat, since it was so late when you called, but I have roast beef with bell peppers on light bread."

"I told you." Hermie spoke to the men in the front seat. "These yokels are something else. What the hell's light bread?"

Big Nose chuckled. "A loaf of sliced bread they bought at the grocers. They don't have bakeries down here."

"Fine." Hermie held out a hand. "Give." Walker passed one of the sacks through the open window, and Hermie jerked a thumb at the other car. "The other one goes in there."

As Phillips passed over the second sack, Walker stood on the sidewalk, shifting from foot to foot. "What do we do now?"

"You know where this Texas Ranger is?"

"Yeah. He has a hotel room here in town, but right now he's in the next town over, Hog Eye. Spent the night there, and I imagine he'll probably be there tonight, too."

Hermie turned to the others in the car. "Town's named Hog Eye." The others in the car laughed with him. "What the hell kind of name is that for a town?"

"They're going to change it to Liberty City soon..."

The look in Hermie's eye told him the man didn't care. His smile dissolved. "How you know he's there?"

"We have a man followed him. Found out from a chippie in a speakeasy in Hog Eye."

"Fine. Lead us out to this Hog Eye."

Walker took a deep breath. "Well, I have something to tell you first."

"What?"

"Y'all are gonna stick out like a sore thumb there. Even though it's smaller than Pine Top, and there's about five thousand new people in town, y'all don't look like you're from around here."

"*Y'all.*" Hermie punched Mad Dog's shoulder from behind. "See *y'all*, these rubes ain't as dumb as you thought. So, country boy, what do *you* have in mind?"

On solid ground for the first time since the wiseguys arrived, Quinn Walker outlined his idea.

Chapter Twenty-Four

Booker Johnston and his buddy Hut Parsons stopped prowling the streets of Pine Top to study something unusual, a clean fifty-five-gallon barrel. It was just sitting by the side of the road on Elm Street, about two blocks from Main.

Always looking for a way to make money, Hut rocked the steel barrel.

"I bet this fell off a truck they were taking out to a rig. I bet we can sell this for at least a dollar to somebody who needs a burn barrel."

"Nobody'll buy a clean barrel for trash." Booker circled the container, looking for holes. "They want one that costs a nickel, or maybe a dime, but you're right. It's sound. Let's go sell it."

They grabbed ahold and found the barrel was heavier than they expected. Booker let it settle back down. "This thing weighs a ton. Maybe we can get someone to give us a lift, and they'll put it in the back of a truck for us."

"I'm afraid they'll start asking too many questions." Hut studied the situation. "On this side of the tracks, people who look like me get the side eye for just walking down the sidewalk. Somebody'll think for sure I stole it. We need to get it out of here before whoever lost it comes back."

"Let's just lay it over and we can roll it."

The boys had some experience in rolling various pieces of equipment for fun. One of their favorite games was to roll a barrel ring or a metal wagon rim down the road, running alongside and using a broken ax handle or good strong stick to push it along.

"Be careful." Hut pointed down the street. "It's not too steep here, but if it gets away from us, it could hit a car or scare a horse, and they we'd get our asses blistered, and after that, I'd prob'ly wind up on a chain gang like Uncle Bubba, and you know colored folks usually die there."

Booker had an idea. "How about one of us gets inside and the other rolls from behind? That way, if it starts going too fast, whoever's inside can just stick his legs out and slow it down. I bet the extra weight'll keep it rolling slow, too."

"Good idea. You're smaller, so get inside and I'll push."

Booker crawled into the barrel with his head toward the bottom. "Go ahead on." Hut pushed and half a turn later Booker found himself flopping around. "Hold on!"

Hut reached over the barrel and stopped its roll. "What's the matter?"

"This way won't work. Let me sit and curl up. It'll be like doing somersaults over and over."

"You'll get dizzy."

"Go slow."

"I have an idea, too."

"What's that?"

"I got this in my pocket." Hut drew out a tangle of jute twine. "How about I tie a loose loop around the middle of this here barrel with enough slack to hold onto? It'll roll inside, and I'll hold it back like the reins on a plow mule."

"Good idea." Booker curled up facing downhill and braced himself. "Okay. Let's give this a try."

Hut scanned the packed-dirt street lined with parked cars and wagons. No one was coming, so he maneuvered the barrel out to the middle and gave a tentative push to get started. The barrel rolled smoothly within the cord, and with Booker's weight, it seemed more stable than when it was empty. Hut walked along behind like a live anchor, pulling on the cord and slowing the barrel down.

"This is fun!" Booker's voice floated back to Hut. "Push a little harder, and then we'll take time about."

"All right. Hang on!" Hut gave the barrel an extra hard shove and it rolled easily...too easily.

Gravity quickly took hold, and before you could say Jack Robinson, it gained momentum. Hut reared back on the cord that had already worn in two from friction. It snapped with an audible crack, leaving him with a handful of limp string. Suddenly frightened, he grabbed on to the barrel, but it was moving too fast. It quickly accelerated, leaving him standing in the middle of the road, watching the large cylinder gain momentum.

"Slow it *dowwwwnnnn*!" Booker's voice crackled as he spun faster and faster.

Hut put both hands to his mouth. "Get out!"

By the time Booker reached the end of the block, the barrel was nothing but a blur heading toward Main. *"Heyyyyyy Urrrrrkkkk!"*

Luck was with him. Instead of a tanker truck or automobile, a wagon loaded with firewood appeared at the exact moment Booker's barrel shot out into the street. It slammed against the rear wheel and stuck underneath the rig like mud thrown against a wall.

He crawled out, dizzy and gagging. A pair of rough hands grabbed the youngster under the arms and jerked him upright. The gathering crowd jostled for elbow room, laughing. The angry man holding Booker checked him out. "You all right, kid?"

Booker gagged again, his head still spinning but clearer. "I think." He swallowed. "I think that was a bad idea."

"You could have killed yourself, kid." The wagon driver gave him a shake. "Or one of us."

"I won't do it again." His head clearing, Booker looked around for an escape. One thing he didn't want to do was have to explain himself to the sheriff. "I need to sit down."

The man turned him loose and bent to get the steel barrel out from under his wagon, talking to the onlookers gathered around him. "Damn kids. A stunt like that'd break a horse's leg or mess up a car." He pointed at a deep scuff in the front wooden hound that fastened the front axle to the wagon tongue. "He's lucky it didn't break."

Swallowing hard to hold the contents of his stomach in place, Booker staggered like a drunk to Quigley's General Store and saw Gene Phillips drive by with Quinn Walker riding shotgun. Neither man looked happy, and he was about to gag again when he noticed two cars following almost bumper to bumper.

Hut arrived, creeping around behind the snarled traffic. He saw Booker sitting on top of several stacked wooden crates, giving him a high-angle view of the action. "Damn. You all right?"

Booker choked down another gag and watched the cars navigating the tangle. When they couldn't get any farther down Main Street, Gene Phillips waved for the car behind him to follow, and they turned left up the street Booker had just rolled down. Even then, they were on each other's bumper.

Booker watched Walker pass in the first car, then the two shiny new Model A's behind. The men inside weren't from around there. Still upset from rolling downhill, his stomach fluttered at the sight of expensive snap-brim hats, tailored suits, and hard faces.

No one like that had ever come through Pine Top, and he rose slightly from his seated position to look inside the second car that crept past. From his higher-than-average elevation, he saw into the back seat and spotted the man sitting there. Beside him were two long guns Booker recognized from the newspapers as tommy guns gangsters liked to use.

"Hut, we need to tell Mr. Bell about this."

"Who's that?"

"A new Texas Ranger that's in town. He'll know what to do."

"What? Are you crazy? Why would we tell a Texas Ranger about you rolling into town in a barrel?"

"Naw, it ain't that." Booker pointed at the retreating Fords. "Those are gangsters, and, for some reason, I think he needs to know." He stood and checked his balance. Seeing that the world had steadied, he flicked a hand at Hut to follow.

"How're we gonna get word to him?"

"Simple, dummy. We tell the sheriff. I bet he'll know where Mr. Tom is right now."

Chapter Twenty-Five

Thick morning clouds blanketed Hog Eye, threatening rain, which would further chill the cool air. In my disguise once again and smelling like cigarette smoke, I was torn between duty and pleasure for the first time in my life. I'd been back to the Hydroxy speakeasy again the night before, but though the clientele changed rapidly, Louise said Ferris was a no-show. I thought about staking out a table, but most of the customers who came in only stayed a couple of hours or so. It would bring on too much attention if I homesteaded a table for very long.

Instead, I figured Louise would hold up her end of the deal, especially if she thought there'd be another five in her future. I considered calling Sheriff Dobbs back in Pine Top to find out about Quinn Walker, but decided against it. Deep down inside, I was sure the sheriff was crooked as a dog's hind leg and was afraid just such a call would warn Walker.

I'd have to investigate myself when I got back to Pine Top the next day.

Adjusting the tweed cap by the bill, I left the hotel and walked down to the Southern Café. The rich, familiar aroma of coffee, bacon, and onions filled the steamy air. Charlotte was there all right, taking an order when I walked in, looking both tired and beautiful.

She did a double take, and dimples formed at the corners of her mouth. "Have a seat, sir. I'll be right with you."

There was an empty two-person table, so I slid a chair around against the wall and waited. She moved around the café, talking easily to the customers. Full of life, she brought sunshine to the dreary day. She paused to speak with an older man and he made a comment that earned a slap on the shoulder and a laugh.

Watching her, I thought back to a slight Mexican girl with the same bright personality. I married Carmelita three months after we met. She had a big laugh when amused, and flashing black eyes when she was angry. We were a close couple for more than two years until a Mexican revolutionary from Pancho Villa's army came across the border one night when I was gone gathering up a prisoner in a nearby town. The Mexican took her life as casually as swatting a fly.

That man now was bones in the desert.

I wondered who Charlotte really was while I waited for my coffee, and why I was attracted to her. Since Carmelita, I never figured to find anyone else in the world who I'd be interested in, and here, when I wasn't looking for anyone, this woman struck sparks the minute she met my gaze. Only seconds after speaking to her, I knew she'd be the perfect companion to walk with, strong in most ways, but fragile in others she'd likely keep hidden.

I couldn't keep my eyes off that little bundle of energy as she crossed the room with my coffee, carrying it carefully so as not to slosh any over the edge. She set the thick brown mug on the table and flipped a page on her pad, all business. "Well, look what followed me home. Howdy, stranger. Didn't expect to see you this morning. Glad you came by."

"Had to drive out here to see you since I didn't figure you'd be in Pine Top today."

"You came all this way to see little ol' me?" Her voice rose in a Betty Boop lilt. "What made you think I wouldn't be there?"

"That I did. Dorothy told me you'd be here this morning."

"Snitch."

"I forced it out of her. You can still trust her."

"Well, it's good to see you, and that's a fact. What'll you have?"

Lacing my fingers around the still-untasted mug, I leaned toward her. "This coffee and a date."

"That second item isn't on the menu. Took it off last week."

"Why?"

"Odd men kept ordering it."

"Oh, what about those who are pretty normal?"

"They're usually boring."

"It won't be tonight."

"You almost have my interest, but it's kinda short notice. What if I have plans?"

"I bet you can change them for a picture show in Longview."

Her eyes lit up. She pushed a stray strand of hair behind her ear and lowered the pad. "I haven't been to the show in God knows when."

"It's a date, then. I'll be here at five. We can drive in and have dinner, one that you won't have to serve, then the picture. I'll have you back here at a decent time."

"What are you going to look like when you come back? A lawman or a roughneck?"

"Which do you like best?"

She tilted her head to study him. "I'm partial to your hat. Goes with the mustache."

"Me too. It feels like my head don't have any protection in

this cap. I'll see you at five, and I'm thinking ham and three eggs over easy sounds pretty good right now."

"A breakfast order *and* a date?" She raised an eyebrow. "Are we starting something here, Mr. Bell?"

"I think we already have."

Chapter Twenty-Six

Clete Ferras watched the Southern Café from across the busy street. He almost didn't recognize the Ranger when he came out from the hotel. In his casual disguise, the lawman looked was almost indistinguishable from the other men in Hog Eye looking for work.

Hat cocked on his head and pulled way down until his skull shaped the crown, Ferras sat on a nail keg outside the hardware store with several loafers. Hiding in plain sight, he fully intended to stay where he was until Tom Bell went into the Hydroxy Mercantile again sometime during the day, but his inner demon pulled him toward the side door while Tom Bell had breakfast.

It was that inner demon that caused him to kill the woman down in the Valley weeks earlier, and it wasn't the first time. It had been building in power for the past several days. It should have been sated with the murder of the farmer and his family, but the wife wasn't enough to satisfy certain aspects that were required.

It was something he neither understood, nor could control. Now, it was clawing to get out.

The girl Louise called to him, speaking in his mind at night, telling him what she wanted. A chippie usually didn't satisfy, though he'd freed more than one from the confines of their earthly shells in years past. But there was something about the way her mouth was shaped that let him know those lips that he could see in his mind right then would feel wonderful against his own.

He unconsciously stuck his tongue out and realizing how odd it looked, plucked at it with two fingers as if a hair or piece of lint was bothering him. While one of the locals told a boring story about a prediction his grandmother had made about a coming drought that would last for years, he thought about the Mexican woman in Laredo who stared up at him in horror as he strangled her beside the corpse of her husband.

She wasn't the first. He'd forgotten the faces of others he'd left in shallow graves over the years. The first was when he was a boy, when a teenage Mexican girl laughed at his advances. She disappeared one night, and they found her floating in the Rio Grande, the apparent victim of an accidental drowning.

The farmer droned on about his grandmother's observations of caterpillars, animals, and birds until the urge inside Ferras boiled with need. He rose and left the group, crossing the street and dodging cars and trucks. A side door off the extremely narrow alley gave him access into the back of the Hydroxy that wrapped in an L-shape around the speakeasy.

The oily man behind the counter saw Ferras enter, but didn't reprimand him because Ferras had the power of the Consortium behind him. He worked for O. L. Caldwell, and that gave him special dispensation that most others didn't enjoy.

Ferras rounded the counter and rapped on the speakeasy's door. The judas hole slid open, and recognizing Ferras, Stump let him in. Louise Cherry looked up when he came through the door, but her shoulders slumped in disappointment when she recognized Ferras.

He joined her at a nearby table. "Did you talk to him last night?"

"Sure. He's still looking for you, *Uncle* Clete."

"That's his story?"

"Yep. I'm supposed to let him know when you get to town. Says he's staying over at the Grand."

Ferras tamped down a shudder. He couldn't let her see the man scared him. The failed attempt in Pine Top should have left him on a slab, instead of the other three. "What'd you have to give him for the info?"

"Nothing." Her eyes gave away the lie. "He bought me a drink and promised another when he came back. He said to let him know in person when you showed up, or if he's not there, then to leave a message at the desk over at the Grand."

Ferras shrugged. He didn't care. "All right. We're gonna wait until tonight. I have some people coming in to meet me here. Now I need to kill some time."

"How are you gonna do that?" She leaned forward and stuck out her chest.

He waved at the bartender. "Two scotches, and make sure they're both the real stuff."

The corner of Hazel's mouth twisted, thinking she wasn't going to make any money from him for watered-down drinks. Her mood brightened when he reached into his pocket and produced a roll of cash.

"Then afterward, you and I are going to have a little party of our own."

Chapter Twenty-Seven

"Leatha Mae, can you come in here, please?"

Mallie Walker still wasn't used to having someone work for her. Quinn told her over and over that she didn't have to ask for service, or to thank Leatha Mae for fulfilling her duties. But Mallie wasn't raised that way, and felt bad whenever she made any type of request, no matter that they were paying the colored woman more than three times what she'd earned keeping house for her previous employers or working in Charlotte's Café.

The two-story Craftsman was bigger than any place Mallie had ever lived. Compared to the dirt-floor shack she'd grown up in, it was a mansion. She was lying on top of the bed, covered with a wedding ring quilt across her legs. She was more than capable of getting up, but once again she simply didn't feel good. It took a couple of minutes before the housekeeper came upstairs into Mallie's bedroom, the largest of the three on the second floor, wiping her hands on a cup towel.

"Yes ma'am?" Leatha Mae's gray hair was short, and she wore a soft-yellow print housedress.

"I'm not feeling good at all again today." Mallie punched at the pillows behind her and leaned back. "Would you make me one of those toddies from that special bottle Quinn bought for me?"

The older gray-haired woman frowned, the wrinkles deep in her forehead. She'd always been a frowner, and the years of chopping weeds in fields within a twenty-mile radius added depth to those marks.

"You're sure taking a lot of that lately. You think you need a dose this time of the day?" Unable to simply stand still, she walked over to the window and raised the shade to admit more light into the room, then adjusted the sheer curtains.

"I do. It perks me right up, and I think the sugar from that Co-cola helps, too."

"It ain't the Coke I'm worried about, though it's right sweet, like you say. Miss Mallie, you say you ain't feeling up to snuff, but you're shore puttin' on the weight. You know I had to let two of your dresses out last week."

Mallie chewed a fingernail already bitten down to the quick. She was always a big girl, but the extra weight she'd picked up was noticeable in her face, making it round and fuller. "It's because I'm not getting any exercise for the past few weeks. I just haven't felt like it since we moved in here. Lordy, girl, I don't even believe I have the strength to go sew in front of the window today, and you know how much I like that."

"It's likely this gray weather that's got you down, it sho' makes me feel blue if it hangs around too long. Why'nt you get outta that bed and go sit downstairs? I'll make up this room and build you a fire. That'll take the dampness out of the house. How about I make you some hot chocolate with that can of Hershey's powder you're so fond of?"

"That sounds good, but would you dose it for me?" Mallie batted her eyes, making Leatha Mae roll her own.

"Lord help us. You still think you need that medicine, then."

"Well, I need *something*. I just don't have any strength. I couldn't even outrun a turtle today if one got after me."

They laughed at the thought of a turtle charging someone.

"Would you like me to call the doctor and see if he'll come by and take a look at you?" Leatha Mae inclined her head, as if the new angle would let her see what was bothering Mallie.

"He said two months ago that I was likely getting close to having diabetes. I'd hate for him to find out that I'm gaining weight."

"He'll surely see that, but I still think he needs to come by."

"All right, but I'd like a stiff hot chocolate anyway." They both laughed again, two girls sharing a joke. Mallie glanced out the window at the changing colors signaling the beginning of fall. "I sure wish Quinn was here. He's always working, and this would be a fine day to sit in front of the fire and talk to him, or listen to the radio tonight. Let's do that. I 'magine he'll be working again. It seems like that's all he's done the past couple of weeks. Would you stay after supper and listen to the radio with me?"

Leatha Mae fussed around, smoothing the quilt lying over Mallie's legs. "I'd love that. It gets lonesome at home now that Brady's gone to glory."

"You know what?" Mallie's voice was low. Conspiratory.

"What?"

"You can have a stiff Coke with me tonight, too. I don't like to drink alone, and I won't tell a soul."

"Honey, now you know I'm a good Baptist girl who don't drink."

"You'll take a taste or two of Bateman's Drops when you feel your liver's acting up."

"That I do, but I buy them at the store. There ain't no prohibition on patent medicines." Leatha Mae shook her head. "Why, you don't even know who cooked that skull pop in there. I had a cousin go blind and die from homemade whiskey somebody drained through a radiator coil."

"Well, Quinn wouldn't buy something like that for me. He gets it special made from a feller out close to Tatum."

Leatha Mae's lips tightened. "That's what he says, but I know these fools who'll buy it off wagons coming through, or even somebody like old man Eckert who won't admit to ever having laid a hand on a jar."

"What do you mean?"

"Well, when my man Brady wanted a quart to keep away the chilblains, he'd go to Eckert's place out there on the county line and knock on the door after he put a bill in the clothespin bucket hanging out on the line. Brady'd back off in the yard and when Eckert came out on the porch, Brady'd say he was looking for a jar he'd lost. Eckert'd wander over to the clothesline while they talked and glance in to see the money, then he'd tell Brady to go kick around over by the hogpen, that he once saw a jar half buried by the fence. Other times a jar'd be buried out by his garden. Customers kicking around always seemed to find a fruit jar half an inch under the ground. Lordy. I wish I could get me some of them jar seeds."

They giggled like schoolgirls.

"Well, anyway, Eckert had a still down by Martin Creek, but it was pretty good stuff. I wouldn't trust some of these other folks, though." She leaned in to speak lower. "You know, I heard somebody whose name I won't speak but lives right close to you here in town is making some pretty fine bathtub gin. I'll have a sip of that with you, if you'd like a pint."

Mallie brightened. "I think I'd like that better than Quinn's medicine. You know, it's pretty strong, and I get light-headed pretty quick, though I feel like I've built up a tolerance for it these last few weeks."

"Well, then," Leatha Mae folded the damp towel, "I'll run over to that place I won't say and get us some so we can have it tonight while we listen to the radio. I do love to hear *The Shadow* and Walter Winchell."

Mallie reached for her pocketbook and dug out a couple of bills. "Here, get us as much as this'll buy."

Leatha Mae's eyes widened. "Why, honey, this'll get more than the two of us can drink in a week."

"Then we'll be feeling pretty good by the time it's gone." Mallie chuckled. "But you go ahead and call Doc Patton and have him come over. Maybe I can get some Bateman's Drops from him while he's here."

Chapter Twenty-Eight

East Texas is a world of water, and that was exactly how it felt as gray clouds hid the pine tops, pouring rain onto the already saturated landscape. Unlike the busy roads in town that were churned into the consistency of mashed potatoes, the county and farm roads were still passable, though slick and boggy in many places. I still had to keep an eye out for low spots that could quickly bury a tire up to the axle.

Me and Charlotte laughed together as we drove in no particular hurry down the county road that late evening between fields, pastures, and woods. The wipers slapped back and forth, clearing water from the windshield. There was still enough light to see clearly, but I'd pulled the headlights on just to be sure.

"I'm telling you, it's beautiful down in the Valley. A lot drier, too."

Full of life, she giggled, shaking her head. "It's the *desert.*"

I was already completely committed to the black-haired woman, we were already planning the future together, though it sounded more like play than anything else. I'd heard tell of love at first sight, but thought it was something from a book or a picture show. An unspoken commitment was already in place, but I planned to wait a respectable length of time before officially asking for her hand.

"Depends on what part you're in. Where I grew up, there's crops and trees, but not like what y'all have here. I think I like that a little better, because you can see more of what's around you."

"There's no *water* in the desert. My skin will dry out and crack like mud in the sun."

"You can rub some of that Pond's cream on every night."

"You men don't understand how it is. Y'all age and the older you get, the more distinguished you look. Women just look old. I don't want to look old before my time by drying out in the desert."

Approaching dangerous territory, I steered the conversation back to my own comfort level. "This is pretty country, and there's no danger any of us'll dry out in the next month or so. Back home we have creeks and rivers just like here, only the trees aren't as thick. They still throw shade. A lot of that water's used for irrigation and crops. I bet you'd like the coast. Sand and palm trees. You'd love the Gulf of Mexico. It's pretty most of the time, but every now and then when the wind blows right and the current cooperates, the water turns clear and the deepest blue you ever saw."

"I'd love to see that. Back where you live, is there a lot of cactus? I hate cactus."

"There's prickly pear and cholla, all right. Century plants farther out west. I'll take any of them over the bull nettle I've seen around here. But we also have cottonwoods and willows on creeks and streams, and sage that's bright green and blooms the prettiest purple flowers in the world, especially after it rains." I snapped my fingers and grinned. "See, we have rain, though seldom as much as this."

She shifted her weight and curled up like a cat in the seat, pulling her ankle-length dress down to cover her calves. "I'm glad you're back in real clothes. You look much more distinguished."

She stretched an arm across the back of the seat and lightly touched the back of my neck with her fingertips. The caress was as much comfortable and familiar as it was welcome. I almost shivered in pleasure.

"I might enjoy a trip there, but it'll be a long while before we can leave, Tom. I have two cafés to run, and with this depression going on, money is getting tighter and tighter, once you get away from all these drillers."

The road made a sharp right angle around a field, then straightened into a thick stand of trees. I slowed even more, cautious on the wet gravel and mud. "You seem to be spread a little thin."

"It was a good idea to open two cafés at the time, but I think I'm gonna concentrate on the one in Hog Eye, because it's growing as fast as Pine Top, and I'd rather be close to home. Besides, if this lease deal comes through, I'll get oil money from it, and that'll make up for the Pine Top café. Then we can do whatever we want."

I didn't miss that "we" part, and it felt good. "Would you ever consider pulling up roots and opening a café somewhere else?"

Her eyes sparkled. "Like down in the Valley?" Charlotte's tone was flat and full of implied humor.

"Well, that's one option. This is a big state, and we could go wherever we wanted. I don't know how much of it you've ever seen. Lots of folks don't have any idea how different it is away from where they grew up."

"How about West Texas? That's always sounded so romantic to me."

"You won't like the Llano Estacado, I don't think, but Big Bend is beautiful." I heard myself saying something that surprised us both. "Like you."

She laughed and squeezed my shoulder.

That light caress was something I'd been hoping for, but my attention locked on a car in the ditch not far ahead. The clouds opened up and rain drummed on the car. The wipers had trouble with the sheets of water running down the windshield, and I squinted at the car ahead. Usually suspicious by nature, I didn't think it was anything but a country road mishap, though it could be anything.

There wasn't much danger of being robbed, but I always felt better with a pistol nearby. Now that I had the big Colt, I kinda wished I'd worn the new gun belt. I hadn't wanted to look too showy with the new tooled leather holster, so instead of strapping on the big Colt, I once again settled for the .38 that was as familiar as the hat on my head.

"Somebody slid off the road."

I wasn't too happy about that. Country custom dictated that we stop and help. That meant I'd, at the very least, get wet trying to pull them out, or worse, find myself muddy to the knees. I hoped we could just give someone a lift into Longview and let them take care of it themselves. I didn't mind helping folks, but this was the one night I didn't want ruined.

It was a 1930 Ford sedan that was half in and half out of the ditch. We coasted to a stop beside the driver's side, and I rolled down the window as the other vehicle did the same. Hanging my elbow out into the rain, I called across the four-foot space. "Looks like you got troubles."

The driver gave a tight grin that electrified all of my senses.

"Sure is good to see you. Slid off a few minutes ago." Instead of addressing me directly, he swiveled toward the passenger, half hidden by shadows on that gloomy evening, as if looking for approval or affirmation.

Alarms jangled loud in my mind, but I couldn't figure out

exactly why. I peered past the slapping wipers and saw the other car's ruts in the red gravel and mud. The clearly defined tire tracks made by the other car angled off toward the ditch and stopped. "Skidded, did you?"

"Yeah. Just started sliding sideways."

There was no evidence of a skid. The driver intentionally steered half into the ditch and stopped. Heart beating fast as a drum, I nodded at the driver and turned to Charlotte and spoke in a low tone. "When I tell you, get down on the floorboard as fast as you can."

"What…"

A flicker of movement from the tree line on her side of the car told me those alarms jangling up and down my spine were valid. "Get down now! Do it!"

Instead of acting, her head whipped around to see what I was looking at.

There was no time for discussion. I threw the shifter in reverse and hit the gas. The back tires spun in the mud at the same time automatic weapons opened up all around us. The spray threw mud and water against the side of the decoy car and the driver recoiled as the slurry flew into his open window.

At least *he* wouldn't be shooting at us, and as close as we were, both of us would have been goners.

Man-made thunder filled the air. Rounds from at least four firearms thumped into the car's sheet metal. The window on Charlotte's side exploded in a shower of wet glass. She shrieked and folded herself onto the floor.

Somehow the .38 was in my fist, and I saw men on my side of the car rise from a tangle of rain-soaked understory brush and berry vines. Muzzle flashes in the flat light were startling, contrasted by the dark woods behind them.

More rounds punched into my side of the car. One bullet

passed through the door, burning a hot crease across my stomach. Another scorched like a heated iron laid against the left side of my neck. A deep groove burned across my left hand that clutched the steering wheel.

Firing across my body and through the open window at muzzle flashes, I kept the car backing straight down the greasy road. Bullets stitched across the fender and door, following our retreat. I sensed more slugs whizzing through the car's interior at the same time my hat came alive, screwing to the side from the impact of hot lead.

A quick glance in the rearview mirror revealed another car coming our way, blocking the road. Thinking it was an innocent local, my stomach dropped. Now someone else might get hurt.

"Dammit! Get out of the way!"

It wasn't until the car whipped sideways and slid to a stop to block the road that I completely understood. We were caught in a well-organized ambush. There was no way to get past the car with the ditches on both sides running a foot deep with water.

Both doors on the new arrival's passenger side flew open, and lightning flashed from the front and back seats as fully automatic weapons opened up. Again, bullets rattled like hail against the back of our car, punching through the back glass that shattered and collapsed inside.

A scream shrill as a catamount's filled the car as I hit the brakes. At the same time, the engine coughed and died in a spray of steam from the punctured radiator. Fluff from the upholstered seats floated inside the car.

The guns fell silent.

Both sides of my face were wet. The left with rain coming through the open window, but the right side was a warm, sticky liquid that ran into my eye. Wiping it away with my sleeve, I threw a look at Charlotte lying half on the floorboard, her limp body leaning over the blood-soaked seat.

The empty look in her slitted eyes, and the gray matter on her door and the dash, told me the whole story, and a cry rose in the car. A full five seconds passed before I realized it came from me.

It was a miracle I hadn't been seriously struck, but it was only a matter of seconds before a bullet found me. Heart pounding, my fury grew until there was nothing but red in my world. It had been years since such a fury took control of me.

When it did, everyone around me died.

Chapter Twenty-Nine

While blood pounded in my temples and a blue jay cried from the trees, I thumbed the cylinder release forward on the revolver and gave it a half flip to the side. Shapes moved in the trees lining the road as the gunmen shifted their positions, seeking advantage.

Mind focused on what was about to happen, I tapped the ejector rod, emptying six empty casings into my lap. Someone shouted, silencing the blue jay that erupted from a tree and flew across the road in a bright flash of color.

Eyes flicking between the road in front and the rearview mirror, I shoved fresh shells into the cylinder.

"Is he dead?"

The high-pitched voice came from the left. Leaves rustled, and sticks cracked underfoot as a man approached the car. "He's moving a little. I think we hit him hard."

"Let him bleed out and don't shoot anymore." That voice came from the other side of the road. "I can't hear a damn thing from all these guns."

I clicked the cylinder closed and thumb-cocked the double-action Colt. The red in the corners of my vision cleared into a white-hot rage. Without another thought, I shoved the door open and stepped out.

The man who'd moved closer was about twenty yards away when he straightened a few inches higher to get a better angle. With the stock of a long rifle against his shoulder, he aimed in my direction. "He's moving!"

I crouched behind the door and lined the sights up on his shape, wondering why'n hell he was waiting. Maybe it was because the light was so dim he couldn't get a good look at me or he was shocked that I wasn't dying or dead. No matter, taking my time, I fired the pistol twice, hitting the man in the chest.

As the fresh corpse dropped, I did the unexpected and charged toward the man's partner, who had the extraordinary misfortune to be changing magazines in his weapon. Guns opened up from two other directions, filling the world with the rattle of war. Bullets snapped through the air, plucking at my coat and ricocheting off the trees. Concentrating with the focus of a hunter after his prey, I ran closer, dropped to one knee, and squeezed the trigger again and again until the hammer clicked on empty.

The well-placed .38s did their job, and the second assailant dropped to the muddy ground not far from his friend's body. Ducking low and out of sight in the tangle of vines and thick yaupon hollies, I closed the remaining distance. The weapons in the hands of my would-be assassins across the road went silent again.

As soon as I was in the bushes, I saw the sprawled bodies. A Browning Automatic Rifle was still in the hands of the first man I'd shot. Taking advantage of the lull in firing, I quickly reloaded the revolver and holstered it. That done, I snatched up the BAR and checked the muzzle to be sure it was clear.

The dead man had several full magazines in his pockets and I transferred them to my own. A single gunshot cut through the limbs several feet away. Breathing hard, and with my heart pounding, I dashed toward a bull pine, intending to use the thick trunk for cover.

Ahead and to my left, the original decoy car made a quick three-point turn and disappeared into the rain. Unseen men shouted questions and orders, their voices muffled. Ears ringing from the gunfire, I couldn't make out what they were saying, but the roar of the retreating engine was distinct.

Water funneled off my hat. I broke cover and slipped through the thick woods, temporarily protected by colorful leaves. The men across the road opened up again, shooting blind and shredding the understory vegetation where I'd just been, I guess hoping the sheer volume of lead would find a target.

All it found was dead space.

I juked to the left to find a clear spot through a thick stand of yaupon hollies. Behind a wide hickory tree, I dropped to one knee, shouldered the BAR, aimed at the muzzle flashes in the trees, and squeezed the trigger. A stream of 30.06 rounds minced the vegetation that hid the shooters. The first muzzle didn't flash again, but to my right, a machine gun from behind the gangsters' car opened up with a steady chatter.

High-power rounds thudded into my hickory tree, making it vibrate. Leaves showered down, and I dropped, getting low and out of sight.

The rounds came too damned close, so I crawled on my belly like a reptile and slipped through the bushes at the edge of the timber. The machine gun across the road opened up again, destroying everything around where I'd just been.

The bottom of the clouds fell out, and the rain became tropical, heavy, and straight down. So much fell at one time it dissipated the gun smoke, working both for and against me. I could barely see where they were shooting from, except for the muzzle flashes, but at the same time it provided excellent cover.

Obviously city people, they had no idea how to fight in such terrain, but it came as natural to me as breathing.

I slammed a fresh magazine into the BAR and studied the car blocking the road, deciding what to do next. Taking aim, I squeezed the trigger, raking the side, punching through the sheet metal and glass. A tire exploded with a soft pop, and men on the opposite side scrambled to use the front axle, tires, and engine block for cover. The powerful 30.06 rounds punched through the body and, hopefully, flesh. A man shouted in either fear or pain and everything went quiet.

When he stopped shooting, I broke from cover and rushed toward the machine gun across the road and the startled man behind it. As my boots hit the muddy road, I saw the assassin kneeling in the bushes. He stiffened and swung a Thompson to bear. The weapon spoke again, but the guy wasn't leading me. All of the shots were behind my racing form before the drum ran dry.

I was damned mad, and the thoughts of personal safety were as gone as Charlotte's spirit.

Two other machine guns opened up from behind the car as I flashed into view and threw a few rounds down the road. The bullets startled them, and they ducked behind the car, still holding the tommy guns over the hood, and though they couldn't see me, they continued firing in my general direction.

That's all that saved me as bullets flew thick as mosquitoes on a still bayou, but they weren't hunters either, and the rounds snapped past as I ran, some ricocheting off the hardwoods and whining away. Midway across the narrow road, I had a brief reprieve as my disabled Ford blocked their line of sight.

With the intensity of a predator, my focus was on only one thing, the man with the Thompson. Three steps later, I was back in Cantigny, France, the last battle of the Great War. This time there was no support from cannons or other doughboys, only one mad Ranger intent on an immediate threat.

I blasted through a stand of brush like a charging bull to find the shooter fumbling with the machine gun that had obviously jammed. When I burst into view, the mobster dropped the useless weapon and clawed at a pistol in the pocket of his coat. Using the man's fear-filled white face under a snap-brim hat as a bullseye, I never broke pace as I switched the BAR to my left hand, snatched the Colt from its holster, and pulled the trigger as fast as possible.

The revolver barked four times and on the fifth, the terrified face exploded in red, and I ran past the falling corpse.

Chapter Thirty

"Oh, God! Oh, God!" Gene Phillips drove way too fast in the heavy rain, rushing back toward Pine Top.

A mile later they flashed past the gangsters' second car parked in a gate turnout. It was the backup getaway car in case Phillips's car and the gangsters' other Ford were too damaged to drive.

Their plan at first seemed so simple. Gene and Quinn would act as decoys to make the Texas Ranger stop, looking as if they'd gotten stuck. Once the Ranger stopped to help, automatic weapons on both sides of the road would open up at the same time, catching him in a cross fire.

"He saw me! He knows what I look like!"

When Phillips heard how they intended to use his car, he was terrified that someone would put a bullet hole in it, or worse, wreck it. He'd argued for a better plan until the gangster named Hermie stopped him cold with a dead look. He knew better than to argue further.

"Calm your ass down!" Quinn Walker ran a shaking hand through his hair.

"You don't understand! I talked to the man. Now he knows what I look like."

Shocked into immobility when the big guns opened up,

Phillips saw the Ranger's eyes widen as he shifted into reverse and shouted at the woman to get down. They'd all expected the first volley to kill the man outright, but when it began to unwind, Walker panicked and ordered Phillips to drive off.

It was the sight of the woman in the passenger seat that almost pushed Phillips over the edge. Charlotte Cain was a distant cousin on his mama's side.

Now the Ranger was out and fighting back, and his car was the least of their worries.

Walker threw a fearful look over his shoulder. "Slow down. We'll be blowed up if we wind up in a ditch this close to that shoot-out."

Phillips took the pressure off the foot feed, slowing some. "You think they got him? It's six machine guns against one man. Surely they rubbed him out." As if to emphasize his words, the rain increased so much it overcame the struggling wipers. Phillips couldn't see through the wall of water and slowed even more. "For a minute there he was getting away, though. It looked like he might get away, but I bet they got him."

"That's what it looked like, but you heard the shooting behind us. I bet you're right, they got him."

"Then they'll come for us. We left them behind."

"I think I can talk my way out of it."

"It's all your talking that got us *into* this. I wish I hadn't ever listened to you."

"But you did, and you're as deep into this as I am. Get us back to town and get ahold of yourself. Dammit, I'm getting tired of telling you that."

Phillips drew a deep breath, staring straight ahead. "Where we going?"

"Dobbs's office. That's where we agreed to meet before they went back to Hot Springs."

Chapter Thirty One

The gunfire stopped. Huddled behind their dead car parked sideways on the sand and gravel road, Ermano "Hermie" Genovese and Frankie "Big Nose" Birger reloaded their weapons with the rattle of full magazines seating into receivers as rain hammered their hats.

Squatting on his haunches, Hermie tucked the Thompson's scarred wooden stock under his shoulder and glanced around behind them, thinking. There was no way the man could have taken out so many of his men in a matter of seconds.

"Cardinella!" They listened, but there was only the rain and water gurgling past in the ditches. "You think he got Mad Dog? Nobody can get Mad Dog."

Holding a BAR across his body, Big Nose waited with one knee on the wet gravel. "I think I saw Gabby fall, so it was just Mad Dog firing those last shots."

"I don't know." Hermie twisted back toward the rear of their car. "Mad Dog! Easy! You guys all right?"

An unseen crow called, its harsh rasp sharp and close by.

"Mad Dog? Can anybody hear me?"

"I told you they were dead." Big Nose licked his lips and

scanned the dripping woods. Water ran off the brim of his hat. "We gotta get outta here. Let's make a break for the other car and leave this son of a bitch behind. For all we know, he could be laying out there in those damned woods, bleeding to death. I bet one of us put a bullet in him. *Somebody* had to, with all the lead we were throwing around. There's no way all of us could have missed him."

"You want to run down this road, in the open? I've never run away from a fight."

"No, but we gotta get outta here, and if we run away from him," Big Nose pointed toward Hog Eye, "we'll have to walk all the way back to that hayseed town, and there's no way we can make it without anyone seeing us."

"Think!" Hermie wanted to slap his friend. "Ferras is supposed to come by in a few minutes. He'll add another gun when he gets here, and when it's over, he can give us a lift to the other car."

They'd met with Clete Ferras earlier that day in a vacant lot at the edge of Hog Eye to hammer out the details of the ambush. Knowing it was Ferras who put together the disastrous attempt at the hotel in Pine Top, Hermie didn't want to take the chance on another failure. He would handle it, but Ferras was going to be part of this job, or else. Cherubino Moretti's instructions were to use the man's knowledge to set up the Ranger, and when it was all done, to kill Ferras, too, before returning to Hot Springs.

But the man hadn't shown as they prepared their ambush, and Hermie threw a silent prayer upward that he was just late. He'd probably stayed up all night with that skirt and lost track of the time. Yeah, that was it. He was on the way right that minute, probably driving fast to make up for lost time.

Uncertain, Hermie and Big Nose waited for several minutes before finally relaxing. The rain settled into a light shower, giving them some relief. Despite their fear and discomfort, a weak smile curled the corners of Hermie's mouth. "Nothin'. It's quiet. I think Gabby did it. I think he plugged him."

"Before he bought it himself."

"Yeah, before he bought it himself."

Putting his hat on the muzzle of his Thompson, Hermie raised it into the air, fully expecting the Ranger to shoot it off. Instead, the only thing that happened was his head got wet.

Big Nose coughed out a tense laugh. "We got him." He shook out a pre-rolled Chesterfield and lit up, exhaling a cloud of smoke into the damp air. "Damn! That was something."

Even though he thought the Ranger was dead, Hermie rose slowly, ready to drop back behind the car, and scanned the trees. "And you wanted to run."

"You did, too. You were as scared as me."

"Yeah, but I didn't want to clear out." Hermie tucked the Thompson's stock back under his armpit and looked around. Brass shell casings littered the road. He pointed toward the woods on their left where the first two men went down. "You go check on the boys there. I'll go over here to see if Mad Dog and Joe are dead."

"No." Big Nose shook his head. The experienced gangster was rattled. "We stay together. I've never seen anyone like that damned Ranger. He *charges* into machine guns."

"Charged. He's dead over there somewhere, or he'd have already opened up on us." Hermie waved his free arm, as if to invite an attack. When nothing happened, he grinned. "I want to see the boys first. They may still be alive, bleeding, but we have to find him before we can leave. The boss wants that badge, you know."

"Fine." Big Nose followed him down the muddy road. Reaching the point where the decoy car's ruts made the turnaround, Hermie paused and looked down the road. "Those two hayseeds ran out on us. I'm gonna kill 'em before we get back to Hot Springs. Nobody runs out on *me*." He jumped over the water flowing down the ditch and stepped into the edge of the low brush.

Big Nose followed him, landing in the wet grass. "I'll help you. The boss won't care when we tell him what we did."

Weapons ready, they pushed through the splintered under-story branches. Giuseppe "Joe" Aldersio and Michael "Easy" Andriacchi lay sprawled in the leaves and pine needles. Big Nose checked them. "They're dead."

Hermie pointed. "Easy's BAR is gone. That's what the Ranger used on Mad Dog and Gabby."

"He shot them with *our* gun?"

"Looks like it." Hermie pointed across the road. "Let's find that Ranger. I'm taking his *head* back with us."

They repeated the process of jumping over the flowing ditch and back to the road, Big Nose paused to scrape mud off the soles of his shoes. Unconcerned, Hermie watched him finish.

Big Nose snorted. "I hate mud. I'm a city guy. I like concrete and sidewalks."

Completely relaxed, the two gangsters had started across the muddy road when a torrent of 30.06 rounds from Easy's BAR cut them to shreds so fast neither knew what hit them.

Chapter Thirty-Two

The echo of gunfire faded, and I rose from cover. "Stop. Put your hands up."

I probably should have said that before pulling the trigger, but those bastards didn't deserve it. When I was sure they were as still as the other four, I stepped out of the woods and waded across the ditch, ignoring the rain-dimpled stream that seeped into my boots. By habit I changed magazines, putting the empty in my coat pocket. Years ago I had learned that an unloaded gun was useless.

The sight of them laying there beside two automatic weapons caused me to fade for a second. "You bastards tangled with the wrong man."

Shouldering the weapon, I emptied it into the still bodies to anchor them in place When the echoes died for the last time, I lowered the monster rifle. Steam rose from the barrel where raindrops struck. Grief washed over me as I knelt and checked their pockets for any information that would lead to the people who ordered the ambush.

The adrenaline rush over, I almost fell and caught myself with one hand. The BAR's stock thumped onto the ground and came to rest against my leg.

Wiping away stinging tears with the other hand, I took a deep, shuddering breath. "Dammit!"

I should have left her behind for a few weeks and come back later.

Nothing heard my anguish except for the silent trees drooping in the rain. Beholding the bodies sprawled on the muddy road, I swayed for a moment. The loss of Charlotte was another scar on my marked soul already tormented by what I'd seen in the shell-blasted battlefields in France.

I added another when a few years later me and two other Rangers found a burned-out house fifty miles north of Hidalgo. It was the time of the Bandit Raids under the rule of President Venustiano Carranza, who launched a bloody attempt to bring Texas back under Mexican rule by attacking small Texas outposts, farms, and ranches.

That day, the still-smoking ruins contained the bodies of a woman and four children all under the age of six. We found a man outside, shot so many times we didn't bother to count. Two blood trails from the dirt yard to the house led us to believe that the seditionist murderers under Basilio Ramos dragged the innocent children inside before torching the home.

The more experienced Rangers and I followed the trail left by the rebel horses and soon tracked down the group of eight bandit raiders who were firing upon a farmhouse defended by two farmers who'd seen the approaching squad of murderers. They had time to herd everyone into the house and grab their rifles, which ultimately saved their lives.

Though I was the youngest of the three Rangers, the others followed as I refused to take cover and exchanged shots. Instead, with the foolish heart of a young man, I kicked my horse into a run and charged the attackers, catching them in a cross fire between us and the house.

The Rangers with me split up and formed a thin line as we

raced ahead. Firing from horseback as fast as I could thumb back the hammer on the Colt .38, death came in a rolling sequence of shots. When the pistol ran dry, I drew a Winchester carbine from the scabbard, and, guiding my mount with both knees, continued to fire until all of the murderers were scattered and lifeless on the hard-packed ground.

Those men fell like cut grass that day, and when my mind cleared, we found that six of the eight men had died by my hand in less than thirty seconds. I vowed that day to keep the dark side of my emotions in check as much as possible, and had been successful until seeing Charlotte facedown in the front seat of the car.

The anger burned down, and my vision cleared. I don't know how much time had passed. Seconds. Minutes. But it was near dusk when I turned from the bloody bodies of the gangsters. The surrounding woods awoke with a chorus of frogs and crickets. Doves fluttered overhead, seeking a roost, and the rattle of a woodpecker was a hollow representation of the tommy guns that were now silent.

It was near dusk when I gathered the strength to approach the car. Knowing what I would find, and numb with dread, I opened the passenger door. Legs folded beneath her on the floorboard, the upper half of Charlotte's body still lay slumped over the soaked and matted cloth seat.

The floorboard was thick with blood. Flies had already found her through the open windows, and their sleepy drone was the crystal finality of her death. I remained where I was for nearly a minute, absorbing the details and hardening my heart. Drawing a deep breath, I opened the back door and returned to her body.

Ignoring the water and muck soaking my knee, I knelt beside her. Using my fingertips, I pulled her hair back from the undamaged side of her head. The opposite side was matted with blood and gore.

"Oh, baby." It was the first time I'd used such a term of endearment for her, and choked with the knowledge that she'd never hear me again, I broke down.

I'm so sorry.

Hitching sobs arose, and that's all I would allow. They broke one at a time and lessened in intensity after several minutes. I'd only known her for a few days, hours actually, but I'd known from the moment I met her that she would be the love of my life. The loss was as deep as when I laid my dad down in his final resting place.

I should have waited until all this was over.

As gently as possible, I lifted her out by the shoulders, taking care not to let her head fall back. I'd seen dozens if not a hundred dead people before, but this time after a quick glance at her cloudy, slitted eyes, I couldn't look at her face and the grievous hole in her temple.

A second jagged hole under her rib cage still leaked blood that soaked my sleeve. Noting the angle, I looked back into the car to see where a round intended for me had shattered the metal steering column, ricocheting off to strike her.

I cradled her limp body and gently laid her in the back seat. A pair of headlights approached. A pickup slowed, worn-out brakes squealing.

Now that my fury had subsided, hot coals settled deep into my soul. As a farmer and his son got out of the truck to help, I tidied my murdered girlfriend's poor body before I went hunting.

Chapter Thirty-Three

Farmers can't work in the rain, and once Booker Johnston finished his chores the next morning, he and his dad went to town once again. While John Henry sat with more than two dozen other locals under the tin roof of an old tomato-sorting shed to talk farming, politics, and the world around them with the other men, Booker set out to find Hut.

Despite the rain, pedestrian traffic on the sidewalks was heavier than usual with roughnecks doing their best to stay out of the falling weather. Men laughed, cursed, and shouted in the street, untangling the snarl of vehicles buried hub-deep and dragging them out only to be replaced by others.

Booker checked their usual place in front of the mercantile and found Hut watching the comedy show of cars, trucks, and wagons sinking in the mud of Main Street. Booker's uncle was there with his team of matched mules, making money hand over fist by pulling one vehicle after the other out of the quagmire that got worse with every drop of rain that fell.

Hut gave him a big grin when Booker sat next to him. Despite the differences in their skin tone, they were like two peas in a pod. They wore shirts faded to an indecipherable color from a thousand washings in homemade lye soap, and soft overalls also stripped of pigment so that they were barely blue.

Booker paid Hut back with a grin of his own. "You ever figure out why Dobbs didn't care that we saw those gangsters?"

Hut didn't take his eyes off Booker's uncle, who was muddy up to his waist, and his mules that were buried up to their hocks, pulling hard against their harness to free another car. "No idy, but I bet he didn't tell your Texas Ranger friend about 'em like he said he would, neither."

"What makes you say that?"

"He asked three questions, and I don't think he was interested at all."

Booker considered the idea. Out of breath the day before from running to the sheriff's office with the news, they talked over each other in their excitement while Dobbs looked down his nose at them. He seemed to be distracted, and asked only superficial questions before hustling the boys back outside.

"You saw that look in his eye." Hut flicked a finger toward his own face. "Adults think we're just dumb kids, and I know how to read some of these old men to tell when they're worried, mixed up, or scared. Dobbs wasn't real scared, but there was something bothering him, I can tell you that."

"Maybe he's scared of gangsters. Those guys in the cars behind Gene and Quinn were some of the meanest-looking men I ever saw."

"In all your *years*," Booker said, cutting his eyes toward his buddy, amused.

Hut countered with the expected response to their usual banter. "All ten of 'em!"

"We should be in vaudeville."

Booker looked to his left to see Tom Bell coming down the busy sidewalk. There was something different about the man.

His walk was stiff as coiled steel and determined, as if looking for a fight. He studied each man as he approached, assessing and dismissing them as they passed.

The Ranger's shoulders seemed broader, and Booker noticed a significant difference, something new. A white bandage on his neck was spotted with red. Another smaller bandage covered the back of his left hand, both homemade and held on with J&J Band-Aid tape.

The *cinco peso* Ranger badge was pinned to his coat for all to see and he now wore matching hand-tooled leather belts. When his coat momentarily flipped back, there was a Colt 1911 on his right hip.

Tom Bell almost didn't stop when he saw the boys, but his pace slowed. The lightning in his eyes faded. "Boys."

Booker stood. "I *figured* you'd come looking for us."

"Why would I do that?"

The Ranger's quiet voice was as hard as flint, and Booker felt a cold chill wash over him. "Uh, well, we thought you'd want to talk to us after you heard from Sheriff Dobbs."

"What?" The Ranger's eyes bored into the youngster. "I haven't talked to Dobbs. I just got back into town this morning, and that's where I'm headed now. What does he have to tell me?"

"I *told* you, Booker." Hut adjusted a gallus on his overalls, really not wanting to meet Tom Bell's hard gaze.

Tom Bell shifted his attention to Hut. "What's your name, son?"

He ducked his head. "Hut Parsons, Mr. Bell."

"Look me in the eye, please, sir. What'd you tell Mr. Booker here?"

The youngster glanced around, nervous, and did as he was told. "That I don't trust Sheriff Dobbs no more'n scared skunk."

Booker cleared his throat, not sure if he was going to get in trouble for not delivering the information directly to the

Ranger, who looked as if he were about to explode. "Well, sir, we saw some gangsters come into town yesterday. We wanted to tell you, but the man at the hotel said you hadn't picked up your key and didn't know when you'd be back. So we went to the sheriff's office and told *him*."

The inquisitive wrinkles in Tom Bell's forehead smoothed, and lightning again flashed in his gray eyes. "How do you know they were gangsters?"

"The way they were dressed, for one thing. We seen pictures in the paper of them Chicago bad men. That's how they looked." The ten-year-old felt the hair rise on the back of his neck as Tom Bell waited for him to fill the sudden silence. In that brief instant, he understood how criminals felt when the Ranger looked at them. "And they had long guns in the back seat, like I've seen in the paper. The kind gangsters use to rob banks."

"Machine guns?"

"That's them."

"Think hard for me. Did any of those guns have drums under them? And the others, were they longer than most rifles? Heavier?"

"Yessir. Both. They went past and turned north to get around this mess here."

"What made you notice 'em in all this?"

"They was driving slow, and I had plenty of time to look while they worked their way around a tangle just like that one." The boy pointed at the action going on mere feet away. "Three cars running nose to tail. Two of 'em were following another car who led 'em around and up that street right there."

"Now how do you know that? Maybe they were just driving around an obstacle."

"'Cause Mr. Gene Phillips was the lead car, and he stuck his arm out the window and waved for them to follow him."

Tom Bell's eyes flashed again, and Booker wondered what was going on behind them. Something was up, for sure.

"Who's Gene Phillips?"

"He's a businessman here in town."

"Anyone else riding in the car with him?"

"Yessir. Mr. Quinn Walker. Lives here now, but he's from Hog Eye. Married a rich oil lady, and they live about two streets over in one of the prettiest houses I've ever seen."

"What's her name?"

"Mallie." Booker stood a little taller. "She's full-blood Indian, and Daddy says she's kin somehow."

"Good to know." Tom Bell reached into his pocket and flipped a coin to Booker. "That's for both of y'all." Tom Bell set his black hat. "Now I think I need to have a visit with Sheriff Dobbs."

He took off down the street, and the boys followed at a distance.

Chapter Thirty-Four

Quinn Walker and Gene Phillips sat across the desk from Sheriff Dobbs's bright-red face. Muddy shoe prints leading from the back door to their chairs were evidence they didn't come in off the street but through the swampy alley. Out front, the sheriff had a place for visitors to wipe their feet.

It was all he could do to keep his hands from shaking. "You two are a couple of goddamned fools!" He stood and pulled down the paper blinds. Turning back to them, he pointed a finger. "Y'all coulda met me somewhere else for this. You should have telephoned."

Walker licked dry lips. "We were shook up, and I imagine the operator listens in on half the calls coming into this office. I couldn't take the chance telling you what happened over the line."

Dobbs glanced at the door, then stepped over and turned the key to lock it. "You're not staying here long. Tell me fast, and then get out. We'll meet somewhere else after I have time to think." A truck backfired out on the street, startling all three of them. Dobbs went an even whiter shade of pale at the sound. "Hurry up."

While Phillips listened and fidgeted, Walker outlined his

version of what had happened the night before on the farm road between Hog Eye and Pine Top, leaving out the part where they ran out on the men from Hot Springs.

Dobbs let him talk to see how closely the story matched what he'd heard close to midnight from Constable Doc Burdine, who'd given him the skinny. Sheriff Dobbs promised to drive out at daylight to go over the scene with him.

Still standing near the door, Dobbs studied the boards beneath his feet as Walker drifted off to end his version. "So how come y'all didn't help those guys?"

"We're not heavies. You have Clete Ferras for that."

"Yeah, but that sunk-cheek son of a bitch wasn't there. *You* were."

"He was *supposed* to be." Walker argued like a child. "I thought he'd be with the others."

"So did I." Sheriff Dobbs studied the two as if they were on display. "Ferras has become a problem. I want you to take care of that."

Walker stiffened. "What?"

"You heard me. Take him out in the woods somewhere and put a bullet in his head, the same way you and him did that Indian woman."

"What am I gonna tell him to get Ferras out there? He'll know something's up, and I'm not a killer. I've done told you I'm not a heavy."

Dobbs's face was impassive. "How's your wife?"

Walker's attention drifted to the floor. Mallie was getting sicker and sicker by the day from the wood alcohol and unknown additive he was giving her in ever-increasing doses. "That's different."

"No it ain't. You're doing it slow. A bullet is quicker."

"I can't shoot Mallie..."

"I didn't say…" His response was cut off when Dobbs raised a hand. He heard heavy footsteps outside the door and lowered his voice. "You know what I mean."

Their discussion ended when someone paused to clean their boots on the scraper before entering. Dobbs jerked a thumb toward the back door, and the men bolted. The sheriff hurried to the door and gently turned the key to unlock it. He grasped the knob as Phillips and Walker slipped out the back. It turned under his hand and he held it tight to gain another couple of seconds before pulling it open to find Tom Bell holding on from the outside.

Chapter Thirty-Five

At first I thought the door was locked when the knob wouldn't turn, but when I tried again, it was almost yanked out of my hand when Sheriff Dobbs pulled it open. I let go, and the sheriff stepped back with a curious, almost fearful look on his face. "Sorry about that, Tom. I was just coming to the hotel to see you."

Dobbs's face was tight, despite the slight grin he'd pasted there. I let my gaze slip off and into the office, thinking I might have interrupted something. The room was empty, but there were two fresh sets of muddy boot tracks leading from the desk to the back door.

"I might not have been there. I came to talk to you about last night. I guess you heard."

"I did. Constable Burdine over in Hog Eye called. I was gonna tell Ranger Delgado what happened, but they told me over at the boardinghouse that he'd taken some prisoners down to Huntsville and won't be back for a couple of days."

"Yeah, it's just me, but I don't need any help. I'm going over to talk with a couple of your local citizens. Quinn Walker and Gene Phillips. Thought you might want to go with me."

The blood drained from Sheriff Dobbs's face, and he

struggled to form a sentence. While he stuttered, I concentrated on not showing any curiosity.

"Who...uh, why them? You think they know anything about it?"

"I don't know. I'll be talking to a lot of folks to find out who murdered Charlotte." Dobbs hadn't mentioned her name, or truly referenced the shooting that was big news all over town. A local woman had been murdered in a shoot-out just outside of town, and the sheriff didn't seem concerned. That bothered the hell out of me.

"Why those two?"

I hadn't answered his first question and he wouldn't let it go. He was more interested in *my* investigation, and alarm bells as loud as those at the firehouse clanged in my head. "I have it on good authority they were seen in the presence of the men who ambushed me and Charlotte. While I'm here, would you like to hear what occurred, from *me*?"

Sheriff Dobbs cleared his throat. His eyes flicked around the office as if looking for an escape, or something to fasten onto. "Uh, yeah, it's hard to believe something like that happened."

"Maybe I need to write you a report real quick." I waved a hand toward Dobbs's desk, drawing his attention to the fresh tracks leading around it and out the back door. The coals in my chest glowed and I could barely keep them from bursting into flames. "You've tracked some mud in through the back."

"Yeah, I forgot how soupy it gets back there."

"So you went out a second time. That looks like two sets."

"Naw, just one. I went back and forth."

To make sure he knew I didn't believe a word he said, I took my time studying the sheriff's shoes that were clean and polished. The cuffs didn't have a speck of muck on them. "So, you want me to write that report?"

"No, don't do that. You don't have the time, I 'magine, and I don't have the time to sit here with you while you do it."

"That's what I thought you'd say. Y'see, Sheriff Dobbs, there's something going on here in this town that not even Ranger Delgado has stumbled onto as of yet. Looks like I stepped in it because I felt an attraction to Charlotte, and I'm afraid that's what got her killed, and that brings me to my point. Do you have anything to tell me that'll help me track down those who ordered that ambush?"

Dobbs shook his head, maintaining his focus on my face. I suddenly couldn't stand still any longer, and stepped over to the closed blinds and lifted the paper shade to watch the cars and pedestrians passing on the street. "For a man who should take his job seriously in this boomtown, you don't seem overly concerned about a shoot-out just out of town, where six men and a local citizen died."

The sheriff cleared his throat again to speak, and I tilted my head, listening, but the words died in the man's mouth.

"You don't need to say anything now. Your time is over. The moment I came in here, you should have told me everything you know, because as a Texas Ranger, I have jurisdiction over this town when it comes to investigative and arrest matters. You should know that."

"I do..."

"That also includes the Sheriff's Department. Didn't Booker Johnston give you some information that I should have heard?"

Dobbs licked his lips. "Well, him and that nigger kid he runs with came in with some holler-headed story about a chopper squad in town, but I don't put much stock in what a kid has to say..."

Instead of jumping astraddle of him over his term of description for Hut, I cut him off and wandered over to the muddy tracks, and nudging the prints with my toe, spread water across the boards. He knew good and well what I was thinking.

"Dobbs, something is going on in this town, and you know more than you're saying. Now, I'm not asking how you're involved, because that isn't where I am right now in this process. You see, if I knew you had something to do with that ambush for sure, you'd be bleeding out on top of those tracks."

"They're my…"

"But you're still standing here in clean shoes, drawing air, and that's where we're gonna leave it for the moment. Now, I'm going over to talk to Phillips and Walker, and based on what they tell me, I'm gonna start digging, and I won't stop until I find out what's going on around here.

"Then once I do, me and Captain Delgado are gonna gather a few other Rangers who're on assignment close to this here oil field and start cleaning house. Have you ever watched a Ranger clean house, Sheriff Dobbs? I won't say it's pretty, but when we're done, this house will be spotless, if you know what I mean."

I turned and hooked a thumb in the gun belt holding my new .45.

"Oh, since we had a discussion about this pistol, you ought to know that last night I picked up the weapons out on the road for evidence. They were the ones used to murder Charlotte Cain, and they're mine now. One's a Thompson machine gun, caliber .45. It'll stay in the trunk of my car, because I really don't like those bulky weapons, but the other is a Browning Automatic Rifle, and I dearly love those things. It fires a 30.06 round, and many more can follow quickly enough. No one wants to be on the receiving end of such a mankiller, for that's the reason they were designed. The rest of the guns are going to Austin. When I find those responsible for the attack on Mrs. Cain, and myself, I'll use this Colt to take them into custody, if they'll allow it.

If they don't, I'll use it or the BAR to take their lives, and, rest assured, I'll feel no remorse when I do.

"See, I no longer have a conscience. I did once, and it occasionally bothered me about certain events in my life. But it died out there last night with Charlotte Cain, and now I'm free of any chain that'll hold me back. I think you know what I mean."

The sheriff's face drained of color, and I nodded. "I see I've struck a nerve. Do you have anything I need to know, or anything you want to tell me before I leave this office?"

Dobbs licked his lips. "I, uh, no. Maybe you want me to go with you?"

"I think not, Sheriff. I'll go alone, for right now." Turning toward the door, I paused. "One more thing. You won't be able to make any calls from this office for the next little while. Before I came here, I stopped by the telephone office and spoke to the switchboard supervisor there. What's her name...? Florence. That's it. I explained to Florence that I'm investigating several murders here in this out-of-control town, and I suspect I'll find many more before I'm through. I told her by order of the Texas Rangers, that no calls will go out of this number until I tell her it's all right."

Dobbs puffed up his considerable chest. "You have no right..."

"I damned sure do!" Pressure filled my head, and I had to swallow down the rising anger. I took a deep breath and continued. "Incoming calls will still come through, so you can respond to local ordinance violations, but the truth is that I don't trust you right now. When I go out this door, I don't want you calling anyone to scat, or come looking for me, or to interfere with this investigation. The operator said she knows your voice and name, and I told her not to put any calls through from you, from *any* phone, until I say it's all right."

"I have duties!"

"Yes, you do, and you can handle them without a telephone. Information and reports can come through just fine so you can keep up with your sheriffing."

"I'm running an investigation, too."

"If you want to call it that. You see, I don't think you're doing much more than sitting back and reading the paper. I think you're part of the problem, right? I think you're playing a dangerous game that's gonna jump up and bite you on the ass pretty soon. So you just stay here and mop the floor for a little while. Your stint as sheriff is about to end. I doubt that'll make much difference to you, because I bet you've made a lot of money here, and that should see you through for the rest of your life."

"Are you accusing me of being crooked?"

"Didn't say that, yet, but now that you mention it, I don't think it'd hurt to lay that star on the desk and go home. Oh, one more thing, I'm going over to the bank in a little while to talk to the president. Over the years, I've learned one thing. No matter what's going on, no matter the crime, it's usually tied to money. I'm going to talk to that bank president and follow some of that money. When I pull on that string, everything around here's gonna come unraveled."

I turned the knob. "I came here to arrest a feller named Clete Ferras. I still intend to do that, but let me tell you something. I'm here to see justice done, on all levels." I stepped outside and threw one last comment over my shoulder. "I intend to do it, too."

I closed the door behind me leaving a visibly shaken Sheriff Dobbs standing alone in his office with Rudy Vallée crooning "As Time Goes By" on his radio.

Chapter Thirty-Six

The phone rang behind the bar in the Ohio Cigar Store, just down the street from the Hazelwood Hotel in Hot Springs. Cigar and cigarette smoke hung low in the speakeasy's still air. Men playing cards and talking at the tables paused and glanced up, waiting to see who it was for.

The bartender answered. "Just a second." He set the candlestick telephone on the mahogany bar top. "For Mr. Moretti."

Chic Marco again crossed the dim club and picked it up, holding the receiver to his ear. "Marco here for Mr. Moretti." He listened, breathing into the mouthpiece, and watching the bartender move away, as was his habit.

Marco hung up and returned to Moretti's table and sat. "Mr. Moretti, Mr. Caldwell on that call. Things went bad in Texas."

Moretti carefully placed his cigar in the ashtray on the table and leaned back. "Talk."

Marco outlined what had happened on the lonely dirt road between Hog Eye and Pine Top. The more he talked, the more Moretti's eyes narrowed as he absorbed the information. Marco finished and sat back, waiting for his boss's response.

Moretti was stunned and angry. He sent his best men, those who had performed the same duties several times in the past in

Chicago, leaving his rivals bleeding on the streets, in barbershop chairs, or lying under restaurant tables. "How many Rangers did he have with him?"

"He was alone."

Moretti shook his head. "Couldn't happen. They were the best button men in the business."

"That's the skinny I heard."

"And this Texas Ranger. He's still alive?"

"Pretty much, but a broad in the car with him caught a round."

Moretti took a sip of scotch from the glass beside the ashtray, then picked up the cigar and took a puff. "We shouldn't have this kind of trouble out of a hick town like that."

The men around him knew better than to speak. Any unsolicited answer could turn his building wrath on themselves. It had happened before, and the survivors in the room had learned their lessons very, very well.

"There's too much money at stake here. Respectable money."

To Moretti, who was used to making cash through the sale of illegal liquor, gambling, and prostitution, gaining a significant interest in the Texas oil boom seemed like a fairly legitimate branch of income, despite ignoring that fact that they were taking land through corruption and murder.

There was also money to be made by hijacking loads, and road crews prowled the back roads, like highwaymen of old. Instead of cutlasses and muzzleloader pistols, they used shotguns and revolvers to relieve drivers of their rigs full of oil.

Only a couple of months earlier, the Texas Legislature passed a law prohibiting the Railroad Commission from regulating production, resulting in a glut of oil that reduced prices. Moretti was making money on "hot oil," crude pumped out over the legal limit and smuggled out of the area by bribing railroad and pipeline employees to look the other way, or filling trucks in the dead of night and slipping out on the back roads.

The idea came from Caldwell in Longview. They'd worked with him before in other rackets over the years after meeting him in a Hot Springs gambling house, both seeing larceny and crime in each other.

"Right now we're gonna let Caldwell roast on his own spit." Moretti took another sip of the amber liquid. "Those guys will have to deal with the mistakes they have made."

He twisted in his chair toward the men gathered around two tables. "That's what happens when you underestimate the other guy."

They nodded, as if that was the most sage advice they'd ever heard.

Moretti finished his scotch and slid the glass away. "Now, we also got this Clete Ferras who's let us down, too. He did a good job down in South Texas, and I thought he'd work out in those oil fields." Knowing he was on stage and his men were watching and listening, he relit his cigar and exhaled a cloud of blue smoke. "He was showing promise, too, when he did that switch angle and got us that big piece of land making us oilmen!"

The toadies laughed as if that was the funniest thing they'd ever heard.

"But he's not holding up his end of the business out there. I want *him* gone, too."

"As in...poof?" Chic Marco took a seat at a nearby table.

"Just like that, and that fast."

"I'll send word to those two in Texas. Make *them* do it."

"Good. That's why you're my right-hand man, Chic. You think good."

Marco gave him a tight smile, not banking anything on the

compliment. "What about our boys that got rubbed out? What are we gonna do about this Ranger?"

"It's time to wrap all this up with a bow. Chic, send some more men down there to get that Ranger for good this time, and have 'em rub out those guys who got us into this."

"All of them, as in the banker and the sheriff?"

"Bring me the sheriff. Cool the banker. That should take care of everyone, then have them stop in Longview on the way back and settle up there, too. I want Caldwell gone, and pay off the rest to keep quiet." Moretti pointed at the Aiello brothers who dressed just alike, except for the gray and brown overcoats they wore. "You guys go for sure. Make sure you get that Ranger. You're a couple of my best droppers."

The brother in the brown coat nodded. "You got it, Boss."

Chapter Thirty-Seven

Half-sitting on the edge of Mallie's bed in the upstairs room of her fairly new mail-order Craftsman house, Dr. Walter Patton closed his scarred medical bag and studied the woman propped up on several pillows. Gray at the temples and sound as a dollar, the doctor had been tending patients for fifty years. "You having any trouble with your breathing?"

"No." Mallie's pale hands rested on the sheets.

"Dizziness, blurred vision?"

"A little. Some mornings are worse than others."

As damp air blew through the open windows, Doc Patton listened to her chest through his stethoscope. "Mornings. Just mornings?"

"Mostly."

"Your lungs sound good. You having trouble peeing?"

Her face flushed. She'd always been shy, but this was truly embarrassing. "Doctor!"

He sighed. "Sorry for being insensitive. Are you having trouble passing water?"

"My kidneys don't act as much as they did."

He frowned. "How're your bowels?"

She stared at the ceiling so as not to make eye contact. A

woman ought not talk about such things to a man, in her opin- ion. In fact, she didn't want to discuss her body functions with anyone, and that included Quinn. "Not acting like they should, either."

"I'm going to pull these covers back so I can palpate your stomach."

"What does that mean?"

"I need to mash on it some." He folded the quilt and sheet back to just above her hip bones. "Hands to your sides." He pressed through her nightgown, feeling for a variety of possible issues such as a mass, hernias, or sensitivity. "Burning in your stomach? Nausea? Vomiting?"

"Yes." Her face reddened again at the word "burning." She thought back to the early days of their marriage, when she and Quinn had relations as much as twice a week. Her mama hadn't told her that having relations could sometimes result in burn- ing...down there. When she went to Dr. Patton about that, he explained why it happened and how to avoid it in the future, much to her embarrassment.

Now, though, Quinn's ardor had cooled, and he only showed interest every now and then, but here she was again, talking with the doctor about very personal issues. "I thought I might be expecting and it was morning sickness, but I got my...time last week."

"Ummm hummm." He listened to her stomach with the stethoscope. "What else?"

"Well, I'm tired a lot more'n usual."

Patton paused and took her hand that was half under the cov- ers. Chewed to the quick, her nails that had never seen polish were tinted. He frowned, ran fingers through his thinning hair, and let out a long, drawn-out sigh. "How long have your finger- nails had this blue tint?"

"About two weeks, but it's so light I didn't think nothin' about it. I've been taking Baby Percy Medicine for my stomach and thought that might be doing it. That's all right, ain't it?"

Fully aware of the orange- and cinnamon-flavored medicine bottled barely 150 miles away in Waco, Patton had prescribed it himself on occasion for teething and colicky babies and to relieve sour stomach in adults by doubling the dosage. The label also suggested its use for "diarrhea, indigestion, cholera infantum, and summer complaints of children."

"Mallie, I'm gonna ask you a question, and your answer won't make any difference in how I look at you or feel about you, and I won't say a word to the laws. Understand?"

Nervous, she nodded.

"Do you drink whiskey?"

"Now you know as well as I do that there's a prohib..."

"Please answer my question."

She sighed. "Well lands sake, I don't see that it's much of a crime to sneak a little toddy or two ever' now and then."

"Well, you're right. It's not a crime." Doc Patton nodded. "I believe you have wood alcohol poisoning, but there's something else going on here, too, and I'm not sure what it is. Wood alcohol, if you drink too much too quickly, can be deadly. You need to stop drinking that stuff and you should get better, if you haven't done any permanent damage to your insides."

"I'm poisoned?"

"Yep. I don't know how bad, but none of it's good." Patton put the stethoscope in his bag. "I've seen several cases in the past few months, but they were all men, and the results came quick after they drank it, because they consumed a right smart amount in a short amount of time. One'll be blinded for life. A couple of 'em died, and two or three more won't last much longer because their organs are shutting down, and there's not a thing I can do about it."

She clutched her throat. "Is that what's gonna happen to me?"

"I don't know. Depends on how much you've drank at a time. I've not run into too many people who just sip at it, like you say you have."

"I can't take much, and I really don't care for the taste. It's too strong for me, so I have a few drops to help me sleep."

"That's why it's creeping up on you. My experience in such matters has been limited up to this point. The others drank a lot of it in one sitting, but you're lucky in a sense. You've been spreading it out over a while, it sounds like."

"I have."

"How long?"

She didn't want to say, because she'd only started drinking not long after marrying Quinn. Well, the truth was that she and her future husband drank a lot of bathtub gin in the whirlwind weeks of courtship. After they married and filed all the paperwork he said needed to be filled out by a husband and wife, he quit bringing home bottled hooch and took to buying it straight from a moonshiner he knew.

"I take just a few sips when Quinn makes it. Sometimes I pour it out when he's not looking."

"Well, you're lucky you have a constitution strong enough to handle it, but it's been accumulating to this point where you're pretty sick. You need to stop it and pour the rest of that mess out."

"That's all?"

"Like I said, if the damage to your kidneys and liver is light, and if you don't drink no more of it, I suspect you'll be all right. You can come into the hospital where I can take some tests. That'll tell me more."

"Oh, no. You won't catch me in no white man's hospital. It's bad enough having you here."

Patton rubbed the back of his neck. "It don't make any difference to me if you're red, white, blue, or black. We're all the same under our skin, but I'll allow there might be some talk if you came in, and that's a fact. You can stay here if the symptoms don't get any worse, but you make sure you don't drink any more of it. I can't say that enough, and as a matter of fact, throw out that Percy Medicine you've been taking and any other patent medicines you have around the house. Most of 'em'll kill you."

"Even the Bateman's Drops?"

"That's opium. It's a drug that's not really good for you."

"It helps me sleep, too."

"Good Lord, what else are you taking to sleep?"

"Well, it depends on how I feel at the time."

"Get rid of it all."

Her answer came quick, before he could ask anything else. She already felt like she'd said too much, and didn't want to get Quinn in trouble. "I'll pour everything out as soon as you leave."

"Good. Would you mind telling me where you got it?"

"I don't want to say."

"You need to."

"I don't buy it myself."

"I didn't think you did, unless you're dropping by the red-light district and some of those tent saloons they think are hid."

"They wouldn't let me in there anyway, seeing's how I'm an Indian and all." She'd been there a time or two, though, with Quinn. As long as she was with a white man, most people wouldn't say anything, thinking she was likely a prostitute. But the last time they went, not long before she'd married, a drunk roughneck put his hands on her, and Quinn had to knock him in the head with a sap he always carried. After that, he decided she couldn't go around such places any longer and picked up the whiskey while he was out.

Scanning the room, as if to see if anyone was hiding close by and listening, she bit her bottom lip. "You won't say nothin'?"

He snorted in exasperation. "I'll have to talk to the sheriff, because wood alcohol can kill you, and if someone is selling that stuff, the law needs to know. I'll keep your name out of it, though. I have plenty of dead men I can hang it on if I want to, but not a one of the living will tell me where they bought it. Now, where'd *you* get it? Tell me, and you can save a whole crop of lives."

She didn't want to get her husband in trouble, and all of a sudden found herself dangling in the wind and didn't know what to say. She'd already implicated herself and was frightened by what Dr. Patton might tell the sheriff. Suddenly terrified by what she'd told, she bit her lip again and pointed to the closed door and whispered the first thing that came to mind, because she'd just been talking about it before the doctor arrived.

"My maid, Leatha Mae, gets it for me from Lyall Brennen."

Chapter Thirty-Eight

A distinguished-looking man with gray at his temples stepped out on Mallie's porch at the same time I came up the walk. A light mist collected on my coat and hat, and seeing it, the gentleman set his own hat and waited.

I climbed the wooden steps and joined him out of the weather. Seeing the worn leather bag in his hand, I nodded. "I see you're a doctor. Somebody sick?"

He nodded. "House call."

"Name's Tom Bell. Texas Ranger."

"Walter Patton."

"I figured." We shook. "Is this Quinn Walker's house?"

"It is."

"He the one sick?"

"No. His wife Mallie."

"I hoped to talk to him, if he's here."

"He isn't." Doc Patton looked back at the closed door and sighed. "Mallie's inside, in the bed. They have a housekeeper waiting on her."

"Hope she's not bad."

"Could have been, but I'm thinking she'll be all right, eventually." The doctor tilted his head in thought. "Say you're a Ranger?"

I pulled back my coat to reveal the badge. "I am."

"And you need to see Quinn?"

"I do. Official business. You have any idea where he might be? I went over to Gene Phillips's house, too, but he wasn't home, either."

"Gene's in the land and oil business now. He could be anywhere the way this town's growing and all the irons they have in the fire. Mind if I ask why you need to see Quinn?"

It was my turn to study the man only three feet away. "Not sure I can say. Why?"

Patton rubbed the stubble on his chin. "I'm not sure I should tell you something, neither, but since you're the law, and I don't think much of the local sheriff or any of those deputies of his, I was wondering if you had some advice for me."

I glanced past the doctor at the windows opened wide enough to let in a breeze, but not so much that rain could get in. The double-hung window was cracked at the top for rising heat to dissipate. It also allowed anyone inside to hear their conversation on the porch, if they had an ear turned toward the porch.

"I have a suspicion of what may be going on here."

Stepping closer I lowered my voice. "I'll trade you."

"How so?"

"For information."

"If I can. I took an oath..."

"I know about your Hippocratic oath. I took an oath, too, to serve this state and country to the best of my abilities. Let's talk. Tit for tat."

"Fine." The doctor angled his body so we faced the street. "I think I have a few cases of wood alcohol poisoning on my hands, and was wondering if you've heard about stills operating close by here."

Feeling let down at the question, I answered anyway. "I

haven't been in town that long, and have been looking for a fugitive, so there hasn't been much talk about making whiskey, but in a place like this, there's always a still somewhere close by. I need more than that to go on. You might need to bring it up to Dobbs."

"I've already said I don't have any use for that man." Doc Patton paused, gathering his thoughts. "This stays between you and me. One professional to another."

"It does."

"Then the lady of the house here has wood alcohol poisoning. She says her housekeeper provides it, and that stuff has made her pretty sick. If she'd kept drinking it instead of calling me, I suspect she'd be graveyard dead in a week, or maybe less, if it's affected her organs."

"I've heard about such, but if you're asking, that's not why I'm here. Rangers usually don't deal with folks running stills. That's more local, with them doing most of the legwork, unless it's big enough to bring in the federal officers."

"Oh, well, I guess I put coincidence before fact, then. I thought you might be investigating the bootleggers around here."

"No, I'm here for another issue, but what you have to say interests me. How do you know the housekeeper's the one buying it?"

"The lady of the house says so."

"Housekeeper." Still suspicious about where he was going with that, I wasn't interested in trying to pin something on other people less fortunate. "Is she a Negro?"

"She is. She answered the door when I knocked."

"Well, she's buying it from someone with the same skin tone, then. I doubt a white man would sell to a colored woman. That oughta narrow things down for anyone who goes looking."

Doc took a deep breath. "You're right. The moonshiner's colored, but it won't be you going after him, huh?"

"Not right now. Maybe your new sheriff will take up the task."

"New sheriff?"

"The one you have now is considering retirement."

"Well, that's good news to me. I haven't heard a word about it."

"I bet you haven't. Just came up." Looking toward the street, I saw Booker and Hut coming up the street. "Good to meet you, Doc."

Instead of ringing the doorbell, I walked with the doctor to the sidewalk. We shook just outside of Walker's picket fence, and he climbed into a flivver and drove away. Booker and Hut stopped, hands in the pockets of their overalls. "Boys, that's a bad habit standing that way. Some folks might think you're lazy."

They took their hands out and straightened. I gave 'em a grin. "That's better. Deputies, y'all ready to go to work?"

Their faces lit up, and Booker spoke. "What do you need?"

"I want to find Quinn Walker and Gene Phillips. Find out where they are and come get me over at Charlotte's Café."

Blinking against stinging tears, I fought a surprising hitch that caught in my stomach at the mention of her name, and it took a moment to regain control of my voice. I felt empty inside, and tried not to think about her laid out over at the funeral home. It was the only way to deal with the fresh grief that seemed to wait like a copperhead until I was most vulnerable.

I'd always been a private man, more so now. Taking a deep breath to steady my voice, I cleared the frog in my throat, hoping the boys hadn't noticed. "I'll be there when you find 'em, but don't let on you're acting on my orders."

"Yessir. Where you think we ought to look?"

"If I was y'all, I'd find a spot around here so you can keep an eye on this house. You can do it together, or split up and one of you go over to Phillips's house and wait there, if you know where he lives."

"You didn't ask some of Sheriff Dobbs's deputies to help you?"

"No. You two are less apt to be noticed than any of them."

I went to find Harvey McKnight, the roughneck who might have some more information for me, while the boys decided what to do.

Chapter Thirty-Nine

It was showering again. Booker Johnston and Hut Parsons ducked under a trash wagon parked just down the unpaved street from Quinn Walker's house to keep an eye out. The ground there was also wet, but they squatted with the ease of youth under the makeshift shelter.

Hut shifted his feet for better balance. "Did you see Mr. Tom was cryin'?"

"Texas Rangers don't cry. It was just rain in his eyes."

"Was too. I saw 'em almost brim over. Men have tears in 'em, same as women. He's grieving for Miss Charlotte."

Booker swallowed a lump in his throat that arose when he thought of the sadness he'd also seen in Mr. Tom's face. "My daddy said if you see anything in Mr. Bell's eyes after what happened last night, it'll be lightning."

A new Ford Model A passed going in the other direction, the big new V-6 engine rumbling with power. Seconds later a wagon stacked with split firewood passed, pulled by a team of mules. Both vehicles were a symbol of the changing times that the kids didn't understand.

Hut drew a deep breath through his nose. "There's a lot of pine sap in that load of wood. I love that smell."

"It'll smell better when it's burning." Booker wrapped both arms around his knees. "I can't wait for it to get cold. I love sitting in front of a fire."

"Not in *our* drafty old house. It gets so cold I have to hug the stove to quit shivering. Even the dogs stay outside 'cause they think it's warmer."

"That ain't true."

"No. My daddy said it, and I thought it was funny."

A Model T just like the one driven by Dr. Patton passed, leaving ruts in the gravelly mud, some of which splashed the boys. Booker used his thumb to rub at a spot on the knee of his overalls. "They say by this time next year all the streets here in town'll be paved or bricked. They're starting on Main and then branching out here."

"That don't make no difference to me. The best they'll ever do out in the country is use gravel. How long you think we ought to sit under here?"

"I don't know. Maybe we could double our chances if one of us goes to Mr. Gene's house to wait there."

Hut studied on the idea for a moment. "But if we do, and one of 'em comes home, then we'll have to go get Mr. Bell, and by that time, they could be gone again. Let's stay here, and if Mr. Quinn comes home, one can stay while the other goes."

"I hadn't thought of that." Booker grinned. "You think like a lawman. Is that what you're gonna be when you grow up?"

"Naw." Hut snorted. "When was the last time you saw a lawman looks like me? Law's white. I reckon I'll farm like my daddy, or maybe run off and have some adventures."

"Like what?"

"Like a cowboy out west. I'd make a fair hand."

"There ain't no colored cowboys."

Hut's brow furrowed. "Are too. Daddy has a cousin went out there and works on a ranch to this day."

"Can you ride a horse?"

"I can ride a mule. Same difference." Hut picked at a scab on the back of his hand. "Or I might go to the city. I've never seen one. Maybe Dallas."

"I'm gonna finish school and go to college."

"To do what?"

"To graduate, of course."

"Then what'll you do?"

"Come back here and make money."

"Sounds like a good plan."

They stopped talking when Gene Phillips pulled up in front of the house and killed the Ford's engine. Booker pointed. "There they are."

"Is that Mr. Quinn in there with him?"

"It is. I'll stay here and you go get Mr. Bell."

"Uh. He's liable to be in the café, and you know they won't let me in. You go, and I'll wait to see what happens."

Booker duckwalked out from under the wagon to emerge into the light shower. Phillips saw the boy rise up but turned his attention back to Walker and continued their conversation while the youngster trotted down the new sidewalk toward Main Street.

Chapter Forty

"What are we gonna do now?" Gene Phillips's hands shook, and he gripped the steering wheel to make them stop.

"Keep our heads low while we do what we've been doing." Quinn Walker was also nervous, but he held it better than Gene. "The problem's Ferras. Things were fine until he showed up."

"We can't run him off. That's the meanest old man I've ever seen."

"Dobbs didn't say run him off. He said rub him out."

Phillips licked his lips. "I don't know how we're gonna do *that*."

"I do. He's still in Hog Eye, laid up with that whore he likes in the Hydroxy. We'll just get him to go for a ride out to where we took that Indian gal Hazel."

"You know that Stanley McCord's fixin' to go to the pen for that one."

Walker shrugged. "Who cares? He's just another oil-field worker. Nobody'll miss him."

"He might get the chair."

"Like I said…"

His stomach in knots, Phillips shifted back to their original conversation. "You think Ferras'll go without asking questions? It sounds suspicious to me."

"I've got that all worked out. I'll tell him we heard the Ranger'll be out there looking around the scene again, and it'll be the perfect time for Ferras to pick him off and he can take all the credit. Then when we get him out there, one of us can blow a hole in him."

"Which one? You know how nervous I get. I'd likely shoot myself, or you."

"All right then. You get him to talking and *I'll* shoot him."

"You ever kill anybody?"

"No, but it's not hard to pull a trigger. With him out of the way, we can finish up what we're doing and lay low while the money piles up." Walker rubbed his palms against his thighs. "Think about it. By the time Thanksgiving rolls around, we're gonna be *rich*."

The decision made, silence filled the car as they pondered the future.

Walker studied the front of his house, wondering if Mallie was awake. She'd taken to the bed lately, proof that their plan was working. It was all he could do not to give her too much at one time. Finesse was the word he liked to think about whenever he considered what they were doing. Finesse was the best because a quick murder could easily double back on them.

He figured old Doc Patton didn't have much experience with slow poisoning by a mixture of wood alcohol infused with oleander. Even if someone started digging into her death, they'd establish that it was illegal whiskey that accidentally killed her, and not the steady doses of the poisonous plant.

No one could prove it was intentional.

It was that kind of crime that brought the whole country's attention on what happened in the Osage Nation up in Oklahoma years earlier. Oil was discovered on the Osage Reservation in 1897, and by 1920, the market had grown so much that three years later the tribe took in more than thirty million dollars, making each member some of the richest people on earth. With that information reaching the headlines, a flood of people arrived in the oil field, hoping to separate the Indians from their money, many of them resorting to murder to make that happen.

Fascinated by the newspaper accounts of the murders, Quinn Walker read everything he could find on the case in the hopes that someday he'd go to the city and meet a rich woman to implement his own foolproof plan. He was much smarter than those Okies. and if the opportunity arose, he'd be one step ahead of the law, which in East Texas was usually no more than a rural constable with little experience other than with drunks, minor theft, and family feuds.

When the oil boom hit Northeast Texas, Quinn Walker found himself in the perfect position. As drillers punctured the earth to suck out what they were calling black gold, he decided to learn from the mistakes made up in Oklahoma. Initially, his aim was low. Find one of the locals who possessed land, marry her, and gently escort the victim out of the world. He would do it smarter, though, in order not to draw attention to himself.

It was working fine until one night when he was drinking with Gene Phillips and told him of the plan. Together they hatched a scheme that involved the two of them. Phillips had been dating Ruby for almost a year and allowed Walker's ultimate goal sounded like a good idea. Phillips didn't have as much ambition as Walker, and decided he'd settle for owning her land and the oil rights, once they got his mother-in-law out of the way. But a brief affair with another woman named Melba Lee bloomed into something completely different, and Walker convinced Gene to join him in moving faster to get Ruby out of the way in order to marry Melba Lee.

As money poured into Mallie's bank account, Walker soon started leveraging land deals, with her permission, of course, making so much money that the bank president Albert Emsworth became interested. Emsworth offered his services to launder the money and they struck a new deal.

After that, Walker wanted to expand even more, and convinced Emsworth that, despite the fact he had little cash of his own in the bank, he'd be the sole inheritor of Mallie's estate someday soon. Even with dollar signs in his eyes, the bank president wanted nothing to with that aspect of their plan, and made it clear that his part would involve money, and nothing else.

From there, the plan expanded like rings in the water from a dropped stone. Emsworth knew Sheriff Dobbs had a larcenous side and was bitter over his low salary in a world of oil money. They'd worked together in a couple of land deals to force black landowners off their farms when they couldn't pay the mortgage.

Once Sheriff Dobbs learned how much cash was involved, he joined in. Playing poker and drinking heavily one night in Longview, he brought O. L. Caldwell into the deal when he accidentally spilled the beans. The idea of making more money than he ever imagined captured Caldwell's attention, despite his fat bank account.

Like those same rings in the water, Caldwell brought Cherubino Moretti into the fold. They'd met two years earlier while soaking in the Hazelwood Hotel's bathhouse in Hot Springs. When Caldwell realized he could use Moretti's specialized services from time to time, they became close allies. Moretti took the scheme up another notch, amplifying Quinn

Walker's original small-time stratagem into the Chicago-based organization, which led to cold-blooded murder and not slow poisoning.

With that takeover, Walker and Phillips were caught up in a wide web beyond their imagination, putting them at the behest of the Moretti gang and organized crime. Once the original masterminds, the two small-town criminals now took orders from three different individuals, and both men did their best to maintain their original course until their wives were gone. After that happened, they'd agreed to cut all bonds with the rest of the consortium, not realizing they were in way over their heads.

Sitting in front of Walker's house while rain drummed on the roof of his car, Phillips cleared his throat. "When are we gonna do it?"

"There's no better time than now. We know where Ferras is."

"You mean right this minute?"

"Why not? Let's get this over with."

Gene shifted into first gear and pulled away from the house. "I wish this was all over. I didn't expect to be involved at this level."

"Neither did I, but there's no turning back now." Walker shook his head. "But like I said, we're gonna be rich pretty soon."

As they accelerated, Phillips glanced to the side to see a young colored boy squatting under a wagon. "What do you think that kid's doing under there?"

Walker twisted around to look out the back glass. "Staying out of the rain, looks like."

Phillips rounded the corner toward Main Street and pulled over. "You have to give me some time to think about this."

"We don't have time."

"You're gonna make time." His voice croaked. "Seeing that

boy under there made me realize my baby's gone and won't never grow up to even be that age." He got out and slammed the door. "This is all happening too fast. Let me think."

"You have an hour, and then you better get your ass back to this car." Walker stepped out and stalked back to his house to kill sixty minutes.

Chapter Forty-One

Hut told me Walker was back at his house, and I rushed back to find he was already gone. Standing there beside that white picket fence I fought down the frustration. Getting ahold of the man was like trying to catch a ghost. The boys stood there quiet as mice, and I figured they were afraid I'd blame them somehow.

"Say they just set there for a while and then drove off?" The light rain soaked my fur felt hat, making it heavy enough to settle down to my ears. The shoulders of my coat were wet, too, adding to everything that was building up inside me.

"Yessir." Hut didn't seem to mind the moisture at all, though his shirt and overalls were also wet.

"I shoulda run faster." Booker hunched his shoulders.

"Not your fault, son." I sighed. "We'll get them…"

A female voice from Walker's front porch made us all look up. "Yooo! Hut Parsons! Is that you standing out there in the rain?"

We turned to see a heavy Negro woman on the porch, drying her hands on a crisp white apron. Hut waved. "Yessum! It's me."

"Who's that with you?"

"It's Booker Johnston, ma'am."

"I know that, Booker. I mean you, sir."

I instinctively touched the brim of my hat. "Tom Bell, ma'am."

"Why is you standing in the rain with them boys?"

"Came to see Quinn Walker earlier, but he wasn't home. Booker here said he'd come in, so I dropped by a second time to catch up with him."

"Y'all get up here on this porch and out'the rain. Y'act like y'all don't have good sense standing around in falling weather, and I declare, I don't like hollering across a yard."

"Me neither." I led the way up the walk with the boys trailing behind like two little ducks. It was much better on the porch and when I removed my hat, water dripped on the painted floorboards. The boys sat on the porch rail. "Thanks for inviting me up."

"You're welcome. My name's Leatha Mae. I keep house for Mr. Quinn and Miss Mallie. Now, how you know he wasn't home if you ain't been to this door? And number two, state your business, please."

Booker started to speak up, but she shushed him with a finger without taking her eyes off me. "You rascals sit there quiet like you was taught to be around adults."

The boys lowered their heads and the corner of my mouth twitched in a grin. I took an instant liking to the round little woman with graying hair. "Name's Tom Bell. I came up a little while ago just as the doctor was leaving. Met him here on the porch, and he said your employer wasn't home, just the wife and she's sick. I didn't want to bother y'all, so I asked these two outlaws here to keep an eye on the place and let me know when he came back."

"Well, he ain't here."

"Yes ma'am. They said he pulled up in front with Gene Phillips and stayed in the car for a while before they left again."

"Is that right?" Leatha Mae pursed her mouth and stared

down at the boys. "Y'all passin' 'round a lot of information about folks that ain't nothin' to either one of you." Not waiting for a response, she met my gaze. "You're right. The missus ain't feeling well today, she's down in the bed, so I cain't ask you in. Can I give Mr. Walker a message for you?"

"No, ma'am. I'll find him directly."

"Mr. Bell. You're with the laws, looks like."

"Yes ma'am. Texas Ranger."

The corner of her mouth turned down in a momentary frown until she apparently came to a decision and turned to the boys. "You two is the sorriest lookin' things I've seen all day." She changed her mind. "All three of y'all needs to come in for a minute." She smiled. "I have some fresh cookies in the kitchen. Y'all can dry off and have one or two with a glass of sweet milk while me and Ranger Bell have a talk, if that's all right with you, sir."

"It is if the missus of the house don't mind me coming in without an invitation."

"She's asleep and she sleeps hard. Likely won't wake up for a while, if these two can keep their voices down while I fix you some coffee." Though the words were stern, her soft eyes told a different story.

———

True to their word, Booker and Hut were quiet as church mice, eating cookies at a small white enamel-top table in the kitchen while me and Leatha Mae visited at the dining room table. The swinging five-panel door between the kitchen and dining room was closed so we could speak in private.

I had a thick mug of coffee as black as tar and hot as sin. My hat hung on the ear of my chair, my coat on the other. While she settled across the table, I took note of the stained beams overhead, and the arts and crafts detail of the home.

"This is good coffee, Miss Leatha."

"Thank you, sir. You don't talk to me like I'm colored."

"Well, I don't see the need to talk down to *anyone*, if that's what you're saying." I was liking the older woman more and more, and a thought tickling the back of my mind kept telling me that what Dr. Patton had said about her was wrong.

"Would you believe what I tell you, then?" She watched me, face impassive.

"I usually know when someone's not speaking the truth." All my life, I've been able to see through most folks and know they were lying. There was something so good about the woman sitting across from me that I knew what the doctor heard was wrong.

She nodded and sipped from a delicate china cup with a chipped rim. She'd poured my mug full, but her coffee came up only halfway to the top. She squirmed in her chair for a minute, and I could tell she was screwing up her courage, but she'd already primed the pump and needed to talk.

"Miss Mallie's sick and gettin' sicker every day. Started feeling that way not long after her and Mr. Quinn got married and bought this house."

"It's a nice one."

"That it is." She looked around with pleasure, as if it were her own. "Finest house I ever been in." She was nervous, so I sipped at the coffee and listened so as not to derail her train of thought.

"See, most folks that hire us don't think too much about us housekeepers knowing one another. We talk all the time, 'cause we're kin, or we growed up together. We see each other at church, of course, but ever' now and then, when we take a notion to go out for groceries and such, a few of us get together for a little chat. We've set a time each week and the folks we work for don't think nothing of us being gone for a while, long as the cleanin's done and supper's ready when they all set down to eat."

"You're talking about the different levels of our society. I understand completely. It's the same down in the Valley, except most of the folks who do your job are Mexican."

"I love that Mexican talk. It's almost like singing to me."

"They say Spanish is the loving tongue."

She grinned. "And I bet the talk amongst 'em is just the same. Rich white folks and their needs and wants."

"I imagine that's true, though I've never had the means to employ anyone. Of course, the door swings both ways on that subject, too."

Leatha Mae stifled a laugh. "You're right about that." Her face fell in an instant. "Mr. Bell, I got to ast you something. It was you in that shooting last night outside of town, wasn't it?"

My fragile mood crumbled and it all came flooding back. Though it seemed like everything happened weeks ago, it was hard to believe that Charlotte had been alive less than twenty-four hours earlier, and here I was, sitting at a table with an attractive Negro woman, sipping coffee like I didn't have a care in the world.

Eyes stinging, I saw the coffee ripple from a tremor. One elbow resting on the white tablecloth slipped, yanking the material sideways, and I nearly upended a vase of flowers. Blinking to clear my vision, I straightened the tablecloth with my palm and smoothed a wrinkle. "Yes, it was."

"You was out with Miss Charlotte." Her eyes softened, and the look she gave me nearly dissolved what little control I had. "We all heard about that, and I'm so sorry."

"Thank you."

Embarrassed, I wiped a tear that threatened to spill over, and

Leatha Mae reached out a hand and rested it on my own. The distinctly human touch and her sympathy finally brought forth the anguish that I'd packed down. Biting off a sob, I slipped my finger from the mug's handle and wiped at a renegade tear that trickled down and into my mustache.

Leatha Mae gave my hand another pat and wiped her nose with the dishrag hanging over her shoulder. The ticking of a black Ingraham mantel clock in the living room was the only sound in the still house.

She broke the silence by speaking soft and low. "It's all right, hon. I worked in the kitchen for her at the Southern Café a while back. I done cried my tears. She was a fine woman and treated everyone just the same. I hated to leave her, but Miss Mallie knew me from when she didn't have no money and offered me a job that paid more'n twice what I was making at the café."

I had to clear my throat to speak. "I would have expected her to treat everyone right."

"She did, and she'd want me to tell you what I...I suspect, you might say."

I put the mug on the table and waited.

"There's something going on around here that my people cain't put their finger on. There's a lot more killin' and dyin' in the last year, and those of us working for white folks is hearing about it when they don't think we're listening. It might have something to do with what happened to y'all last night."

"Go on."

She glanced at the kitchen door, then checked the closed pocket doors leading into the living area. "Can I ask what day you got to town?"

I told her.

"That's another piece of this puzzle." She took the dishcloth from her shoulder and wiped at a nonexistent spill on the table.

"A white feller called up Miss Ambrosia Roosevelt that same day to come fix up a hole in his friend's stomach. He was over in that tent camp east of town, but they didn't want nary doctor to know he'd been shot."

"She has some medical training?"

"You might say that. She's been taking care of my people for years, stitching up cuts, healing whatever ails 'em, and delivering babies. White folks who want to keep secrets also call her. She's midwife'd more'n her share, all right, and once even got caught up in a fight between families when a little ol' white country girl had twins out in a shack on the Sabine."

"Fight between the father's people and her people?"

"Oh no. One of the well-to-do families over in Hog Eye couldn't have their own children, so they sent word to that little girl sayin' because she was poor as a church mouse, they figured she couldn't feed two babies, she should give 'em one to raise as their own."

"That takes some backbone."

She nodded and took a delicate sip. "It does. Well, Miss Ambrosia marched herself right over to that uppity woman's house and told her that if she said one more word about taking one of those babies, she'd tell the whole town about why she couldn't have her own babies after what a back-alley doctor done to help her get rid of what she was carryin' before she got married."

"That took some backbone too, for a colored woman to get involved in a dispute between white people. I imagine that clammed her up, though. Before we get too far off, tell me about this man who was shot."

"Somebody put a hole in his stomach with a target gun. The reason I bring it up, he got a high fever and got to talking out of his head and said he was shot down on the creek. Said he was sent down there to check on the dead. Come to find out, the more he talked, they understood that someone sent him out to where Hazel Freeman was murdered to see how much of her was left.

"Sounds like he hoped they was nothin' but bones left after the animals and ants got through with her, but somebody showed up at the same time and shot him. Then we all heard that a lawman came to town, telling he'd found a body and wanted to report it. That was you, wasn't it?"

Hoping she wouldn't ask anything more, I nodded.

"I heard tell young Mr. Booker Johnston in there was with you."

"Met him out on the road that day. He's the one who led me to her."

"And Booker was squirrel huntin'."

"How would you know that?"

"'Cause Frieda Jackson works in the kitchen at the Pine Top Hotel and she cleaned them squirrels for him."

"Y'all have a pretty solid grapevine here."

"We do, and 'cause of that I know he hunts squirrels with a target rifle."

Giving myself time to think, I sipped coffee. "People don't think *Booker* shot that man."

I couldn't have that.

"No, and I cain't put an answer to why you'd use that little gun of his, but all that lets me put two and two together."

"You should be a lawyer. What happened to this feller? You have a name?" I knew who she was talking about, and she had a name, of course, but I wanted to see just how much more detail she'd admit to. I didn't mind her holding her cards close. It showed me that she'd keep a few things back in order to protect herself, her friends and family, and maybe even me, if it came to that.

"Nossir. She said he never give a name and no one had ever seen him before, but that's not unusual these days, not with all these people pouring into town looking for jobs." She tilted her head, watching my face. "She patched him up and he went on. She figured he passed away. Miss Ambrosia says them little .22 rounds are worse than gettin' ice-picked, you know. It's hard to fix one of them little holes. That bullet gets inside of people and can go anywhere if it glances off a bone."

Unmoved by the man's possible death, I was glad that I had a resolution to that shooting in the woods I'd kept from Sheriff Dobbs.

"Well, anyway, me and the girls were talking about how there's so much death these days, and all of a sudden we realized that we're all working for folks rich with oil money, and ever' one of 'em has a new outside man in the family."

Apparently the fire in my gut gave my emotions away. Leatha Mae paused, nodding her head as if I'd spoken. "So I see you're getting my drift, Mr. Bell."

"I knew there was something going on in this town."

"There is."

We sat in silence broken only by the ticking of the clock on the mantel.

"I've heard bits and pieces from a few folks, but haven't been able to put it all together until now. You're not pointing any fingers at anyone, are you, Leatha Mae?"

"It's not my station to do that, sir. I'm only telling you what I know and have heard spoke for the truth. There's a lot of coincidences around here."

"Does one of your housekeeping friends work for Gene Phillips?"

She nodded. "And Sheriff Dobbs."

My stomach fluttered. "You don't know where Quinn Walker might be?"

"Nossir. He leaves the house without telling Miss Mallie a thing. Says he's going to work, but that man works some odd hours, I can tell you that. I 'magine he's with either Gene Phillips or Jack Drake."

"That's a new name. I reckon you know someone who keeps house for him, too."

"I do, and like Gene Phillips and Mr. Quinn, he married a girl who came into oil money only a few months earlier."

As I listened, she told of coincidental or unsolved deaths in the county that resulted in the men who married in becoming wealthy. When she finished, my coffee was gone. I laced my fingers on the table. "No one's been brought to trial that you know of?"

"None, 'cept for Stanley McCord, who they have in jail for killing Hazel. There'll be a trial soon, I 'spect."

Mind racing, I saw the shadows from two sets of feet flicker under the swinging kitchen door. Pointing with my head, I silently told Leatha Mae the boys were just on the other side. She leaned forward and we met over the table. The smell of coffee was strong between us, as was the aroma of onions rising from her hands.

"Do you have any idea why Mallie's so sick?"

"I think it's from something Mr. Quinn's doing. He likes his whiskey, and she does, too. Brings home a bottle ever' other week or so. They have a drink ever' night, but he always makes his from a different bottle. He mixes hers with Co-cola, but takes his with a few chips of ice and that's all. She feels worse ever' morning."

"You said he brings it home. You don't get it somewhere for her?"

"Nawsir. All my people buy it from…" She paused, startled that she'd almost spoken a name. "We have one person we buy from, but it's easy to get. Stills 're popping up all over this county to keep these oilmen from going thirsty, and some of the whiskey's bad. Miss Ambrosia's been called on a right smart number of people who've gone blind or died from that stuff."

"You know where he's getting it?"

"Heard 'em out on the porch one night. Mr. Gene knows a man."

There it was. Leatha Mae wasn't buying the whiskey like the woman upstairs said. The dominoes in my head were starting to line up, and I had a sneaking suspicion it was Walker himself bringing the whiskey home. The wife likely got scared when Dr. Patton asked her about it and blamed it on the easiest target she knew of, the hired help.

I drew a deep breath, reaching a conclusion. "I got to go. I've taken up too much of your time, and the missus is liable to wake up soon, though I'd like to sit here and wait for Walker."

"You can."

"I don't think so. I have a little pokin' around to do." I drained the last couple of drops and sat the mug down. Fine grounds dribbled down the inside. "Leatha Mae, it has been a pleasure to visit with you."

"You won't say nothin', will you?"

"Not a word." My voice rose slightly as I stood. "And neither will those two deputies of mine, if they know what's good for them."

The shadows under the door disappeared and I gathered up my hat and coat. "Thanks for the coffee and the talk."

She came around the table and laid one hand on my arm. "God bless you, Mr. Bell."

"You can call me Tom."

"No, I cain't, but thank you just the same, Mr. *Tom*."

She leaned in and for a second I thought she might hug me,

but instead, she rose on her tiptoes to give me a kiss on the cheek as light as a baby's breath. Somehow that brief, almost imaginary, contact drained all the grief from my mind, leaving me clearheaded and strangely calm.

With an embarrassed smile, she opened the swinging door and released the boys from the kitchen's confines. "Time to go, boys."

With the kids in tow, I left feeling as light as a feather and with a head full of possibilities.

Chapter Forty-Two

I stepped through the polished wood and glass doors the next morning and into the artificial brightness of the Pine Top Hotel on Main Street. The showers finally stopped, and the number of men going about their business under a lead-gray sky was slightly less than usual, but still busy.

Behind the desk, the day clerk threw up a hand in greeting. I waved back and saw the roughneck, Harvey McKnight, sitting on a red settee in the lobby, surrounded by opulence that didn't belong in such an obscure oil town. He rose. "I hear you've been looking for me. The boss said you came by the rig when I wasn't there."

"I did." I pointed toward a table far away from the desk and elevator. I took a seat close to the window to see outside and watch the door at the same time. I placed my hat crown-down on the table. "Still haven't seen Clete Ferras?"

"No. I've looked everywhere I go."

"We'll find him. I know you didn't grow up here, but have you ever heard the names Quinn Walker or Gene Phillips?"

"Can't say as I have. Heard about what happened to Charlotte, though. Were they involved in it? People are talking all over town about how you shot six men by yourself."

I ignored his question "I'd like to talk to them."

"You all right?"

"No. I'm not all right, but I have things to do. I'll deal with all of this later."

McKnight pursed his lips. "I thought Charlotte was some punkin'. Most of us who ate there thought a lot of her, and word got out pretty quick that she'd taken up with you." He seemed to lose his train of thought. "I really don't know what to say..."

"There's nothing *to* say."

"Well...you need to know that rigger you had a little talk with is passing the word that he's looking for you. Says he'll be ready the next time and it'll just be you and him and it don't matter if you wear that badge."

"The redhead. Harold Guinn."

"That's his name." He snorted. "You put down six men in as many minutes, and this pissant thinks he's gonna punch your ticket."

"Well, ol' Harold don't want to tangle with me right now."

"You keep an eye out. He's the kind who'll catch you looking the other way and knock you in the head with a pipe."

Looking past Harvey, I watched two men swagger into the hotel lobby. The city-cut overcoats they wore cost more than six months' wages for a farm hand. They went directly to the empty front desk. One of the men with a long white scar that ran from his left eye all the way down to the corner of his mouth slapped the bell impatiently. The other leaned over to look through an open door leading to the office.

"Thanks for the warning." I stopped talking when a pale-faced man in a rumpled suit hesitantly entered the lobby, and seeing the two of us sitting together, came close with his hat in his hand.

"You're Tom Bell."

"I am."

"I'm Gene Phillips," his voice broke, "and I have a confession to make."

"You've done something wrong."

Blinking back tears, Phillips nodded. "I'm in over my head in this."

"In what?"

Phillips swallowed. "They'll kill me for telling you, but I can't keep it a secret any longer. You got to promise me that I'll be protected."

The driller raised his eyebrows. "You want me to leave?"

"Naw, we need to talk some more." I pushed out a chair with one foot. "Phillips, sit down. I don't want to look up at you anymore."

Close to sobbing, the man dropped into the chair.

"All right now, get it off your chest."

"My baby's dead, and it's all my fault."

"You kill it?" If there was one thing in the world I despised, it was a child killer.

"Not directly."

"Buddy, you're about a hair away from me mopping this floor up with you. Get to talking while you can."

"I'm sorry! I got into something with some other people and it swarmed out of control and now my baby's gone. I was talking to Jack Drake about it last night, and he's in it too and he said that we need to get out and leave town for a while, but I can't decide what to do and wanted to tell someone and he said if we gave out all the names of them that's in this with us they'll kill us all, even Emsworth, and he ain't done nothing but push papers and…"

"Slow down. We're gonna have to take this one step at a time."

A shout from the side entrance stopped his confession.

Booker rushed through the side door and grabbed my arm. "He's *dead!*"

I stood. "What's wrong, son?"

"Hut's been run over and he's dead! Hurry!"

With no other option, I reached behind my belt for a pair of handcuffs. "Stick 'em out."

Phillips stretched his wrists across the table, and I clicked the bracelets on. "Wait with Harvey here and don't you dare leave." I slapped the driller's shoulder. "Keep an eye on him till I get back."

Chapter Forty-Three

The Pine Top Hotel's day clerk stepped out of his office. "Help you gentlemen?"

Obviously from the city and equal in height and weight, the only discernible differences between the pair of new arrivals were their wool overcoats. One was brown, the other, gray.

Brown Coat kept both hands in the coat's pockets. "Looking for someone maybe staying here. Tom Bell."

"Sure enough." The desk clerk pointed. From his vantage point, an ornate column hid the Texas Ranger, though the two men on either side were clearly visible. "He's sitting right over there."

They turned as one and sized up the tough-looking man in khakis and a white shirt who reached out and adjusted the hat beside him. An empty chair separated him from the pasty-faced individual in handcuffs. The prisoner planted his elbows on the table and rested his forehead on both hands.

The city people spoke softly to each other for a moment, apparently undecided about something. Finally making a decision, the men in overcoats exchanged a look and crossed the lobby.

Gene Phillips heard their footsteps and glanced up to see

their approach. He gasped, realizing who and what they were, and thinking they were after him, he tried to reach into his pants pocket for a little pistol, but the handcuffs stopped him.

Chapter Forty-Four

Booker whirled and charged down the sidewalk, leading me at a run. I was halfway down the block before I realized I'd left my hat. That's unusual for me, especially in such weather, but it was ridiculous to turn around and go back.

Two blocks down, I saw a cluster of men gathered around an empty pickup truck idling in the middle of the muddy, churned-up street. The door to the cab was open, but I couldn't see much else.

"Coming through!" I pushed through the crowd to find Hut half-buried in the soft mud behind the front tire, moaning. Relieved that he was alive, I slogged through the muck. A frightened farmer in faded overalls and a sweat-stained felt hat shifted back and forth beside the boy he'd run over, keeping everyone back.

"Y'all don't touch him."

He saw my badge and relief flooded the man's face. "He just darted out in front of me. I stopped after the front tire rolled over him."

"What're you just standing here for?" Dropping to one knee, I ran my hands over the youngster's body everywhere I could reach.

The farmer took off his hat. "I's afraid to move him. Sent my boy to find one of his people."

"Sent him to find somebody the same color, you mean, so you wouldn't have to touch him." I didn't take my eyes off Hut, who raised a weak arm. "Hut, how bad are you hurt?"

"Didn't know what else to do." The farmer looked around at the men around us, as if he needed to explain his actions to strangers.

Hut waved his muddy hand. "My other arm's broke, I think."

"Everything thing else still have feeling?"

"Yessir. I can wiggle my toes and everything."

Relief flooded through me, and my stomach unclenched. I couldn't help but grin at the kid covered in mud. "You're lucky this ground's so soft and that truck was empty. He mashed you into the mud instead of crushing you."

"This broke arm ain't lucky, Mr. Bell."

"At least you're breathing." Grasping Hut under his good arm, I gently pulled him out from under the truck with a wet, squishy sound.

Hut wasn't about to be carried, and planted his feet. "I want to walk."

Understanding how he felt with the crowd gathered around and watching, I made sure he could stand and turned loose. "I would, too." I looked around. "Anyone send for a doctor yet?"

One of the drillers guffawed. "Not for no *nigger* kid. He should have had better sense than to dart out like that."

My brief sense of relief turned to white heat that flared up. For a moment, all I could think about was smashing the smug man's face with a fist, but it wasn't the time.

I tamped it down and pointed at Booker, who stood nearby, shifting from one foot to the other in concern. "You ever hear of Miss Ambrosia?"

The youngster nodded. "Yessir."

"How far is she?"

"Couple of miles, if she's home."

"Dammit. Hut, let's go sit down there on the sidewalk for a second."

"Mr. Bell, I'm sick. I think I'm gonna puke."

"Broke bones'll make you sick at your stomach sometimes. Come on."

We slogged straight at the roughneck who'd made the comments. Others parted, but standing between us and the sidewalk, the man held his ground until he saw I wasn't going to hesitate or turn.

It was Hut who defused the situation. He puked all over the man's leg, and I laughed big.

Folks got out of the way after that, and pretty soon I sat him on the concrete sidewalk that was eighteen inches higher than the street and placed the boy's broken arm across his chest. "Use your good arm to hold it in place and I'll be right back. Booker, stay with him."

As I stepped onto the sidewalk, a man in muddy overalls rushed toward us. Booker pointed. "Here comes Uncle Dan."

The farmer hurried as fast as he could through the crowd. A number of men, recognizing him as an Indian, refused to get out of his way, intentionally slowing him down. Others glared at the farmer, daring the Choctaw to touch them or speak to them.

To avoid a challenge, he stepped off the sidewalk and slogged through the mud until he reached where the boys sat. "I heard a boy'd been run over, and somebody said it was Booker."

"It's Hut, Uncle Dan."

"I can see that. How bad's he hurt?"

Turning to put my back to the wall before answering, I made sure everyone around us could see the badge on my shirt. "Broke arm, as far as I can tell."

Chapter Forty-Five

Gray Coat's hands were in his overcoat pockets when he was clear of the support column. "Tom Bell?"

Harvey McKnight nodded and pointed at the hat beside him. "Yep, that's…"

His response was cut off when Gray Coat raised a sawed-off pump shotgun from underneath his overcoat at the same time Brown Coat produced a similarly hidden Thompson machine gun.

"Hey, wait!" Phillips half stood, still struggling to get the pistol free of his pocket. He managed to get his fingers around the little grip and pulled it out.

Both weapons opened up at the same time. Gunfire hammered through the hotel lobby as Brown Coat hosed McKnight with the Thompson. Riddled with bloody holes and dead before he hit the floor, McKnight fell from the chair as the window collapsed behind him. Brown Coat kept his finger on the trigger, riddling the still body.

Gray Coat saw the pistol in Phillips's hand and turned the twelve-gauge pump on the handcuffed man, shucking shells through the shotgun's chamber as fast as he could pull the trigger. Five swarms of buckshot pellets tore into Phillips's falling body, and he collapsed before he could fire the little pistol that dropped onto the hard floor.

"These hayseeds don't have enough common sense to pat down their prisoners." Gray Coat chuckled and thumbed shells into the shotgun's empty magazine. "Let's scram."

Their job finished, the shooters bolted for the door as rivers of blood poured from the fresh corpses.

Chapter Forty-Six

"I'll take him." Booker's uncle reached for Hut.

I patted him on the shoulder. "You can't carry this boy two miles to Miss Ambrosia's house."

"My *mules* can." Dan made money pulling stuck cars free of the mud and a team of mules would eat up the distance in no time.

Gunshots rang down the busy street, and my head snapped toward the direction of the gunfire. Despite the drilling noise from hundreds of nearby oil rigs, it was obvious one of the guns was fully automatic. The commotion around us ceased as everyone turned toward the Pine Top Hotel.

"I'll come check on him as soon as I see what that shootin's all about."

"And nobody better get in my way." Picking up the boy, Uncle Dan pushed through the crowd, followed closely by Booker.

The crowd ringing the boys wavered and charged toward the Pine Top Hotel to see what was happening there. Damp and muddy from the knees down, I rubbed my palms together to dislodge the sticky muck and jogged back to the hotel.

When I reached the side door I'd left through only minutes earlier, a crowd of onlookers blocked the sidewalk, peering through the door.

"Texas Ranger! Make way!"

Hearing the authority in my voice, the roughnecks and townspeople parted, allowing me to push inside to find Harvey McKnight's riddled body dead on the floor. Gene Phillips lay facedown in a pool of blood beside the overturned chair on the other side of the table. Rank smoke lingered in the still air, leaving the distinct smell of spent gunpowder.

Seeing there were no immediate threats, I spun toward the desk clerk. "What'n hell happened here?"

The shaken day clerk pointed at the main entrance. "Two city fellers! They thought one of 'em was you!"

Scooping up my hat from the table, I ran across the lobby through the scattered spent brass and empty shotgun shells on the polished floor. The main entrance was also clotted with onlookers. This time they fell over themselves to get out of the way when they saw the big Colt automatic in my hand. When I reached the sidewalk, others pointed south, shouting.

"They ran down the block and around the corner!"

"Two men!"

"One had a machine gun!"

Knowing it was already too late, I rushed to the corner to find they were gone.

Chapter Forty-Seven

Quinn Walker came outside after an hour to meet with Phillips only to find Jack Drake's butter-yellow Nash parked on the dirt-and-red gravel street in front of the house. Seeing the bright car, he at first thought Gene was in there also. Drake had been laying low, like he was supposed to. Coming to the house was still another bad idea.

Staying on the sidewalk, Walker stopped at the passenger door and peered inside. Finding no one but his cousin, he rested a hand on the open window frame. "Something wrong?"

"You bet." Nervous, he checked over his left shoulder and motioned for Walker to get in. "We need to get out of here and talk."

Sighing, Walker climbed in. The Nash pulled away from the curb, leaving an odd set of marks. The Nash car's front wheels were slightly inset from the back tires, leaving two sets of distinctive tracks.

"What's wrong?" Walker shook out a Lucky Strike and snapped a match alight with his thumbnail.

"We're in trouble, cousin." Drake flicked a finger in the direction of town. "Two men went to the Pine Top Hotel's lobby and cut down Gene and another man with a shotgun and a machine gun."

Startled, Walker paused, the flame several inches from the end of his toonie. "Killed 'em? Gene's dead?"

"Deader'n hell. Shot 'em to pieces."

"I didn't hear nothing." Walker paused, realizing the gunfire two blocks away was muffled by the building and the extraneous noise of vehicles and drilling rigs. "What was he doing at the hotel..."

Walker's comment drifted off and he stared straight ahead, thinking as the match burned toward his fingers. Feeling the heat, he shook it out, wishing he wasn't in such a bright car that would draw attention to them.

He snapped another match to life and lit the cigarette. "Did you see the bodies?"

"No." Drake shook his head. "But everybody in town's talking about it, and the Ranger had been there, but then it was like he knew something was about to happen. The story I heard was that two men came into the hotel and when the Ranger saw 'em, he slipped out the side. After the shooting was done, he came back in and acted like he was going after the triggermen."

"The Ranger was there?"

"Didn't I say he was?"

"No."

"Well, I'm rattled. Gene was with the Ranger and that other guy."

"Who was the guy?"

Weaving through streets that weren't much more than trails winding through the edge of town, Drake drove them out of town. "He was a driller. Him and Gene were sitting together in the lobby when the shooting started." Once Pine Top was behind them, he relaxed and drove at a slow, steady pace. "Gene was in cuffs, so that means the Ranger knew something."

Walker's mouth went dry. "This is going from bad to worse."

"So what do you think happened?"

"I have no idea, but somebody came to get rid of that son of a bitch." Walker took a long drag on the Lucky Strike and let the smoke out through his nose.

"Maybe they were after Gene."

"The problem now is we don't know if Gene had time to talk before the Ranger skipped out. He could have all our names. For all we know, he's looking for us right now. We may be all right, though. Even if he spilled his guts about what we're doing, the confession died with him."

"So that's good, then, you think?"

"I don't know what to think. Did anyone have a description of the shooters?"

"City people in suits. Fedoras and fancy overcoats. That's how they got the guns in without anyone noticing. Those coats have holes in the pockets so you can reach through and get after whatever's in your suit coat or pants pockets. They simply swung the guns up into their left hands and started shooting."

"City people? Gangsters, sounds like. You think Moretti sent some more guns out here?"

"Maybe, but I wish this was all over."

They drove past barren fields with water standing in the middles, and half a mile farther along, fields with cotton hanging low and muddy. Nothing outside the car registered with Walker, who was working out a plan to handle the situation. "This needs to move fast. Take me to Hog Eye."

"What's there?"

"Clete Ferras. I changed my mind, though, take me to the bank first."

"Why? You fixin' to talk to Emsworth?"

"No. I'm gonna use the phone booth in there. I'm calling Moretti to find out what the hell's going on."

Chapter Forty-Eight

I sat in one of only two wood and glass phone booths in Pine Top, the one located in the hotel lobby, and asked the operator to get me Quinn Walker's house. Leatha Mae answered. "Walker residence."

"Leatha Mae, it's Tom Bell."

"My lands. I just sat down at this telephone table to call you and get somebody to find you. Mr. Walker came in this house without me knowing it. I's up with Miss Mallie and never heard him come in. Ain't no tellin' how long he was here. He just left a minute ago, saw him through the window."

"Do you know where he's going?"

"Nawsir. This time he climbed into that yeller car drove by Mr. Jack Drake. They went off without telling anybody where they's going."

"What make of car is it?"

"Mr. Tom, I don't know nothin' about cars. I can't tell one make from another, but it's the only butter-yeller car I've ever seen."

As I pondered her information, she added something that piqued my interest. "There's one thing about that car, though. I was standing in the upstairs window when they pulled away, and it don't leave tire tracks like other cars."

"How so?"

"One set of tracks is inside the others. They don't line up like a regular car or wagon."

Something itched in the back of my mind. Two sets of tracks. I snapped my fingers. There were similar tread imprints down near where I'd found Hazel's body that first day in town. Then I thought there might have been two cars, but now I realized it was only one, and the likelihood that it was Jack Drake I'd shot in the stomach was very real.

"Anything else you can tell me, Leatha Mae?"

"I heard through the grapevine that Mr. Phillips is dead. Killed in a shooting at your hotel."

"Grapevines work faster than telephones."

"They've been around longer. Is it true?"

"It is." I watched Sheriff Dobbs enter the lobby. "I'll call you later, or send word to me here at the hotel if Walker comes back."

Hanging the receiver back on the hook, I opened the polished wood and glass door and stepped out. Dobbs caught the motion and appeared startled when he recognized it was me.

He scowled. "Official business, but somebody had to come find me at the office. If you hadn't…"

"Wouldn't have made any difference. Those two were shot down while they were waiting on me. Seems suspicious, don't it, after our little talk?"

Dobbs blanched. "You don't think I…" Biting off the remainder of his comment, he glanced around to see if anyone was listening. No one paid attention. They were all watching two men from the funeral home wrap sheets around the leaking bodies.

I stepped close to Sheriff Dobbs, intentionally crowding him. "Looks like this is all coming to a head. Tell me about Jack Drake and a man named Emsworth."

The look on the big man's white face spoke volumes.

"That's what I thought. Give me that six-shooter on your hip. We're going to your office to talk."

Chapter Forty-Nine

Jack Drake nosed the Nash at an angle to the plank sidewalk out front of the Hydroxy Mercantile in Hog Eye. The wide main street bustled, but with less chaos than nearby Pine Top. Men in work clothes bustled in and out of the various buildings, dodging horse-drawn vehicles, cars, and trucks, as they crossed to the other side.

"I'll wait here." Drake killed the engine.

"You understand Moretti's orders, then." Quinn Walker opened the door and put one foot on the ground. His stomach was in a knot, and he swallowed to keep the contents down.

Drake nodded and lit a cigarette.

———

Before they left town, Walker had called Moretti, who took his own sweet time coming to the phone. "Mr. Moretti, this is Quinn Walker."

"You already told my man who you were. That's why I'm talking to you."

"Oh, right, well sir, something happened here and I wanted to find out if you had sent some men to get rid of that Texas Ranger that's hanging around."

"You bet I did. They made it happen, huh?"

"Well," Walker swallowed, "they tried, but it was the wrong guy."

"Who was it?"

"An oil worker, and one of our people. They chewed 'em up pretty good, but the Ranger wasn't with them. Some say he ran away before they started shooting, but I don't know. I didn't see it."

"Son of a bitch!" Glass broke on the other end of the line, and Walker waited for Moretti to come back on. "Did they get Ferras?"

"No, sir. I don't think so."

"How have things down there gotten so tangled up? It should have been a simple job, and your people seem to be the problem."

Shocked, Walker gripped the receiver tight. "It wasn't us. We've been doing all this by the book, that is, until Ferras showed up. Did you know he killed a whole family to get their land?"

There was silence on the other end. "A whole family. Kids?"

"Yessir. And a wife. The whole thing could come unraveled the way he did it."

"Where's Ferras now?"

"I'm not sure. He might be in Hog Eye, messing around with a whore."

"I hate the name of that town. Hog Eye. You hayseeds kill me."

"They're gonna to change the name to Liberty City soon…" Walker trailed off, realizing his entire response was inane.

"I'm tired of all this. My boys will get that Ranger. Don't worry about that. But I'm tired of that hick Ferras. He's more trouble than he's worth, and he won't do what he's told. I want you to rub him out. That's *your* job now if you want to keep breathing."

"I'm not a button man!"

"You are now. Shoot the son of a bitch, or I'll have my crew finish up down there with you. You understand me?"

"Yessir."

"You call me once it's done. I want to hear your voice tell me he's no longer a problem. Understand?"

"I do."

"Good, then I want you in Longview. I'll set up a meeting with Caldwell and you and some people I'm sending down there. Meet them at the…" He spoke to someone out of earshot. "Right, the Daisy Drugstore. We're cleaning all this up right now."

"Cleaning up?"

"You'll see what I'm talking about. My man will give you the lowdown and then you can go back and finish this deal the right way. I have too much money invested in this. Once I get my cash, I'm outta that damn state that's giving me a headache."

Both frightened and relieved, Walker nodded into the phone as if Moretti could see.

"Are you nodding or shaking your head? You still there?"

"I'm here, sir."

"Good, then get it done and let me know when it's finished."

The gangster slammed the phone down, and Walker walked out of the phone booth, terrified at what he'd been ordered to do.

———

Jittery as a new bride, Walker closed the car door and after glancing around for the gangsters who'd killed Gene, stepped up on the sidewalk. A bell tinkled over the door, announcing his arrival. He waited, annoyed by the loud music coming from a radio, until the clerk drifted down the counter. Walker pointed at the speakeasy's entrance.

After throwing a glance out the window, the man rapped on the door, and the judas hole slid back. A few seconds later the door swung open to admit Walker into the dim interior full of customers and cigarette smoke hanging low overhead.

He scanned the room and finally spotted Clete Ferras at a table with a young woman, laughing at something she said. He sobered when Walker approached the table.

"What are you doing here?"

"Looking for you. All hell's broke loose back in Pine Top. We need to go somewhere and talk."

"Who sent you?"

Walker looked around to be sure no one was listening. "No one. Look, we can't talk here."

Skeptical, Clete Ferras came to a decision and tilted a glass, draining the contents. "I'll be back later, baby." He rose and followed Walker out to the car.

When they emerged onto the sidewalk, Drake flicked his cigarette butt out the window. Ferras climbed into the back seat, and as soon as the doors closed, Drake backed the Nash out and drove out of town.

The trio rode in silence until they were back in the country. Walker finally turned to speak over his shoulder. "Something's come up. Gene Phillips is dead. Shot to death in the lobby of the Pine Top Hotel."

Ferras shrugged. "Someone have a beef with that boob?"

"I think he was bumped off by Moretti's men."

"What for?"

"I don't have any idea." Walker shrugged and twisted around with his arm across the seat back to better see Ferras. "There was a driller with him, and he's dead, too."

"You think Moretti's mad at us about something?"

"Maybe. I have an idea. I let him down. He gave me an order

and I didn't follow it, like when he told you to be there when his guys rubbed out that Ranger."

"There was something I had to do." Ferras scowled. "They were supposed to be the best button men in the country. They should have handled it without me."

"You might have made a difference."

"Okay. Maybe. So what do you want me to do about it now?"

Walker shrugged and went cold. It was a moment he saw everything with complete clarity and the fear, anger, and frustration pushed him to his final limit. He turned even more so he could swing a pistol around. At the sight of the .38, Ferras's eyes widened and he had started to raise a hand in defense when Walker shot him three times in the chest with the double-action revolver.

The man shouted at the first impact and jerked at each successive shot. One of the soft-nosed bullets pierced his head, and Ferras fell sideways, already in Hell by the time his head hit the soft material covering the back seat.

Not expecting Walker to shoot Ferras in the car, Drake screamed and nearly skidded off the muddy road and into the bar ditch. His head snapped around to see Ferras lying in the back seat, leaking blood.

He instinctively braked and slid to a stop in the middle of the road. Jumping out of the car, he ran around to the side and yanked the door open and grabbed the body by the lapels. Jerking the limp corpse upright with a grunt, he dragged the man clear and toppled him into the ditch.

"Shit! What are you doing? We were supposed to take him down to the river. You said the Sabine would take his body away."

Spinning around, he saw Walker, white-faced, sitting in the passenger seat, the smoking gun still in his hand and resting on one leg. Drake leaned in and saw three bullet holes in the seat back.

Rubbing a shaking hand over his forehead, Walker finally

found his voice. "I had to do it. I lost my nerve and figured he'd know something was up by the time we got there. I couldn't wait. I had to do it right then."

"But you shot him in my car!" Drake shouted, flinging an arm toward the corpse lying facedown in the ditch. "I have bullet holes in my *seat*. How'n hell am I gonna explain that? And the blood!" He reached in and touched a fingertip to a drop soaking into the cloth seat. "Look at this!

"You said it would be simple. Marry in with someone who had land and we'd be rich in no time. All we had to do was give them a dose of that crap you're getting for them to drink and before long they'd pass away by what looked like natural causes, you said."

Drake's voice rose. "We had someone to do the dirty work, you *said*! Dobbs would cover everything up for us, you *said*! Even Emsworth was in on the deal so it would all be legal on paper, you *said*!

"I got a goddamned hole in my stomach that still leaks blood from that damned Texas Ranger, and if this all comes unraveled they're gonna strap us in Old Sparky and we'll ride the lightning. Shit, man, you don't have a plan for *any* of this!"

Walker leaned out and gagged, bringing up nothing but bile. "Everything's out of control. It's not supposed to happen this way."

Drake rushed around to the driver side and slipped behind the wheel. "We need to get out of here."

"We can't just leave him laying here. Somebody'll remember he got in the car with us."

Hands on the wheel, Drake waited. His voice calmed. "So what do you want to do?"

"Put him in the back seat and dump the body in the bottoms. We're not far from the Sabine. We throw him in, just like we planned."

"Just like *you* planned, but look at him. He's wet, muddy, and leaking blood. It'll get all over the seat. What are we gonna do about that? The first person that looks in the back and sees that mess will know we had something to do with his disappearance."

"We'll figure that out once he's in the river and gone."

Chapter Fifty

Sheriff Dobbs's considerable bulk filled the visitor's chair sitting against the wall across from where he usually sat in the sheriff's office. Hanging his head and with his hands cuffed behind his back, he sat on the edge of the seat. I reached out with a hand and ripped the badge off Dobbs's shirt.

He struggled to stand, and I stopped him by pointing at his nose with my index finger. "Don't!" He sat back, stunned at what was happening.

Pitching the badge into the hat lying crown-down on the desk, I picked up the Colt revolver beside it. Pulling the ejector rod, I flipped the cylinder and slapped five rounds free of the chamber. Slipping the .38 back into its worn holster, I half sat on the desk and crossed my arms.

"I told you I'd get to the bottom of this. A man like you knows good and well Texas Rangers won't quit. You should have left town when I told you. You might have got away up in the territories with me swamped with all this mess. Now, who's behind it all. Is it you?"

Dobbs talked to the floor. "It was the money. The city council don't pay me beans for doing this job, and they have the money to give me a raise. They're tighter'n Dick's hatband, and I deserve more than they'll allow."

"I didn't ask you why. I asked you who."

The sheriff's full face quivered with fear, though the scars on his chin and one cauliflower ear were evidence that the man wasn't a stranger to fists or violence. His eyes flicked up to my face, then back down again, as if he were too embarrassed to speak directly toward me. "They'll kill me if I tell you."

"I've already heard that once today. You'd better spill it before I lose the rest of my temper and kill you myself."

"Look, I'm not afraid of the people here in town, except for Clete Ferras, but those guys from Chicago don't fool around. They'll shoot us all and go have dinner."

The mention of Chicago surprised me. That explained the machine guns, both at the ambush the night before and at the hotel. For the first time in my life, I found myself at a loss for words.

I shifted to better see the window and anyone approaching the office. "What have you gotten into?"

"It was a grift. A con in some ways. They were just gonna pull a little swindle, that's all. Get some names changed on deeds and whatnot, but...but it got worse. A lot more than I'd bargained for."

"*You* kill anyone?"

"No! I wouldn't do that." He deflated even more. "At least *I* didn't. Ferras did, and Drake, I think."

"Well, a man's hypocrisy will only go so far, I guess. Spill it, and look me in the eye when you do. I'm not laying on the floor."

Dobbs's shoulders squared and he straightened up in the chair. He talked fast for the next five minutes, so fast I couldn't keep up with the names and incidents. Like opening a water hydrant, information poured from the sheriff, who knew what would happen to him when he went to prison. While he talked a blue streak, I rounded the desk and took names and notes with a chewed pencil.

The flow slowed to a trickle, and the former sheriff finally trailed off. "I think that's all I know."

The pencil stub needed sharpening by the time he finished. "No it ain't. I need the head of this snake. You haven't told me the name of who's running it."

Dobbs licked his lips. "O. L. Caldwell in Longview, but he answers to a guy named Moretti."

"I can find Caldwell. Where's this Moretti?"

"Right now he's in Hot Springs, or that's what I've heard."

"Who's the bootlegger?"

"That I *don't* know. Drake's in charge of that part of the deal. Any time I bust a still, I have to check with Drake to make sure they're not our people."

"What's in the whiskey?"

Dobbs shrugged. "A little bit of something called oleander in it, a plant of some kind, I guess."

"Slide down and sit there on the floor."

"Can't I have a chair? I'm a big man. It'll be hard for me to get up."

"It'll be even harder to get up if I knock you down. Now do it."

Knees popping, Dobbs squatted and then dropped the last few inches to sit on the floor with his legs splayed out. I picked up the phone and dialed one number. "Operator, Florence? Good. Give me Doc Patton's office."

I waited as she plugged the phone plug into the appropriate jack. A moment later a male voice came through. "Ahoy-hoy."

His greeting almost made me smile. Alexander Graham Bell, the inventor of the telephone, suggested that was the appropriate way to answer a phone. However, Thomas Edison preferred to answer hello, and that one stuck. Patton had a sense of humor.

"Doctor Patton, this is Tom Bell. We met on Quinn Walker's porch."

"I know. How can I help you?"

"I think I have some news you can use. I just heard from a source that someone is putting oleander in wood alcohol. I think that might be what's going on with Quinn Walker's wife, making her sick. Does that give you something to go on?"

A heavy sigh came through the receiver. "It does. Mr. Bell, you might have saved that woman's life. I suspected the wood alcohol, but never in a million years would I have figured out the oleander poisoning was added in. This information came before it was too late."

"It's fatal, then."

"Oleander is highly toxic, but it usually reacts quickly. If what you're saying is true, then whoever is providing it has figured out a way to mix this poison in extremely small doses so that it works much slower."

"I'll figure that out later. I just wanted you to know."

"I'll go over there right now. By the time I'm finished cleaning her out, she'll be up and around in a day or two. Mr. Bell, you saved that woman's life, and maybe a couple of others. Ruby Phillips and Calpurnia Drake."

"Those names are familiar."

"Are they? Well, I have to go." With that abrupt announcement, he hung up.

I replaced the receiver and thought for several long seconds before making up my mind. "Stand up."

"What're you gonna do?"

"I plan to give you a taste of Ranger Delgado's trotline."

Chapter Fifty-One

Gravel crunched under the Nash's tires as Drake drove in silence through the pines. Occasionally, the hardwoods growing on both sides of the road met over the middle, creating dark, leafy caverns that gave way to more pastures.

A packed-dirt road covered in fallen leaves veered off to the right, and he slowed, steering carefully through the narrowing channel. Youpon hollies and berry vines crowded the car, making him feel as if he were actually driving through the woods instead of following what wasn't much more than a pig trail.

Now that the initial shock was over, Walker finally took a deep breath to speak. "We're getting close to the river."

"Anywhere here is fine." Drake looked around as if there might be people peering at them from behind the trees.

"I don't want to dump him out on the road where somebody can find him. There's a turnaround not far from the water."

The trees thickened the closer they got to the Sabine, but at some point in the distant past, someone had cut down several trees right on the bank for a campground. It was big enough that Drake could steer around a blackened firepit. He killed the engine parallel to the river, which was moving heavy and sluggish several feet below. Much of the understory brush had been cleared away to make fishing easier.

He opened the trunk and was startled by Ferras's white face and one dry eye that seemed to be watching him. Walker joined him, and they grunted the limp body from the back. Shuffling and huffing, they dragged Ferras's body to the edge of the river that was so high it had eaten away at the bank.

Relieved that they wouldn't have to roll it down to the water, Walker took a better hold under the body's arms. "All right, on three, we swing him out into the water."

Drake nodded and counted. "One, two, three!"

They let go at the same time, and Ferras splashed into the current that immediately took him downstream. They watched in horror as he only went a few feet before tangling in a sub-merged bush jutting from the bank.

"Now what are we gonna do?" Drake voice sounded as if he were close to crying.

"Nothing. Wait."

The limbs that caught Ferras's jacket finally lost their hold, and he spun out away from the bank. The muddy water took hold, and the body soon floated out of sight.

More relieved than he cared to admit, Walker straightened and grinned. "That wasn't so bad, was it?"

"I still have bullet holes and blood in the seat."

"I have that figured out. We go to my house, get my shotgun, and come back down to the river someplace. I angle the shotgun in the back seat and pull the trigger like it went off by accident. Bang! And no more bullet holes."

"What about the blood?"

"We get some water and scrub it down. Nobody'll think nothing of it. They'll be too impressed with how close one of us came to getting killed while we were out hunting. I'll pay for the new seat, and we're home free."

Drake took a deep, relieved breath and straightened his shoulders. "Even back when we were kids, you always could figure things out."

"That's right." Walker clapped him on the shoulder and gave a harsh laugh. "One more problem out of the way, and, before you know it, you are I are gonna be living in the lap of luxury."

Chapter Fifty-Two

The gray clouds over Pine Top quit weeping, giving the town some relief.

In the flat light, I snapped a padlock into place and stood back to study the situation. A short trace chain linked the handcuffs on Sheriff Dobbs's wrists, his *own* handcuffs, to the heavy log chain Iron Eyes Delgado put into place months earlier.

Sitting on the wet ground, four other prisoners were spaced several feet apart, and they looked on with interest after recognizing the sheriff. The nearest man with uncombed hair and a scraggly beard barked a laugh. "Look what's on the trotline today."

Dobbs frosted me with a furious glare, but there was nothing he could do but sit there as water soaked the seat of his pants and wait for what came next.

"Dobbs, I'll be back directly with another'n. I'd advise you not to talk to anyone about any of this."

"You don't have to do this, Bell."

"Yes, I do, and you're lucky this is *all* I'm doing right now."

Without a backward glance, I walked away from the crowd gathering around the former lawman, who sulled up and refused to make eye contact with anyone.

Walking fast to bleed off anger and energy, I made my way down to the Pine Top Bank and Trust. Located on the intersection of Main and First streets, the building's fan-shaped lobby widened from the glass door in the corner. To the right was an office protected from prying eyes by frosted glass on the door with gold letters reading PRESIDENT.

A guard stood watch only a few feet away. "Texas Ranger. Here on business, so you keep that six-shooter in your holster. No matter what happens."

The stocky man took in the situation in a flash, paying particular attention to the Ranger badge. "Yessir. Anything I can do to help?"

"Stay right there and hold this door for me when I leave." I crossed the lobby, ignoring the tellers who watched with interest. Without knocking, I twisted the knob and burst in to find a weaselly banker with oiled hair leaning back in a wooden desk chair, fingers laced across his stomach.

On my side of the polished desk was a dejected gray-haired farmer who slumped in his chair. The workingman jerked upright when I blew through the door, almost dropping his sweat-stained hat. Feeling sorry for the man, because I suspected why he was there, I held out a hand to keep him seated.

The banker jumped to his feet in outrage and pointed a finger at the open door. "See here! You can't just come barging…"

"You Emsworth?"

"I'm bank *President* Albert Emsworth, and who are you to come charging in here this way?"

Like vengeance under a Stetson, I circled the desk and grabbed the man by the lapels. Slapping him hard, more for effect than anything else, I yanked the vulture around to slam him into the wall. A framed diploma fell, the glass shattering at their feet.

"Texas Ranger. You're under arrest."

Emsworth's face went deathly white. "What for?"

"Everything I can think of." One hand full of lapel, I spun the bank president around and pushed him back against the wall as the farmer escaped the office, face alight with pleasure.

"Who are you, and what is this?"

I cuffed his hands behind his back and said, "Name's Tom Bell, and I suspect you know exactly why I'm here, or your mouth wouldn't be opening and closing like a fish out of water."

He gasped for air as I pushed him through the office and into the lobby where several customers and bank employees had collected to see what was going on.

With one hand full of the back of Emsworth's coat collar, I shoved him toward the entrance. As requested, the guard turned the knob and held the door as we passed, nodding. "Have a good day, sir."

"It's getting better."

———

I frog-walked Emsworth to the courthouse while he sputtered and complained all the way. Once there, the bank president's shaking legs gave way, and he collapsed to the ground. I snapped a padlock through the trace chain and the handcuffs.

"You can't do this to me! I have rights!"

"Yes, you do, but right now you're gonna set right here until I get back."

It was then that he looked to his left to see Sheriff Dobbs several feet away, and realization swept in. "Oh, no."

Dobbs struggled upright, his face red with fury. "You have no warrant for arrest. You're holding me and Emsworth without legal authority."

"Been thinking while I was gone, huh?" I took a long, deep breath to study my handiwork. "I'll have the paperwork in less than an hour, so sit there and be quiet."

Emsworth sputtered at the former sheriff. "It was you who got us into this. Fix it!"

"Shut up, you idiot."

"You can't tell me to shut up!" Emsworth kicked at Dobbs, who was out of reach.

Even so, Dobbs kicked back at the little banker. "Don't say a word until we get a lawyer, you fool." The air went out of Dobbs's anger. His voice lowered as he looked around at the onlookers watching the action. "Look, Bell, I'm out here in the open with no way to protect myself. I've put a lot of people in jail over the years and some of 'em are likely to be right here. What if someone wants to get even?"

Hearing that comment, Emsworth moaned. "Good Lord. You don't know how many people are mad at me, too. I've had to foreclose on farms and call in loans. It wouldn't take but one vengeful man with an ice pick to settle up."

"You might have a good point. Dobbs. How many deputies do you have? You do have deputies, don't you?"

"I do. There are four, but only two are on duty, Bill Rollins and Sam Knott."

"Where are they?"

"How'n hell do I know? Out working somewheres."

Thinking and fiddling with my mustache, I turned to survey the men gathered around. "Anyone know where Deputies Rollins or Knott might be?"

"I do."

I almost laughed at the familiar adolescent voice as Booker pushed through the circle.

"Howdy, Deputy. How's Hut?"

"Miss Ambrosia's fixing him up. Said he'll be right as rain soon as that busted wing heals up."

"Fine then. Where are those deputies I still haven't laid eyes on?"

"Well, Bill Rollins is usually hanging out over at Timmon's Meat Market, and Sam Knott's likely at the Blackstone Café next to the Rex Theater."

"The meat market?"

"Yessir. Mr. Bill's half owner there."

"Which is closest?"

"Sam Knott at the picture show."

"Hie on over there and bring him back. Tell him I said to hurry."

Booker took off like a shot, and I addressed the gathering. "You men, pass the word. I'm a Texas Ranger. These men are my prisoners as much as if they were in a jail cell. The first man who lays a hand on them, or interferes with these arrests, will find themselves chained up here, too, and I can promise you, I'll make damn sure that they find themselves on a work detail down in Huntsville along with these two, if they're lucky."

Emsworth moaned. "I can't go to prison."

A farmer waved his hand. "What'd they do?"

"Broke the law." Not inclined to answer any questions, I held the man's gaze until he looked away.

Five minutes later, Deputy Sam Knott arrived, led by Booker. The man slid to a stop at the sight of the sheriff and bank president cuffed like the others on the trotline. "What'n hell?"

"They're my prisoners."

Knott grinned and reached into his shirt pocket for a plug of chewing tobacco. "Never thought I'd see the day. What do you want me to do?"

"Get your shotgun and stand guard over all these prisoners until I get back. I don't want any of them injured."

"You bet. Where you going?"

"To get some arrest warrants," I nodded toward the courthouse, "and then pick up a few more people."

Chapter Fifty-Three

Jack Drake saw a crowd blocking the street ahead and turned off Main to make his way toward Quinn Walker's house. "Wonder what's going on over there?"

"Probably somebody stuck in the mud, or a fight. Hell, these roughnecks spend most of their time drinking, screwing, and fighting."

They drove two blocks before turning onto Walker's street. Drake killed the engine in front of Walker's house and sighed. "Thank God that's over."

"It's not. I need to get that shotgun." He jerked a thumb over his shoulder. "Once that's done, *then* we can relax."

Before he could open the door, a neighbor passing on the sidewalk saw the two of them in the car and stopped. "Howdy, Quinn."

"Hello, Buford." He didn't want to talk, but decided he had to be neighborly before sending the man on his way. "Where you headed?"

He pointed. "Down to the courthouse. Have you heard the news?"

"No. What news?"

"Sheriff Dobbs and bank president Emsworth's on Ranger Delgado's trotline."

Again that now-familiar feeling of terror washed over Walker. He glanced over at Drake, who sat there openmouthed. He drew a deep breath to settle his voice. "What'd Delgado arrest them for?"

"Wasn't him. There's another Texas Ranger in town. Tom Bell. Nobody knows why, but he hauled Dobbs over first and cuffed him to the trotline, then went away for a while and came back with Emsworth. They say he slapped him around first, but now he's cuffed there, too. I heard he's gone again, after someone else, but nobody knows who."

While the man talked, Walker chewed the inside of his lip to get some saliva flowing so he could speak. Choking down his fear, he nodded as if considering the news. "Wonder who he's after now?"

"Well, I don't know. Since them gangsters shot up the Pine Top Hotel, I figure he's on a roll. It'll probably be the shooters themselves. Can you imagine Dobbs and Emsworth chained up with gangsters? What's this town coming to?"

Buford slapped a hand on the windowsill to punctuate his point and walked away.

Drake checked up and down the street before turning to Walker. "What do you want to do?"

"Get the hell away from here for a while."

"My house?"

"Hell, no! I meant get out of town."

"If you tell Mallie, I gotta tell Calpurnia."

"No! We don't tell anybody." Walker looked behind them. "Drive."

As Drake pulled away, Walker slumped in the seat. "Dobbs probably won't talk, but that little weasel Emsworth'll spill his guts in a second. Right now that Ranger's out looking for us, or Ferras. We have to get out of here."

"But where? We can't leave all we've worked for here."

"We have two choices. Hope that Ranger doesn't have our names yet. If that's the case, then we can figure out where he's going and kill him."

"You're talking out of your head. We can't kill a Texas Ranger. They've already tried it and see where it got us?"

"Fine then. The other choice is to get the hell out of here." Walker snapped his fingers. "He's already arrested Emsworth. Drive us to the bank; he won't be going back there right away. We'll empty out our accounts. That'll give us traveling money."

"You can't close out an account that big without the bank president signing off on it."

"Dammit! I didn't think of that." His heart sank at the thought of all that money he couldn't touch. The house, the other properties and deals they'd been working on, all gone up in smoke. Now that dumb wife of his would be rich and not know what to do with it at all.

"It's over, then."

"No, it's not. We're supposed to meet Caldwell at the Daisy Drugstore in Longview tomorrow. Moretti's sending someone down to talk with us. They'll know what to do."

"And then what?"

"We do like we're told."

Chapter Fifty-Four

An hour later I left the municipal courthouse with warrants for Walker and Drake, along with the paperwork for Dobbs and Emsworth. The sidewalk and street were jam-packed with onlookers squeezing forward to get a look at their former sheriff.

The skies were still gray, but nothing had fallen for several hours, sparking hope in everyone that their little spell of bad weather was almost over. The new had worn off the sight of Sheriff Dobbs in cuffs, so the crowd of onlookers around Delgado's trotline had dissipated.

Deputy Knott was there where I left him, keeping watch over the prisoners with a pump shotgun cradled in his left arm. Young Booker Johnston stood close, as if he'd been assigned a duty. Both Dobbs and Emsworth sat dejected, barely acknowledging my return. "Howdy, Sam. Any trouble?"

"None to speak of. A couple of fools came by to spit on Emsworth. I believe he'd foreclosed on their farms, but for the life of me I can't understand why anyone would spit on a person. It ain't decent."

"Civilization is gauze-thin and even more fragile. We're half a second away from total anarchy at all times, so I'm not surprised."

"Anarchy?"

"I'll explain it later. Where's the other deputy...Rollins, is it?"

"Right. Bill Rollins. Haven't seen him." Knott indicated with his head for me to follow, leading away from everyone. We stopped halfway between the road and the municipal courthouse. "Sir, I doubt you've heard, but there's talk that Bill is fairly close to Sheriff Dobbs, if you know what I mean."

"I think I do. You're saying I chose the right man to guard our prisoners."

"I ain't saying for sure, but I'm glad it was me here, else the sheriff might have slipped his cuffs."

I thought back. At no time during his discussion with Dobbs did he mention Bill Rollins as part of their criminal organization. "What's Bill done?"

"Nothing much, and that's the problem. He's half owner of Timmon's Meat Market, and though he ain't the kind to rob someone, he's not above a certain amount of larceny. He tends to look the other way when something happens, if you know what I mean. A little cash in his pocket will go a long way toward keeping his mouth closed."

That comment prompted a question. "Y'all shutting down any stills around here that Rollins might have been involved in?"

"Nossir. Not that I know of. Like I said, Bill spends a lot of time hanging around the meat market and don't often get off the street here in town. I remember once when Sheriff Dobbs sent him out to make an arrest east of town. Bill bucked and snorted about it, saying that was work for the constable out there. He went after a while and they brought the man to town, but he'druther not get his hands dirty, if you know what I mean."

"Do you *know* of any stills operating around here?"

"Well, I know of stills, but if I was to go looking for one of them, it'd be hard to find. These old boys been at this a long time, and they're hid back up in the woods. Now, a constable, like I mentioned, would have a better idea of where one might be operating."

"Quinn Walker and Jack Drake. You ever have any dealings with them?"

"Yessir. I know 'em both. Businessmen here in town."

"I have warrants for both of them."

A raised eyebrow was his comment.

"All right. Here's what I want you to do. You have a car?"

"Yessir. The county give us three."

"Load Dobbs and Emsworth up and take 'em to Longview for me. Let Rollins know what's happening so he can keep watch over Pine Top best he can. I don't want to leave this town without some law in place. I'm gonna telegraph the Ranger headquarters in Austin."

"Will do. Now?"

"Yeah, we need to get those two out of here. You can't stand guard over 'em all night, and I want them both locked up safe and secure."

"Then what?"

"I'll tell you when I know something. Here's the warrants for those two. Stick these in your pocket until I get back with these others." He waved several more papers.

"Be glad to." Sam chewed at a wad of tobacco in his check. "How long you reckon they'll be here?"

"Until I get back."

A newspaper photographer snapped a photo, and a reporter with a notepad stepped in front of me. "Ranger Bell. Ben Klarner, *Pine Top News Messenger*. Can you give me a statement for the paper, sir? Why are the sheriff and bank president on Delgado's trotline? Is Deputy Knott an arresting officer also? What's going on?"

"What's going on is simple. These men are under arrest."

"What for?"

"For getting in my way."

Klarner blanched and stepped to the side. "What kind of investigation is this? Are there others that you intend to arrest? Neither Sheriff Dobbs or Mr. Emsworth will give me a statement."

"Well, at least they're finally showing a little sense." I pushed past the man. "I'd suggest you leave them alone until I'm finished."

"Finished what?"

"Dispensing justice." I paused at the sight of Ranger Delgado making his way down the street and waited until he stopped beside the sheriff. "Enrique."

The slender Ranger studied the scenario without expression, his cold eyes taking in every person gathered around. "Looks like a lot's happened since I been gone. Why're Dobbs and the bank president on my trotline?"

Deputy Knott passed him the arrest warrants and spat a stream of tobacco juice dangerously close to Dobbs, who glared up at him. Delgado studied them before speaking. "Looks like a lot was going on right under my nose."

"Well, you weren't sent here to clean *this* mess up. You've been busy with the oil workers."

"There was a crime going on and I missed it. You found it, and *you're* after Clete Ferras."

"Yep, and I almost missed it, too." I pointed at Booker. "My young deputy there's helped more than anyone else."

Delgado scanned the crowd. "Any trouble from these people?"

"Nope. Deputy Knott there's gonna ventilate anybody who messes with our prisoners. Here's the other arrest warrants. I'm going after these guys."

"You need help?"

"Naw. There's only about six or eight of 'em."

"Good." Delgado said. "Walk with me."

Chapter Fifty-Five

When Enrique Delgado and I were a distance from the courthouse, we walked side by side. The older, more experienced Ranger cut his eyes at me. "Tom, I heard what happened last night. The folks over at the boardinghouse couldn't wait to tell me. They say you had feelings for that little gal. I'm sorry."

"I did."

"You're after justice. Is it to uphold the law?"

Surprised, I almost missed a stride, making a little stutter step before catching back up. "Why do you ask?"

"Because of that badge on your shirt. God will sort it out in the end with divine justice, but if you're on the hunt, it has to be legal in the eyes of Texas law."

"Both, I guess, but I'm afraid I'll be stretching it a little anyway. One of those names on my list is O. L. Caldwell over in Longview, and the other is a Chicago gangster by name of Cherubino Moretti who's in Hot Springs right now."

"You could telegraph Hot Springs and have Moretti picked up."

"You know as well as I do the law there is corrupt. I've heard stories that they have the police department in their pockets, and no one'll touch them."

"I've heard that, too."

We came to Delgado's boardinghouse and stepped up onto the porch. There were half a dozen rocking chairs there, along with a porch swing. We took the two rockers at the far end. "So what do you intend to do?"

"I'll pick Caldwell up. That shouldn't be any problem."

"And Moretti?"

"I'll cross that bridge when I come to it."

"I doubt they'll go down without a fight."

"You may be right, but if I send word to the laws up there and tell 'em I'm on the way, him and those men of his'll head back up to Chicago, sure as shootin'. Dobbs told me Ferras has been working for Moretti, too, and that he may be headed to Hot Springs to meet up with them. Maybe that'll get me in without those gangsters knowing about it."

"I wouldn't bet my life on it."

"I won't. But before I do that, I suspect there are a couple of their thugs still here. Did anyone tell you about what happened at the Pine Top Hotel this morning?"

"They did. You don't think they're gone?"

"I don't know. They may be. They were after me, but killed the wrong man. Maybe they left without finding out. I mean, who would they talk to or ask? They didn't stop by Dobbs's office, I believe him about that. Men like that stick out like sore thumbs."

Delgado rocked, thinking. "You want me to go to Hot Springs with you?"

"I could use the help, but one of us crossing state lines without *official* authorization from the governor is enough."

"Even though you're going up there after Ferras, you're liable to lose your badge."

"I don't intend to let them go home."

"Hang on a minute." Delgado stood and went inside. I rocked, forcing myself to relax while I had the chance, and wondering what he went in for. Minutes later, the Ranger came outside, using one boot heel to keep the screen from slamming. In his hands was something I'd heard about, but never seen.

"Is that what I think it is?"

Delgado held it out with both hands, as if offering to help me turn around and slip it on. "I 'magine. It's a Dunrite Bulletproof Vest. Made by the Detective Publishing Company in Chicago."

The pinstriped wool vest was lighter than I expected, though in my estimation it weighed close to fifteen pounds. The elastic straps on the back were adjustable to better fit the wearer. Surprisingly stylish, it could be worn unnoticed under a suit coat. "This thing really stop a bullet?"

"Most, they say. Saw one demonstrated once. A guy with a .38 six-shooter stood about five feet way and shot the man wearing it in the left side of the chest. He barely flinched."

"Steel plates. Two in front and a big one in back. Guess they figured someone might need it if they were running away."

"That wouldn't be us. Take it, but I wouldn't walk into something heavy like that .45 on your hip, or a Thompson, and expect to wake up the next morning. And in my opinion, it won't turn a 30.06, neither. At best it's just a little extra protection. Anything else I can do to help?"

"Not that I can think of right now. I'm gonna have Deputy Knott take Dobbs and Emsworth to jail in Longview. I don't want them sitting outside on that chain for much longer. Somebody might come by and shoot 'em before they have a chance to testify. While he's doing that, I intend to track down Quinn Walker and Jack Drake."

"I can help you with that part. I have a few honey holes around here that might be holding those two, even though they're locals." Delgado rocked again, watching the street. We fell silent when a man left the boardinghouse and nodded howdy and we responded the same way.

Once he was gone, Delgado tapped the arm of the chair with a forefinger. "You know, Tom. I have a feeling that Rangering is about to change. Last time I was in Austin, I heard rumblings that our organization is liable to back Ross Sterling, who's making noise about running for governor next year. If that happens and Ma Ferguson wins again, she's gonna be pretty damn sore."

"She's running again?"

"Says she is."

Miriam A. Ferguson, or Ma as she was known, served as a controversial governor from 1925 to 1927, and made no bones about disliking the Rangers, who swung a wide loop that came dangerously close to putting her crooked husband behind bars.

Delgado paused, thinking. "I know for a fact that she don't much like us, saying we run too free and easy with what we do, but that's how us Rangers have always been, and that's why we're so effective. I'm afraid she'll disband us all if she gets in, and if that happens, you and me and the rest of us will be looking for work. I was talking to Frank Hamer in Huntsville yesterday, and he says if she wins in '32, he's gonna resign. Frank Hamer, one of the best Rangers I've ever known."

"What're you telling me?"

"Just what I said. You have time to think about it."

A well-dressed man came up the walk and went inside. Once he was out of earshot, I stood, holding the vest. "Enrique, if the Rangers aren't around in a couple of years, this state's going to hell. I don't like Ma Ferguson one damn bit, but she'll win.

"I'm headed to Longview to lock up Caldwell, and then I'm going to Hot Springs. I may or may not have a job when I get back, but after what you just told me, I think none of us will be

Rangering pretty soon." I stepped off the porch. "Many thanks for the gift."

"You bet."

I stopped on the sidewalk and nodded back at Delgado, a man I'd admired from the first moment I met him a several years earlier. "I think I'm doing what you'd do in my situation."

Delgado's voice floated over the quiet, shaded yard. "Yep, and that's what worries me."

Chapter Fifty-Six

Someone rapped on my door as fast as a woodpecker only a minute after I was back in the Pine Top Hotel. Standing to the side and avoiding the bullet holes that were still in the shiny wood, I opened the door with one hand, holding the .45 in his other.

It was Booker. "Mr. Bell. Troubles."

"What kind?"

"The bank president, Mr. Emsworth, was shot dead in front of the courthouse."

"Dammit!" I hurried to the bed for my coat. "What happened?"

"A car pulled up to the trotline and someone shot 'em to pieces from a car, but that ain't the worst."

"What?"

"They shot Deputy Knott, too. He's hurt bad, and they took the sheriff."

"Who did? How many men?"

Booker followed me, both of us almost trotting down the hall. "Four, at least that's what I heard."

"How'd they get them cuffs off Dobbs?" We took the stairs two at a time, anxious to reach the scene. "I have the only key to that padlock, and it run through the links of both chains."

Booker ran behind. "They didn't unlock it. Mr. Bell. They left his hands behind."

————

It was chaos on the street. A black Ford with yellow wheels was pulled up to the curb, with the back door open on the sidewalk side, presumably Deputy Knott's vehicle to transport the two prisoners. A wide bloodstain on the ground and splatter on the cloth seat was evidence of where Knott had stood when he was gunned down.

His shotgun lay on the ground. I picked it up and checked the loads. He'd gotten off one round. A man in a light-colored shirt and slacks stepped forward. "You must be Tom Bell. I'm Deputy Bill Rollins."

"I've heard of you. Where were you when this happened?"

"I wasn't quite here yet. Heard the shots and got here just as a car took off."

"You get a look at the shooters?"

"Nossir. Like I said, I was just coming up. I've talked to several witnesses who saw it. They say there were four men."

"What kind of description did you get?"

"Well dressed. City people. Machine guns. All of 'em hard dark hair under dress hats."

Booker chimed in. "Two of 'em were in overcoats. One gray and one brown." My little deputy was observant.

It was a terrible, bloody scene. Two gray, ham-sized hands lay on the walk beside empty handcuffs. Only feet away was Emsworth's leaking corpse with both arms held upright by the chain. I counted at least a dozen holes in the man.

The other prisoners on the trotline sat silent and pale in shock.

"Somebody's cleaning house here, Rollins. Let me tell you this, buddy. If I find out there's any connection between you and these people, I'm not taking you to jail. I'll put you in a shallow grave somewhere. Do you hear what I'm saying?"

Rollins swallowed. "Sir, I just didn't get here in time."

"I know where you were." Dismissing the deputy, I turned toward the oil workers gathered around. "Who saw what happened here?"

One man stepped forward. "I did, sir."

"Who're you?"

"Buford Hill."

"Tell me."

"I's just passing by when I saw the crowd. Didn't know the sheriff was on the chain, but when I got here, that deputy who was shot had opened the back door and was digging in his pocket for something when a car with two bad men pulled up. One of 'em got out and opened up on the deputy and Mr. Emsworth."

"You knew Emsworth?"

"Yessir. His bank took my farm, so I had to go to work on the rigs. Anyways, one guy in a gray overcoat shot them fellers and went over to the sheriff, who was a-squalling like a little baby. The other one held a big gun on him and they started to shoot, but I heard one of 'em say they needed to talk to him. About what, I don't know, but the one in the brown coat said they didn't have much time, so he went back to the car and opened the turtle hull and came out with something like I ain't never seen before."

Hill took a breath, spat, and worked a chew back into his cheek. "Long, wide blade, sharp as a razor, I reckon, because he gave one swing on each wrist and them hands fell off smooth as silk."

"It was a sugarcane cutter." An oil worker chimed in. "Saw

'em used down in Louisiana and south Arkansas. That's what it was, all right."

Hill nodded, as if they'd already discussed it. "The other feller tied ropes around his wrists, I reckon so he wouldn't bleed to death, and they stuffed what was left of him in the back of the car and took off."

"Which way'd they go?"

The witness and several others pointed northeast.

Chapter Fifty-Seven

The next morning dawned clear and cool. Fall had officially arrived in East Texas, and the busy streets seemed even more chaotic. The blue sky covered the piney woods for the first time in days, filling the world with autumn light and bringing color to the world so bright it didn't look natural. I stared downward from the window, watching the mass of men, vehicles, wagons, and horses pass by on their way to hundreds of destinations.

Slipping on my coat, I settled my hat and walked down the stairs to the lobby to find the day clerk leaning on the counter watching two colored men on their knees scrubbing the floor clean of yesterday's blood and matter. "Morning, Mr. Bell."

"Howdy."

The desk clerk turned and plucked something from the room cubby. "I have a couple of messages for you."

"Many thanks." Taking the slips of paper, I started toward my usual table, but paused. Though they were doing their best to erase all signs of bloodstains, splintered pockmarks in the dark wood from the chopper squad's bullets almost glowed.

The desk clerk noticed. "Uh, I have a man coming today to fix those."

"Is he gonna get around to my room, too?"

He swallowed. "Yessir."

Intent on the flowing script on the top note, I took a seat against the wall on the opposite side of the lobby. Seconds later, Booker came inside and perched on a chair next to me. I noted the boy's bare feet and the frayed hem of his overalls. "Morning Deputy. It's cold outside. Where are your shoes?"

"Morning sir. Outgrew 'em, and they hurt my feet. Daddy says I'll get a new pair for Christmas. This may be the last day I can see you. Daddy says once the fields dry out I'm going back to work."

"I imagine that's about right. Did you eat, yet?"

"Yessir. Had some bacon in a biscuit this morning and then rode in with Uncle Dan. He figures to pull a few more cars out of the mud today with his mules, then they'll go on back to the field, too."

"Good. Let me read these messages."

The first note was from Dr. Patton.

Ranger Tom Bell,

Just wanted to drop you a note saying that based on your information, I have taken the appropriate actions to treat Mrs. Mallie Walker. She has already responded with significantly better results and I feel that she will be fine in a day or two. It is my theory that the dosage she'd received was light, but cumulative. Oleander is extremely poisonous, and even the water in a vase full of blooms is dangerous. Good luck with your investigation.

P.S. The other two ladies I've treated were, I believe,

suffering from similar poisoning. Though I don't know for sure who provided the tainted alcohol, I believe their poisoning too was also intentional.

P.S.S. Deputy Knott is in good condition and I feel he will fully recover.

Doctor Walter H. Patton, M.D.

The second note was from Mallie herself.

Ranger Bell, thank you for saving my life. I would have died if not for your visit. You are a godsend. I have to confess now that my head is clear that I lied. Leatha Mae did not supply the whiskey like I said. I was trying to shield my sorry husband, but now that I know from the doctor what he did, I want to come clean. You can find my soon to be ex-husband at the Daisy Drugstore in Longview, which is really a blind pig. He won't be coming back here, because Leatha Mae's brother is here with a shotgun and has orders to shoot him if he comes through the front door with those damned flowers again. Yours truly, Mallie.

Flowers.

I'd noticed fresh flowers on the dining room table while me and Leatha Mae talked.

"Booker. Run over to Mallie Walker's house and tell her housekeeper Leatha Mae to throw all the flowers away that were on the dining room table, and any others like them in the house, and then pour the water out because it's likely poison. Got that?"

The youngster repeated the message verbatim.

"Good. Go fast."

Booker started for the door and I called him back. "Yessir?"

I opened my billfold and handed him twenty dollars. "This is for your service up to today. Take it and go buy yourself some shoes, socks, and a couple of new pairs of overalls. You have a coat?"

"Well, yessir, but it's a little short in the sleeves. It's from two years ago."

I felt Charlotte's presence at my side and knew what she wanted. I pulled out two more twenties, more money than Booker had likely ever seen at one time in his life. "Get you a coat, and a couple of new shirts. Then give Hut that same amount of money you spend, for him to get the same thing. Got it?"

His eyes were wide as saucers. "Yessir, but there'll be some left over."

"Give half to your dad, and half to Hut's daddy. He has one, don't he?"

"Yessir."

"Good. Make sure you do all that. How's he doing today?"

"I heard he's fine. I reckon I'll see him soon enough."

"Fine then. I'm leaving town soon, so I'll look you up when I get back."

He hesitated, and I grinned. "One more thing, you've made a fine deputy. Maybe that's what you can do when you get grown, or you might make a Ranger."

"I'd love that!"

"Me too. Now, hoof it on out of here and do your business."

Like I ordered, he hoofed it out of the hotel. I caught the desk clerk's attention. "Is there a flower shop here in town?"

"Nossir."

"Thanks." I studied on the answer for a minute. "Wait, if I was to want to send flowers to a girl, or a funeral, how would I do that?"

"Well, sir, lots of folks grow their own, so you might find somebody with a nice flower garden and ask them if you could cut some."

"Is there anyone in town that might have a lot of flowers around their house?"

He thought for a moment. "You know, there's a place out on the north side of town where Mr. Leonard Perkins sells some from time to time. We have an old negro healer here that gets some of her herbs and roots from him, too."

"Miss Ambrosia?"

"Why, that's right."

"You ever hear of oleander?"

"Why, I sure have. Mr. Perkins had a couple of big oleander bushes in his front yard, I believe. Big red flowers that sure are pretty."

"Whereabouts is his house?"

———

I borrowed Ranger Enrique Delgado's car and found the house easily enough, following the desk clerk's directions to go north of town after turning left at the oil workers' camp, then four miles to a tin barn with a Guernsey cow in the lot on the east side and turn right. The house sat in a grove of pine trees, surrounded by large shrubs and a flow of blooming fall flowers.

I pulled up the drive and tapped the horn in case Leonard Perkins had a dog, which he did. A liver and white German shorthair came from under the porch and tuned up to announce my arrival.

A slender man bent by age opened the screen door and stepped onto the porch, hitching up a pair of Hercules wool pants that had seen better days. "Shut up, Sally! Get out and come on up here. She won't bite."

Taking the man for his word, I stepped out of car. "I believe you might be Mr. Perkins."

"I am, sir. How can I help you?"

"By answering a few questions." I paused to rub the bird dog's head, and then stopped at the porch steps. Flowers and shrubs grew all around the house, giving it a homey feel. To the side was a huge garden planted with fall vegetables. "Mr. Leonard, I understand you have some oleander bushes."

"Yessir. You're the law?"

"I am. Texas Ranger. Name's Tom Bell, and I was wondering if you get much call for oleander blooms."

"I sure do, this time of the year. They sure are purty and right smart of folks like to decorate with them."

"You know they're dangerous, right?"

"'Course I do, but I don't have any kids, and Sally don't mess with 'em. I sell lots of blooms, but I tell everyone to keep them away from little ones and pets, though I don't believe I've ever seen a kid chew on 'em before." He chuckled and wiped his large nose with a handkerchief. "Little ones'll chew on anything else, though."

"You know the names of your customers?"

"Mostly. Ever' now and then somebody I don't know'll come by."

"Anyone regular?"

"Sure. Miss Ambrosia buys the herbs she can't grow on her own." He chuckled. "Some folks just can't raise certain things. I have a cousin that can't raise a radish to save his life. I dig roots in the woods, too. Miss Ambrosia caint get down and dig like she used to, neither, but I can still root like a hog."

"I've heard of her. Anyone else?"

"Jack Drake's been coming around a while. Buys 'em for his wife, I believe."

"Anyone else a regular?"

"Art Stevens, Miss Rosemany Minx, Dretha Plummer. Those are the only ones I can think of right now."

I started back to the car. "Much obliged, sir."

"You bet. You need some flowers?"

All the energy drained from my body. I'd almost forgotten Charlotte's funeral. "Yessir. Would you bundle up say, fifty dollars' worth of different kinds for me?"

The old man's expression was comical. "You say fifty dollars? Son, that's a lot of flowers."

"It is. They're for a lady."

"Aw. I'm sorry. You must have thought a lot of her."

"More than she knew. Listen, I'll have a man come by in the morning to pick them up for me."

"They'll be ready. Sorry for your loss."

"Much obliged, and I appreciate the information." I went to find Booker's Uncle Dan to pay him for transporting flowers to the funeral home. I wouldn't be there, though.

Charlotte would understand.

I headed to Longview, and then Hot Springs, Arkansas, figuring Delgado wouldn't mind if I kept his car a little longer.

Chapter Fifty-Eight

The Daisy Drugstore in Longview was nothing special. A brick and glass building located between the E-Tex Café and the Tyler Café, it had a nondescript entrance. I parked my borrowed Ford by angling into the curb like all the rest of the Model A's. The paved street was a welcome relief from Pine Top's mud.

A team of mules clopped by, pulling a log wagon bearing the enormous girth of a single pine rising high above the driver's head. It was followed by a second wagon, and then a third of similar size. Presumably the same tree trunk cut into manageable lengths, it was destined for the sawmill on the outskirts of town. Despite the oil boom in Pine Top, only seventeen miles away, the logging industry was alive and well in the East Texas piney woods.

Preferring the smell of pine sap to crude oil, I drew a deep breath of clean air and stepped onto the sidewalk. The drugstore's window displayed a variety of signs, patent medicines, cigar and cigarette offerings, and what appeared to be an electrical device "guaranteed to provide relief from female hysteria and nervous diseases."

A bell rattled overhead when I entered. Loud music from a radio behind the counter filled the drugstore that smelled more like cigarette smoke than powders and liniments. A solemn man with oiled hair and a white mustache waited behind the counter as I closed the door and surveyed the drugstore's uncommonly short interior. Instead of a teller-like cage in the back, there were four ten-foot-tall shelves full of thick jars of unidentifiable powders and pills. Three doors separated the stacks of shelves.

"Help you, sir?"

Flashing a smile, I closed the short distance, noticing an opening in the counter to allow easy passage. The linoleum there was worn, while it still had a pattern everywhere else. "Coming into a nervous place like this makes me jumpy."

The man's eyebrows went up and he relaxed. "Ahhh. Then you know the drill."

"I do." Without stopping, I rounded the counter without invitation. Shocked, the man reached under the counter, but I grabbed his nearest wrist and twisted it at the same time a weighted leather sap dropped into my hand where I had it in my sleeve.

It cracked the side of the counterman's head, just behind the ear. His eyes glazed and his knees wobbled as if he were standing on a ship. Pulling hard to keep him off balance, I saw a sawed-off pump shotgun laying on the shelf beside a black button. "Nope."

Recovering his wits faster than I expected, the man pulled back against my grip to free himself. Instead of getting into a shoving match, I used his momentum against him and pushed hard. When the clerk instinctively resisted the shove and drove forward, I again went with the force and yanked him close and into a second, harder blow from the sap.

This time the man's knees went weak and watery. Using a handful of hair to keep him from falling, I slammed his forehead into the counter, holding him there. "You hear me, mister?"

Counter Clerk groaned. "Yeah."

"How do I get in back there without triggering an alarm?"

The clerk swallowed and put one hand on the counter to steady himself. "Push that buzzer."

The sap's third swing landed on the back of the man's hand. Bones snapped and he shrieked. "All right! No more."

"The next one's back against your head, and I'll keep working on you until someone opens a door to leave. Now, do you want to wake up in the hospital three days from now, or this afternoon? All right. The alarm warns them the law is out front, right?"

"Yes."

"Three doors. Where do they go?"

"The one on the left is a dummy. When you open it, an alarm sounds. The one in the middle is an office. Nothing else. That one on the right end takes you inside."

"Inside what?"

"What do you think, feller? Into the bar."

"Is someone watching back there?"

"Of course. Knock shave and a haircut, but end it with three raps for the two-bits part, and not two. Buster'll open up."

"Buster armed?"

"Pistol."

"He shoot quick?"

"Never has."

"Lay down on the floor." I picked up the pump shotgun and checked the loads. "Thanks for the gun." I leaned over and applied the sap one last time, and the clerk went out like a light.

Taking a deep breath to calm my nerves, I tucked the sap into the small of my back where it usually rode, and rapped the code. Half a second later, the door opened, and I followed the shotgun's muzzle into the bar as cigarette and cigar smoke mixed with stale beer and spilled whiskey washed over me.

Chapter Fifty-Nine

It was dark inside the wide room that took up more of the building space than one would imagine. It appeared that the speakeasy was wider than the drugstore, taking up considerable space behind a number of businesses. The surprised doorman didn't change expression when he registered the bore of the sawed-off twelve-gauge shotgun aimed at his midsection. He raised both hands, and I plucked a snub-nose revolver from his waistband.

"You make enough money to die here?"

"Hell, no."

No one in the gin joint paid any attention to what was going on at the door. They were too busy with drinks and conversation. Keeping the shotgun low and out of sight, I focused on the stout doorkeeper.

"Don't start none, and there won't be none. Understood?"

He nodded.

"You know the names of who comes in here?"

"Some?"

"Quinn Walker. Jack Drake."

"I know Mr. Walker."

"He here?"

The man started to shake his head, but something in my

demeanor changed his mind. "You the law, or mad about something?"

"Both. Texas Ranger, and I have half a dozen other Rangers out front and out back. We can do this easy or hard, but if you're stupid, you're gonna get hurt or dead. Which is it?"

"Mr. Walker is here. Sitting at a table in front of the bar."

"How many back exits?"

"One."

"Lead me over there, and if there's an empty chair sit down. If not, turn and put both hands on the bar and don't move a whisker."

"You're crazy to come in here like this."

"I know it. Turn around, and let's go."

Chapter Sixty

Carrying the shotgun muzzle-down against my leg, I followed the frightened doorkeeper as we wove between the tables toward the bar. Soft music from the largest radio I'd ever seen filled the air, along with a heavy cloud of tobacco smoke. I wondered what those people did for a living, if they were in a speakeasy at that time of the day. You could almost understand if the place was packed in the evenings, but the number of drinkers so early was surprising.

The sight of a badge threw me for a loop. A Longview police officer in uniform sat at a table with a man wearing a suit and hat. With gray temples and a matching trimmed mustache, he looked like a politician. Their presence made things even more difficult. If Walker did something stupid, I'd be faced with trouble from several sides: the obviously crooked cop, the man with them, and the murderer himself.

The doorman reached Walker's table, and I rested a hand on his shoulder. "Sit."

The two customers at the table looked up in surprise as the uninvited doorkeeper sat down. I did the same, and once in the chair, I leveled the stubby shotgun out of sight under the table, pointed directly at the taller man's midsection.

"Arthur, what'n hell are you doing?" The dark-haired man frowned. "We don't know you well enough for this."

The doorkeeper swallowed and was about to speak when I took over. "Quinn Walker?"

His eyes narrowed. "Yeah, what of it?"

"My name's Tom Bell, Texas Ranger. You are under arrest, now sit still and be quiet."

Walker stiffened and exchanged looks with his partner, who slowly set a half-empty glass of beer on the table and waited.

"Don't be stupid, Walker. I have a sawed-off shotgun under this table and it's pointed right at you. If I have to pull this trigger, there's no way I'll miss, and it'll cut you in half at this distance."

Walker placed both hands flat on the table, a dark drink between them. Still keeping the twelve-gauge pointed where it was, I turned my attention to the other person at the table. "Hey, buddy, what's your name?"

"Jack Drake."

"Pick up that cigarette in the ashtray and take a puff to settle your nerves. You look like your head's gonna spin off."

Hand trembling, he followed instructions and let the smoke out in one long stream.

"Now, boys, y'all take a swaller of those drinks so it all looks good."

They obeyed and replaced the glasses.

"Good. Now here's what we're gonna do. I want you both to finish those drinks, and Mr. Drake, you keep smoking that toonie like you don't have a care in the world. Have you paid for those drinks yet?"

They nodded as one.

"All right then. It's good to see you're conscientious customers who won't try to walk out on their bill. Now, when I say, y'all stand up and we're gonna walk out of here slow and easy, just the way y'all planned to when you finished drinking. Mr. Doorkeeper, you're part of this little circus act, so you lead the way out the door you were supposed to be watching and don't even roll your eyes at anyone in here. We get to there, you have a seat back on your stool while we leave and act like you're so tired you won't never get up again.

"Outside, Mr. Walker and Mr. Drake will walk to my car that's parked right straight in front of this building. Mr. Walker, you get in the back, slide over to the other door. Mr. Drake will follow. Y'all take a drink and, Mr. Drake, you take a drag on that cigarette."

Just four friends at a table.

"Now, once in the car, I want y'all to turn your backs to a door and put your hands behind you. I'll put on the cuffs, and we'll leave without any trouble, because I don't like trouble, and that kind of thing irritates me. You don't want to irritate me, boys. Understand?"

They nodded, and I saw Jack Drake's attention flick to the side and then back.

"Mister, I saw something in your eyes I don't like. Smile at me and do it now."

Drake built a weak smile, and I forced out a fake chuckle. "That table behind me. How many men are sitting there?"

"Four."

"Mr. Walker. Are they with you?"

"Yes."

"The police officer and his friend, too?"

Walker smiled. "You bet. Looks like you got a tiger by the tail, don't it?"

The pit of my stomach fell out. Dammit! I'd violated my own rule in a room full of strangers. The hair on my neck rose when I realized there was no telling how many guns they had between them.

Everything was clear. The gangsters, Walker and Drake, the Longview police officer, and possibly the well-dressed man with him were all there to meet with someone. There was no other reason for all of them to be in the same place at the same time.

My mind raced. Who could it be? Moretti? No, such a man wouldn't come to Texas to meet with underlings. A man like that would lose respect if he did. So who was it? Someone important for all of them to be there.

Time was running out. The unconscious "druggist" behind the counter would soon be discovered, judging by the number of customers already in the speakeasy. It was only a matter of minutes before someone found him. If it was a regular customer, he might disappear, understanding something was wrong. If it was a good citizen, they'd raise the alarm, thinking the drugstore had been robbed.

I took several deep breaths to slow my heart. "Walker, I'm only going to ask you once. Give me the name of the man all y'all are here to meet."

Reading the situation, he smirked. "O. L. Caldwell."

The name was a punch. "The oilman?"

"The one and only."

"He's mixed up in your scam?"

"How do you know anything about what may or may not be my business?"

"Sheriff Dobbs told me, right before those men behind me shot the bank president."

Drake stiffened. "They shot Emsworth?"

"They did. Right in front of the courthouse, before they cut off Dobbs's hands to get him out of the cuffs."

Terror flooded across their faces. Maybe for the first time they realized what they'd tangled with. Men who would cut off a man's hands just to get him out of a set of cuffs would do anything.

"They didn't do that." Walker shook his head. "You're just trying to scare us."

"I figure they took him out in the woods somewhere between here and Pine Top and squeezed all the information out of him they could, before he bled to death or died from shock. You boys are fools if you don't think that chopper squad is here to clean up a mess. They'll get all y'all in one place and it'll all be over but the crying in a few seconds."

Walker and Drake focused on the men behind them, as if watching a nest of rattlesnakes. When Walker's eyes widened in fear, I realized the jig was up. The gangsters knew something was wrong.

Two heartbeats later, four sets of chair legs scraped across the wooden floor.

Chapter Sixty-One

Like a stick of dynamite only half an inch from a lit fuse, the situation was about to explode.

"It's that Ranger."

I stood in a crouch and whirled toward the four armed men in long overcoats coming to their feet. The flash of a pistol coming to bear was the beginning of the detonation. Swinging the shotgun on the man with the pistol, I shouted. "Don't do it!"

Ignoring the order, a second man tucked a hand under his brown overcoat and another weapon appeared. I pulled the trigger, and a streak of fire shot from the large bore, lighting the room like the flash from a Speed Graphic's flashbulb. The first gangster to reach for his gun took most of the load and folded over the table, his groan drowned out by a shriek as the man behind him absorbed more than one of the double-ought pellets.

"Put his lights out!" A short, squatty gangster with .38 in hand became the next target as he brought the pistol to bear. He snapped off a round as I lost half a second shucking another shell into the chamber and pushing the forepiece forward.

Finger still holding the trigger back, the shotgun exploded again.

The gunman twisted in agony and dropped the pistol, clutching his chest. He disappeared behind the table as I racked the shotgun, which detonated a third time. The fourth gunman went over backward, dropping his unfired .45.

The one in the gray overcoat who'd caught pellets from the first round came closer than any of them to getting off a clean shot, but the shotgun still held two more rounds. They went off as fast as I could jack the shells, and he went down as well.

Blinded by the muzzle flashes and my hearing muffled from the blasts in such an enclosed space, I threw the empty shotgun at the doorkeeper's head as the terrified man stumbled back to the bar. Snatching the big Colt from its holster, I swung back around toward Quinn Walker and Jack Drake, to find them gone. The flicker of light at the back of the speakeasy as the exterior door closed showed where they'd disappeared, along with the police officer and the man I'd assumed to be a politician.

Customers flowed toward the doors like water, and my "prisoners" were gone.

Chapter Sixty-Two

Longview Sheriff Lonnie LaPierre and I stood on the sidewalk in front of the Daisy Drugstore. Sitting on the sidewalk and cuffed with their hands behind them, the druggist lookout, doorman, and bartender waited for someone to take them to jail.

Just like in Pine Top, a crowd of onlookers clotted the sidewalk and meandered back and forth across the street, blocking traffic and watching the three prisoners who wouldn't raise their heads. I scanned the crowd, hoping to see the two men who'd dodged out on me while I was busy trying to stay alive. By the time I'd made sure the gangsters were no longer a threat, the customers had all cleared out, including the police officer and the individual I'd guessed was likely a politician.

The sheriff had already talked to the prisoners. Pulling at his ear, thinking, he was the most expressive person I'd ever met. I watched him go through a variety of such actions including scratching his cheek and blowing out his cheeks as he absorbed all that had happened.

"Say you shot all four of 'em?"

"That's what happened all right. I'm concerned, though, about Walker and Drake getting away. I'd appreciate it if you'd have your men on the lookout for a yellow Nash. They can't be far, and something that bright shouldn't be hard to find."

LaPierre pointed at his sheriff's car parked parallel to the sidewalk, blocking in several civilian cars and a truck. "I have a radio in there. Give me a minute to raise a holler."

"Go ahead on." We moved out of the way of a dozen men flowing into the front of the "drugstore," carrying rolled-up stretchers.

The sheriff was back a minute later. "They'll keep an eye peeled. The problem is, we don't know which way they went." He ground out a cigarette butt with his boot and plucked a pack of Chesterfields from a shirt pocket. "Look, I know you're on the wrong end of this questioning, and to tell you the truth, I'm uncomfortable as hell doing it. I just need to know what happened."

He shook a fresh cigarette from the pack and smoked for the next several minutes while I outlined the events that led up to the shoot-out. The animated sheriff listened, frowning, grimacing, raising his eyebrows from time to time, and finally tilting his hat back at the end, as if spent.

"Whoo wee, that's the damnedest story I believe I've ever heard." He spoke without taking the Chesterfield from his lips. "I knew you Rangers were hell on wheels, but I never understood up till now that them wheels run on greased tracks. I believe I'd've pissed my pants when those men stood up."

"It was an uncomfortable moment, for sure."

The stretcher-bearers emerged, burdened by one covered body after the other. The crowd grew silent and parted to allow them to load the bodies under the bloody sheets into the back of a pickup.

The truck pulled away as onlookers closed in to catch a glimpse of the corpses on their way to the funeral home. The

Daisy's door was propped open, as well as the one leading into the speakeasy, and a steady flow of mixed odors blew outside in the strong draft.

I went inside and the sheriff followed. We stopped beside the counter. "You say you didn't know about this place?"

"Nossir. Ranger Bell, you and I both know that there's likely to be a dozen speakeasies here in Longview. I heard they're more than ten thousand in New York, and likely half as many in Chicago. I have half a dozen deputies to help here in town, and a handful of constables scattered within a twenty-mile radius. Hell, the police department hasn't been in place but for a year, and I don't recognize the officer you described."

"I believe you. These places pop up like weeds, but right now I'm more interested in my two fugitives that slipped out while I was busy. All I got out of them was they were there to meet O. L. Caldwell. That name mean anything to you?"

"It sure does. He's a well-known oilman around here."

"Where does he live?"

"He has more than one house. One's here in Longview, though. Can't say about the others."

"Can you send one of your deputies over to pick him up for me?"

"On what charges?"

"Just bring him in for questioning. He's somehow tied into a case I'm working on. I'll handle the rest."

"The police chief should be here any minute, and I'll leave this mess to him and go with one of my boys to bring in Caldwell." His radio crackled loud enough for us to hear it. "Hang on."

Sheriff LaPierre went out and sat in the car. I leaned against the doorjamb, surveying the crowd that was starting to disperse now that the gangsters' bodies were gone.

He was back a minute later. "Two bits of news. The Nash is parked in an alley about a block away, with bullet holes in the back seat that's stained with dried blood. There's dozens of dirt and gravel roads that splays all out through that country. No telling where they went, or how.

"I've had that happen a hundred times. One of these days we'll get a better handle on how to chase these people down, but I guarantee that a good driver can run these roads for months, staying just out of reach. The other news is that Mr. Caldwell's housekeeper says he left last night and didn't say where he was going. Said that's unusual for him, but he seemed in a hurry."

"I bet he was."

A uniformed police officer pushed through the crowd. I gave him the once-over, but it wasn't the man in the bar. He stopped, glancing between us. "Sheriff. We've found a car parked just down the street that I believe belonged to those four dead gangsters."

"What makes you say that?"

"Well sir, we opened the back and it's full of tommy guns and rifles like I ain't never seen. There's four grips, enough ammunition to start their own country, more guns in the back seat, and even a couple stuck under the front seat, but that ain't all. There's a dead man back there with no hands. They been cut off. Looks like he bled to death."

"Show me."

A photographer was taking pictures of the car and its contents. Somehow they'd located the owners of other vehicles that were parked nearby and moved them to make room enough to open the doors and trunk. Weapons leaned against the Ford, and half a dozen pistols lay on the front fender. Ammunition was stacked on the ground.

The sheriff whistled when he saw the rolling arsenal. "Lordy mercy. Who travels with that many guns?"

"I do, now." The sheriff almost lost his dinner when we

glanced into the bloody trunk. I'd seen worse in the war. "Officer, there was a policeman in the bar a little while ago, sitting with an oily politician with a crooked nose. The policeman was about thirty, heavyset with eyes that droop at the corners."

"That's Carver."

"Sheriff LaPierre, you need to tell the police chief that's who I saw inside. Y'all can figure out from there who the man was sitting with him. I don't have time to fool with it."

"What're you gonna do now?"

I glanced up and down the sidewalk in both directions. Signs attached to the overhanging awnings offered everything except what he wanted. "Where's the nearest telegraph operator?"

"Down thataway, not far from the bank."

"Much obliged."

"Where you going?"

"To tell my captain that I'm heading for Hot Springs to pick up some prisoners."

"They have them waiting for you?"

I threw the answer over my shoulder. "Nope."

"What am I gonna do about this mess you're leaving behind?"

"Send 'em to the funeral home, and I'll make a report when I get back."

"Oh, and that's Pine Top's Sheriff Dobbs, if anybody asks."

Chapter Sixty-Three

The next morning, Cherubino Moretti padded across his room on the fourth floor of the Hazelwood Hotel, puffing a cigar that trailed smoke like a steam engine. "What'n hell is going *on* down there?"

His right-hand man, Chic Marco, shrugged and rested his elbows on the table by a window. He absently rubbed at the long white scar on his face, knowing better than to offer an explanation or opinion. Right then Moretti was doing what he did best, blowing off steam.

"I send guys down there to rub out that damned Ranger, and poof, they're all gone. Then more guys, and four of 'em can't handle him in a bar full of our people!" His voice rose and he puffed harder. "Gimme a scotch."

Their room had been the one Al Capone preferred when he was in power. It was a special feeling to take his place because Moretti felt that soon he'd be running Chicago himself. Just like Capone, he'd reserved the entire floor for his men, but some of the rooms were now empty, all because of one measly Texas Ranger.

Marco poured three fingers of Cutty Sark and dropped in a single ice cube. He handed it to the boss, who took a long swallow as he continued to pace. Returning to the table, Marco slid into a chair. "Well, at least those two rubes took care of Ferras. I never did like that asshole."

"They *say* they rubbed him out. Right now I don't believe a damned thing I hear from Texas. Tell me again how that Ranger got the drop on four of our guys while people in my pocket were sitting only a few feet away."

Marco shook a butt from a deck of Chesterfields and fired one up, glad he'd sent the boys to Longview instead of doing it himself. It wasn't his fault they ran into trouble.

He drew in a long breath of smoke. "They had a safe place in Longview, or thought it was safe. Walker and Drake were waiting for O. L. Caldwell to come in so they could take that Texas turd out in the boonies and put him in a shallow grave."

"Because it's getting hinky."

It was like they'd practiced a vaudeville bit. Both men knew the story, but it was Moretti's way to work through a problem.

"That's right, Boss. It's all screwed up. The guys were there at the next table. They'd finished the job in Pine Top and were gonna rub out Caldwell and those two Texas jerks when it all went to pieces."

"That's right." Another swallow of scotch. "And right there we had a cop and a city councilman ready to help."

"Yes sir. Then the Ranger walked in."

"By pasting the counterman and offering to do a little chin music on the doorman."

"Boss, I think a gun in the stomach is a little more than chin music."

"You're right, but the big maroon should have been on his toes. Anyway, the next thing we know, this cowboy is at the table with a shotgun and cuts loose on our guys. Kills all four."

"But Walker and Drake got away. They followed the payroll cop out the door and everyone split."

Moretti drained the scotch. "And now we don't know where anyone is."

"No sir. The councilman called after it was all over and said Caldwell didn't show, and he thinks those other two are on their way here."

"What makes him think that?"

"They mentioned it before everything went crazy in that gin mill."

"What are we supposed to do with 'em if they come here?"

"I don't know. Maybe they think we'll cover for 'em, or maybe you have a plan."

"My plan was to make money down there without any trouble." Moretti faced the window overlooking Central Avenue and spread his hands. "Look at this place. It's a goddamned money machine because it was done *right*. Since the Flynns and the Dorans settled things forty years ago, this town has been wide open."

The two families were the orchestrators of the Hot Springs gambling industry. After the Hot Springs gunfight in 1899, the competition calmed, and the town became a hotspot for cards and casino gambling of all kinds. Though illegal, the gambling, saloons, and prostitution were no secret to most of the local authorities; everyone from the police to judges to the mayor turned a blind eye to the potential felonies. Payoffs meant silence, and the amount of money filtering to once lint-filled pockets guaranteed it was an anything-goes kind of town.

Moretti paused. "If those two palookas bring their trouble up here, I'll have them pushing up daisies."

"Maybe you should just clean house." Marco lit another Chesterfield off the butt. "Start all over."

"Hey!" Moretti turned and smiled. "That's a helluvan idea. What do we stand to lose?"

"Everything, if we don't."

"So we pull out of the property business down there."

"That's a good idea, Boss. You're making a bundle off the hot oil, so you don't need that land. Like you said, it's been nothing but a headache. It's a plan those hicks came up with, not yours. It was bad from the start."

"I said that?"

"Sure."

"So it's settled. Those guys are on the way up here for a new plan, so we'll give 'em one. Get word to Caldwell that we're finished with the land deal. We're still working the Chinese squeeze on the oil business, and that's that."

Moretti laughed, feeling a weight lift off his shoulders, and held out his empty glass. "Pour me another one and let's celebrate ending the land part of this Texas job."

Marco rose to refill the glass.

"And get that little blond up here. She was something."

"Right, Boss."

Chapter Sixty-Four

Bright blue skies followed me to Arkansas. The road leading through the mountains changed from pines to hardwoods in bright fall colors. Cool, clean air flowed through the Ford's open windows, blowing away the Texas humidity. The breeze caressed my face, and it would have been a pleasant drive had it not been for the memories that still hung heavy in my mind.

Nestled in a mountainous bowl, Hot Springs was a colorful resort city filled with clean, expensive cars of all makes and models. I drove north on the broad boulevard of Central Avenue. Wealthy visitors walked the promenade on Bathhouse Row, strolling in the sunshine and enjoying the fresh air of the Ouachita Mountains.

Traffic moved slowly, giving me time to get my bearings. The architecture of one bathhouse after the other was only the tip of what drew visitors to the area. For decades, the natural hot mineral waters were the draw, and the spigots flowed night and day. But as I knew, such glamour also brought the criminal element to town, and with so much money to be made, corruption became the norm.

Gambling, prostitution, and liquor all served to tarnish the gem that was Hot Springs. As recently as 1899, the Garland

County sheriff's department and the Hot Springs Police Department shot it out over who would control the gambling industry in that town. When the smoke cleared, five men lay on marble slabs and little had changed.

I didn't care who was in charge of the organized crime in the area, though at some point I'd have to speak with both agencies regarding my presence in their town. I hoped to slip in, locate Walker and Drake, and get out of town with them in tow to put the criminals in a safe lockup where they'd be secure. After that, my plan was to come back and deal with the man who was the architect of Charlotte's death.

It was a tall order for one man, but there's nothing more determined than a mad Texas Ranger who is in the right.

I passed one glamorous bathhouse after the other. The Buckstaff, Ozark, Quapaw, and Fordyce were only a few that registered. Restaurants, oyster houses, and what were obviously houses of ill repute bearing names like Fannie's Place, Roxie's, and Sweets, sat side by side.

Head on a swivel, I noted Dante's Five and Dime, the Ohio Cigar Store, and the Southern Club, all apparently doing a booming business and virtually ignoring Prohibition. I flipped through memories of conversations. Out Malvern way was the Pythian Hotel and Baths, where steam not only came from the hot water flowing from bathhouse spigots, but from sweaty dancing to jazz music in hot, smoky clubs.

Windows on the second and third floors of several buildings on the west side of Central were wide open, curtains of lacy female underwear and hosiery fluttering in the breeze, advertising female distraction.

A scantily dressed, short-haired blond leaned out of the window and called down to a male passerby on the sidewalk. "Hey, handsome! Hey, hon! You got time to come up for a quick visit?"

He glanced up, touched his hat brim with a grin, and continued on.

"Ah, keep goin' ya big baboon!"

Good Lord, what a town.

As I drifted up Central, the Hazelwood Hotel rose like a behemoth where the broad avenue split, the left maintaining the same name, and the right fork evolved into Fountain Street and followed the incline to North Mountain. The hotel's front doors opened on the corner of Central and Fountain at the top of a wide set of concrete steps rising fifteen feet above street level. An extensive veranda stretched the length of the building along both streets.

Feeling gritty from road dust, I decided the massive hotel was what I needed to clean up and get ready for what might come next.

Chapter Sixty-Five

"So what do we do now?" Jack Drake sat on the bed in their room at the Park Hotel, a fairly new seven-story hotel just off Bathhouse Row in Hot Springs.

"We go see Moretti." Walker shrugged. He was out of steam and had little interest in coming up with anything else.

"You think he's going to open his arms wide and hug us? Think about it for a minute. That guy came in and took everything over. He just wants money, and he'll say we cost him everything he had back home. He's going to put all of this on *us*."

"He can't." Walker puffed his chest out and opened the window. "We did everything we were supposed to. It was his meddling and Clete Ferras that caused it all to come unraveled. Ferras worked for him, so he wasn't our responsibility. I'll just explain what happened, and point out that it was *his* guys who missed two chances at that Ranger. He'll understand when he hears it straight from the horse's mouth."

Drake barked a laugh. "You've lost your damn mind."

"No I haven't. It'll be all right."

"Then I suspect he'll just send us back home to start over. Have you forgot that Ranger and the fact that Dobbs and Emsworth's gone?"

Walker deflated. "You're right. We're spinning our wheels being here."

"Maybe not."

"What do you mean?"

"You've been the brains behind this deal since we were kids, but now you need me."

"Fine. Spill it."

"You said it a minute ago. It was all good until Moretti got involved. When it was just me and you, everything was fine. So the simple solution is to get him out of the way."

"Pay him off somehow?"

"No." Drake took a revolver from his pocket. "We kill Moretti. Once he's gone, all we have to do is head back home and get our own sheriff back on the payroll. We start all over."

"You forgetting the Ranger?"

"No. But I've learned something from Moretti. We quit trying to do all of this ourselves. We put together enough men to handle the Ranger."

"You kill one and there'll be fifty tomorrow."

It was Drake's time to deflate. "I didn't think of that."

They sat in silence, listening to the traffic and voices coming from below. Walker felt like giving up and disappearing, catching a train, and joining the thousands of people riding the rails. They could go to California and start over. There were jobs there, and big towns. It would be easy to get lost in the flood of westward-bound migrants and find another easy way to make money. It was out there without working too hard for it. Money was always there; all they had to figure out was how to get their hands on it.

That's when Drake came up with a plan.

"I'm still gonna kill Moretti. Because of him, I have this hole in my stomach. Then, once we're finished here, I say we go back to Pine Top, rob the bank, and get all our money back. Then we can go to California and start over with cash in our pockets."

No longer in charge, Walker shook his head. "We're not bank robbers."

"It'll be easy. Look, I've been reading the papers. Pretty Boy Floyd, George Birdwell, and a couple of new hard cases named Barker and Karpis are all making a pretty good living off banks." Drake leaned forward. "But here's where we're different. Smarter. I learned that from you. Think smarter. We don't try to make a *career* out of banks. We just hit the one and we're gone. It'll be easy since Dobbs is dead, and they have only a deputy or two." His excitement built. "It's perfect! We just need to get Moretti off our asses."

"And how do we do it? He's gonna have men all around him."

"Easy. We find out where he stays when he's here, and then wait in the lobby. He walks off an elevator and we plug him and everyone with him. I've thought this out. You know what it's like when the elevator doors open. Everbody's ready to get off, so they just come spilling out. Plug the first guys you see, 'cause they'll likely be bodyguards. That leaves him standing right there in the open. Shoot him and then just walk out and drive off. It'll be a turkey shoot."

Walker licked his lips and patted empty pockets for a cigar. "And then?"

"We drive back to Pine Top, hit the bank, and catch a train for Dallas. Next stop, California."

"Sounds like a good idea."

"I think it's the best we can do."

Chapter Sixty-Six

Cherubino Moretti closed the door to room 443, once Al Capone's suite, now his. He'd specified that particular number since Capone was occupying a different room in the U.S. penitentiary in Atlanta. The moment he stepped into the wide hallway in a light cream-colored suit, other doors opened and four of his men appeared. Their dark suits and tilted hats were in sharp contrast to the boss's dress.

Chic Marco came forward. "Where to, Mr. Moretti? You'd said you might be interested in going to the theater tonight."

He started toward the elevator as two men closed in the front, followed by two more behind. "Oysters."

"Sounds good. I have four new men down in the lobby."

"Good. When'd they get in?"

"Got off the train about an hour ago. There are four more down the hall. Didn't figure we'd need that many tonight." Marco punched the elevator's call button and glanced up to see it was coming down from the eighth floor.

Chapter Sixty-Seven

It was late by the time I'd cleaned up, and it was time to go to work. Not wanting to look like a Texas Ranger, I left the gun belt in the room, tucking the .45 inside the belt in the small of my back. Two magazines went into my left pants pocket.

Opening the window to vent the stuffy air, I felt a distinctive draw that flowed across the room and through the shutter vents in the upper half of the hallway door, pulling air from the outside and into the wider-than-average hallway.

Well-dressed people strolled along the sidewalks and promenade on Fountain Street below. Not on official business, I put the *cinco peso* badge into a jacket pocket, just in case I ran into the local constabulary.

The big-brimmed cowboy hat was a dead giveaway, so I traded it for a snap-brim fedora with a wide ribbon hatband. The image reflected in the mirror with the hat in a rakish tilt over one eye made me look like most of the men on the street.

Closing the door, I peered upward through the shutter vents, just to be sure no one could see inside, confirming the design was true and guaranteed privacy. Satisfied, I walked past the elevator and took the stairs down from the third floor.

I'd never seen anything like the Hazelwood Hotel. I'd thought the lobby of the Pine Top Hotel was nice, but the vast opulence around me made the small-town hotel in Texas seem nothing more than a hall closet.

Spanish Colonial arches rose high above the open second floor where guests sipped iced drinks that I suspected were laced with liquor, enjoying the view from small tables overlooking the lobby. Getting the lay of the building, I followed a wide opening into a lounge. The big dance floor between an inset bandstand and what once was a long bar was empty, but by dark, I suspected it would be filled with people enjoying the music.

The stairwell opened into a short hallway near the restrooms. Farther down, the elevator dinged and opened as I approached the doors. Two men were waiting to get on and paused as the crowded elevator unloaded. One of those waiting to get on slipped a hand into his coat pocket at the same time his friend pulled back his own coat and reached for his belt.

Chapter Sixty-Eight

As usual, Moretti remained where he was as Chic Marco and Lando Regio stepped off the elevator and quickly scanned the lobby. Two men in suits were waiting to get on.

One reached into his coat pocket.

His friend pulled back his coat.

Moretti shifted his weight to get off, but Chic Marco held out a hand to hold him back. Sensing something was up, he grabbed for the .45 in a shoulder holster.

The bodyguards behind Moretti pushed forward, also reaching for their weapons as the crime boss backed against the rear wall. Dean McGurn and Jerry Barbera placed themselves as the next level of defense against whatever might come.

The hotel guest reaching into his coat pocket pulled out a pack of Pall Mall cigarettes and lipped one out. His friend tucked his shirttail in and backed away from the others spilling into the hallway. "Excuse me."

Chic Marco let go of the Colt and relaxed. Their demeanor changed in a flash, and the mobsters formed a barrier between the guests and Moretti, who threw up a hand in a wave and turned toward the hotel ballroom.

A serious-looking man with a thick mustache and fedora paused to let them pass. Moretti barely gave him a glance.

Chapter Sixty-Nine

Quinn Walker and Jack Drake walked shoulder to shoulder past the Hazelwood Hotel's grand entrance. Walker paused to look up at the towering building. "Damn, we shoulda stayed there."

"Too much money." Drake paused. "But nothing's cheap in this town, that's for sure."

A tight group of men left a brightly lit ballroom, pausing to light up. Smoke billowed into the still air from four cigarettes and one fat cigar.

"Now those guys have it made." Seeing the men light up gave Drake a craving. He lipped a Pall Mall from the pack and watched the quintet get into a cab. "We'd be that rich soon if it wasn't for that damned Moretti." He flicked his thumbnail to light a match.

Chapter Seventy

An elderly colored bellman was standing near the staircase and nodded as I passed. Eyes closed, another colored man dressed in white pants and a white shirt was beside him.

"Evenin' Cap'n."

I stopped as the five men from the elevator disappeared into the lobby. "How are you gentlemen?"

The bellman smiled and touched his friend on the arm. "I told you he looked nice." He gave his feet a little shuffle. "Fine. Just fine. Can we help you?"

"I'm looking for a little relaxation tonight."

The man's eyes twinkled. "We sure got enough of that to go around, sir."

"I suspect you do."

The other man turned his head toward me. I realized he was blind.

"Come downstairs with me and get you a soak and a rub-down. I'll do it myself."

The bellman nodded and smiled, revealing more than one missing tooth. "This here's the best masseuse in town. Been doing it how long, sixty years?"

"Nearbouts."

"Well, thanks, I'll remember that, but right now I'm thinking about a cigar and a drink."

"There's plenty of places for that, too. You know of anyplace special you want to go?"

"Nope. New in town. What can you recommend?"

"You from Texas, I 'spect."

"Shows that much, huh?"

"Yessir, but I have a lot of experience in placing where our guests come from. You from Texas, and there's others here from Chicago, New York, some from Tennessee who sounds a lot like us, and even Florida."

"That's a pretty wide spread. Other than the bathhouses, what do you think?"

I slipped a hand into my pants and came out with two silver dollars, one for each of them.

One disappeared in the bellman's palm as if he were a magician, a talent perfected over the decades. He dropped the other into the blind man's pants pocket. "For that cigar, you might try the Ohio Cigar Store. You can have that drink in the back, if you're of a mind. Then there's the Silver Fox, the Arkansas House, and if you like a place nice as this, and gambling, you might drop by the Southern Club. That's a favorite around here."

"Much obliged. Say, what's your name? I might need to check in on that bath later."

The gray-haired bellman shuffled his feet as if dancing. "Silas Golightly, sir. Light on my feet I was, at least when I was young. This here's…"

"The man who's gonna give you your next rubdown. Just ast for Blind B."

"That's a deal, Blind B. Silas, I bet you could still cut a rug, if you was to want to."

"Yessir, that's a fact." He quickly looked down at the floor as the group of men from the elevator came back through and stepped out onto the veranda.

I waited until they were outside. "Who was that, Silas?"

Keeping one eye on the men who passed through the twenty-foot arched opening and onto the broad veranda. "Sir, that's Mr. Moretti, from Chicago."

"Thanks, gentlemen."

The knot of men climbed into two cabs that quickly disappeared into the traffic.

I pushed through the doors, but before they closed, I heard Silas. "Told you he was nice."

With no concrete plan in mind, I crossed catty-corner to the west side of the business district. At present, I had no interest in checking out the bathhouses. There was no way to investigate beyond the lobbies without checking in and undressing.

The flow of tourists on the busy sidewalks was different than the harried roughnecks back in Pine Top. Here there was much laughter and everyone seemed more relaxed. Well-dressed women in brightly colored skirts and tops walked arm in arm with men in double-breasted and three-piece suits. Blue, medium brown, and dark gray tones were predominant in the long coats. Unusually self-conscious in my three-year-old dress jacket and light wool slacks, I couldn't help but admire the European cuts.

Brightly lit signs advertised everything on the street from vaudeville theaters to candy and general stores to haberdasheries. My first stop was the Manhattan Room, a bustling restaurant. Hungry from traveling, I ordered oysters, a steak with all the trimmings, and finished with a liquid "dessert" recommended by the waiter who wore a bow tie and a pencil-thin mustache.

The man returned with an old-fashioned and set the drink on the table as if prohibition had been abolished that day. There were several similar drinks in front of people who couldn't have cared less that they were drinking illegal hooch in public.

"When in Rome." Ice tinkled in the glass as I took a sip of the sweet, fruity liquor and closed my eyes when it warmed me all the way down. "That's real rye whiskey."

"Yes, sir. It is. Only the finest for our customers."

"How do y'all get by with that?"

The waiter adjusted his bow tie and leaned in. "That's the chief of police over there with those other men. He likes a drink every now and then, too."

"I get it. This is a pretty wide-open town, huh?"

"It's different, that's for sure. First time in our fair metropolis?"

"That's the second time I've been asked that in an hour. Yep, I plan to see the sights and maybe meet up with a couple of old buddies I've been looking for."

"Where are they staying?"

"I'm not sure."

"The Hazelwood has a fine ballroom, if they like music. You might try the Goddard Hotel, or if they enjoy a drink or two, look into the Southern Club or the Ohio Cigar Bar." Once again the waiter leaned in. "They say Al Capone used to visit the Ohio. It was his favorite place. They're going to miss him."

"You talk like he was popular around here."

"Oh, he was. Mr. Capone ate here a lot, and brought his whole family down from time to time to vacation."

"And just strolled around wherever he liked."

"That's a fact. He'd take the whole fourth floor of the Hazelwood, for him and his men. He always had a lot of men around, though he never needed them here. It's a safe place for everyone."

"Safe as in..."

"Lots of people from Chicago and New York come here,

because it's pretty easy to be yourself when the police and sheriff departments work so well with them, if you know what I mean."

"I believe I do. Many thanks for the info, oh, by the way, I read in the papers about a...um," I dropped my voice. "A real gangster named Moretti. Does he come here too?"

"He's the top dog now that Capone's in the slammer." The waiter grinned with the self-importance of someone with information few people have. "If you were to visit the Ohio, you might get a glimpse of him there. Just say Horace McClusky sent you. That's me. Moretti likes the speakeasy back there because it has good music and there are a lot of friendly girls upstairs."

"Wow. This is a regular Sodom and Gomorrah."

He winked. "With *gambling*."

Chapter Seventy-One

It was easy to get into the club at the Ohio Cigar store. Horace McClusky's name opened the hidden door behind the counter, and I was in. The place was packed with a laughing, exuberant crowd enjoying themselves under a blue cloud of smoke.

Music from a band at the back of the room filled the air as three bartenders at the mahogany bar to my right struggled to keep up with the orders. I stopped at the end of the bar and waited. Eventually, a young man with a scrawny mustache saw me and stopped. He leaned close to hear. "What'll you have?"

"Beer."

"We have liquor, you know."

"Just had one. Now I want to wash it down."

The bartender grinned. "You're a man after my own heart. You know how to drink, not like most of these bluenoses in here who think they can drink it all in one night."

"Bluenoses?"

"Prudes."

"They don't look like prudes to me."

"Most of 'em are fancy pants who come down to take the water. They come in here for the excitement, but most of 'em can't hold their liquor. They like to feel dangerous."

"I've heard it could be. They say Capone used to come in."

"He did, but they held the door a little more for him and wouldn't let everyone in."

"It's more relaxed now, then."

"It will be until Mr. Moretti comes in. He's in town and likes to drink and gamble. The owner offers him the same consideration in the evenings. Moretti's here a lot during the day when we're not so busy. He uses the place like an office."

"Do tell."

"You always know it's him, because he has bodyguards all around." He looked around. "Let me give you a tip, if you want to see him, wait until tomorrow in the daylight hours. I doubt he'll be in tonight, as packed as the place is."

The beer arrived, and I was half finished when Quinn Walker and Jack Drake came in. Turning my back to the room, I watched through the corner of my eye as they took a table. Confident they wouldn't recognize me in a business suit and fedora, I kept an eye on them and nursed the beer as they ordered liquor.

Keeping to themselves, they continually scanned the room, and I figured they were looking for someone, maybe Moretti. I nursed two beers for a couple of hours until they staggered to their feet and left.

Sober as a judge, I followed the pair outside and bumped shoulders with a drunk. The man, with a good-looking woman on his arm, felt slighted. "Hey, buddy! Watch where you're going!"

He shoved me back, and the next thing I knew, I had his arm twisted so far up behind his shoulders, he screeched. "Hey! I give!"

I slammed him against the wall. "Get lost."

When I turned back around, there were so many people on the street Walker and Drake had completely disappeared.

Chapter Seventy-Two

It was noon by the time Cherubino Moretti crawled out of bed. "Marco! Coffee!"

Chic Marco pushed through the bedroom door with a tray containing a steaming pot and two cups. "How much did you win last night, Boss?"

In only his pants and an undershirt, Moretti shrugged at Marco's question. "More than I lost the night before." Instead of going to the Ohio the previous evening, they'd dropped by the Southern Club. "And enough to irritate Sigmund."

Marco didn't care for the Southern Club's owner. "I didn't know he was mad."

"Not so's you could tell it. The man's a pro, but you can see it in his eyes when money goes out the door." Moretti rubbed his stomach. "Let's get a little lunch."

"Oysters again?"

"Nah. Larry's Steaks. I want to take a look at their operation in back while we're there." He drained the cup. "Gimme a minute and we can go."

Marco opened the door and peered into the hallway. Seated in a chair near the elevator and not far from the stairwell, Lando

Regio was leaning back against the wall. Hearing the door, he rose. "We moving?"

"In a few minutes, yeah. I need to shave first."

When Moretti was almost ready, Marco walked out into the hall. Two doors farther down, a new guy's head popped out. Marco waved. "Just going to lunch. All quiet. The rest of you guys get something to eat and come on back."

Jack Rawlings waved back. "Georgio went for sandwiches. He should be back any minute."

"Good thinking." Marco crossed to a room and rapped on the door. "Moving."

By the time Moretti came out adjusting his hat, Marco had pushed the elevator button and his men were formed up and ready. The well-oiled machine went into motion when the doors slid open and they stepped inside.

The short ride ended with a smooth stop and for the second time they were presented with the sight of two strange men waiting for the elevator. This time one of those waiting had a gun in his hand.

Marco was reaching for his own weapon when a blur came in from the right as Georgio Meloy dropped his sack of sandwiches and grabbed the gunman's wrist. With an expert twist, he forced the man to drop the revolver and at the same time, knocked him into his associate, who stumbled against the open elevator door.

Both men disappeared inside as several pairs of hands grabbed them in a flash. The elevator doors closed, leaving the sack full of sandwiches behind.

Chapter Seventy-Three

Gun in hand, I answered the knock on my hotel room door to find a familiar face in the wide hallway. "Iron Eyes Delgado. What'n hell you doing here?"

The slender Ranger answered, his voice soft as velvet, "I'm here to help you out, Tom."

"Come on in."

Delgado removed his hat and stepped inside. Glancing around for somewhere to put it, because it's bad luck to put a hat on the bed, he rested it beside mine on top of the dresser.

"Didn't expect to see you here. You're here to...?"

"To keep you out of trouble." Delgado adjusted his gun belt and sat down.

"That's a full-time job."

"I'm starting to learn that."

"So want to talk me out of what I plan to do?"

"No." Delgado reached into his back pocket and produced several folded pages. "I brought two arrest warrants for known fugitives Quinn Walker and Jack Drake. I also have a new one for Clete Ferras, for murder, but you won't need it."

"How come?"

"They found what's left of him in the Sabine. Shot to death and gator-chewed."

"Well, that settles his hash."

"It does." Delgado flipped through the papers. "Here's one for O. L. Caldwell, which you should have gotten before you left Longview..."

"I was in a hurry."

Delgado held up a hand. "I'm milking this duck, Tom. Let me finish. There's also a warrant for someone named Cherubino Moretti, from Chicago."

"Good. What's that one for?"

"Racketeering, prostitution, grand theft," he looked up, "that's oil he's skimming from the drillers, solicitation of murder, and murder."

I should have gotten the warrants myself.

Delgado seemed to see inside my head. "You were blinded by anger, son. I wasn't. After you left, I did a little digging and talked to Mr. O. L. Caldwell out in Longview. I 'magine you got that name just before you shot those four at the drugstore.

"He's too well known to hide for long, so I talked with some folks he does business with and told them it'd be in his best interest to come in and give himself up. So he did."

"And he ratted Moretti out."

"He did. So I understand this Chicago gangster is in town and figured you came this way with the intention to settle with him. I figured it'd be more legal if you had an arrest warrant." He smiled with his eyes and dropped the papers on the bed. "So, here you go. Now you're here all legal."

"Enrique, I didn't intend to bring him in."

Delgado nodded. "I know you didn't, but you're too good a Ranger to lose it and go outlaw. You and me, we're not done yet back in Texas, no matter who wins the election. There's a lot of bad folks who need bringing in, or killing if that's the case, and they need the Rangers whether they know it or not. You're a born lawman, and that's something most people don't understand. It's your calling, son."

"So now I guess we go to the sheriff's office and the police station and show them these warrants, to be all legal. Then just go pick those guys up."

"Hell, no. This place is as crooked as a barrel of snakes. They'd pass the word we were here and these guys'd scat. I just want the paper to keep us on the up-and-up. There's three more Rangers drinking coffee downstairs. We figured to help you gather these guys up and go on home."

Finally taking a deep breath, I studied Delgado's creased face. "Why'd they come with you?"

"Because those old boys understand the value of the law, and good friends."

A shiver went down my spine. There were men here with him, men who valued me as a Ranger, and friend. I'd do the same for any one of them. Emotions rose along with a lump, and we waited for several moments, listening to people pass in the hallway.

I drew a deep breath to steady my voice. "When do you want to do it?"

"Just as soon as we find out where Moretti and those other two are."

A tiny grin touched the corners of my mouth. "Moretti's right under us, but he ain't holed up. The man travels this town like he owns it."

Iron Eyes looked at the linoleum under our feet. "That makes things simple. Reckon he's there now?"

"The desk clerk told me he was, about twenty minutes ago. I was just fixin' to go up there and say howdy."

"Well, let's get the boys and go to work."

"We still need to find Walker and Drake. I had 'em last night, but they slipped out of my hands."

"Let's get the bird in hand first, then we'll worry about the other two in the bush."

———

We met the other Rangers in the lobby, and I knew them all. John Ward, Luke Clarendon, and Sam Evans were all experienced Rangers. They rose, adjusted gun belts under their coats, and shook, drawing stares from the other guests who saw five hard-eyed men in western hats and matching badges.

"Good to see you, Tom." Ward flicked a hand toward the elevator. "Y'all missed the damnedest thing."

"What was that?"

"Pretty good scuffle a little while ago when the elevator opened. There were a couple of guys in business suits yanked inside about two seconds after the door opened. Somebody got their blocks knocked off, and we think it was the businessmen."

"What floor did it go to?"

"Fourth."

I glanced up at the floor indicator above the elevator. "Describe the pair you saw."

"One about your size. Oiled hair and no hat. The other one was shorter and had a pretty good gut on him."

I looked at Delgado. "You don't think they were Walker and Drake, do you? That might explain the scuffle and the car stopping on the fourth floor." I turned back to Ward. "You notice anything about the fat guy?"

"He kept rubbing a hand on the right side of his belly while they waited for the car."

"The other one. Hooked nose. Big one?"

"That's right."

"It was them. Good Lord, Enrique. We have 'em all penned up on the same floor. We need to move fast before they all come back down."

Chapter Seventy-Four

What was left of Quinn Walker and Jack Drake was tied to chairs in Chic Marco's room. Sitting shoulder to shoulder and facing the tall windows, both sported already blackening eyes, bloody noses, and puffy lips they'd acquired on the short ride back up to the fourth floor.

Their bloodstained coats lay on the floor. More blood covered Walker's blue shirt. Drake's shirt would never be white again.

An obviously agitated Moretti paced back and forth in front of the window, alternately glancing outside and then back to the men sitting with their heads down. The room was packed with his men. Two waited outside.

"What'n hell is this? Who are you two idiots?"

Walker cast fearful eyes upward at the furious mob boss. Drake spat out a broken tooth. "Drake. Jack Drake."

"You're the rubes from *Pine Top*?" Moretti's voice rose. "You have the balls to try and knock *me* off? You two come here! To my hotel! With guns?"

Drake chuckled deep and wet. "Bad idea, huh?"

Moretti saw blood seeping from the man's right side. "Did someone shoot him? I didn't hear a shot. If he was shot, the cops'll be here in a few minutes." His voice rose in either fear or anger.

"Nobody shot, Boss." Marco yanked Drake's shirt open to reveal his large stomach covered by a sleeveless undershirt. Buttons rattled off the floor and a nearby chifforobe. Blood seeped through the material. "No hole in his shirt or undershirt. Looks like an old wound that's trying to heal. Somebody shot you, Mac?"

He nodded. "Yeah, that Texas Ranger none of us can kill."

His head snapped sideways from a sharp-right fist. Marco stepped away, rubbing his knuckles wrapped in a wet washcloth. "Watch your mouth, you dumb palooka."

"You telling the truth?" Hands in his pockets, Moretti studied his prisoners. "It was you who shot at that Ranger?"

"Yeah." Drake held his head down from the pain, as a string of blood ran from his mouth to his stomach.

Moretti turned to Walker. "You were the brains of this outfit when you started. Now you're quiet as a mouse. What's with you? You afraid to talk?"

Pain flashed across Walker's face as he tried to speak. What came out was wet and mushy, almost indecipherable. "Yeth, oken yaw."

Lando Regio laughed. "Hey Meloy, you broke his jaw."

"Knock it off." Moretti raised a hand as if to strike. "You guys don't talk. Only me and Marco."

Regio realized the danger of annoying his boss, and his mouth became a thin line.

"All right, back to you, rube." Moretti paced the room. "You intended to shoot me in the elevator."

"That was the plan." Drake groaned and tried to sit straighter, but his bonds kept him slumped forward.

"Then what? You think you can just walk out of this town

after *shooting* me? These guys are the best in the business. That's why you're sitting there and I'm standing up over youse. I'm the big dog in this town when I'm here! I got the cops in one pocket and the mayor in the other! I'm on a first-name basis with the sheriff and the police chief, and you try to come in here and murder *me*?"

Drake cleared his throat and spat to the side. "I figured we were doing what you'd do."

Moretti laughed, his eyes glassy. "This one's got balls, like I said. So you can think like me, huh, rube? All right. Tell me what I'm gonna do right now."

"Well, you're gonna beat on us some more, then likely kill us, or walk us down to a car and take us for a drive. You'll come back, and we won't."

"And I thought *this* one was the brains."

"But you're missing something, Moretti."

"What's that, tough guy?"

"I don't think you'll have time to get the job done."

"I'm getting tired of this. Why won't I have the time?"

"Because that Texas Ranger is in town looking for you. We saw him down in the lobby for a second this morning when we got here. You're next."

Chapter Seventy-Five

Fifteen minutes later, the other Rangers were back up from their cars. They gathered around my double bed, loading an arsenal of weapons. Each man strapped on a Dunrite Bulletproof Vest.

I took mine from the dresser and slipped it on. "Looks like you bought the whole lot."

Delgado tucked one of his matched .45s back into his holster. "I got a good deal on them. And boys, I want them all back in the same condition they're in right now."

"That was my plan." John Ward chuckled and settled a black, hand-tooled, two-gun rig on his hips. It carried matching ivory-handled Colt .44 revolvers. Each shell loop that wrapped from the left side and around to the back was filled with extra ammunition. He stuffed five fat rounds of number 4 buck into a Browning twelve-gauge automatic shotgun and hung a bandolier of shells over one shoulder.

Clarendon's .45 revolver hung near his hand in a low-slung holster. His long gun of choice was a short auto-loading .35 Model 8 Remington rifle with a detachable twenty-round magazine, a caliber that could put down any big game on the North American continent.

A man of few words, Sam Evans checked the action on a

Navy model Thompson submachine gun. He snapped a fifty-round drum to the tommy gun and belted on a bandolier holding five twenty-round magazines. A powerful Colt .38 Super Model Automatic rode on his right hip.

Delgado rested his hands on matching 1911 pistols on each hip. He also had a Thompson machine gun with a twenty-round magazine locked into the well. A bandolier similar to the one Evans wore lay beside it.

I unwrapped the Browning Automatic Rifle and double-checked a bandolier of spare magazines. Delgado eyed the rifle. "That new?"

"Yep. Picked it up on the road here while-back, along with a tommy gun that looks a lot like yours."

"I bet you did. All right, boys. This is Tom's dance. We're here for backup. Tom, how do you want to handle this?"

I watched the men gathered in my room. "The good news is that there's no one on this floor but Moretti's men. He thinks he's Al Capone, and that's how he does things. He has at least eight men, according to the desk clerk, but that may not be all. There's a lot of rooms here, so he may have others close by. It wouldn't surprise me if some of these rooms have girls in 'em. They all like the prostitutes."

Ward always tilted his head when he was listening. "What room is he in?"

"443."

"That's directly below us, if the numbers are the same."

I nodded. "That's right. So take a look at the hall when we get out there to get your bearings. We go down the stairwell. I expect a guard to be in the hall, but I have an idea how to put him out of the dance."

"Then we hit that room?"

"John, take a look around you and tell me what you see."

Clarendon surveyed the room. "Bed. Bathroom. Chifforobe. Window, and three doors."

"That's right. Every room has a door from the hall, and two on the side. The connecting doors lead to the rooms on either side, so if you were to open them all up, a man could see down the entire length of the building. That worries me. If we get into a gunfight, this bunch could go from room to room without getting out into the hall. If I was Moretti, I'd make sure all my men could move around that way."

Evans scratched an ear. "Let's just put someone at the far end, and he can plug that hole if they try to get away."

"Can't." I shook my head. "The hotel folks locked the doors on that stairwell in this wing, so you can't get in from the third or fifth floors."

"That'd be bad if the hotel was to catch fire." Evans fingered the rounds in his belt loops, as if counting them.

"Sure would, but nobody's gonna say a word since it's Moretti."

"I'd be willing to bet that you can open those doors from the inside, though. They'll use it to get away if they have the chance." Delgado drew a deep breath. "Not something I like, but there's nothing we can do about it. There aren't enough of us to cover every escape route. Y'all ready?"

"I'm going through Moretti's door and making the arrest." I didn't have to tell the others why. I was sure they'd heard the story of Charlotte's murder on that lonesome road and understood that it was me who had to arrest the man who ordered the ambush. "Y'all can handle the others. Arrest 'em, or kill 'em. I don't care."

"We have to do this fast," Delgado said. "Even though the local law looks the other way when it comes to vice, they'll frown on us arresting one of their benefactors, and if the shooting starts, they'd be determined to arrest *someone*, and that'll be us."

Clarendon adjusted the Dunrite vest and put on his dress coat. "I doubt any of the laws will come in if we start shooting. These people seem to avoid confrontation."

Nods all around.

"Once we have our prisoner, we go out the back and follow the foot trail that leads down to Fountain Street and our cars. Sam, you know how to lead us out of here, right?"

"I do. Came here about a year ago with my wife so she could take the water. Didn't help, though. She's still mean as ever."

We laughed, bleeding off tension, set our hats as if getting ready to ride a horse in a strong wind, and I led the way.

Chapter Seventy-Six

The elevator door opened on the fourth floor and a drunk staggered into the hallway, fumbling for his key. Hat tilted back on his head, he squinted down the hallway as if lost.

Seated in a chair outside Moretti's room, Dean McGurn shook his head in disgust.

"Hey, buddy. You're on the wrong floor."

The drunk didn't hear him, concentrating on digging in his pants pocket. He ricocheted off the wall and paused, swaying as he focused on what he was doing.

McGurn rose to stop him from going farther. "Hey, pal. You're lost. Turn around and get back on the elevator."

The drunk's voice slurred. "To where?" He closed one eye and frowned at McGurn.

"Your room, ya' dope! You got wax in your ears? You're on the wrong *floor*. Get outta here." He reached out to shove the drunk back down the hall.

The man's slow movements vanished in an instant when his hand shot out and a sap cracked the gangster's skull right behind his left ear. McGurn's knees buckled at the same time his eyes rolled back in his head.

Texas Ranger Sam Evans caught McGurn under the shoulders

and dragged him backward through the stairwell door held open by Ranger Delgado. He gave a mirthless chuckle. "Damn, you knocked the *dog* out of him."

"Pretty good acting there, Sam." Once the unconscious man was out of the way, I led the way around the corner and into the hallway, followed by Rangers Delgado, Ward, and Chandler. Evans straightened his hat, picked up his Thompson, and brought up the rear.

Outside, church bells rang, announcing the noon hour.

Chapter Seventy-Seven

Moretti stared out the fourth-floor window and chewed his cigar, trying to decide what to do with Walker and Drake. He considered leaving them where they were and going across the hall into his own room to think, but his men were waiting, and putting it off would show weakness.

Walker's eyes were closed from the pain of his broken jaw. There was something about the man Drake, who looked to be fat and slow, that smelled dangerous. Some of Moretti's best guys looked soft, but were hard as nails. The talkies always showed gangsters as rail-thin, barely strong enough to hold up the tommy guns they shot on screen. He knew better.

"Drake, I like you. I really do. If you'd come to me earlier, I would have taken you in as one of my guys. I always need a good button man, and you'd work out just fine, not like this sack of shit sitting next to you."

Walker roused up enough to mumble something else. "We illed Feas ff you."

"What's he mumbling about?"

Drake snorted a clot of blood from his nose and spit on the carpet. "Says we killed Ferras like you said."

Ignoring Walker's attempt to please him with the news,

Moretti threw up both hands. "Now look at that. You realize all the rooms on this floor are rented in my name? Now I gotta pay for that rug." He grinned at his men. "Whadda ya think about that? These Texans don't have any manners at all."

They chuckled, waiting to see what he decided.

"All right, boys. We can't kill 'em here. It'll be too hard to drag the bodies downstairs without being seen. Get 'em up on their feet and walk 'em down the back. Pour some whiskey on 'em so they'll smell like they're drunk, put 'em in a car, and take them both for a ride."

He turned toward Chic Marco. "I don't want these stiffs found, you got that?"

He grinned. "They ain't stiffs, yet, but I gotcha, Boss."

"Good. Hurry back. I feel like going to the Ohio for a drink or two this afternoon. Then I gotta call a couple of people and tell them we're out of the land and cattle business in Texas for a while."

Marco waited to see if he had any further orders while church bells rang outside.

"Land and cattle business. Get it? We're through with going legit with property there."

"Oh." Marco grinned. "I get it."

A loud crash outside the door shocked everyone into immobility.

Chapter Seventy-Eight

Room 443 was silent when I put my ear to the door. Bristling with armaments, the Rangers took up positions around me, covering the expansive hallway and Moretti's door.

Delgado whispered. "You think they're gone?"

"That guy wouldn't have been sitting out here if they were. Maybe he's asleep."

"He could have a woman in there."

I shrugged and stepped back. "Let's see." My boot slammed just below the latch and the wood splintered. "Texas Rangers!" I followed the muzzle of the BAR inside.

Instead of a single room, I found myself in an empty suite.

Chapter Seventy-Nine

The abrupt sound of splintering wood in the hall launched Moretti's men into action. Chic Marco pointed at the connecting door. Lando Regio yanked it open. Pistol in hand, he rushed inside, looking for an escape route.

Moretti waved both hands and hissed. "Quiet!"

A loud voice came through the upper have of the louvered door. "Texas Rangers!"

"Shit!" Marco spun to face Moretti. "They're here! In *Arkansas!*"

Stunned and immobile, the mob boss was suddenly incapable of thought.

Regio popped back in the room. "This way, Boss!"

Seeing a way out, Moretti bolted for the next room, leaving Marco to clean up the mess tied to chairs.

Gritting his teeth, Marco withdrew a straight razor from his pocket and opened it up. Walker moaned softly through his broken jaw. Drake's face went slack with the knowledge of what was about to come.

"Sorry, guys, but you were already dead anyway."

Chapter Eighty

I came out of the empty room to find the Rangers all facing outward, covering the hallway and elevator. Delgado flicked his eyes toward the door across the hall. "Heard somebody talking in there through the louvers."

Feeling light as a feather and full of energy because I just *knew* I was close to Charlotte's murderer, I kicked the door in. "Texas Rangers!"

Two dead men tied to chairs faced the door. Heads lolling, blood still trickled from their slashed throats and ran down to the floor and a fresh lake of blood.

The unexpected sight almost took my breath away, and it took a second to regain my wits. Choking it down, I knew it was too late to help either of them. Avoiding the widening pool of blood under the bodies, I tried not to look at the terrible wounds that stretched from ear to ear. After making sure the bathroom was empty, I checked behind the bed.

Satisfied there were no immediate threats, I saw the connecting door to the next room was closed. Standing to the side, I tried the knob and fell back as machine-gun fire chewed through the door. My fears about how they might use the system of interconnected rooms were answered.

Son of a bitch!

I threw myself backward across the bed.

From outside in the hallway, more automatic weapons opened up in a heavy roll of thunder.

Chapter Eighty-One

Fine dust and powdered plaster filled the air as incoming rounds walked up and down the connecting door until a magazine on the other side ran dry. Metallic clicks came through the holes as the shooter reloaded. Whoever was on the other side grew still.

I let out a groan and using the bed as a makeshift cover, knelt on one knee in the classic shooter's position and shouldered the BAR, focusing on the door. Through the bullet holes and drifting dust, I saw shadows and shapes moving on the other side. There were so many. I recognized the figure of a man pressing up close to the other side to peer through one of the punctures.

The big rifle came alive in my hands, sending twenty 30.06 rounds through the existing bullet holes and remaining wood. The heavy gas-operated rifle absorbed much of the recoil, allowing me to concentrate on where I wanted the rounds to impact.

The satisfying sound of a falling body told me at least one bad guy was out of business.

Ejecting the spent magazine, I inserted a fresh one and slapped it hard from the bottom to make sure it locked into place. "Coming out, boys."

"Come ahead on."

I emerged to find the hallway carpet littered with spent

rounds. Holes in the wall and the door two rooms down on the left were evidence the Rangers had been in the fight as well.

Delgado pointed. "Somebody opened that door and opened fire on us."

"Bet *that* was a mistake."

Ranger Clarendon pointed with the muzzle of his .35 Remington. "There's people in rooms down that way on the right side. A couple of doors opened, and somebody shot at us while we were in the thick of it. I threw a few rounds down that way, and they quit, for the moment."

"That's what I was afraid of. They're going through the rooms toward that end of the wing."

Ranger Ward knelt on one knee with the Browning twelve-gauge snugged against his shoulder. "We concentrate on one side, they could come back this way without us seeing them. We can't let 'em get behind us."

I considered our situation and looked at Delgado for guidance, but the calm, more experienced Ranger waited for orders. Even though he was the senior of the group, no one had the authority to issue orders. The others came into the engagement with the explicit knowledge that I would lead the way if and when Delgado gave me the nod.

It was my dance.

"All right. Enrique, you come with me. Ward, that scatter-gun'll clear the hall if you go to shooting, and that includes us. Follow us a little bit, then cover back where we came from."

Ranger John Ward nodded and backed against the only wall safe at the moment, the one separating Moretti's room 443 from the hall.

"Sam," I pointed at the room he'd just vacated. "You take that side to keep 'em from coming back this way. We'll clear 'em, and you follow along, but stay inside and not out here."

Ranger Sam Evans allowed a flicker of a smile and ducked into the room.

"Luke, you do the same on the other side. Delgado and I'll kick the doors all the way down."

Ranger Luke Clarendon nodded and, avoiding the clotting blood on the floor, took up a position where he could see the connecting door that was shot up so bad it barely hung on its hinges.

A door slammed farther down. I concentrated on the long hall. "We're gonna have to do this one room at a time."

"It won't be fast." Ranger Evans threw a look back toward the elevator. "I wonder how long these local boys will hold off before someone comes charging up here."

Delgado snorted. "They'll wait until the shooting stops."

Chapter Eighty-Two

Cherubino Moretti's shirt was wet with the sweat of fear. He'd never been in such a perilous position in his life.

Chic Marco was calm as a cucumber. It was almost as if he was enjoying his newly elevated position. "These guys are good. I think Barbera bought it."

"That's one tommy gun down." Lando Regio held his own as-yet unfired Thompson tucked under his arm. The left pocket of his coat held two more magazines.

"Let's just get the hell out of here!" The panic in Moretti's voice showed he wanted nothing more than to bolt like a rabbit and run.

"Can't." Marco, who survived the battle of Verdun in France, knew how to fight. Most of his experience was in trench warfare, but he'd cleared his share of shattered buildings. His quick thinking showed that he was more than a gofer to Moretti. "They'll cut us down if they have a man down at the far end. They have to move a helluva lot slower than us, because they don't know what we're going to do."

He shouldered past Moretti, who waited by the bed. "They don't know which rooms we're in, so they can't do the same as us. That gives us the edge, that and our guys scattered up and down this wing." He paused. "I just wish I remembered where they are."

He pitched an ashtray against the connecting door and waited. "This is Marco. Anybody there?"

No answer.

Backed up by Regio holding a sawed-off shotgun, he turned the knob and waited. When no one fired, he let out a deep breath and stepped through. A second later, his hand reappeared and waved them in.

They were now one room down and one room closer to the stairwell at the far end.

Dean McGurn closed the door behind them and lodged a chair back under the knob. "That'll slow those Texas bastards down."

Chapter Eighty-Three

The sound of a closing door came to us as we crept down the hallway. I pointed left, and when Ranger Delgado was ready, I fired a short three-round burst through the vents and kicked the door open.

A body lay on the floor beside the unmade bed. In nothing but a pair of boxer shorts and a sleeveless tee shirt, the gangster lay in a pool of blood, a .45 still in his hand.

Realizing it was the first man who'd engaged the Rangers, I kicked the weapon under the bed. "Sam! Clear!"

The connecting door opened, revealing the Ranger Evans and his Thompson.

I returned to the hallway. Ranger John Ward still had the rear covered. I pointed at the door on the opposite side, and Ranger Delgado repeated his actions.

Three-round blast. Kick in the door.

Two made-up double beds. Empty.

Call Ranger Clarendon to move up through the connecting door.

My turn to repeat on my side.

One unmade double bed. Empty.

We moved on.

Chapter Eighty-Four

Chic Marco pushed forward to take control of their retreat, followed by Lando Regio. Moretti came next, with McGurn bringing up the rear.

"We got more guys than this." Moretti's head was on a swivel. Sweat ran down his face, and he wiped it away. "Where are they?"

"I know there's four in a room somewhere on the other side, but I don't know about the others. Some of the new guys that came in last night might be checking out the town. I sure hope not." Marco shook his head at the mob boss' fear. "Hang on, Boss. The rest're probably doing the same thing as us, heading toward the exit."

McGurn joined in. "I think there's some more of our guys farther down."

"Why were we so scattered?" Moretti's eyes were glassy with fear.

Marco raised an eyebrow. Some of the rooms farthest from Moretti were party rooms, where they kept the connecting doors on the opposite side of the hall open all the time to move freely from one to the other.

Those on their side were used for the prostitutes after Moretti settled in for the night.

"To keep an eye on things, Mr. Moretti. We didn't want all of us bunched up in one place. We have you covered from both sides."

"You're a good man, Chic." Moretti patted his shoulder with a soft, damp hand. "Get me out of here, and I'll make it worth your while."

"You bet, Boss." Standing to the side, Marco picked up another ashtray and pitched it against the door. "It's me."

Moretti barely raised an eyebrow at the feminine underwear on the bed. Marco opened the door and Moretti stepped on a camisole on his way through.

Chapter Eighty-Five

Halfway down the hall, the rats who gathered in one room on the right couldn't take it anymore. The door opened, and one of the gangsters who'd been listening to the fight's progress stepped into the hallway with a tommy gun.

Half crouching, he braced himself and fired, leaning into the recoil. A stream of .45s ripped down the length of the hallway. Or at least that was his intention. Thompsons tend to rise up and to the right on full automatic. The first few rounds went close to where he wanted, but the rest stitched the wall almost to the high ceiling.

The hammer of detonations was as physical in the enclosed space as the bullets looking for flesh. Leaving a cleared room, I was halfway into the hallway when the man started shooting. A round bounced off the metal plate on my vest's right side, spinning me back and out of sight.

The gangster's rounds were met with Delgado's own Thompson. Instead of holding the trigger down, the slender Ranger limited his response to three-round blasts, bringing the weapon back to bear each time. Calm as a preacher in church, he returned fire again and again. The battle of machine guns ended quickly when the gangster fell, but he was replaced by a triggerman who leaned out the door with another Thompson.

This one knew how to hold the tommy gun level and intended to rake the hallway. Delgado disappeared into a doorway to reload at the same time I saw red and reemerged. The gangster crouched and took aim at Ranger Evans, who ducked into Moretti's room. The heavy blasts of my BAR came a split second before the gangster's Thompson opened up.

A long burst broke out, chewing the man apart as bullets plowed into wood and flesh, splashing a red mist onto the walls. He fell back inside, followed by a continuing stream of lead from the BAR. Men shouted from farther down the hall, and more doors slammed.

Dust and fine particles floated in the air, drawn on currents through the door held open by the gangster's riddled body. I slapped a new magazine into the BAR. Delgado crossed the hallway to get a better angle and poured a fresh stream of lead through the wall. Thunder rolled and debris flew as he swept the Thompson right, then back again left, eating through plaster and lath.

Inside, Luke Clarendon saw something he didn't like in the connecting doorway leading to the same room Delgado was hosing. Clarendon's .35 Remington sprayed the wall at waist level.

Clarendon's Remington fell silent. Delgado rammed another magazine into the tommy gun at the same time a scream of pain faded into groans. Delgado backed up a couple of feet so he could see and pointed to the hole in my Dunrite vest that was twisted on my body from the bullet's impact.

I adjusted the vest and flashed Delgado a weak smile. "It works."

Chapter Eighty-Six

Throwing caution to the wind when more than one machine gun opened up, Chic Marco rushed into the next room, which smelled of cigarette smoke, whiskey, and sex. A naked woman hiding behind the bed screamed when a .45 pistol went off, the round hitting the doorjamb.

Marco and Regio opened up on the half-dressed man who dissolved into a red mist of blood, tissue, and hair. It was only after he hit the ground that Marco realized the corpse was one of their men.

"Goddamn it! That was one of our guys!"

The prostitute continued to shriek as Moretti merely glanced at the man's body and backed against a wall to allow Marco to open the next door in line. Finding the room empty, Marco waved for Moretti to follow.

The woman stood on the opposite side of the bed, holding a pillow in front of her body. "Mr. Moretti! It's me, Bobbi! Help me!"

He threw a look at the little blond who'd been the center of his attention in the Ohio Club only a couple of days earlier. Not recognizing her, or caring, he followed Marco and Regio. McGurn again blocked the door behind them.

Giving her a quick once-over, he followed his boss out of the room.

They were almost clear.

Chapter Eighty-Seven

Behind the advancing Texas Rangers, the elevator dinged at the far end of the hallway. The door slid open, revealing three men in suits and wearing fedoras tilted over one eye. All held pistols, cocked and ready to use. They stood there as if the elevator car was the safest place in the building, despite the fine plaster dust and gun smoke filling the air.

Seeing Ranger John Ward on one knee against the wall, the tallest of the three misread the situation and pulled the lapel of his coat back to reveal a badge. "Sheriff's Department. Put down your weapon."

Ranger Ward whirled, throwing the shotgun to his shoulder. "Texas Ranger! Official business. Get down or get out of here!"

Gunfire rattled at the far end of the wing. Torn between what could be coming from behind him, and the three lawmen still standing like fools in the elevator car, Ward remained where he was.

"That's one of those damned Texans."

Ward's face reflected the shock he felt when all three men pointed their guns not down the hall, but at *him*.

The tallest lawman fired, hitting Ward in the chest. Again, the steel plates in the Dunrite vest stopped the round. Barely registering the impact of the light .38 at a distance of thirty feet, Ward did the only thing he could do as the other two opened fire. He pulled the trigger on the Browning shotgun and kept firing as the autoloader sent death down the hallway and into the car.

The rounds spread as they were supposed to, and the three crooked lawmen soaked up most of the hundred and twenty-five #4 buckshot pellets that shredded their bodies. They dropped to the elevator floor and were still, as Ward thumbed more shells into the Browning's magazine.

Chapter Eighty-Eight

Lights flickered overhead, and the smell of woodsmoke filled the air. Possibly the bullets that penetrated the walls around them had cut through electrical wiring, shorting it out. Despite the cotton feeling in my ears from all the gunfire, the hissing spray of water from punctured lines was loud in the brief silence.

Ranger Delgado and I took half a second to absorb the carnage behind us in the elevator. Ranger Clarendon stuffed the last fresh shell into his Browning and concentrated on the stairwell.

Nary a crease appeared on Delgado's face. "Guess I'll have to eat a little crow. Someone *did* come up."

———

"All right." Chic Marco planted his feet. "On the count of three, you two guys hit the hall and lay down covering fire. Me and the boss will come out behind you and into the stairwell. You guys follow us."

Lando nodded he was ready. Looking uncertain, McGurn hefted his .45.

Marco called across the hallway. "Boys, if you can hear me, let's go. One, two!" He twisted the knob.

"Three!"

———

Delgado and I whirled at the sound of the last two doors on the far end of the hallway discharging armed men. Someone had been counting down and they poured into the hall, firing a variety of weapons and sending a swarm of lead down the hallway.

———

Three gunmen from the opposite side joined Regio and McGurn. Five men opened fire as Marco pushed Moretti out behind them.

Crouching, he followed. The hallway exploded in thunder.

———

Unable to shoot past us, Clarendon dropped to the floor. Me and Delgado held our ground, trusting the Dunrites and returning fire into the clustered mass of desperate men. Concentrating on the front sights of their weapons, we poured round after round into the men, who wilted in place.

Chapter Eighty-Nine

Ears ringing and hands shaking, I handed Ranger Delgado the BAR and dropped the bandolier of extra magazines. I charged down the hallway. "Y'all get out of here! I'm going after Moretti!"

I disappeared into the stairwell as the Rangers reloaded. The air was filled with dust, powdered plaster, pieces of wood fine as sawdust, and gun smoke.

The hiss of punctured water pipes in one room identified the source of the hot, steaming mineral water soaking the carpet at their feet.

———

Still facing the elevator, Ranger Ward cleared his throat. "So what now?"

Ranger Delgado drew a deep breath to calm his nerves. "You boys have done your do. Those two that Tom's after are headed down to the street, and he'll catch 'em or he won't. This place is going to be crawling with Arkansas laws in a few minutes. We take the back stairs like we planned and get out before they start looking for us."

"I hate to leave Tom behind." Ranger Clarendon rested the

Remington in the crook of his arm and took Tom Bell's still-hot BAR from Delgado.

Delgado agreed. "Yep, but now he has these others off his back, so it's between him and Moretti."

"There's still that other guy."

"He's had worse odds." Delgado clapped Sam Evans on the shoulder. "Let's get the hell out of here before any more crooked lawmen show up."

Chapter Ninety

As always, Chic Marco knew how to escape when the need arose. He led the whimpering Moretti down the staircase and into a spacious landing intersected by three different doors. There was no need to decide which one to use.

He yanked open a familiar door and they charged through into an echoing marble hallway that ended at smaller, lavish staircase leading downward into a humid reception area. A number of half-dressed people rushed past them and into the main part of the hotel.

"Which way?" Moretti's voice reverberated against the marble and tile.

There was no need to consider which way to go. Marco had been to the bathhouse more than once to soak in the volcanic mineral waters, and afterward, enjoy a hot steam, shower, and massage on one of the many tables.

"The exit is at the end of this room!" Marco pointed past a line of vacant massage tables and led the way at a run. "It leads out to the parking lot."

"Look at us. Everyone who sees us will remember what we look like." Both men were covered in grime and blood splatter. "And besides, the car is on the other side of the hotel."

Marco jogged past the tables with a pistol in each hand. "We'll go down the street and cut through the woods in back."

"Po-lice out there."

They slid to a shock at the sound of a strange voice, noticing for the first time an old colored man who stepped out from behind a tiled support column. Marco pointed his .45 at the old man's face before recognizing him as a masseuse who'd given him a massage in the past.

"What's with him?" Moretti pointed at the man standing stock-still.

"He's blind."

"I am," the old man spoke with slow deliberation, as if concentrating on making himself understood. "But I know there's a carload of po-licemen out there."

"Now what are we gonna do?" Moretti's voice rose in fear. "Listen. We can't go back that way. Somebody's coming."

The old man felt for a massage table and eased down to sit on the fresh sheets. He pointed at a line of doors. "In there. I'll take care of this for you, Mr. Marco."

Moretti's head snapped toward Chic. "You know him?"

"Gave me a massage or two. There's no way out of those steam rooms."

"I'll just sit here and point toward the back door when they gets here, then you can slip out back up the stairs and away. They won't know where you went."

Marco slapped the old man on his bony shoulder. "Thanks, old-timer."

"It's my pleasure, Mr. Marco."

They slipped into the steam rooms as a single set of footsteps came down the staircase.

The door closed and the silence inside the four-by-four room was broken only by Moretti's panting. They sat in the dim light coming through the tiny window and waited.

Chapter Ninety-One

A door slammed somewhere far below as I reached the stairs. The Colt .45 in hand, I took the steps two at a time to the ground floor. Pausing, I considered the signs pointing to more than one exit. LOBBY, NORTH WING, and BATH HOUSE.

It was doubtful they went into the lobby to push through a crowd of terrified guests with firearms in their hands. There'd likely be lawmen there, too.

The second exit led to more guest rooms. That was a possibility, but it would be a long run to still another exit at the end of that wing, leaving them in the open way too long.

The third had my attention. Without consciously knowing why, I pushed through the door and into an ornate hallway leading to the Hazelwood's bath house below.

Another door slammed, and a male voice said something unintelligible. The voice had a note of fear in it, and that was all I needed to hear. I trotted down the hall, footsteps echoing off the marble floor. Gun still in hand, I reached a landing with more steps leading downward into the lower level that housed the spa area.

One hand on the dark wooden rail, I advanced with even more caution, keeping an eye on an empty receptionist's desk.

Forcing myself to breathe slowly, I listened for a sound that would indicate an ambush.

Lit by a single schoolhouse light high above, damp towels lay in white puddles in front of a detailed wooden door bearing a brass plaque that said BATH HOUSE.

Another door. Damn, I'm tired of doors.

The hotel was built into the side of a mountain, and despite the narrow, horizontal windows up near the ceiling, it felt like I was entering a basement or a cave. The air was damp, swampy. Taking care not to slip on the white penny-tile floor, I pushed the swinging door open and stepped into what appeared to be a waiting room. Chairs lined two walls, but the long, white room full of massage tables had my attention.

Everything was white—the tables, sheets, cabinets, and a dozen more doors on the left-hand side. Each door had a tiny, dark window. Enormous white soaking tubs added more steam to the air, some still full of bubbling mineral water and separated by pony walls offering little in the way of privacy. Two rows of tiled support columns stretched toward the distant wall, glowing in the sunlight from a glass exit door.

In the middle of the great barn-sized room, a line of massage tables stretched the length of the spa. Some were made up, waiting for the next guest's relaxation. Used sheets dangled off the others, where those who'd been lying there had left in a hurry.

It reminded me of hospitals back in France during the war. The only thing missing were the pitiful human casualties, struggling to survive their wounds and get back home where they belonged.

Backlit by the sunshine flooding that end of the room through the glass door, an old Negro man in a white uniform sat with his eyes closed on one of the tables, facing the wall full of doors. Obviously an employee, he seemed at peace with the silence, maybe enjoying the unanticipated break in tending to pampered guests. I remained where I was, taking in the expansive bath house.

Forming the short leg of an *L*, a larger area to his right extended forty feet, divided into cubicles by portable screens. One was open, revealing an unoccupied massage table. The floor was littered with more towels, articles of clothing, and one shoe. Light from the high windows backlit the screened areas, revealing the shape of even more tables reserved for guests requiring extra privacy.

The .45 up and ready to fire, I moved as quietly as possible. However, each careful step sounded incredibly loud in the silence. I was suddenly lonesome for people and wished I hadn't told the other Rangers to leave.

The impossibility of what I had to do was almost overwhelming. Reasoning that the two gangsters wouldn't try to hide amid the flimsy screens in the dead-end massage area, I sidestepped to an unfamiliar line of doors.

Mouth dry, I reached out and turned the knob, aiming the big Colt into the darkness within. Hot, dry air boiled out of the tiny cubicle. A description popped into mind.

Sweat lodge.

Familiar with the Indian custom of sitting in hot lodges to sweat out impurities, or for religious purposes, I'd never seen a modern steam room. Taking a deep breath to calm my nerves, I advanced to the next.

The old colored man continued to sit as still as a stone without opening his eyes.

I had a clear view of the first soaking tub full of steaming water. Relieved that each step would allow me to see into each consecutive horseshoe-shaped cubicle, I checked the next steam room.

Another belch of hot air.

I hate this!

Fully dressed and still wearing my plaster-covered coat and hat, I was soon drenched in sweat. The entire bath house was uncomfortably warm, and I wondered how anyone could tolerate the heat day after day as the old man did.

Another step, and the white-haired old man took a deep breath and turned his face in my direction. His eyes were still closed, and by his movements, I realized the old man was Mr. B, the blind man. I'd met him a day earlier in the lobby. As slow as molasses in the wintertime, a gnarled, bony hand rose to chest height. His bent finger pointed to the exit at the far end of the cavernous room.

But then he did something unexpected. A slight smile formed on his lips, and he shook his head. The hand and finger again moved with glacial speed and came to stop on a door directly across from where he sat, and not three feet away.

Distant voices floated down from above.

"Booker! Where's Mr. Booker? Mr. B!"

A chill went up my spine when the elderly gentleman's head turned toward the voices. They'd left the blind man behind in a frenzied panic to escape whatever was going on up on the fourth floor.

He nodded, again unhurried, as if savoring the last few moments alone.

Mr. B. The old man's name was Booker. What a damned coincidence, or was it? One part of my mind wondered at the reason, or maybe divine providence behind it all.

Or was it Charlotte's doing?

Booker's hand descended just as slowly as when it went up, coming to rest once again in his lap. A heartbeat later, he rose, turned toward the way I'd come, and made his unhurried, silent way toward where I stood.

Pausing when he came abreast, the old man spoke barely above a whisper. "Careful, sir. They's in there fo sho."

"Thanks, my friend. How'd you know it was me?"

"Didn't, till I heard your voice just now. Don't much like criminals is all." Passing a support column, the elderly man gave it a pat to reassure himself he was on the right path and walked out of sight.

Steadied by the wonder of it all, I considered my choices.

There was another tiled column not far from where Booker'd been sitting. Three quick steps and I was there, using the support structure as protection. Left shoulder against the smooth white tile, I had a perfect, clear view of the steam room's door.

"Moretti!"

My voice echoed off the hard walls and floor.

"This is Tom Bell! Texas Ranger! The man you've been trying to kill. I'm damned aggravated right now, and I have a .45 pointed at that little room you're hiding in! Y'all throw out your weapons and come out with your hands where I can see 'em, or by *God* I'll shoot through that door until it falls apart!"

After a moment's hesitation, the door cracked and a .45 slid across the tiles. "We're coming out!"

"Come ahead on."

The door opened wider, revealing a man who appeared to be holding the inside wall for support. His eyes were dead when he found my position.

I knew that look. "Don't."

The sweat-soaked man hesitated, then planted his left foot. Years of firing weapons told me he'd just steadied himself in a shooting stance.

I didn't shout another warning.

I shot him three times with the Colt, the big slugs letting the life and soul out of the gangster who collapsed outward onto the wet floor, still holding a cocked revolver in his right hand.

He twitched and grew still. Red blood stood out in stark contrast to the white floor.

"Don't shoot! Don't shoot! I'm coming out. I don't have a gun. See? Here are my hands." A pasty-faced, slightly overweight man emerged, holding his hands ridiculously high. Blood splatter covered his shirt from the dead man's exit wound. "Please don't kill me!"

"Moretti!"

Tears rolled down his plump cheeks. "Yes! Yes! Please don't shoot! I'm unarmed."

Looking down the .45's barrel, finger tightening on the trigger, I saw Charlotte's bloody body slumped across the car seat back on that dark Texas road. The man who was responsible stood clear and distinct in my sights. Only a couple more pounds of pressure, and the one who'd caused her death would be gone.

"Please! I'm doing what you want. Please don't shoot me." Moretti's voice trailed off as he stared into the eternity that was my .45.

Finger curled even more against the trigger, compression increased another pound, nearing the point where the sear would break, the hammer would fall, and it would all be over. My head seemed about ready to explode as the familiar red rage once again engulfed my consciousness.

Here it comes again, and I'm gonna let myself go.

Moretti's eyes widened, and his mouth fell open. He said something, but I couldn't hear through the roar that filled my senses. Though it hadn't yet happened, I could feel the trigger's break.

The snap.

The detonation.

The recoil as the Colt automatically loaded another round.

Then another shot.

And another, as the mobster, who was now fouling his pants and filling the moist air with his stench, would soak up every round in the pistol until it locked back.

The red filled in, and I still hung on by a hair against the rage I'd been trying to control my whole life.

A gentle voice cut through my consciousness. At first it was young Booker speaking so softly I couldn't make out the words.

Then it changed and it was Charlotte.

Again, I couldn't make out the words, but the meaning, the message that seeped through the anger melted it away like snow in the summertime became clear.

The enormous weight that had been on my shoulders evaporated along with the fury that drove me to Hot Springs. My vision cleared and there was the figure standing before me not as a target, but a terrified criminal.

I took a deep breath, let off on the trigger, and spoke softly. It was all the strength I could muster to speak. "Get down on your belly."

Moretti frowned, unable to understand.

Texas Ranger Captain Enrique Delgado's voice rang out sharp and clear, echoing throughout the spa.

"He said get your ass on the ground right now or I'll shoot you myself, you slimy son of a bitch."

Moretti fell as if he had been shot, and a figure wearing a cowboy hat pushed past and dropped a knee to the man's back. Moretti grunted, and Ranger Sam Evans snapped on a pair of cuffs.

"Tom, you can lower your pistol now. It's over."

Exhausted almost to the point of needing to sit, I let my

hand drop. I turned to see Captain Evans and Captain Luke Clarendon stationed between me and the bath house entrance. "I thought I told y'all to get."

"You did." Ranger Delgado looked inside my soul with expressionless eyes. "But I got a call on Clarendon's radio as soon as we got in the car. Governor Sterling sent word that we're here to bring Moretti back to Texas. Seems like the governor here is looking to bank some goodwill for the next election and agreed it was all right.

"So we're driving out of town down the main drag without anybody bothering us. Getting rid of that old boy laying there won't change things in this corrupt town, but it'll serve justice back home."

The other Rangers dragged the stinking, blubbering gangster toward a shower stall in the back.

"As soon as they get the shit washed off that son of a bitch, we're gonna wrap him in a towel and head back to Texas and Old Sparky. He'll ride the lightning, for sure."

I holstered the .45 and watched them drag Moretti off the ground. "It's over."

"Yes, it is." Delgado gave me a gentle pat on the shoulder, the only way he knew to show affection. "Good job, Ranger."

AUTHOR'S NOTE

It's been ten years since I started this journey as an author, and it's flown past like a rushing stream. To date, there are now a dozen mysteries and thrillers bearing my name, and more in the works, because ideas come to me at all hours.

Hopeful writers just starting out, and students and fans in the many classes and panels I sit on, often ask where my ideas come from. They seem to have trouble finding a subject, but that's never happened to me. For instance, this novel in your hand was sparked by a drive through deep East Texas on my way to visit my friend and fellow author, Joe R. Lansdale.

I took the long way from my home near Dallas because I wanted a quiet drive through the country. Passing through Kilgore, Gladewater, and Liberty City, I realized that most of the people on the road, and many of them living in houses, both old and new, tucked into the piney woods, had no idea about the rich history in that part of Texas.

The oil boomtowns and the lawlessness that came with the drillers who discovered the East Texas oil field have faded from memory, for the most part. You can still find those stories, but it takes some digging. So when I got home, I dug.

According to the American Oil and Gas Historical Society, this huge oil field discovered in 1930 "has produced more than five *billion* (italics mine) barrels of oil—and continues to produce. The 1930 discovery revealed a field 43 miles long and 12.5 miles wide. It remains the largest and most prolific oil reservoir ever discovered in the contiguous United States."

During my research, certain names kept coming up. Drillers J. Malcom Crim, H. L. Hunt, C. M. "Dad" Joiner, to name only a few, were making the news in the early 1930s, as did a tough Texas Ranger named Manual T. "Lone Wolf" Gonzaullas.

Lone Wolf is legendary in the way he dealt with criminals back in that day, and I suddenly realized that my fictional Texas Ranger from the Red River series, Tom Bell, could have been right there with him in Kilgore, which was then known as "the most lawless town in Texas."

That's where fiction separates from fact. I didn't want to write a book about Gonzaullas, or the real Kilgore, but I did want to put Tom Bell in a similar situation during the Great Depression. I've been fascinated by that time period since I was kid, after hearing stories from my parents and grandparents who lived through those difficult years.

It's in my nature to place my characters in a situation and ask myself, what if? What if a young Tom Bell arrives in a similar boomtown on the trail of a murderer? What if he met a woman there? What if he discovers a body, and further investigation leads to corrupt officials under the thumb of Chicago gangsters who regularly visit Hot Springs, Arkansas? What if...

Readers will notice a vague reference to another atrocity in Oklahoma about that same time when oil was discovered under land owned by the Osage Nation. They became incredibly rich, but soon members of the tribe began to die under mysterious circumstances. J. Edgar Hoover turned to former Texas Ranger Tom White to find out what was happening and to solve those murders. In a story that will raise the hair on the back of your neck, he discovered that corrupt officials and ruthless men were marrying into the Native American tribe and murdering their wives and her relatives to gain their inheritance and all that liquid gold underfoot.

So what if that happened in East Texas in a similar fashion and Tom Bell was there?

Fans of the Texas Red River series gave me a lot of grief when I "killed off" retired Ranger Tom Bell in my third novel, *The Right Side of Wrong*, set in rural Northeast Texas in 1966. I didn't realize his popularity with readers until touring for the fourth novel, *Vengeance Is Mine*. People *love* Tom Bell, and many readers had a crow to pick with me about his demise.

"He was one of my favorite characters. Drown Pepper in the Red River if you want, but bring Tom Bell back," one said. "You shouldn't have killed him!"

But did I?

I didn't remember the exact verbiage of how I left it, so I went back and read my own work. *Huzzah!* I didn't say Tom Bell was *dead*. The novel ends with the old Ranger shot up and providing cover fire for Constable Ned Parker and Cody Parker as they escape a Mexican prison and head for the Rio Grande and home.

So I revived that character, and folks thanked me for it. But they wanted more. It was then I wondered what Tom Bell would have been like as a young Ranger, one without as much restraint and experience as he has later in the series. What if he had a love interest? What made Tom Bell turn out like he did later in the series?

The Texas Job fleshes out his history, and in it, we see the origin of this tale that began in *The Right Side of Wrong*.

Several people believed in that idea. My longtime agent, Ann Hawkins, thought it was a great story, and we pitched it to Dominique Raccah, the founder, publisher, and CEO of Sourcebooks. She loved it, and with the help of her hardworking team, this book became a reality.

My thanks to Ann and all of those great folks at Sourcebooks for supporting my work, and as always, to my friend, brother from another mother, and mentor John Gilstrap for all that he's meant to me the past ten years. Thanks also to those who have helped me along this rambling path.

Thanks to my wife, Shana, for always being there for me. She is the love of my life.

And finally, many thanks to all my faithful readers!

—*Reavis Z. Wortham*
Prosper, Texas
March 27, 2021

ABOUT THE AUTHOR

© Shana Wortham

Spur Award–winning author Reavis Z. Wortham pens the Texas Red River historical mystery series, and the high-octane Sonny Hawke contemporary Western thrillers. The Texas Red River novels are set in rural Northeast Texas in the 1960s. In a Starred Review, *Kirkus Reviews* listed his first novel, *The Rock Hole,* as one of the "Top 12 Mysteries of 2011." *The Rock Hole* was reissued in 2020 by Poisoned Pen Press with new material added, including an introduction by Joe R. Lansdale.

"*Burrows,* Wortham's outstanding sequel to *The Rock Hole,* combines the gonzo sensibility of Joe R. Lansdale and the elegiac mood of *To Kill a Mockingbird* to strike just the right balance between childhood innocence and adult horror."

—*Publishers Weekly,* Starred Review

"The cinematic characters have substance and a pulse. They walk off the page and talk Texas."

—*Dallas Morning News*

His series from Kensington Publishing features Texas Ranger Sonny Hawke and debuted in 2018. *Hawke's War*, the second in the Sonny Hawke series, won the Spur Award from the Western Writers Association of America as the Best Mass Market Paperback of 2019. In 2020, the third book in the series, *Hawke's Target*, won a Spur Award in the same category.

Wortham has been a newspaper columnist and magazine writer since 1988, penning nearly two thousand columns and articles, and has been the humor editor for *Texas Fish & Game Magazine* for twenty-three years. He and his wife, Shana, live in Northeast Texas.

All his works are available at your favorite bookstore or online, in all formats.

Check out his website at reaviszwortham.com.